Amy Perry's Assumptions

Amy Perry's Assumptions

Laura Starkey

First published in Great Britain in 2023 by

Bonnier Books UK Limited
4th Floor, Victoria House, Bloomsbury Square, London, WC1B 4DA
Owned by Bonnier Books
Sveavägen 56, Stockholm, Sweden

A CIP catalogue record for this book is available from the British Library.

ISBN: 9781471415241

This book is typeset using Atomik ePublisher

Embla Books is an imprint of Bonnier Books UK
www.bonnierbooks.co.uk

To all the kind people who asked, 'Are you writing another one?' and 'When can I read it?' This book is for you.

I do love nothing in the world so well as you.
Is not that strange?

William Shakespeare
Much Ado About Nothing, Act IV Scene i

Prologue

Amy Perry breathed in the green smell of a fading summer evening and watched the last of the day's sunshine disappear behind Rowton Hall, the eighteenth-century stately home that stood tall and proud beyond the village of Rowton-in-Arden.

Shards of pinkish light bathed the building's vast, slate-grey roof, illuminating its array of chimneys. As its picturesque sandstone front was plunged into shadow, the copse of trees beyond its lawns suddenly felt dense and dim.

Amy shivered slightly in the growing gloom, shifting the position of her back against her favoured old elm tree and realising that it probably would have been smart to head home half an hour ago. Gran would go spare if she popped her head into Amy's room and discovered she wasn't there.

Technically Amy shouldn't be here at all, either with or without permission from her legal guardian. While the Ainsworth family – owners of this land, as well as pretty much everything else within a five-mile radius – were happy for people to walk through the little wood during daylight hours, the gate was closed at night and a sign warned that trespassers would be prosecuted.

Amy couldn't help a derisive snort at this: it wasn't like she'd done any harm by sitting here watching the sun go down, leafing through the latest *NME* and putting away most of a packet of ginger nuts. Besides, how much wealth and property did one family really need exclusive access to? As someone who'd spent much of her childhood in a two-bedroom flat with no garden, Amy had little sympathy with attempts to restrict her access to this spot.

The copse was her favourite place in Rowton, partly because she knew her dad had loved it too. He'd once confessed that – unbeknown to Gran – he'd regularly sneaked out on nights when his teenage head was too full of noise to sit still. Amy found it comforting to think of them both seeking solace in the same secret routine at different times, then creeping home undetected.

They had moved in with Gran when Dad's doctors explained that, while treatment might keep him comfortable, there was nothing more they could do for him. Though Gran's help had been a huge relief, the culture shock had hit sixteen-year-old Amy hard. Coming to Rowton had felt like stepping into a Jane Austen novel, and weirdest of all was the presence of an actual, real-life lord of the manor: Roger Ainsworth, aka Viscount Waverley. A member of the House of Lords, he liked to be addressed by his full title, and kept a determined distance from the commoners, many of whose homes he owned.

Amy fished in her bag for a final biscuit, and a familiar voice cut through the quiet air as she closed her fingers around it.

'Got any more of those?'

She jumped in surprise, dropping it into the dry, dusty grass. *Argh*.

Sam Ainsworth – owner of the voice and heir to the very ground Amy was currently sitting on – flopped down next to her. He angled his elbows behind him and slouched back to look up at the deep navy sky.

'*No*, I haven't,' Amy said, willing herself to sound cool and unflustered by his sudden appearance. 'That was the last one. And you shouldn't creep up on people like that. You should wear a bell – like the ones people put around cats' necks to stop them killing birds.'

He grinned at her, his white teeth flashing in the shadows. 'Well *you* shouldn't be out here by yourself,' he retorted. 'It's dark. You never know who might be hanging around.'

'Apparently not,' said Amy. 'I suppose you're going to head home now and dial 999, since I'm breaking His Lordship's rules? Or find a footman to throw me off the premises?'

Sam threw his head back and laughed, and Amy averted her eyes from his long, lightly tanned throat.

'Seriously, though,' he said, sitting up a little straighter. 'Why are you on your own? Celebrating the end of exams with all your dearest friends?'

He spread his hands to indicate the clear absence of other people, and Amy stuck her tongue out at him.

Unlike Sam, she wasn't exactly popular at college – but in fact she *had* been invited to hang out with several of the cool girls from their English class after their papers went in earlier. She'd walked with them to the riverside park near the Royal Shakespeare Theatre and sat on the grass as a bottle of warm white wine was passed around, along with the latest gossip. The hot topic was who might pair up with who at an eighteenth birthday party that had become the big end-of-exams event that Friday – but Amy had kept quiet when it was her turn to spill.

'Duhhh. She has her secret thing with Hari, remember?' Amy frowned at the memory of Vicky McBride giggling, her over-plucked eyebrows raised so high they almost disappeared into her mass of brown curls. Rather than point out that there was nothing *remotely* romantic between herself and her best friend, Amy had soon made her excuses and left, catching the bus back to Rowton in time for tea with Gran.

Yes, Hari was the only person in Rowton that Amy felt fully at ease with, but she'd never liked him in *that* way – and she was one hundred per cent sure he didn't fancy her either. Their friendship was based on a shared love of indie music, and a connection that transcended their superficial differences. At college and among the locals Hari was gregarious and well liked, whereas Amy – quiet, studious and fond of black clothes – had a reputation for spikiness. However, both had 'lost a parent', as their sympathetic neighbours might have put it. Their experience of grief bound them in a way their more fortunate peers couldn't fathom.

'Really, where's Hari? Off answering a call of nature?' Sam said, reclaiming Amy's focus.

'For God's *sake*,' she grumbled, trying not to laugh at Sam miming binoculars with his hands, aiming his face at an overgrown shrub as though Hari might be lurking behind it.

'Hari and I aren't a two-for-one special, you know,' Amy went on. 'We are occasionally seen separately.'

'*Very* occasionally,' Sam said, arching an eyebrow. He and Hari were also friends, and together the three of them – the only people in their year who lived in the village – formed a slightly strange trio: Hari the ever-affable link between the other two, whose chief form of communication was banter and sniping.

Amy's raised voice drew the attention of Max, the Ainsworths' chocolate Labrador. Presumably, Sam had been sent out to walk him before the family went to bed.

Max abandoned Sam to rest his warm, heavy head on Amy's lap and, within a few short seconds, he had located her lost biscuit. She stroked his floppy ears as he munched it, loving the feel of their velvety softness between her finger and thumb.

'Traitor,' Sam muttered. He shook his head at the dog and then yawned, stretching his arms high above his head and lying back down on the ground, his face to the sky. Amy quickly pulled her gaze away from the sudden tightness of his T-shirt across his chest.

'Hari has his last exam tomorrow,' she told him, fervently hoping the dusk would obscure the ridiculous blush she could feel burning her cheeks. 'Further Maths. I think Mrs Chauhan has him under house arrest until he's completely done.'

'Sounds about right,' Sam laughed as he flipped himself onto his side to face her. 'But tonight aside, I can't remember the last time I saw you on your own.'

He said it lightly, but his eyes caught Amy's and held them. Not sure what to do with his full attention, she felt her face grow hotter.

Amy found Sam infuriating and intriguing, in proportions that seemed to shift and fluctuate so frequently she could never quite be sure whether she liked or loathed him. She never missed a chance to poke fun at his insanely privileged upbringing and well-to-do accent; she'd once informed him that he sounded like a BBC newsreader from the 1930s. She had also openly berated him when she found out he'd refused to do A levels at the posh independent school he'd been at previously. Amy would have given her eye teeth to be at the sort of school where classes weren't rammed, expectations were high and resources weren't strained. Everybody hates a tourist, she regularly informed him. It riled her that he seemed to be cosplaying a normal person, when he was born into the English peerage and would probably never have to work a day in his life.

Amy was further annoyed by her increasing awareness of how good-looking Sam was. Until recently, his attractiveness had mostly been theoretical to her; like the date of the Battle of Hastings or the positions of the planets in the solar system, it was something she'd filed under 'indisputable, but not of immediate interest'.

Lately, though, Amy had *felt* his allure as well as recognising it as fact – most recently in the exam hall this afternoon, staring up the row of single-seater desks to where he was sitting, square-shouldered and scribbling furiously in the blazing light that spilled through a nearby window.

Sam had hair the colour of something delicious you might find in the window of a French patisserie: the same shade as the warm, glossy sheen on a fresh croissant, or the gilded top of a perfectly singed crème brûlée. His eyes were a rich, chocolatey brown, framed by the sort of thick, perfectly curled lashes nature always bestowed on boys who – in Amy's view – could never truly appreciate them. His skin was a clear, soft beige that freckled and tanned in the summer, which she also resented. At this time of year Sam positively glowed, while Amy lived in sun hats and fervently hoped she wouldn't burn through her factor 50.

Even worse, Sam was tall and lean; a lifetime spent playing sport had given him the sort of triangular torso that effortlessly raised pulse rates. Despite Amy's disdain for his army of female admirers – and her determination never to become one of the hangers-on who seemed content to wait around in the hope he'd notice them – she could sort of see their point.

Most disturbing of all was his mouth, from which issued many ill-formed arguments and sarcastic comments, but which was also a full, perfect pout. She'd once ranted to Hari that Sam's lips were set in a permanently surly expression, only to realise she'd said 'sultry' by accident. Hari had laughed his arse off about it, and Amy's slip of the tongue had sparked days of relentless piss-taking.

'So you two haven't declared your undying love for one another yet then?' Sam asked, one corner of his troublesome mouth lifting in a wry smile that didn't quite reach his eyes.

'It isn't like that,' Amy huffed, insistent. 'Ugh. I'm done with this topic today. And I should head home anyway.'

'I'll walk with you,' Sam said, heaving himself back up to standing.

'You don't have to do—'

'I need to stretch Max's legs anyway,' he cut in, 'and it'll be pitch-black out here by the time you're over the bridge. Only a proper arsehole would knowingly let you go alone. I'll follow you at a respectful distance if I have to, but I'd really rather not stalk you back to your gran's.'

'*Fine*,' said Amy, and before she could register what was happening Sam had pulled her to her feet, both her hands somehow in his.

A moment later, he loosed them to bend down and pick up Max's lead. Amy's palms tingled.

The bracelet around her wrist jangled as she pushed her dark hair out of her face, willing herself to calm down. It was some assortment of green crystals on a stretchy band, sent to her by her mother from California. Lily Godwin, whose name had never been Perry because she didn't believe in marriage, was what Gran called 'a flighty type'. After a whirlwind romance with Amy's father, John, she'd had their baby but soon decided infant Amy would be better off brought up in the sort of stable environment her aura could never provide.

Leaving Amy's father heartbroken, she'd gone travelling and eventually settled in America, in an apartment stacked full of tarot cards, astrology charts and antiques, permanently fuggy with joss stick smoke. She and Amy – or Amaryllis, as Lily had originally named her daughter – kept in touch, but their relationship was casual rather than close.

'So, how did you find it this afternoon?' Sam asked as they made their way out of the little wood and walked towards the village centre.

'*Don't* tell me you want to dissect the English Lit paper,' Amy said, laughing. 'I didn't think stressing about tests was your style.'

'It isn't,' Sam said amiably. 'You were the one who wanted to change the subject. Ten quid says you picked the question about the meaning of love in *Much Ado About Nothing*, then wrote two thousand words arguing it's about the patriarchy's need to control women.'

Amy felt her face flush again and sniffed indignantly. 'So what if I did?'

'Well, it's a bit blinkered, in my opinion,' Sam said, 'and *very* bleak – but I have every confidence you'll get an A star. You always make a compelling, if depressing, case.'

Amy threw him a withering look. 'And what did *you* write about?'

'I answered that one too, but in my version love is redemptive: Beatrice's heartbreak over her cousin forces

7

Benedick to face how he really feels – how he's *always* felt about her. That love, finally declared, makes a happy ending possible for pretty much everyone. What can I tell you?' he went on, smirking. 'I've spent two years defending literary romance in the face of your committed cynicism. No reason to stop now.'

Amy's stomach began to do something strange and utterly treacherous as he spoke. She hated slushy movies, happy ever afters and soppy songs – in fact, she loathed the whole sentimental circus of love as much as her father had adored it. At the same time, she was acutely aware of how close Sam's arm was to hers.

For a fraction of a second, Sam's hand brushed hers and she felt a powerful urge to grab it. Instead, she shoved her fists into the pockets of her oversized hoodie.

'So,' she said, to cover her suddenly shallow breathing. 'You're off to Cambridge in the autumn.'

'If I get the grades,' Sam confirmed.

'You'll get them. You know you will,' she chided. Sam wasn't just handsome and popular; sporting and academic achievements seemed to come so easily to him that they were practically automatic. He was, quite literally, the village golden boy.

Next to him, Amy felt every bit the short, somewhat weird interloper: the pale, petite nerd with no parents who was more comfortable reading books by herself than getting pissed with her peers in the park. She couldn't imagine what it was like to be so self-assured, so *visible* – to be comfortable with attention in the way that Sam was. She supposed it helped if people gawped at you because you were gorgeous and clever, rather than because you were an almost-orphan who dressed like a goth.

He shrugged again, oblivious to her unease. 'Honestly, I'd be quite happy going to Sheffield instead. I haven't admitted this to anyone else, but I might even prefer it. It's my parents who want Cambridge – they pushed me to apply. It's UCL for you, right?'

'Yep,' she nodded, her chest feeling full and heavy with the pleasure of sharing his secret.

'Ah. You always were desperate to escape to the big city,' Sam said.

It wasn't a question, so Amy didn't answer. In all honesty, she couldn't wait to taste true independence – not to mention enjoy a little urban anonymity.

As she and Sam approached the bridge over the stream that separated the old and newer halves of Rowton-in-Arden, Amy admitted to herself that he'd been right: blackness had smothered the village like a blanket, and she might have felt jumpy walking home on her own – even though Rowton's extremely zealous Neighbourhood Watch group had arguably rendered it the safest place in Warwickshire. She didn't tell *him* this, obviously. Instead, she teased him: 'When was the last time you set foot on my side of the water? I hope you've had your jabs.'

It was a joke, but like all wisecracks it contained a kernel of truth. The wealthier residents of the village lived on the Rowton Hall side of the stream, which had been mentioned in the Domesday Book and was where almost all the buildings were deemed 'of particular historical significance'. Over the water was a hotchpotch of pretty old cottages, allotments, the village primary school and newer housing, much of which dated from the 1970s when the village had expanded.

Sam laughed and shook his head. 'No, but you're worth the risk. Can't have you heading back to Dodge with no defender.' His voice was low and rich. It made her feel like something inside her was melting.

As Amy and Sam crossed the bridge, their fingers somehow twined loosely together. Amy wasn't sure who'd initiated the hand-holding or even how it had begun, but the sensation of his skin on hers was electric. The touching of their palms felt like a circuit being completed – like a light coming on. She didn't dare to look at him in case it flickered off again.

Neither of them spoke as they walked towards Amy's house. Max lolloped along just behind them, tired now and clearly wondering why he was being taken on such a long walk at this time of night.

When they reached the small, timber-framed cottage owned by Amy's grandmother, she led Sam away from the front door and instead stopped outside the old lean-to her long-departed grandad had built onto the kitchen before she was born. A large-ish window, waist-high from the ground, had been left slightly ajar.

'You're going in through *there*?' Sam asked.

Amy nodded. 'Makes less noise than the door, and she doesn't know I'm out.'

Sam stared at her, eyes wide. She realised he couldn't decide whether to be impressed or disapproving and laughed out loud at his baffled expression: pleased, just this once, to have left him lost for words.

He glanced down at their still-joined hands, then raised his eyes to her face and said: 'I like you, Amy. Really. Like, a lot.'

It came out in a rush, as if he hadn't planned to say it but couldn't hold the words in. He made a wincing face and then brought his gaze up to her eyes, searching them.

She said nothing, but thrilled at the tightening of his fingers around her own. She squeezed back gently – her hand apparently several steps ahead of her brain, which was yelling at her that she needed to stop this before she got hurt. Sam's easy charm meant he was never short of female attention, but he also never seemed serious about anyone he dated or hooked up with. By contrast, Amy was *inherently* serious – totally incapable of letting someone in and then shrugging it off as if it didn't matter.

'I'm pretty sure you think I'm a posh twat,' Sam went on. 'And I find you absolutely *maddening* most of the time. But I like you. I argue with you even when I don't disagree with you just to get your attention . . . You *are* wrong about *Much Ado*, though, just for the record.'

Amy threw him a withering look. 'Do you have a point, My Lord?'

'Eurgh,' Sam said, kicking the toe of his trainer against a gap in the concrete slabs beneath their feet. 'You know I hate that, *Amaryllis*.'

Amy grinned, pleased that she'd undercut the tension between them and scored a point – even at the expense of being called by the hated name on her birth certificate. Sam smiled back, then stepped closer. Her breath caught in her throat.

'My point,' he said, in a voice that was almost a whisper, 'is that there'll be no more classes, now. No more heated debates about Shakespeare or war poetry or Arthur Miller. So it's time to settle the argument I've been having with myself for two years and just *ask* you whether or not you like me back. Whether it might be okay for me to kiss you.'

His hair was shining like warm caramel in the weak light from the window and his dark eyes, almost black in the dimness, were wide. She felt like he could see right through her, right down to her bones, which seemed to be slowly dissolving.

Amy's heart stuttered in her chest, her lungs beginning to burn as she reminded herself to breathe. Sam stepped a little closer and her pulse jumped, blood rioting in her veins. He dipped his head towards hers and she exhaled softly as she nodded, his lips grazing her mouth and coaxing it into a kiss.

Every romantic trope she'd ever scoffed at felt too small and tame for the sensation that seized her as Sam's hands found her waist. The kiss deepened. Her fear of feeling it all too much diminished with every press of his lips, until what was left was a simple, frightening fact. She liked him, too. Really. Like, a lot.

Even now she couldn't bring herself to utter the words out loud – she just kissed him harder, hoping that when they broke apart her shining eyes and shy nod would say enough.

Sam gently tucked a lock of inky hair behind Amy's left ear, his thumb skating across her cheekbone as he withdrew it.

'So . . .' he said, sounding shyer and less sure than she'd ever heard him before. 'Does that mean you'll come to Mike's birthday with me this Friday? To the party for his eighteenth?'

'Yeah. It does,' Amy said, despite her general aversion to social events and a vague dislike of Mike. He'd once referred to her as 'spooky doll girl' on account of her (lack of) height, goth-y wardrobe and huge blue eyes – and the nickname had stuck, becoming widely used among their peers, even though Mike had no doubt forgotten he originally coined it.

Sam's face split in a smile that made Amy feel like her heart was fracturing.

'I should go in,' she told him. 'Gran'll do her nut if she realises I've sneaked out.'

'OK,' Sam said. He touched his lips to hers again: a light but lingering kiss this time.

'Thanks for walking me home,' Amy whispered as she scrambled up onto the window ledge and pushed her way into the house.

'That's OK,' Sam said, smiling again. 'I've been waiting for an excuse all year – constantly thwarted by Hari and his driving licence.' Then his face fell and he frowned. 'Do you really think he'll be alright with this?' He moved his hand to indicate his proximity to Amy.

'I really do,' Amy promised him. 'Trust me, I'll talk to him. He's going to be fine about it.'

'Really?' Sam said doubtfully. 'How can you be so sure?'

'Because,' Amy said, poking the top half of her body out of the window and reaching for his hand, '*this* leaves less time for what he refers to as our "relentless bickering".'

Sam smiled then, giving in to her good humour. He stretched up to kiss her one last time before disappearing into the darkness.

'Relentless bickering?' he murmured, laughing. 'Something tells me we'll always find time for that.'

ROWTON-IN-ARDEN & COPLEY HERALD ONLINE

06:21 GMT
Saturday 21 June 2008

LOCAL TEEN DIES IN RIDGE LANE CRASH

A Rowton-in-Arden teenager has been killed in a car crash on Ridge Lane – the most serious incident to occur at the 'accident hotspot' in recent years.

Hari Chauhan was travelling in a Vauxhall Corsa towards Copley on Friday afternoon, apparently on his way to a venue where a birthday party was due to be held that evening.

The 51-year-old driver of a Ford Transit van, which was seriously damaged in the collision, has been treated for minor injuries and is expected to make a full recovery. The cause of the crash is not yet clear.

Kenneth Bradley, principal at Shakespeare's County Sixth Form College where Chauhan studied, said: "Words can't convey my heartbreak at this news. Hari was among our most gifted students and had such a bright future ahead of him."

Chauhan, expected to achieve four A level A-grades, was due to take up a place to study law at Balliol College, Oxford, this autumn.

A spokesperson for Warwickshire Police commented: "Friday's incident is the most horrific we've seen in the Rowton area for many years. The loss of this young man is simply tragic."

Police are asking for anyone who witnessed the collision to notify them immediately. Information can be provided via the incident hotline, on 0800 545 123.

Chapter 1

'One for the road,' Kit announced, plonking a cocktail down on the table in front of Amy. They were in a dimly lit Mayfair bar that seemed to be ninety per cent mirror. Almost every surface was shiny – made of glass, granite or some polished metal that meant you had to look at yourself from a new angle each time you moved your head.

The place was heaving, which wasn't surprising given it was Saturday night. Everyone in here was tall, slender, attractive and well dressed – no doubt because anyone with a normal amount of appearance-based insecurity wouldn't be able to stand more than a few minutes of constant confrontation with their own reflection.

While catching sight of herself every few seconds wasn't exactly enjoyable, Amy did like the fact that most people in this place were far more interested in themselves than others. In that sense it was rather like a mini London: a sea of individuals pursuing independent courses who, quite frankly, had neither the time nor inclination to wonder who you were or where you were going. She liked the anonymity this afforded: the freedom to wander the city streets alone and unencumbered.

'*Kit*,' Amy moaned as he sat down opposite her. 'You said you were going to the gents! I was supposed to head home almost an hour ago. Also, this place is really starting to get to me . . . I think I need to do some sort of pore-minimising face mask, or maybe get one of those electric toning wands that shrink your jowls.'

'You do *not* have jowls,' Kit said, rolling his eyes. 'And your pores are fine. Now drink up and stop complaining.

14

It's weeks since I've seen you properly, and it's your birthday eve! We're supposed to be celebrating.'

Amy pulled her glass further towards her and assessed its contents. The heavy-bottomed tumbler was full of orange liquid, its sugared edge garnished with lime and a lurid red cherry. The drink smelled sweet but strong: cloyingly alcoholic. 'Mai Tai?' she guessed, lifting the glass.

'Got it in one,' Kit said, clinking his martini against it. Amy sipped her drink, enjoying the burn-y sensation that bloomed in her throat as multiple spirits slipped down it.

'So, what's Hugh got planned for you tomorrow? Assuming he doesn't bin you off for being back late, obviously.'

Amy cringed and took another gulp of Mai Tai. Kit and Hugh didn't particularly like one another, and neither bothered to make a secret of the fact. Kit was Amy's best friend: they'd hit it off eight years ago on her first day at Howard-Knight Publishing, where all three of them worked.

Kit suspected that Hugh was unhappy about how close they were, despite Kit's dating life mostly involving buff guys he met at the gym. Though Amy refused to admit it, Kit wasn't far wrong. In truth, Hugh was uncomfortable with Kit's obvious hotness. He looked a lot like the guy who played the Duke of Hastings in the first season of *Bridgerton* – and although she'd never felt even slightly attracted to him, he was, objectively speaking, very pretty indeed.

Kit's antipathy to Hugh occasionally hit nerves that Amy wished he'd steer clear of. While she could live with criticism of what Kit called Hugh's 'middle-aged man at Harvey Nicks' wardrobe and questionable taste in music (like an idiot, she'd let slip that he owned several James Blunt albums), rants about her boyfriend's 'possessive psycho streak' made her uncomfortable. Granted, worrying excessively about what time she'd be home wasn't Hugh's *best* quality, but by most people's standards he had all the makings of A Great Boyfriend. He was clever, handsome and financially solvent, as well as good company . . . most of the time. What's more, his personal hygiene was impeccable and his flat was always tidy. In short, Hugh was a fully functioning adult – something an alarming number of men, in Amy's experience, definitely couldn't claim to be.

Amy and Hugh were attracted to one another. They were compatible, and together they enjoyed a highly Instagrammable relationship that didn't involve any drama. If Amy was honest, one of Hugh's key advantages was that – like every other boyfriend she'd ever had – he seemed slightly more attached to her than she was to him. It was probably dysfunctional, but she might as well face it: she'd always avoided being the more emotionally vulnerable partner. Hugh's insistence on knowing Amy was safe was irritating, but not a deal-breaker – rather an outward sign of a dynamic she was very used to.

'Don't be daft, Kit,' Amy said briskly. 'Hugh isn't going to dump me because I'm back a bit later than planned.'

This was true, but her dismissiveness was also deliberately misleading. Amy knew she'd probably get the silent treatment for a while if she stressed Hugh out by going dark on him this evening, and she suspected she was no more than half an hour away from receiving an anxious WhatsApp with a terse request for her ETA. She found herself pricing in his inevitable annoyance: it was the cost of staying out a bit longer, and worth paying to spend extra time with Kit.

'Hugh has some big mystery day out planned,' she said, in an attempt to take the conversation elsewhere. 'He's point-blank refused to give me any details about it but I'm sure it's going to be exciting.'

Amy did her best to *sound* excited, but in all honesty she was nervous. She hated surprises and (although she'd asked a *lot* of leading questions) had totally failed to get a read on what was in store.

Kit sniffed out her apprehension immediately. 'Sounds like your worst nightmare,' he stated baldly.

Not for the first time, Amy found herself wishing that her boyfriend of six months knew her as well as her friend did.

When she neither confirmed nor denied his accusation, Kit changed tack. 'How's it going with him, anyway?' he asked. 'Now you're living together, I mean.'

'We're not *living together*,' Amy said. 'Not really. You know that.'

'Ames,' Kit protested, draining his martini. 'Do you or do you not currently reside in Hugh Howard's South Bank flat?'

'Well, yes, but—'

'And have you, or have you not, had your post redirected to his address?' Kit pressed on.

'Yes, but that's for security reasons,' Amy cried. 'Bank statements and—'

Kit held up his palms, signalling for her to stop. 'The prosecution rests.'

'I do not *live* with Hugh,' Amy said, exasperated. 'It's way too soon for that. I'm just staying with him for a while. It isn't *my* fault my landlord decided to sell up, then asked me to leave within four weeks. It was good of Hugh to suggest I crash with him – especially when you consider the size of my shoe collection.'

Come on, she thought. *Laugh at my crap joke so we can lighten the mood and move on.*

'Mmm,' Kit murmured, annoyingly non-committal. 'So you're looking for a place of your own, still? How's that going?'

His Yorkshire accent had bounced back to full strength after a few drinks, Amy noticed. She liked it: broad, warm and unapologetically Sheffield, without the edges shorn off by the need to sound 'more professional' in an office soundtracked by Received Pronunciation.

Like Kit's, Amy's was one of only a handful of 'regional voices' at Howard-Knight. A shared determination never to pronounce Bath with an 'r' in the middle had bonded them on a work trip to the city during Amy's first week at the firm.

'It's going verrry slowly,' Amy admitted, grateful for the change of subject. 'We've seen a few places, but none of them have been right so far.'

Kit's black eyebrows pulled together. 'Why is Hugh involved in helping you flat-hunt? Does he get a say in where you live now – or, perhaps more accurately, where you *don't?*'

Amy squirmed, realising she'd somehow managed to make things worse. 'He's just trying to be helpful! He wants me to find somewhere nice – somewhere decent – not rush to spaff half my earnings on the nearest available hellhole.'

Kit snorted. 'Something tells me you could find an apartment in Kensington Palace for fifty quid a week and he'd still say it wasn't good enough for you.'

Although trying to avoid his gaze, Amy accidentally caught his eye in one of the many mirrored tiles that surrounded them. His face was soft with concern, despite his derisive tone.

'Seriously . . . Be careful, Amy. Please. I know I take the piss, but you need to make sure his overprotective behaviour doesn't become something more . . . sinister.'

'*Sinister*?!' Amy forced a laugh. 'I think you've overdosed on erotic fiction – or maybe been on too many dodgy Tinder dates. I've seen every corner of Hugh's flat, and I can tell you with complete confidence that there's no red room of pain.'

Kit wrinkled his nose and shuddered theatrically. 'I wasn't implying he's some sort of closet Christian Grey.'

'He *definitely* isn't,' Amy said, slurping what little was left of her cocktail.

'Oh dear,' Kit said, raising an eyebrow and grinning. 'Is he boring in bed? That's a blow. I mean, Hugh's not really my cup of tea, but shagging the CEO's posh nephew should at least be *kind* of hot . . . ?'

Amy felt herself flush. 'He's perfectly fine in bed!' she cried, desperate to shut Kit up. 'Hugh and I have a very straightforward, fuss-free relationship. It's exactly what I need, and we both know where we stand.'

'*Ouch.*' Kit was belly-laughing now, every inch of his

gym-honed, tight T-shirted chest shaking. 'Damned with faint praise.'

'Listen, Kit,' Amy said, giggling too but doing her best to sound indignant. 'We don't all want to be embroiled in the kind of sexual mega-drama you seem to find each time you swipe right. You know I'm not a swooner. I like an intelligent man with clean fingernails who can hold a decent conversation and – if we're being ambitious – knows how to cook a carbonara. Being in amorous thrall to anyone is just . . . not my style.'

'Despite all evidence to the contrary, I still struggle to believe you mean that,' Kit said. 'Surely at *some* point you've had a knee-trembler: a crush so powerful you thought it might stop you breathing, or a kiss so gorgeous you look back and wonder how you didn't spontaneously combust?'

Amy narrowed her eyes at him, allowing her expression to tell the lie she didn't want to put into words.

'Tragic,' Kit said, shaking his head. 'Truly tragic.'

Amy laughed again and punched his stupidly solid arm. 'Bearing in mind that you brought me out tonight to celebrate my birthday, this amount of teasing seems excessive – even for you,' she said.

'I am who I am,' Kit simpered, his eyes bright with mischief. 'But you're right, I'll stop laughing at your lust-free life for now – you only turn thirty-one once. Shall we have a final round? I think they're about to call last orders.'

'I thought this' – Amy pointed at her empty glass – 'was one for the road? But yes, I think I *do* need another overpriced cocktail now you've reminded me how old I'm going to be tomorrow.'

As Kit bolted for the bar, Amy felt her phone buzz inside her handbag. Hugh, probably. She decided not to reply for now: it would only spark a back-and-forth she didn't want to get into, although the thought of dealing with him later sent a prickle of unease down her spine.

'French 75s,' Kit said as he reappeared. 'Had to be done.'

He handed Amy a flute full of fizz, then kissed her on the cheek. 'Happy birthday to my beautiful, clever, hopelessly *un*romantic BFF,' he said, lifting his glass in salute.

'To Amy Perry. May the year ahead be your very best yet.'

Chapter 2

The following morning, Amy was sat in the passenger seat of Hugh's shiny silver Audi, saying nothing and trying not to chew her gel-polished fingernails. She felt vaguely queasy, partly thanks to the varied mix of drinks she'd put away last night and partly as a result of her nervousness. She still had no idea where they were going, or what awaited them when they got there.

When she realised they were leaving London, she'd felt a fleeting hope that they might be on the way to a fancy boutique hotel – maybe even one with a spa . . . However, that idea had evaporated within seconds. As far as Amy was aware they had no luggage with them, and Hugh wasn't the spontaneous, 'let's just go in the clothes we're stood up in' type.

'I'm taking you for an afternoon out in the countryside, Amy, not to prison,' Hugh said, side-eyeing her as they exited the M25. He wore a wry smile but his gaze was cool. The atmosphere inside the car was tense and brittle, and Amy could tell he was annoyed by her uneasiness. Nor had he fully forgiven her for coming back to his flat last night tipsy and two hours later than planned.

Amy smoothed down her charcoal wool sweater and stared out of the window as greyness gradually gave way to green. The car travelled on, ranging up and down roads that, as they got further from the motorway, became narrow lanes, then muddy tracks lined with trees. She frowned, beginning to fear for her footwear. The Grenson boots she was wearing had cost way more than she could really afford – a sum that hadn't even made it onto her latest Visa statement yet.

Ruining the beautiful pale suede would be nothing short of a disaster.

'We're here,' Hugh said, slowing and stopping the Audi alongside a worn wooden stile. Amy's heart sank, landing somewhere in the region of her soon-to-be-trashed boots. Why hadn't she brought wellies? Why didn't she *own* wellies?

'We're . . . where?' Amy asked, desperately trying to sound enthusiastic. She was now almost certain she was going to hate whatever Hugh had in store for her this afternoon, but she didn't want *him* to know that. He was trying to do a nice thing for her birthday, however cack-handedly – and hurting his feelings would only make her feel worse.

'At our destination,' Hugh grinned, getting out of the car and striding around it to open the passenger door. He was starting to enjoy her confusion, which was a tad grating. Amy decided to look cheerful, despite the muted sense of panic that had taken up residence inside her ribcage.

'So . . . you've brought me to a field for my birthday . . . ?' she said, painting on a whimsical smile designed to project anticipation. She hoped that the sunnier she seemed, the quicker Hugh would explain what the bloody hell was happening.

'It's not just any field,' Hugh said, pulling Amy to her feet and smiling expansively. She widened her own grin in response, hoping the expression didn't look as phoney and manic as it felt.

Hugh made it up and over the stile in a single fluid movement. It was set in a wall of low, leafy hedges that denoted the end of one person's land and the start of another's. For a split second it made Amy think of the Ainsworths and Rowton Hall: the careful demarcation Sam's father had always maintained between his land and the common ground beyond.

'Come on,' Hugh beckoned. Excited and impatient, he extended a hand to Amy again, offering to help her climb across.

Amy's mouth had fallen open and she was already looking past him. Even at five foot three, she could easily see over the hedge line to the expanse of grass behind it. She was staring at a huge, rainbow-striped swell of fabric as it swayed in the breeze. It was gossamer-light, bright as a flame and undulating like a snake about to strike. There was a large basket anchoring it to the ground.

'Are you serious?!' The words bubbled up and out of her mouth before she could stop them.

Something like anger briefly shadowed Hugh's face. Amy cursed herself, swallowed, then tried again. 'I mean, er . . . Is that . . . ? Are we . . . ?'

'Yes,' Hugh said firmly. 'I thought a balloon ride would be great fun.'

His eyes had widened, and Amy couldn't work out whether he was pleading with her to go along with this or daring her to disagree with him. For a moment she felt irked that someone who purported to know her could possibly think she'd consider this *fun*. She wasn't good with heights and she'd never enjoyed flying; in fact, Hugh had complained that she'd gripped his hand so hard she left bruises during take-off on a trip to Rome a couple of months ago.

The fear of being a thousand feet up in the air in *that* thing – oscillating with every slight shiver of wind – was already sitting like lead in her stomach. She felt nauseous, a little embarrassed and, in some corner of herself that she was working hard to keep contained, utterly terrified.

What was more, it was late March in England. The weather wasn't *bad*, but the temperature was hardly tropical – and everyone knew it rained every five minutes at this time of year. Amy was going to freeze, flying around the countryside in only a jumper, jeans and a light jacket.

'Okay,' she said, ignoring the slow, churning sensation in her gut. 'I mean . . . Why not?'

Recognising success when he saw it, Hugh's face lit up with a smile so brilliant it could have advertised toothpaste.

Amy found herself examining him as he helped her cross the stile. His face was symmetrical, classic – almost Disney-hero handsome. It was hardly surprising he wasn't used to hearing the word 'no' all that often, especially when you took his background and social connections into account.

Hugh kept hold of Amy's hand and she let him lead her in the direction of the hot-air balloon. Beside it was a rangy, slightly grizzled-looking guy waiting to greet them.

'Steve,' he said by way of introduction, holding out a hand to each of them in turn.

'I'm Amy,' she said. 'Bit nervous, to be honest.' She smiled at him apologetically, hoping for some encouragement. Surely he'd encountered plenty of jittery passengers in his time, and had some standard reassuring patter prepared?

Steve merely raised one eyebrow and said, 'You'll be fine,' entirely without sympathy. He had the distinct air of someone who would rather be doing something else with his Sunday; a sentiment that Amy couldn't help sharing.

After Steve got aboard, and with a little help from Hugh, she climbed awkwardly into the basket. It was lined with thick leather padding – presumably there to prevent broken bones in the event of passengers being jostled around in-flight. Its presence was in no way comforting.

Steve readied the balloon for take-off, adjusted the intensity of the burner flame and then released the tethers that secured the basket to the ground. Seconds later, the balloon was drifting upwards.

Amy watched the ground fall away, and it soon became a mishmash of rolling hills, fields, roads and housing estates. The sun anointed every different colour with soft spring light: grassy green, bright yellow, brick red and slate grey. Amy couldn't deny there was beauty in it, but her palms were damp and her pulse was thudding in her veins. The view from up here was pretty, but it certainly wasn't relaxing.

Hugh, on the other hand, seemed delighted. His face ablaze, he moved closer to stand beside Amy, resting his left hand on her right. 'Isn't this AMAZING?' he cried into the wind, not noticing the whiteness of her knuckles on the edge of the basket. Nor could he hear the refrain of 'Shit, shit, *shit*,' currently repeating on a loop in Amy's head, keeping perfect time with her too-rapid heartbeat.

'It's . . . quite something,' Amy replied. He kissed the top of her head and she felt faintly patronised – as if this was her reward for not saying the wrong thing.

Before the spark of irritation this inspired could ignite, Amy felt Hugh's arms wrap around her. He turned her 180 degrees, guiding her so she was facing him and her back was to the sky.

He stared down at her, his ice-blue eyes piercing and intense, then kissed her lightly on the lips and knelt down.

No.

No. Motherloving. *Way.*

Amy felt her jaw drop and her legs start to wobble. This couldn't be happening – but at the same time it definitely, undeniably was.

Hugh took her hand in his and pulled a red velvet ring box from his trouser pocket. Before he'd even opened it, Amy's whole body was quivering. She concentrated very hard on not throwing up.

'Amy Perry,' Hugh said, sure she must be trembling in eager anticipation of the big question. 'I adore you. I want you to be mine forever. Will you marry me?'

He pressed a tiny gold button on the box to reveal the ring he'd chosen for her. Amy noted that, probably without meaning to, he puffed his chest out slightly as the lid flipped up. To be fair to Hugh, it *was* an incredible ring: a huge emerald-cut diamond flanked by two smaller, sparkling baguettes. The band was almost certainly platinum and Amy couldn't begin to imagine what it must have cost.

It was beautiful, but she knew with sudden clarity – a little like that of the flawless gem before her – that she could never accept it. For a moment she felt like she was floating somewhere in the sky alongside the balloon – as if she were out-of-body and watching all this happen to someone else.

From that vantage point, everything looked like it was supposed to. *This* was how proposals were made on TV or in romantic movies – not that Amy watched them. The trappings of a textbook moment to remember were all in place: a handsome man, a speechless woman and a gigantic jewel, all gilded by sunlight sliding through clouds.

As someone who didn't believe in true love – who could barely utter the words without retching – none of this should have meant anything to Amy. But the disconnect between Hugh's grand gesture and their rather prosaic affection for each other was so stark it exposed the uncomfortable truth. She wished she *had* been moved by his proposal – or, perhaps more accurately, that it had come from someone she had real feelings for.

Hugh's performance of passion she was sure he didn't possess – and which she definitely didn't return – brought to mind the only time in Amy's life she'd ever been swept up by an emotion that might have been love. She chased the memory away, then swallowed hard.

She and Hugh had only been together six months. By any measure this proposal was too much, too soon – and that was probably what Amy would tell him when she was calm enough to speak. How strange, then, that a small but unwavering voice inside her should be pointing out the opposite: that this moment, this man and these feelings were actually not enough. Entirely to her own surprise, she discovered a deep-seated, cast-iron certainty that she couldn't enter into a lifelong commitment on the basis that she and Hugh shared interests, made happy housemates or could build a prosperous future together. She needed something more than that.

Slowly Amy's head began to shake, though her mouth still refused to form words.

Hugh seemed to think she was awestruck, perhaps unable

to believe all this was really happening, but Amy realised Steve had clocked her turmoil. He'd angled his body away from them and was staring intently at a wisp of grey cloud that seemed to be getting closer, his face set in an expression of horrified mortification. She noticed there was a picnic basket at his feet, and she glimpsed the neck of a champagne bottle poking out of one side.

Fuuuck.

'Hugh,' Amy managed to say, finding her voice after what felt like several years. 'We need to talk. Please . . . Can we just talk about this?'

Finally, it seemed to hit him that she hadn't said yes. That without actually saying no, she was turning him down.

Hugh's eyes flashed with hurt, or maybe fury, but he screwed them shut before she could feel their full force. He closed the ring box with a snap, pulled himself up to his full height and huffed out an angry sigh.

Amy slumped down and sat on the floor of the basket with her head between her knees. *Keep breathing,* she told herself. *In and out. Maybe this isn't as bad as it seems.*

For a moment, Hugh looked at her with some mixture of longing and disdain, then turned his back on her to address Steve.

'How soon can you land this thing?'

Chapter 3

Several hours later, Amy was perched on a stool next to the breakfast bar in Kit's kitchen with her head in her hands. Her overnight bag, stuffed with 'essentials' rapidly grabbed from Hugh's flat, sat forlornly on the floor. Its seams were straining.

She clearly hadn't packed light, but at this point she had no idea what was in there. The past few hours had been a horrible blur, and it was entirely possible she'd discover she had three different eye creams and no clean underwear when she came to investigate later.

Right now, she had to explain to Kit why – instead of enjoying what remained of the weekend with Richie from HIIT class – he was sloshing emergency measures of gin into two chunky tumblers and cancelling his plans.

Amy looked up to see him riffling through his stainless steel fridge for a lemon, then pouring an alarmingly small measure of cold tonic water into the top of each glass. He sat down opposite her, pushed a drink in her direction and raised his eyebrows expectantly.

'It was awful,' Amy said. '*Beyond* awful. I have done an awful thing.'

Kit frowned and took a sip of his G&T.

'Ames,' he said, his tone bracing but kind. 'From what you told me on the phone, it seems pretty clear you did the *right* thing. An awful thing would have been to say yes when you didn't mean it.'

She flopped a little on her seat, sinking her elbows onto the countertop and resting her forehead on her fingertips again. 'I just don't understand how this has happened,' she said.

'How could he have thought we were ready for marriage after just a few months together? Especially when he knows I'm not even *interested* in weddings . . . I don't understand how we got here.'

She groaned and poked at a cube of ice that was protruding above the rim of her glass. For some reason it made her think of the iceberg that sank the *Titanic*.

'I should never have moved into his flat,' Amy sighed. 'You were right . . . Even though I said it was temporary, he didn't seem to hear me. He didn't *want* to hear me. I shouldn't have let Hugh – or his walk-in wardrobes and underfloor heating – persuade me to stay there, not even for a few weeks. *Garrrgghh* . . . I should have just taken that overpriced fleapit in Kentish Town, or the houseshare with the guy who'd dyed his beard bright green. Maybe I shouldn't even have gone out with Hugh in the first place.'

Kit patted her shoulder and shook his head.

'Drink up,' he said, gesturing at her untouched glass. 'And don't be too hard on yourself. I'm hardly Hugh's biggest fan and even I didn't see *this* coming. You felt like you had a handle on things, and some of the time I thought you did too – but looking back, hasn't he been pushing you for more time, more attention, more commitment from the very beginning? Think about how many months he spent showering you with compliments – not to mention *gifts* – before you finally agreed to let him take you out for dinner. He just wouldn't give up.'

'I guess that's true,' Amy said miserably. 'But what kind of shallow idiot does that make me?'

'You know you're not an idiot,' Kit said, 'and you're not shallow. Not compared to me, anyway.' He struck a pose, showing off his undersized Comme des Garçons T-shirt and the rippling muscles beneath it.

This earned a watery-sounding laugh. 'Really?' Amy asked.

'*Really*,' Kit told her. 'You and I both know you do a flawless impersonation of someone whose prime concerns are her career, her credit card balance and her designer handbag collection . . . But I've always believed there's more to you than a sharp eye for good writing and killer accessories. There's a soft, squidgy centre lurking beneath that impeccably groomed exterior, even if you wouldn't admit it for a Chanel 2.55.'

Amy took a fortifying gulp of gin, first to numb her cold wash of panic at the words 'credit card balance', and secondly because she didn't know what to say. Kit was her best friend and she was closer to him than almost anyone else in the world, but if she conceded he was right he'd never let her forget it. If she told him about her soppy moment yesterday – that second where, so briefly, she'd wondered how she might feel if someone else had proposed to her – she wouldn't be able to take it back.

Sensing that Amy didn't want to plumb her own hidden depths right now, Kit went on: 'If you want total honesty, I have no doubt Hugh genuinely wanted to be with you – but I also think he saw you as a challenge. He wanted to be the one to melt the ice queen – he's one of those guys who loves the chase, and you gave him the best game of his life.'

'*Ice queen?*' Amy demanded. 'God. Is that how people see me?'

'I mean . . . pretty much,' Kit said, sounding rather as if he regretted his choice of words. 'People who don't really know you, I mean. I – er – thought that was the look you were going for . . . ?'

'Hmm,' Amy said, finishing her G&T to cover the muddle of feelings this revelation had set loose. 'Maybe. Yeah. I suppose it was.'

Amy and Kit spent the evening binge-watching crime documentaries on Netflix and eating the sort of carb-rich, nutrient-free foods they usually denied themselves. One two-hour film – in which a suave con man diddled a succession of bright, attractive women out of tens of thousands of pounds – only underlined the problem with society's romance obsession, in Amy's view.

'They were all too suggestible,' she ranted at Kit. 'Even though they all had qualifications, careers and healthy social lives, they still wanted the perfect man and the happy ever after. *That's* what made them vulnerable.'

'Maybe,' Kit mused. 'Or perhaps he's just a super-convincing liar who's really great at sex.' Amy threw a cushion at him then, but didn't bother trying to press her point home.

That night, after Kit had gone to bed, she examined her tired face in his bathroom mirror. Her cornflower-blue eyes – which people usually said were her best feature – were ringed with purplish shadows that looked strikingly awful against her pale skin. She'd barely slept since Friday night; Saturday's 'rest' had been a fretful, booze-soaked stretch of only around five hours. Her dark hair, cut in a blunt bob that fell to just above her shoulders, was haphazard and wavy. Dimly, she wondered how much effort it was going to take to wrestle it into its usual sleek silhouette tomorrow morning.

Tomorrow morning.

Work.

She was going to have to walk into the Howard-Knight office a mere nine hours from now as though nothing had happened: as if she hadn't just split up with the CEO's nephew, who also happened to be the firm's finance director and heir apparent to the top job.

As Amy brushed her teeth over Kit's unnecessarily snazzy sink – one of those tiny glass bowl affairs that looked great but was totally impractical if you wanted to wash your face without also soaking your feet – she seethed at her own stupidity.

She kept remembering Hugh's livid face on the drive back to London after his sky-high proposal. 'I'm afraid you'll have to move out,' he'd said, almost the second they got back inside the flat.

Then there was the way he'd looked at her as they sat

opposite one another on his hideously expensive sectional sofa: his eyes tight and hard, his mouth a thin, resolute line. This was the shuttered, detached expression he'd worn as he informed her that saying no to marriage meant saying no to everything: that now she'd rejected him, there was nothing between them worth salvaging.

When they'd first started seeing each other, Hugh had been at pains to convince Amy that being with him wouldn't affect her career in any way. Now, as she recalled the stiff set of his shoulders and the clinical way he'd informed her that he expected all trace of her gone from his flat by the weekend, she marvelled at her own naivety.

Given his almost Soviet-style determination to erase her from his life, it seemed vanishingly unlikely that being in the same building as him five days a week would go well. It was typically enterprising of Hugh, she had to admit, to have told her what she wanted to hear in order to achieve his desired outcome.

Working for a publishing house had always been Amy's dream, and it had taken her years to reach her position as a senior editor of literary fiction. Now – rather like the sort of love-focused fool she usually wrinkled her nose at – she'd got in over her head and ended up messing with a man who *literally* had his name on a brass plaque outside the office door. She couldn't help fearing that as far as her future career prospects were concerned, she might as well have dropped a bomb on Howard-Knight's Baker Street HQ.

The following morning, Kit woke her with a cup of hot black coffee.

'Time to get your game face on, Ames,' he said. 'It's going to be a shit day, but once it's done, it's done. You and Hugh will be old news before the week's out.'

Amy sipped from her mug and dipped her head in what she hoped passed for a nod. She appreciated Kit's frankness and optimism, but didn't share his confidence that the mess she was in could be cleared up in a matter of days.

In fact, the more she thought about the long-term implications of finishing with Hugh, the more anxious she felt. His good looks and family connections meant he was popular with pretty much everyone at work. By contrast, Amy knew that while she was respected among her colleagues, she was too reserved to be well liked outside her small circle of friends.

When the news that their relationship was over began to circulate, Amy suspected her status as the villain of the piece would be established all too easily. What's more, Howard-Knight was a *publishing firm* – to a large extent, populated by people whose main passion in life was storytelling. Though she tended to stay out of their hushed conversations, Amy was familiar with her colleagues' enjoyment of juicy office gossip – not to mention the power of a prevailing, if not entirely accurate, narrative.

'I'm not sure I can cope with this,' she moaned, plonking her coffee down on the side table next to the sofa bed and burrowing back inside her sleeping bag.

'You have to. And you can,' Kit told her. 'Now neck that, get in the shower and let's get this shitshow on the road.'

He poked the sleeping bag, making contact with Amy's stomach, which was empty and beginning to rumble. 'I'm not going to tell you to style this out,' Kit said, 'or pretend it's not a total nightmare. But you and I both know that if you don't go in today, it'll only be worse tomorrow.'

Amy emitted a vaguely affirmative groan from beneath her thick cocoon.

'Attagirl,' Kit said. 'Now, sort yourself out and I'll make us something superfood-y for breakfast.'

Roughly ninety minutes later, the two of them emerged from Baker Street Tube station and began the familiar walk up Marylebone Road. The Howard-Knight office was just a few minutes' stroll away from Regent's Park, housed within a red-brick, five-storey town house with gigantic windows and a wrought-iron balcony.

'Why did I *do* this to myself?' Amy whined as they approached.

Kit threw an arm around her shoulders. 'You know I wasn't Hugh's biggest fan, but I don't know any woman – or bloke for that matter – who wouldn't have had their head turned by fancy trips to Europe, dinners at Michelin-starred restaurants and fresh flowers every Friday.'

Amy sighed and grit-grinned at him, abundantly grateful that he was on her side but didn't feel the need to patronise her.

'Like I said the other night,' Kit went on, 'even I didn't imagine he was about to get down on one knee, and I've been calling him a possessive lunatic for months. None of this is ideal, but you *are* going to get through it.'

Amy leaned against him, breathing in the smell of some heady designer cologne. It was comforting and quintessentially Kit, if a tad overtly sexy for 9 a.m.

Within seconds she checked herself, ducking out of his loose embrace before they could be seen. The last thing she needed today was anyone implying she and Kit were having an affair.

They made their way up the stone steps and through the heavy double doors into the Howard-Knight reception area. Jo was perched behind the desk this morning, looking pretty and owl-like in her on-trend oversized glasses.

Kit bestowed a dazzling smile on her and earned a bashful giggle in response. On the other hand, Amy's 'Hi Jo,' was greeted with a weak, silent smile.

'She knows!' Amy hissed as she and Kit passed through another set of doors into the stairwell. 'Which means *everyone* knows. Shit, balls and bollocks.'

They climbed four winding sets of stairs and arrived at the entrance for the second floor, where Amy's team was based. Kit would leave her here before heading up another flight of stairs to his own desk in the PR and marketing department. He turned to her, placed his hands on her shoulders and whispered, 'As the French say: *courage, mon brave.*'

34

Amy allowed herself a brief whimper, then stiffened her spine and nodded at him.

'See you outside at six?' he asked. 'I'll take you to the pub for a restorative drink before we head back to the flat. And Amy . . . You can stay with me for as long as you need to. You know that, right?'

'Thank you,' Amy said, 'I do . . . and six it is. If I make it that far, the drinks will be on me.'

Chapter 4

Amy arrived at her workstation, unlocked the cupboard beneath her desk and retrieved her laptop. She tried not to focus on the fact that everyone had suddenly stopped talking.

The hush was horrible: the gloomy, ominous kind of silence that falls when a vicar stands up to begin a funeral service. She willed herself not to look up and survey the room, though she was certain people were staring at her. The thought of meeting eyes full of questions – or worse, judgement – had turned the skin between her shoulder blades cool and clammy.

As she sat down, Amy scanned the selection of brightly coloured Post-it notes she'd stuck to her desktop monitor last Friday: reminders of her priorities for immediately after the weekend. It felt like a lifetime since she'd scribbled on them.

Desperate for another caffeine hit, Amy debated whether she should risk going to the kitchen and joining the scrum that was bound to be gathered in pursuit of tea and coffee. After a brief internal struggle, she decided that waiting in line for the machine would be a very particular kind of torture: even if nobody asked outright what had happened between her and Hugh, she'd know that at least some of her colleagues were wondering. She hated the sensation of being talked about; it made her want to turn invisible.

She tried to relax into her seat and calm her disorderly breathing, but rapidly found herself wishing the chair would grow a gullet and swallow her. Marcia – a fellow editor who specialised in bloody horror stories and thrillers, but always dressed as though she were off for high tea at Fortnum & Mason – stood up from the desk opposite Amy's and disappeared in the direction of the kitchen, her floral maxi dress swishing behind her. Usually she'd offer to bring Amy a drink back too, and her silence – not to mention her refusal to look Amy in the face – did not bode well.

To Amy's left, Jeremy – a slender cycling enthusiast and non-fiction editor – had his AirPods in. He was keenly focused on his computer screen.

Amy sank back behind the potted palm sat between their desks and instructed herself to calm down. She must be imagining it: whatever people's opinions on the demise of her relationship might be, surely there hadn't been a collective decision to give her the silent treatment.

She worked through the morning's to-do list, scrunching her notes into tight balls that she threw into the recycling bin at her feet. At around 11, when she finally decided to come up for air, Amy faced the fact that nobody had said a single word to her since she'd arrived. The sense that she was being frozen out was palpable.

She clicked into Slack and typed a message to Kit:

No one is speaking to me. Literally, not a word. They're giving me the kind of wide berth you'd usually reserve for people carrying open cans of cider on public transport.

A moment later, his reply appeared:

Okaaay. But have *you* spoken to anyone? Allow me to offer you a little PR expertise: people are worried they'll look like they've taken your side if they're overtly friendly today. You're going to have to make the first move.

Amy made a face at the screen, then sighed. Perhaps he had a point.

'Jeremy, Marcia,' she said, in a slightly too-loud voice that, to her dismay, betrayed nerves. 'Do either of you want a tea or coffee?'

Marcia's green eyes widened as Amy got to her feet. A beat

or two later, she shook her pretty auburn head and muttered a high-pitched 'No! Thanks!' as if it had just dawned on her that Amy was expecting a response. Her rabbit-in-headlights expression was grimly amusing, and Amy wondered how Marcia handled graphic descriptions of brutal murder if simply being asked whether she fancied a cuppa freaked her out.

Jeremy – his AirPods finally removed – rolled his eyes in Marcia's direction and said, 'Cheers, Amy, but I'm all right, ta.' He shot her an apologetic glance that seemed to say, *Sorry – I've got nothing against you personally, but it's clear that talking to you this morning would be career suicide.*

Now that Amy had said she was going to make coffee, she'd have to actually do it. *Bollocks.*

She stood up and started walking across the office, feeling a little like Cersei Lannister suffering through her walk of atonement. Based on some of the stares Amy was getting, there might as well have been someone shuffling along behind her, ringing a bell and shouting 'SHAME!' every three seconds.

Finally at her destination, Amy ducked through the kitchen doorway and let out a powerful sigh – only at that moment realising she'd been holding her breath.

Her relief was short-lived. Hugh was standing next to the coffee machine, deep in conversation with Rupert – an old family friend and his uncle's overpaid, underqualified executive assistant. Rupert was both very rich and deeply unpleasant: a practised shit-stirrer who never missed an opportunity to bitch about someone when silence would suffice. He threw Amy a satisfied leer as he slunk from the room, the motion putting her in mind of the way a spider might slip behind a skirting board.

Amy realised that she should have considered the possibility Hugh could be in here. The walk-through kitchen she was standing in had been placed at the centre of the building's second floor, serving the editorial department on one side and finance – the department Hugh managed – on the other.

Yes, he typically bought his coffee from the swish deli on the corner, but that shouldn't have distracted her from the reality that, in the aftermath of their wrecked relationship, the company's Nespresso maker lived in No Man's Land.

'What's the matter?' Hugh demanded. Amy realised she was staring at the spot where Rupert had been, her mouth hanging open. She closed it immediately.

'Nothing, I'm fine,' she mumbled, even though she wasn't. 'How are you?'

Hugh's face darkened and she instantly realised she'd said the wrong thing. His eyes narrowed to cold blue slits. 'How do you think I am, Amy, after you *broke my heart*?'

Amy flinched at the venom in his voice. At the same time, she felt like protesting: they'd never been sentimental with one another, and this was the first time he'd ever mentioned hearts as far as she could recall. He hadn't even said he loved her during his actual proposal of marriage, so to claim he was in impassioned agony felt more than a bit rich.

Before she could come up with an adequate answer, Hugh hissed, 'Do you have any idea how *humiliating* this is for me? To have offered you the world, and then to be refused so brutally?'

'Hugh,' Amy choked out, 'you know I never – *we* never—'

She'd been going to say 'talked about marriage' or 'discussed a long-term commitment', but there was a lump in her throat that speech couldn't get past. A prickly heat was gathering behind her eyes and she fought to regain control of them. She'd never cried in front of anyone at work before and she didn't intend to start now.

'I never meant for this to happen,' she finally whispered, entirely honestly. 'I never wanted to hurt you.'

He scoffed at her, either disbelieving or disinterested – she wasn't sure which. Nor was she sure that 'hurt' was the right word for his reaction to what had happened between them; 'outraged' felt closer to the mark. It was as if he thought a yes to his proposal was merely his due – that after six months of wooing and spoiling her, and in return for more of the same, agreeing to 'be his forever', as he'd put it, was the least she could do.

The attention he'd lavished on her, Amy now saw, was payment upfront for her future compliance; he was furious that she'd reneged on a bargain she'd never even realised she was making.

'You've made a fool of me, Amy,' he said bitterly, 'and you've made a mockery of the life we were building together, both personally *and* professionally . . . God, I had such hopes for us – I thought we'd be a husband-and-wife team, eventually running this place together. Surely you knew that? We'd have been incredible. *Unstoppable.* Yet now . . . Well. I wonder whether we should be working anywhere near one another at all.'

He spread his hands as if to draw her attention to the space they were standing in – as if to remind her that this whole place and everything in it belonged to his family. This was their business, and had been for generations. On the other hand, despite her long years of grit and graft, H-K was a workplace that Amy had no roots in, that she could easily lift herself out of . . . Or be unceremoniously *ousted* from, in just the same way as she had been from the South Bank flat.

As for Hugh's claim that she must have intuited his plan for them to take over one day . . . Absolutely not. But dangling a dream job in front of her at the same time as implying that she might be advised to leave her current role was a brilliant way to drive home what refusing to marry him might have cost her. It was a clear manipulation, so cold and contrived that it made Amy's stomach turn.

'Well,' Hugh said, almost smiling at what Amy knew must be the slack expression on her face. 'Something to think about, perhaps.'

Then he turned and strode from the room, leaving Amy immobilised with a still-empty mug in her hand, clutched so tight she thought it might crack.

'Amy?' said a voice behind her. Carolyn's. *Great*. Her boss wasn't renowned for her sensitivity – more for 'getting shit done' with the least regard possible for individuals' personal preferences, problems or opinions. Ordinarily, Amy rather admired her – but right now she didn't feel capable of shoving her troubles down far enough to discuss next month's upcoming publications or the effectiveness of this or that marketing push.

To her surprise, she felt a hand settle gently on her left shoulder. The motion was so unexpected, she jumped in shock.

'My office,' Carolyn said. 'Let's go.' She twisted and bent forward so she could look at Amy's face, which was still turned towards the coffee maker. Carolyn pressed her lips together and shook her head slightly. Amy wasn't sure whether she was being warned not to cry, or if Carolyn was simply betraying a shade of exasperation at the intrusion of emotions into the workplace. Without saying anything else, she lightly steered Amy out of the kitchen and back through the editorial team towards the door to the stairwell.

'Head up,' she said, her voice quiet but clipped. 'You're not Hester bloody Prynne.'

Somehow, despite everything, this made Amy want to laugh. She swallowed the urge before it could seize her, and she and Carolyn began to climb the stairs.

They went up two floors to the part of the building where Howard-Knight's senior management team was based. Amy's feet felt like dead weights by the time she'd dragged them up four twisting flights of steps, but Carolyn marched as though she would brook no delay.

When they arrived at her office, she gestured for Amy to sit down and then shut the door. Amy felt like a problem pupil who'd been summoned by the headmistress. She couldn't remember the last time she'd been in here; in fact, she was pretty sure her last two performance reviews had taken place at Carolyn's favourite wine bar.

Carolyn lowered herself into the leather-upholstered desk chair opposite Amy and brushed a swoop of silver hair off her forehead. 'So,' she said, her voice heavy. 'It's all gone tits up with Hugh Howard.'

Amy nodded assent as Carolyn folded her arms and sighed. She looked as elegant and businesslike as ever in a chic, single-breasted black blazer, matching cigarette pants and a sea-green cashmere sweater. Carolyn's hair, Amy thought, was her trademark: an unfussy but immaculate crop, cut tight into the nape of her neck but left longer and more textured on top. On some women it might be dowdy, and Amy was pretty sure a style like this would render her a dead ringer for a prepubescent schoolboy. On Carolyn, though, it was insouciant and sexy – more so than ever since she'd embraced going grey.

'Well, I hate to say I told you so,' Carolyn went on, wiping a short-nailed but carefully manicured hand across her face.

'You didn't tell me anything!' Amy cried, sounding wounded and rather more curt than she'd meant to.

'Didn't I?' Carolyn asked, apparently surprised at herself. 'Oh. I really should have. Workplace relationships are almost always a disaster. Trust me, I have age on my side – not to mention three ex-husbands.'

Amy buried her face in her hands. While she was frustrated with Carolyn, she was also grateful for her temporary removal from the office floor. When she looked up Carolyn was studying her, a speculative look in her precisely lined grey eyes.

'He *promised* me that if things didn't work out, we could go back to being just colleagues,' Amy said. Even to her own ears, she sounded callow.

She tried again. 'We promised one another that *this*' – Amy flapped her hands, gesturing around her at the building – 'would stay completely separate from *that*.'

Carolyn rolled her eyes and Amy winced, sure she was about to get a lecture on how stupid she'd been. Instead, Carolyn wrinkled her nose and snorted: 'And now, I suppose, he's strongly implying that your future here is in doubt because your romantic liaison is over. It's amazing how promises to be forbearing are forgotten the moment a man like Hugh's pride gets hurt. No doubt if he'd been the one to end things, he'd be strutting around with his head held high – oozing magnanimity but explaining that it was all too much, too soon.'

This assessment of Hugh immediately struck Amy as both uncharitable and one hundred per cent accurate. She knew in her bones that Carolyn was right: that if it had been him who'd chosen to finish their relationship, he'd have told everyone they'd decided to be 'just good friends', then expected Amy to take the high road and keep things professional no matter how she might be feeling deep down.

'The trouble is, under these circumstances Hugh can claim emotional ruin – and it's clear he's going to make life at H-K difficult for you if you stay,' Carolyn said bluntly.

She wasn't known for pulling her punches, but this really hurt. It was painful for Amy to think that anyone – especially someone whose bed she was sharing just a few days ago – could hate her enough to want her hounded out of her job. Even worse, it was nauseating to think that in this day and age he might actually manage it.

'Surely I can't be sacked for refusing to marry someone?' Amy heard herself say. 'This is 2022, not 1822.'

Carolyn looked down her long, straight nose at Amy, her eyebrows knitting together. 'Of course you can't,' she said wearily. 'But be realistic. He has cards to play that you can't match – the sympathy card, as well as his family connections. Julian is his uncle, and they're close . . . Their family owns the bloody building.'

Amy's stomach cramped and she stared at her shoes.

'So, I'm supposed to just . . . leave?' she asked, sad and seething and sounding like a sulky adolescent. 'Jump before I'm pushed? It's . . . it's not *fair!*'

'You're bloody right, it isn't fair,' Carolyn said with feeling, sounding genuinely sympathetic for the first time since they'd come up here. Possibly for the first time in their eight-year acquaintance, Amy thought.

'No,' Carolyn went on. 'I didn't ask to speak with you so I could recommend you resign. Far from it.' Wordlessly, she slid open a desk drawer, retrieved a box of Kleenex and handed it to Amy, who dabbed gratefully at her suddenly leaking eyes.

'What, then?' Amy asked.

'I have a proposition for you,' Carolyn said. 'Howard-Knight has been toying with the idea of setting up a new imprint for some time. It's taken me *months* of persuasion, but I finally have the green light for a digital-first commercial project – and it's always been my plan to try and base it outside London. As a business, we're dogged with an old-fashioned "metropolitan elite" label that, in my view, is putting promising young authors off signing with us.'

'Okay,' Amy said, intrigued but very confused. 'This is interesting, but what does it have to do with me? You know I've no experience with commercial fiction. It's not my area.'

In truth, she didn't *want* it to be her area – she was very happy where she was, working with authors whose artistic credentials were impeccable, even if their sales were hit-and-miss. Popular stories weren't her bag: too often they came with the sort of bland happy ever afters she'd never been able to stomach as a child, let alone an adult.

That kind of fiction also reminded her of her dad – of how badly burned he'd been by believing in soulmates, true love and its ability to conquer all. His whole life had been blighted by her mother's choice to leave them, though he'd worked tirelessly to try and hide it. He'd been a kind, thoughtful, fun-loving father – the sort who hosted board game tournaments, jumped into swimming pools and nursed cut knees – but he'd never stopped missing Lily or longing for her to come back. He'd never stopped hurting.

'You're talented, Amy, and I don't want to lose you from

the team,' Carolyn insisted. 'In fact, I'd say you're ready for a new challenge. I'd like you to build the author list for this new imprint, and I want you to do it from a different city. Birmingham has always been my preferred option, and you're from there, aren't you?'

'I'm from Warwickshire,' Amy said. She resisted the urge to point out that the Midlands was a pretty big place, much of it nowhere near Birmingham.

'So . . .' she went on, 'you're telling me you want me to leave, but *not* leave? You want to send me away? For how long?'

Carolyn sniffed impatiently. 'I don't want to *send* you anywhere, Amy. You're a person, not a parcel. However, I am strongly suggesting this as a sensible course of action bearing in mind what's happened. This is your chance to turn a potentially career-stalling calamity into an opportunity for growth – a way to take some time away and do something new. Something I'm sure you'll be good at.

'As for how long . . .' she continued, spreading her hands in a 'let's not worry about that now' sort of way. 'I suppose that depends on how things go, as well as how long it takes our friend Mr Howard's injured feelings to heal.' She wrinkled her nose at this, betraying a dislike of Hugh that Amy had never previously suspected.

Amy sat with Carolyn's suggestion for a few minutes, turning it over in her mind. She felt hot and cold and immediately sweaty at the thought of leaving London: she'd been here since she was eighteen and had never seriously entertained living anywhere else again, despite the pollution, the crime and the insane property prices.

But Birmingham wasn't *un*appealing . . . Amy had a vision of the massive Selfridges there, then remembered that several of her university friends had ended up with jobs in the city. It might be nice to reconnect with them. And as much as she had no desire whatsoever to spend time in Rowton-in-Arden, it would be nice to see her grandmother more: their weekly

FaceTimes were always awkward affairs, not least because Gran's broadband was useless. The freedom to pop by in person on a regular basis would be novel, and something inside her warmed at the thought.

Plus, based on this morning's frosty reception from her colleagues – not to mention her unpleasant encounter with Hugh – there seemed little sense in saying no to Carolyn's offer. If she stayed, Amy might get to continue working on her preferred kind of fiction – but she might also face a long period of strangeness and silence from people she'd formerly worked well with.

What's more, while Hugh couldn't have her sacked, between them he and Rupert *could* conspire to see her sidelined from every project she wanted to work on. Who knew: she might be pushed out of her role in lit fic even if she dug her heels in and refused to slink quietly away. She might end up editing books about knitting, origami or cage fighting – all valid topics for enthusiasts, she supposed, but very far from her wheelhouse.

Carolyn's arms were folded. She raised both her eyebrows as Amy took a deep breath and met her gaze.

'I'll do it,' Amy said. 'I never thought I'd leave London for more than a holiday, but for now I think this makes sense. Thank you for offering me a way out of this mess.'

'You're welcome,' Carolyn answered, nodding. 'And I'd have asked you to do this anyway, personal disasters aside. It's a smart step for you.'

'Great,' Amy replied, trying hard to settle the butterflies that had taken flight in her stomach. 'When do you want me to start?'

Carolyn picked up the box of tissues Amy had left on her desk, deposited them back inside her drawer and closed it.

'Taking everything we've discussed into consideration,' she said, 'I think Monday might make sense.'

Chapter 5

'Man alive, this is nice,' Kit sighed as his jam-packed Kia made its way up a single-track, tree-lined road towards Rowton-in-Arden. 'It's *so* green and lovely here. I feel healthier just for breathing the air.'

'That's air con. The windows are all closed,' Amy pointed out, cringing as they approached a sharp bend. She knew exactly what would happen when the car rounded it.

'Fuck ME,' Kit practically yelled, his eyes wide as he stared through the windscreen at the stately home that had suddenly come into view. 'It's fucking PEMBERLEY – as if from nowhere!' His face was aglow with excitement.

Amy groaned. 'It isn't Pemberley, and I think you'll find it's been there since the late eighteenth century.' She threw Kit a glare that she hoped sent the message *I expected better from you*. Also: *don't you dare start droning on about men in wet shirts*.

'It's Rowton Hall,' she explained, 'owned by the family whose estate the village is on. Nothing to do with Jane Austen, though it was supposedly the inspiration for the manor house in *Anne of Arden* by Georgiana Scott.' Amy made a face, as though this knowledge tasted bad.

'Hmm. Never read it, but I bet my mum has. Nice gaff, anyway,' Kit said, whistling and slowing the car by degrees so they wouldn't speed past it too quickly. 'Is it a National Trust place? Can you go in?'

Amy barked a short laugh. 'No,' she said. 'So don't go getting ideas. It's still a private residence. As far as the current owner's concerned, opening to the public is very much an "over my dead body" situation.'

'Isn't it always an "over my dead body" situation when these places get passed into the care of the nation? Some posh old white guy dies and his offspring discover there's no money left?'

'How should I know?' Amy grumbled, willing Kit to put his foot on the accelerator.

Failing to notice her discomfort and still thrilled at the sight of the Hall, Kit said: 'So you know the owners, then? Like, personally? Who are they?'

Amy sighed. 'Viscount Waverley and his family,' she told him. 'Everyone in the village has had dealings with them at some point – but from what I remember, *His Lordship* isn't exactly a man of the people.' She wrinkled her nose at the memory of Roger Ainsworth's stand-offish superiority.

'So there's a wife? Kids?' Kit asked.

Amy found herself wishing very powerfully that she'd hired a van and driven herself back to Rowton.

'Yes and yes,' she said.

They were past the house now, in sight of its landscaped gardens and the rough little scrap of woodland Amy had always loved. The memory of being caught there after hours by Sam Ainsworth swooped down on her, and before she could stop herself she was recalling their walk back to her grandmother's cottage – the fizz and crackle of tension that had ended in their kisses outside the kitchen window.

'*And?*' said Kit, clearly dissatisfied with Amy's monosyllabic response.

'And what?' she answered him, playing dumb.

'You are being *very* evasive,' Kit said, narrowing his eyes as Rowton Hall and its surrounds retreated in the rear-view mirror and the car picked up speed.

Damn him. He knew her too well.

'You know what I'm talking about,' he continued. 'I'm asking what the rest of the family is like, if the dad's a pompous old mardy-arse. Are they awful, too?'

Amy burst out laughing. *Pompous old mardy-arse* was the rudest and most accurate description of Sam's father that she'd ever heard. She wondered what Sam would have made of it.

'The Viscountess – Pamela – is as snooty as you might imagine,' Amy told him. 'Only ever seen in riding gear or a skirt suit. Multiple strings of pearls at all times . . . Carefully coiffed hair that would probably survive a tornado. You get the idea.'

'And what about the children?' Kit asked. It was too much to hope that Amy's efforts to describe Mrs Ainsworth might sate his curiosity about the family.

'Two, I think,' Amy said vaguely, even though she knew full well there was only Sam and his younger sister, Megan.

'Male or female?' Kit demanded.

'Bloody hell, Kit, are you building some sort of dossier? One of each.'

'How old?'

For fuck's sake!

'The son is my age,' Amy conceded, her throat suddenly dry and her voice a little rusty. She considered stopping there, then reasoned she might as well offer a little extra information rather than have it squeezed out of her. Reluctance to confess that she knew Sam would only supercharge Kit's nosiness if he uncovered the facts later, which – given his relentless mood – he was bound to.

'He and I were at the same sixth form,' Amy said. 'We had English classes together and a few mutual friends.'

There, she thought. That was more than enough detail, delivered in a way that wouldn't rouse any inconvenient suspicion.

'The daughter's a few years younger, I think,' Amy went on, hoping she could push the conversation past any further need to focus on whether she and Sam had been close. 'Sweet girl, from what I remember.'

'And was the lad sweet as well? Did he have a name?' Kit

asked, smirking, a knowing gleam suddenly bright in his brown eyes. Amy felt herself starting to redden and cursed her parchment-pale complexion.

Nothing she said now would exonerate her. Kit had clearly decided there was something Amy wasn't telling him, and since she had no intention of spilling it, she was better off keeping her mouth shut. He could spot half-truths and outright fibs at fifty paces, and obfuscation would only convince him there was something juicy to find out. Amy wasn't sure why she wanted to keep her history with Sam off the agenda with her best friend – but for some reason it was suddenly very important.

Kit shook his head at her silence and snickered. 'He *was* sweet, then.'

Flushed and annoyed, Amy stared resolutely out of the window. 'Sweet' definitely wasn't the word she'd have used, if she'd been prepared to use one.

'All right, Perry, keep your own counsel,' Kit said, smiling in satisfaction. 'But let the record show that whatever you're hiding may pertain to your secret soft centre, as discussed last weekend. You don't fool me: you're the human equivalent of a dark chocolate caramel. Hard, shiny and a little bitter on the outside, but sweet and squishy – maybe even a little *salty!* – beneath the surface.'

Amy sighed heavily.

They travelled for a further few minutes without talking. When they turned onto Rowton-in-Arden's small high street, though, Kit began exclaiming again.

'This place is STUNNING,' he enthused. 'First the Regency manor, and now this! It's just like where Kate Winslet lives in *The Holiday*. I can't believe you never told me it was so pretty here.'

Amy shrugged. 'It never came up.'

Kit scowled at her, then waved his hand at the little parade of old-fashioned shopfronts they were crawling past – most of which boasted carefully tended window boxes or hanging baskets overflowing with bright spring flowers. 'I mean, just *look* at it. It's a delight.'

Amy observed that the village cafe had changed hands since the last time she was here; it looked cute but modern, and the delicious smell of fresh coffee was drifting through her now open window. As an avid caffeine lover, she decided this was promising.

One or two of the shops had had facelifts, too, and several were even open. Back when Amy lived here, the whole village shut down each Saturday evening – and after that only the pub and the church welcomed visitors on Sundays, which had made for a serious lack of excuses to avoid homework.

Rowton's architecture was a ragtag mix of wattle and daub constructions with exposed wooden beams and Georgian red-brick properties. The older places had windows sunk inches-deep into thick walls sporting hundreds of years' worth of render. Their front doors were from another era – a time when people were shorter and didn't have to worry about getting troublesome things like three-seater sofas into their homes.

The Regency buildings dotted here and there stood taller, their elegant sash windows often bordered by traditional shutters that were visible from the roadside through their mottled panes. Vases of flowers, pot plants and the occasional cat stared out from many of them, hinting at the small worlds of contentment that existed behind the glass.

Kit drove past the clock tower at the centre of the village and stared, as if in wonder. The road widened to accommodate the tower for a few metres, with the left- and right-hand carriageways splitting around it. Wood-framed noticeboards were attached to either side of the brick structure and – as Amy recalled they'd always been – were peppered with posters, advertisements and local announcements. There was a worn stone trough at its base – presumably from a time when travellers who passed through Rowton would have had horses to water.

There was a strangled sound of excitement in Kit's throat as he glanced left and saw the bridge that connected Amy's side of the village to the older part they were driving through. 'Oh my God, is that a bridge? Is that a fucking *stream*? Amy, this is so picturesque I might cry.'

'Stop being such a drama queen,' Amy said. 'You sound like a presenter from one of those daytime property programmes. An unusually sweary one.'

Kit ignored her. 'This is proper chocolate-box territory,' he ploughed on. 'Perfect for a lovers' weekend getaway.'

'Take the next left and we'll come to the road bridge,' Amy said, exasperated. Kit nodded and flicked on the car's indicator.

A few minutes later, they pulled up at the kerb outside Amy's gran's cottage. They tumbled out of the car, stretching their legs before pulling the first of many bags from the back seat onto the pavement. Kit was enchanted by the simple loveliness of the place. The front garden was neat and tidy, its lawn freshly trimmed and bordered by beds packed with softly scented bluebells.

Amy and Kit struggled up the narrow path, dragging a holdall and several sacks full of Amy's possessions with them. Before either could ring the doorbell, a thunderous barking commenced.

'What. The fuck. Is *that*?' Kit hissed, a line appearing between his perfectly groomed brows. 'Has your gran got a Dobermann in there? Why the hell would you not mention the presence of a *terrifying guard dog* in your childhood home?'

Amy found herself laughing – properly convulsing – for the first time in days. First, she'd had no idea that Kit was scared of dogs, and his fear seemed very off-brand for a man who, in almost every situation, oozed the sort of self-confidence you'd associate with James Bond. Secondly, her grandmother absolutely did *not* have a Dobermann . . . Far from it.

'That'll be Bertie,' Amy said, wiping tears of mirth from her cheeks. 'Gran's very annoying, very loud, very *miniature* sausage dog.'

'*What*?' Kit burst out, just as Amy's gran opened the

front door and a small creature on extremely short legs shot through it, barrelling down the garden path and back up again at lightning speed.

The dog circled Amy and Kit, barking and jumping and wagging his tail madly. Kit froze when Bertie leapt up to place two glossy black paws on his knees, his tan-splotched nose sniffing the newcomer with enthusiasm. A moment later, it was Amy's turn.

'You already know me, Bertie,' she said irritably, but the dog clearly saw her as an interloper. Amy couldn't help feeling this reflected poorly on how regularly she visited the only living relative she knew.

'Can we come in now, Bertie?' Amy complained.

'Of course you can,' Amy's grandmother said, smiling broadly. 'Bertie! Come!'

The dog tipped his head to one side, as if considering whether obedience was likely to offer him any advantage. The brown patches above his deep, dark eyes looked almost like eyebrows, arched inquisitively. Again – and to her own surprise – Amy found herself laughing.

Only when Gran rustled the packet of treats in her hand did Bertie scamper back towards her, making room for Amy and Kit to follow.

As she watched the slow, ungainly shuffle of her grandmother's feet, Amy felt her blood turn icy. While Gran looked as elegant and beautiful as ever – her white hair short and neat like Judi Dench's, and her blue eyes quick and alert – she also looked stiff. She seemed suddenly older and less stable than she was supposed to be, and the shock of this made tears spring to Amy's eyes.

In Amy's head, her grandmother remained as active and irrepressible as ever – but now it was clear things had changed since the last time she'd come to Rowton. And when *was* that? Six months ago? Nine? Guilt broke over Amy like a wave.

Something was wrong, and she didn't know what – because Gran hadn't told her, but also because she hadn't asked.

Chapter 6

Once Amy's stuff had been dumped at the bottom of her grandmother's small, steep staircase, the older woman took Amy's hand and pulled her into a tight hug. When she released her a moment or two later, she placed a soft-skinned hand on Amy's cheek, assessing her face.

'You look tired, my girl,' she said, her voice tinged with concern. 'Still as pretty as ever, mind.'

She turned to Kit before Amy could pass any return comment on the awkwardness of her grandmother's movements, or the flash of pain her eyes had betrayed as she'd bent to push a still-rambunctious Bertie into a sit.

'I'm Grace,' she announced, seizing both Kit's hands in hers and pumping them up and down enthusiastically. 'Amy's gran.'

When she let his hands drop, he took one of hers, turned it over and kissed it.

'Kit,' he said. 'Pleased to meet you.'

Amy rolled her eyes, muttering something sarcastic about Sir Walter Raleigh and his cape having nothing on *this* – but no one else was listening.

Grace fanned herself with her fingertips and laughed. 'Goodness, aren't you a charmer?'

She turned to Amy. 'Are you two . . . ?'

'*God*, no!' Amy spluttered. Kit made a wounded face. 'I mean – no. We're just friends.'

'Nice,' Kit said, smiling sardonically. 'Really nice. I think what Amy meant to say there is that while I am *obviously* a catch, she and I aren't very well-suited in a romantic sense.'

'Ah,' Grace said, and nodded in understanding. 'Your tastes tend another way?'

'Mostly, but not always,' Kit explained. 'I'm attracted to some women – just not this one.'

Amy scowled at him and Grace laughed. 'I see,' she said. 'You like the wine, not the label.'

Amy felt her mouth fall open. 'Since when do you watch *Schitt's Creek*?' she asked.

Grace shrugged. 'Since Barb and Dave got the Netflix,' she said. 'It's quite *marvellous*, isn't it? Now, shall I make a pot of tea while you start putting your things upstairs?'

Kit laughed hollowly. 'We need to finish unloading the car first . . . I'm sorry to break it to you, but this' – he gestured at the clutter in the hallway – 'isn't the half of it.'

'Dear lord, Amy,' Grace said, shaking her head. 'How many clothes and shoes does one person need?'

Amy pouted. 'There are toiletries and books and work things, too,' she argued. 'And it won't be in your way for long – only until I can sort myself out with a flat.'

'Of course,' Grace said. 'Though you know you can stay for as long as you want? This is your home, too.'

Amy felt a surge of emotions she couldn't untangle: warmth, gratitude and the almost physical ache that came with spending time in a place where the absence of people she'd loved and lost loomed as large as the presence of those who remained.

Before Amy could say anything in response, Grace moved into the kitchen with Bertie at her heels. She pulled the door closed behind them so he couldn't abscond or make a nuisance of himself as Amy and Kit brought in the rest of her belongings.

A short while later, they had each drunk several cups of tea and made a sizeable dent in a recently baked carrot cake. They'd also dragged every last box, bag and case Amy had brought back to Rowton up to her old bedroom.

It was clean and tidy, with a vase of freshly cut flowers on the windowsill. They'd probably come from the back garden, Amy thought, as she glanced out of the window to survey the postage stamp-sized patio and the flower beds beyond it. Then her forehead creased in concern; she hoped Gran hadn't taxed herself too hard to get this room ready for her. Not only was she clearly unwell, Amy wasn't planning to be here long.

'Is this him?' Kit asked softly, pointing to an old polaroid still stuck to the mirror on the dressing table. 'Hari?'

'Yeah,' Amy nodded, smiling with fond sadness at the image. She was in it too: Hari's arm thrown over her shoulders, both of them open-mouthed and laughing at whatever dumb thing their photographer had said seconds before. She looked broadly the same as she did now, minus a few fine lines.

'Good-looking bloke,' Kit said, reaching out to stroke Amy's arm in sympathy. 'He had kind eyes. I'm sorry you lost him.'

'Thanks. It was the worst kind of shock,' Amy said, swallowing. 'Hari was one of the few people in our year with a car, so he was helping transport stuff to the venue for a mate's eighteenth birthday party later that day. He lost control going round a bend. The police said later that he'd just misjudged it – that he wasn't used to having so much weight in the vehicle.'

'Awful,' Kit said simply, pulling Amy closer. After a moment, he asked: 'Who's that off to the side?'

Amy stifled a groan. She knew who he meant. Sam was also in the picture, though not the focus of it; he was standing on Amy's other side, almost but not quite out of shot. His eyes were on Hari and Amy, his expression unreadable but his cheekbones razor-sharp in the murky light of whatever party they'd been at. His golden hair was mussed and there was a pint of cider in his hand.

'Oh, no one – can't actually remember his name,' Amy said, regretting the lie as soon as she'd uttered it.

Kit raised an eyebrow in evident disbelief. 'He looks to me like the kind of guy you'd remember,' he said. 'And he's looking right at you, even though you're dressed like Wednesday Addams.'

Amy shrugged, not wanting to dig herself any further into her fib. Not wanting to think about the silence that had swollen between her and Sam in the aftermath of Hari's car crash – the fact he hadn't sought her out at the funeral, that instead he'd seemed determined to stay away from her. She batted away a sudden recollection: Sam's eyes briefly meeting hers across the aisle in the crematorium, full of sorrow, regret and something she could almost have mistaken for longing. He'd looked away almost immediately and she'd felt broken. Abandoned. Vulnerable. Stupid.

'Do you fancy a walk around the village?' she asked Kit. 'We could take Bertie. Based on the amount he's jumping around, I'm guessing he's not been out today.'

'Hell, yes!' Kit said, seeming to forget the mystery man. 'Show me *everything*. Show me the pretty stream! And maybe the pub . . . ?'

'Done,' Amy nodded. 'The least I can do is buy you a pint for wrestling all my stuff up Gran's stairs.' She meant it, too: Grace's staircase was narrow and practically vertical – the kind of construction that wouldn't be allowed in a modern house. Amy wondered how Gran was managing it.

'Too right,' Kit said. 'Could I use the loo before we go?'

Amy led him back down the stairs and through to the extension at the rear of the cottage. Like her bedroom, the bathroom was suspiciously clean. The mirror above the sink was gleaming, spotless, and there was a stack of neatly folded charcoal-grey towels on a stool next to the bath.

How was Gran staying on top of all this, Amy wondered. The housework, the dog, the cake . . . Not to mention the front *and* back gardens, both of which looked immaculate, considering how slowly she seemed to be moving.

Amy returned to the kitchen where she found her grandmother reaching down to fetch a new bottle of washing-up liquid from the cupboard beneath the sink.

'Don't do that!' Amy said, more sharply than she'd intended. 'Let me get it.'

Grace stepped back and sighed, seeming both grateful for the help and annoyed that it was required.

'I'm popping out to show Kit around the village,' Amy said. 'We thought maybe we could take Bertie with us, since he seems a bit lively.'

'Yes, that would be a help – I'll make Kit some sandwiches for the road while you're out,' Grace said, stretching up to retrieve Bertie's harness and lead from the hook by the side door.

'Gran, don't!' Amy yelped. 'You'll hurt yourself.'

Grace raised her hands, as if in defeat. Amy grabbed Bertie's things, then stared at her as the dog leapt around joyfully at her feet.

'Are you going to tell me what's going on?' she asked, eventually.

Grace drew herself up to her full height of five feet. She squared her shoulders and met Amy's gaze without flinching – and, to Amy's relief, it was suddenly very clear that despite the stiffness of her limbs, Grace was undiminished in spirit.

'Don't be so dramatic, love,' Grace said, her voice steady and her tone just this side of dismissive.

'Gran,' Amy murmured, wanting to tread carefully but determined to get an answer. 'I'm worried about you.'

'Honestly, I am *fine*,' Grace insisted. 'You've nothing to be concerned about.'

'But you're clearly struggling,' Amy said. 'Is it your arthritis? It seems worse than ever. I've no idea how you're keeping this place so spick and span, it must be—'

Something in Grace's face shifted, and Amy felt understanding descend on her.

'It's not you, is it? Someone's helping you out. Who is it? Barbara?'

'She's helping with the house, yes,' Grace sighed. Then she stared at the floor like a child who'd been caught out in a lie.

'If you don't tell me right now why she's cleaning for you, I'm going to ring Barbara and make *her* tell me,' Amy declared.

'You wouldn't dare!' Grace cried, outraged but visibly admiring of Amy's nerve.

'I absolutely would,' Amy said.

For a moment they simply stood, eyeballing each other. Grace gave in first, as Amy had hoped – not least because she didn't have Barbara's phone number.

'There was a minor accident,' Grace reluctantly acknowledged. 'Dr Novak described it as me "having a fall", if you can believe it – like I'm some feeble old dear who can't be trusted to walk in a straight line.'

Amy felt the ground beneath her wobble – or perhaps it was her legs.

'You fell over?' she asked.

'I tripped on some uneven pavement and stumbled on the high street,' Grace said. 'Barb was with me and I was seen to straight away – she and Dave took me to the hospital and I was discharged a few hours later. It was barely worth mentioning.'

'I can't believe you didn't tell me,' Amy said, unable to keep the hurt out of her voice.

'I didn't want you to feel like you had to come rushing back here in a panic,' Grace said. 'You have your own life to live . . . your job, your friends. And I know you much prefer being in London.'

Grace was simply being truthful, not trying to wound – but the words cut Amy anyway.

'I had a right to know,' she said, indignant but also painfully aware that her gran's motives weren't selfish.

'When did this happen?' Amy asked.

'About six weeks ago,' Grace replied, inspecting something on the lino.

'SIX WEEKS?'

'Yes.'

'But . . . If it was that long ago, why are you still . . . ?' How could Amy put this? Unstable? Unsteady? In pain?

Grace sighed again.

'It seems that knocking my left leg has indeed caused my arthritis to flare up,' she explained. 'When they scanned my hip at the hospital to check nothing was broken, they were concerned by what was rather charmingly called the "excessive wear and tear" on the joint. That, plus the pain I'm still in, is why they've put me on the waiting list for a hip replacement.'

'A hip replacement?'

'Yes. Is there some problem with your ears?' Grace asked, knitting her eyebrows sarcastically.

'Don't make jokes!' Amy cried. 'This is serious. A hip replacement is a big bloody deal!'

'Do *not* swear at me, Amy,' Grace instructed. 'You might be an adult and I may be temporarily infirm, but I'm still your gran. I am well aware this is major surgery and that it'll take me a while to get back on my feet after it's done.'

'And when will that be?' Amy asked.

'I don't have an exact date yet,' her gran said, 'but Dr Novak seems to think it could be within the next couple of months.'

'And . . .' Amy could hardly believe she was about to say this, but she knew she had to: 'if I hadn't ended up coming here this weekend – if things hadn't kicked off between Hugh and me – would you have told me when your appointment came through? Would you have let me know what was happening then?'

Grace was silent, but consternation was written all over her face.

Amy struggled for the right thing to say and came up with nothing.

'Sorry,' Kit suddenly interjected. 'I've been ages. I love a nose around a new bathroom . . . Are you ready, Amy?'

Amy realised she still had Bertie's lead in her right hand,

which she'd long since bunched into a fist. The dog was sitting next to her, whining and staring up at it plaintively.

'Yes,' Amy said, slightly shrill. She knelt down to wrestle Bertie into his harness, trying to shake off the conversation she'd just had with Grace.

'Do you want anything brought back from the village, Gran?' she asked, her voice flat and thick.

Grace shook her head. 'I'm fine, thanks, love.'

'We'll see you in a bit, then,' Amy said. Then she made her way to the front door with Kit right behind her and Bertie scrambling desperately for escape.

'So. What was that all about?' Kit asked as soon as he and Amy were away down the street. 'I hung back on purpose because I thought I heard raised voices . . . ?'

Amy inhaled a deep breath, then let it all out in a rush. A second later, she jerked forward as Bertie tugged on his lead, impatient to be trotting faster.

'I asked Gran what's happening with her health,' Amy said, then recounted what Grace had just told her.

'Wow,' Kit muttered. 'Do you really think she'd have gone ahead with the op and not mentioned it? I mean, not to be morbid or anything, but these procedures come with risks. Why would she go under the knife without telling you when there'd be a chance – however slim – that she might not make it?'

'I don't know,' Amy said, tears pricking at her eyes. 'Maybe she'd have thought better of keeping it to herself and told me, even if I hadn't turned up here out of the blue. As for why . . . Gran and I love each other a lot, we speak every week – but I haven't exactly spent much time here since leaving for uni. I think she didn't want me to feel obligated to come back, which is thoughtful but also horribly misguided . . . And it makes me feel like an absolute shit.'

Kit took the hand that wasn't holding onto Bertie and squeezed it.

They walked on, crossing the bridge from New Rowton

into the older half of the village. Kit oohed and ahhed at the quaintness of everything in a way that didn't require Amy to respond, and she was grateful. Only as they began strolling up the village high street towards the clock tower did he ask, 'So what now, then?'

'Well,' Amy said, sighing again. 'I think my plans to rent a cute little pied-à-terre in the Jewellery Quarter need to be iced. I can't sod off to Birmingham and leave her alone. It seems her friends and neighbours have been helping out with the house and garden – which is the least *I* should be doing. I would have been, if I'd known what was going on.'

'So you're going to stay with her?' Kit asked. 'Amy Perry, archetypal city girl and committed Londoner, is going to live in a cottage in the country?' He smiled.

'I've done it before,' Amy said, smiling back. 'I can do it again. At least for a while.' She sounded bracing – so resolute that she almost convinced herself, as well as Kit, that being back in Rowton wouldn't drive her absolutely nuts.

Kit nodded, and as Amy looked at him, she saw his handsome face suddenly crumple in disgust. At the side of the road, Bertie was hunched over in a posture that could only mean one thing.

'*Poo bags*,' Amy groaned, closing her eyes and tilting her face to the sky as if praying for deliverance. 'I forgot the bloody poo bags.'

'Ah,' Kit said gravely, then laughed. 'Proof, if any were needed after the events of the past week, that shit really does happen.'

Chapter 7

A fortnight ago, Amy had spent her Sunday afternoon at a gastropub on the South Bank. She, Hugh and several of their mutual friends had gathered for food, drinks and chat, then settled in for the afternoon.

Replete with roast chicken and sipping from a chilled glass of Sauvignon, Amy had perused the Sunday supplements in quiet contentment when everyone was all talked out. She'd read in quiet comfort, her Veja-trainered feet tucked neatly beneath her on an artfully distressed leather couch.

It was safe to say that, two weeks later, life appeared to have changed beyond recognition. Today Amy found herself single, back in the place where she'd spent her most awkward teenage years and fishing dog faeces out of the gap between two cobblestones with a slightly ragged tissue.

Kit was still laughing.

'This,' Amy said, brandishing the poo-filled Kleenex in his direction when she straightened up, 'is *not* funny!'

Kit yelped and jumped away as she advanced on him, and she cackled at the momentary terror on his face. Satisfied, she threw the offending thing into a nearby waste bin.

'Maybe you don't think it's funny yet,' Kit said, breathless from giggling, 'but I reckon you will after a drink. Pub?'

'Yes, *please*,' Amy said with feeling. 'You can get them in while I scrub my hands in the ladies.'

They meandered up the high street towards the Old Oak – Rowton's only pub and the site of several hapless attempts to buy booze during Amy, Hari and Sam's college years. Living in a village where everyone knew one another made it pretty tough to get hold of alcohol before you were supposed to;

even casual acquaintances knew roughly when each other's birthdays fell, and every adult had a vague idea of how old the local youngsters were.

Added to this was the pub landlord Jed's fear of finding himself on the wrong side of Grace, Mrs Chauhan or – God forbid – Roger Ainsworth. The Oak, like many of the buildings on this side of the water, was part of the Viscount's estate, so allowing his underage son and heir to get publicly hammered wasn't something the ruddy-faced, lifelong publican – despite his generally convivial nature – could countenance.

Amy remembered the Oak as an old-fashioned boozer: the kind where the same middle-aged men propped up the bar night after night, the dartboard was always in use and the paisley-patterned carpets felt sticky under your shoes. When they reached it, though, it was clear there had been changes since she'd last set foot in the place: the formerly tired-looking exterior had been repainted a clean, soft white, and the old rickety wooden window frames scrubbed, repaired and stained an elegant, olive-y green.

They stepped inside and Amy all but gasped. Gone were the pub's floral wallpaper and fussy pendant lights, as well as the dark-wood furniture that had seen better days. In their place were smooth walls painted a gentle shade of grey, framed prints and neatly arranged tables and chairs. They looked, fittingly, as if they were made from oak – and probably by hand. It was lighter, brighter and *nicer* in here than Amy had ever known it. Some sweet, tantalising aroma wafted past her as she made her way towards the toilets. A waitress was hurrying by, carrying a tray with three portions of what looked like sticky toffee pudding. *Yum.*

Once Amy had washed her hands several times with the lime and mandarin-scented soap in the pub's renovated bathroom – all white metro tiles, chrome fittings and marble-topped sinks – she found Kit at a small table a few metres from the bar.

'Nice place,' Kit said approvingly as he pushed a large glass of wine in Amy's direction.

'Didn't used to be,' Amy told him. 'I think I might be in shock.'

'*Amaryllis Perry* – is that you?' a voice boomed from several feet away.

Amy cringed and took a sip of her drink. *And so it begins,* she thought.

Kit whipped his head up to look at her. '*Amaryllis?*' he hissed, eyes bright with unconcealed glee.

'Not. Now,' Amy said, through gritted teeth. 'I'll explain later.'

'Looking forward to it already,' Kit murmured, grinning. 'In the meantime, you'd better see what that scary-looking lady wants.'

Amy turned to see Gran's friend Barbara and her husband Dave, surrounded by empty plates that suggested they'd recently enjoyed a hearty meal. Bertie – who presumably knew Barbara well – was scrambling to reach their table, no doubt in the hope of claiming any leftovers.

Reluctantly, Amy scooped him up from the floor, which she noticed was no longer carpeted. Instead, large rugs sat atop what she assumed must be the building's original flagstones, restored to their former glory. She plonked the dog on her lap and waved in Barbara's direction.

'Hi, Barbara,' she said. 'Yes – it's Amy. Nice to see you.' She hoped this emphasis on her name would indicate a preference – and that she could avoid a protracted catch-up conversation.

Moments later, though, Barbara was pulling up a chair to sit alongside her, offering Bertie something tiny, brown and pungent-smelling from a ziplock bag she'd pulled out of her coat pocket.

'And who's this young man?' Barbara asked, blunt as ever and nodding in Kit's direction. 'Are you going to introduce us?'

'This is Kit,' Amy said. 'My friend from work. He's helped me move all my stuff up from London today. Kit, this is Barbara – Gran's best friend and something of a local legend. Are you still involved with the WI, Neighbourhood Watch and the animal sanctuary?' Amy asked.

'Absolutely,' Barbara nodded emphatically. 'As well as the parish council.'

'Pleased to meet you,' Kit said, twinkling at her.

Barbara was a handsome woman, rather than a pretty one; she had symmetrical, even features that were attractive but somehow austere. Amy had always thought she had the sort of face you'd see carved into the prow of a ship – strong, bold and spirited. She was tall, particularly by Amy's petite standards: at least five feet ten, with the sort of wiry frame that suggested constant busyness – a determination to happen to life, rather than let life happen to her.

'Thanks so much for helping Gran with the house, Barbara. And for getting her to the hospital when she fell,' Amy said.

'Not at all,' Barbara muttered, waving a hand. 'Grace is well-loved in this village, as you know – Dave and I aren't the only ones pitching in.'

Amy gulped and nodded. Frustration that she hadn't been there to help her own grandmother formed a guilty lump in her throat.

'Now, don't take on,' Barbara said, patting Amy's shoulder in the way you might do an anxious dog. 'I told her she should have let you know what happened.'

Amy nodded.

'But,' Barbara continued, a dangerous glint in her eyes, 'now you're back, you could certainly be helpful with a few things – especially while your Gran's less mobile than usual. I've a number of events coming up where I could do with an extra pair of hands – fundraisers and the like. Are you any good at baking? How are you with sponges? Meringues?'

Kit almost choked on a mouthful of locally brewed ale.

It was fair to say that while Amy had many talents, baking wasn't one of them.

'I'm afraid not,' Amy said, giving Kit a swift kick under the table. 'But I'd be glad to help out in any other way. Here, let me give you my number.'

As she added herself to the already bulging contacts list on Barbara's mobile, Amy wondered what repercussions this small act might have. A moment later – and with a victorious smile that made Amy even more nervous – Barbara reclaimed the phone, stated her intention to be in touch soon and announced that she and Dave were off home.

'Well. I don't think we're in Kansas anymore, Toto,' Kit said as he watched them go, looking as dazed as Amy felt.

Then he turned to her and asked, 'So tell me, *Amaryllis* – are all the locals like that?'

'*Please* don't call me that,' Amy said, smiling gamely but allowing her voice to betray her deep discomfort. 'It's the name my mother gave me, but it's not exactly "me", is it? So flowery and fussy . . .'

'No,' Kit agreed. 'You're no more an Amaryllis than I am a Christopher. You could have told me, though.'

'I know.'

Amy shook her head and decided to change the subject. 'In answer to your question about Rowton's residents, Barbara's a special case,' she said. 'But this is definitely another country compared with London.'

Kit cast his eyes around the room, taking in what must be a combination of village residents and visitors. Many a pair of muddied walking boots peeked out from beneath the tables. The lunch service was probably over, but it looked as though the Oak had done a roaring trade. Amy spotted the day's specials on a chalkboard at the end of the bar: breaded brie; pan-fried wild scallops with linguine; triple-layered chocolate and raspberry cake with Amaretto ice cream. No wonder the place was packed.

'If we *are* in another country,' Kit murmured, looking

over Amy's shoulder, 'it seems that some of the natives are *delightful*. I'm almost done with this drink, and yet I feel very thirsty indeed.'

'What are you on about?' Amy asked.

'Twelve o'clock,' Kit whispered. 'Well, six for you. *Don't look*, you'll give the game away!'

Amy rolled her eyes. 'If there really is some talent behind me, he almost certainly doesn't live here. Most of the men in this village are of pensionable age.'

'Hang on . . .' Kit said softly, narrowing his eyes. 'I recognise him from somewhere. I've definitely seen that face before. I wonder if he's famous . . . ?'

Amy itched to turn around in her seat and find out who Kit was ogling. The BBC had been known to film in and around Rowton – perhaps there was some period drama shooting nearby.

'Oh my God, it's the lad from your photo,' Kit breathed. 'The one with the just-had-sex hair, the brooding look and the pint in his hand.'

Oh. Dear. God.

'I'm sure it isn't,' Amy insisted, praying for this to be true rather than really believing it. 'You're imagining things.'

'It *so* is,' Kit told her. 'I'm certain.'

She was going to have to look. There was no way she *couldn't* look.

Amy twisted in her seat, moving gradually and slowly so as not to draw any attention.

Once she'd turned far enough around, she immediately saw that Kit was right. Her stomach spasmed, then made some movement that felt like a furious backward roll.

Sam had hardly changed: he was a broader, manlier – and yes, arguably even 'hotter' – version of his teenage self. Amy longed to look at him properly, slowly – to check him for changes that might not be obvious at first glance.

She didn't dare. Instead, she let her eyes roam briefly over his face: still as well proportioned and fine-featured as it had always been – that moody, smart-arsed mouth quirked up in a half-smile at something he'd just heard.

Enough. She'd seen enough.

She whipped back round to face Kit, realising too late that she'd spun more quickly than was wise.

'Amy?' said a voice behind her. *His* voice. 'What are you doing here?'

'I could ask you the same question,' Amy said haughtily, resenting the implication that she ought to be somewhere else.

'I live here,' Sam said. He smiled lopsidedly, amusement dancing in his dark eyes.

They were the colour of dark chocolate Lindor balls, Amy noticed. She *hated* that she noticed. She'd also forgotten about his dimples, which should probably be illegal. She shook herself slightly and tried to gather her suddenly scattered wits.

'At the pub?' she asked, intending to sound witty but coming off as stupid. He laughed at her.

'In the village. At the old house.'

Now it was Amy's turn to laugh. 'Ha! You make it sound like some run-down old shack.'

'Shack, no. Run-down? Very much so.'

Amy snorted.

Kit was looking from Amy to Sam and then back again, trying to parse exactly what he was witnessing. He stared at Amy meaningfully, as if to demand an explanation. When she ignored him, he took matters into his own hands.

'I'm Kit,' he said, holding his hand out to Sam so he could shake it. 'Amy's friend from work.'

'Sam,' Sam said, nodding. 'Amy and I are old friends.'

Amy made a dismissive noise and avoided Kit's eyes. '*Interesting*,' he said to Sam, his tone dripping mischief. 'I've known her eight years and she's never mentioned you.'

'I'm wounded,' Sam complained, looking at Amy and flashing her an amused smile that suggested he was anything but. He folded his arms across his chest, which was clad in a white cotton shirt, sleeves rolled up to expose golden-skinned forearms. He eyed her speculatively.

Amy sighed and pouted at him. 'I'm sure you'll live.'

'Are you two visiting?' Sam asked, addressing Kit. 'Is Amy showing you the sights?'

'Kind of . . . ?' said Kit, looking at Amy as though he wasn't sure what he was allowed to say.

'I'm here for a while, actually,' Amy said, her tone clipped and chilly. *Channel Carolyn,* she told herself. *Be more Carolyn.*

'Ah,' Sam nodded, swivelling in her direction. 'Taking care of Grace?'

Amy dipped her head to confirm this, then took a deep breath to cover her ire. It was bad enough that Barbara, Dave and Gran's other friends had known what was going on with her when Amy didn't – but she was incensed that Sam Ainsworth of all people should have had the full picture while she remained ignorant.

'Well then,' Sam said smoothly, 'no doubt I'll see you around. I've been back here a few years now.'

'Oh . . . ?' Amy said vaguely. She hadn't expected this.

On the occasions when she'd looked him up on social media, usually late at night, it had always seemed as though he lived between London and whichever exotic location he was currently holidaying in.

She didn't feel bad about stalking his Instagram from time to time – it was a perfectly normal thing to do in this day and age, she told herself. In any case, she mostly checked out Sam's photos for the sake of curling her lip at them. He was typically in some sun-soaked, rich-person setting, surrounded by people who were doubtless called things like Tarquin and Barnaby and Araminta.

'A story for another time, perhaps,' Sam said, smiling as he retreated. 'Have a nice evening.'

With that, he walked off in the direction of the bar. He settled on a stool and immediately became embroiled in conversation with Jed, who looked the same as he always had but with greyer, wilder hair.

Once Sam was safely out of earshot, Kit said: 'You have some explaining to do, young lady.'

'Urgh,' was all Amy could manage by way of response.

'*He's no one, I can't even remember his name,*' Kit sing-songed, reminding Amy of the lie she'd told him earlier. How long had that taken to come back and bite her on the arse?

'Spill,' Kit instructed, before leaning back in his chair. 'God, I wish I wasn't driving. I could definitely sink another pint while you get into this.'

Amy put her face in her hands, willing the situation to go away. When she straightened up again and looked at Kit through her fingertips, his eyebrows were so high in his forehead they were mere millimetres from his hairline.

'That was Sam,' Amy said.

'Yeah, he told me that himself. What I want to know is, who is he – or *was* he – to you? My spidey senses are tingling.'

'Sam is the son of the Viscount,' Amy sighed.

Kit's mouth dropped open. 'Whoa. So he's an aristo-in-waiting *and* looks like Heath Ledger at his hottest? Clearly there are times when God gives with both hands.'

'He looks nothing like Heath Ledger,' Amy insisted, even though she could see what Kit meant.

'Oh my *God,*' Kit said softly, closing his eyes as if in understanding. 'He's Heath Ledger and you're that blonde lass – the one that wanted to get into Juilliard.'

'*What?*' Amy boggled at him.

'Julia Stiles! That was her name. The actress who was in *Save the Last Dance*. Then in *Ten Things I Hate About You*, opposite Heath.'

'First-name terms now? You know I don't watch romcoms.'

'*Ten Things* is based on a Shakespeare play, I'll have you know. *The Taming of the Shrew*. Heath and Julia bicker and argue all the while but are secretly hot for one another. That's the vibe here, there's no point denying it.'

Why did Kit always have to hit so close to the mark? It was infuriating. But there was no way Amy was going to admit to having harboured a continent-sized crush on Sam as a teenager – it was simply too embarrassing.

Anyway, that sappy girl wasn't really her, and nor had it ever been. Those avid, breathless weeks when she'd been borderline obsessed with Sam were a blip on her otherwise sane and sober record – never repeated and never revisited.

'Sam and I never really got on,' Amy told Kit. This was the truth, if not the whole truth. Sam's quiet coldness in the wake of Hari's death had stamped out any feelings she'd had for him, except dislike. He'd been awkward, aloof and stiff-upper-lipped in the aftermath of their mutual loss, seeming to enforce a careful distance from Amy – almost as if he feared her anguish might contaminate him. She'd felt like she lost them both that summer, and it had devastated her. When Sam jetted off to spend a year travelling with some old family friend, she didn't even say goodbye.

'We had classes together, during which we mostly disagreed about poetry, plays and novels,' Amy said. 'Sometimes we ended up hanging out because he was friends with Hari and so was I. Hari was, like, the glue that stuck us together . . . Or the neutral zone between two warring factions.'

'But you never liked him?' Kit asked, his narrowed eyes doubting and playful.

'No,' Amy said, emphatically – relieved that Sam and Jed had sloped off in the direction of the pub kitchen and she no longer risked being overheard. 'He was always so smug. So arch. So *annoying*. He pretty much got himself kicked out of some private school that cost thirty grand a year so he could come to the state sixth form in Stratford . . . Talk about pissing all over your privilege.'

'Politically dubious, perhaps, but I do love a rebel,' said Kit, shivering theatrically.

'During our first year he got a job here collecting glasses. *Collecting glasses* for minimum wage, for fuck's sake – the boy who was, who *is*, going to end up owning the pub.'

'Well, it's unorthodox,' Kit said reasonably, 'but it's not like he was out there whoring and pillaging the local peasants, is it? What's your issue, Ames – poshos coming over here, taking our jobs? Did he get in the way of *your* glass-collecting ambitions?'

'Of course not,' Amy snickered. 'I just always hated the "man of the people" shtick. He might as well be from another planet, so why not just *own* that? Live in his separate sphere and just . . . lord it over everyone like he was born to, the way his family trained him?'

'He could lord it over me anytime,' Kit said, winking.

Amy shook her head in disgust.

'Anyway. Now you know,' she said, sipping the last of her wine and putting her glass back down on the table. 'He was never mentioned because he isn't important.'

'Did you really not know he was living in the village?' Kit asked. 'This is a small place. Seems weird that you never ran into him when you came back to visit your gran.'

Amy shot him a dark look, not least because she felt quite guilty enough about how infrequently she'd visited Grace over the past year or two. 'No idea at all,' she said.

In honesty, she felt grateful to the universe for never having thrown Sam in her way before – though she'd hardly given it many opportunities. She'd generally restricted time spent back in Rowton to hours rather than days, and she'd certainly never asked Gran or Barbara about what Sam was doing with himself. Perhaps aware there was something sensitive they didn't know, neither of them had mentioned his name to Amy in years; the last solid intel she'd had from Barbara was that he was based in New York and working for some big corporate firm from a corner office. At the time, she'd sniffed indifferently at this – but later, when her online snooping suggested he'd moved back to the UK, she hadn't been able to help wondering why.

'I'm sure our paths will barely cross while I'm here,' Amy told Kit now. 'Even if he is living at "the old house". . . Which, in case you missed it, is what he calls that stately pile we drove past on the way here.'

'Pity,' Kit said, pushing his chair back to confirm it was time to go. 'A few heated exchanges with His Lordship-to-be might have provided some entertainment, at least. Sounds like you'll have to start making cakes if you don't want to die of boredom over the next few months.'

'I think I've had *more* than enough excitement recently,' Amy commented as she led the way out of a side door of the Old Oak, avoiding Jed and Sam. 'I'm here to work and spend time with my gran, not resurrect old squabbles or start training for *Bake Off*,' she decreed. 'This next little while is going to be a quiet, calm time for me – and that's exactly what I need.'

Chapter 8

Despite Carolyn's suggestion that she begin her new role without pausing for breath, Amy decided to take a few days of leave after returning to Rowton. She wanted time to get her stuff unpacked and settle in, especially now she was planning on being at the cottage for the foreseeable future, rather than just while she was flat-hunting. It felt surreal, but not unpleasant, to hang up her clothes in her old wardrobe and arrange her vast collection of skincare and makeup products in baskets on the dressing table – though the process *had* made her wonder whether she was equipped for country living. Her array of strappy sandals and spendy flats seemed unlikely to get much airtime in the village, and she sensed several 'sensible shoe' purchases hovering on the horizon.

It wasn't until Thursday morning that her workday alarm went off at seven o'clock – later than it would have done in London, as for the time being she'd only need to commute as far as Gran's kitchen table. Her stomach cramped painfully as her mobile phone trilled, and after tapping the 'stop' button Amy got up to grab a box of tampons and a packet of paracetamol from a nearby drawer. *Of course* the universe would see fit to send her her period today, when she needed to wade through hundreds of emails and start getting her head around her new responsibilities.

She made her way to the downstairs bathroom and chugged the tablets with a tumbler of cold water, then washed and dressed at a snail's pace while she waited for the painkillers to kick in. The sensation in her lower belly was gnawing and urgent – as if someone was trying to dig through layers of skin and muscle with a spoon. It was at moments like these that Amy wondered how on earth women coped with childbirth.

When she stepped from the bathroom back into the kitchen she found Gran already there, preparing Bertie's breakfast and making two cups of tea.

'Oh love, you look poorly,' she said to Amy. 'What's wrong?'

'I'm OK,' Amy said, sitting down. 'Honest. It's just . . . *women's troubles*, you know?'

'Ah,' Grace nodded sagely. 'I remember how badly you used to suffer. I'll do you a hot-water bottle.'

Amy opened her mouth to protest, then closed it again as a fresh wave of pain squeezed savagely at her insides. She felt her eyes start to shimmer with unshed tears – the combination of discomfort and surrendering to her grandmother's care threatening to overwhelm her. It had been a long time since anyone had looked after her when she felt ill.

Grace opened a cupboard and pulled a scrappy-looking thing down from its lowest shelf. With a start, Amy recognised it as the furry, sad-faced, sloth-shaped hot-water bottle she'd used pretty much every month during her teenage years.

She felt strangely emotional at being confronted with this worse-for-wear, bad-taste relic from her past – this ugly thing that Gran had kept, presumably for no reason other than that it had been Amy's. When Grace handed the filled hot-water bottle over, Amy gratefully hugged it to her stomach.

'Thanks,' she said.

'You make sure you take it easy today,' her grandmother replied, briefly placing a hand on Amy's cheek and then putting a mug down in front of her. 'Don't work too hard.'

Amy smiled and shook her head. 'That's the sort of thing I'm supposed to be telling *you*.'

'Oh, I'm all right,' Grace said. 'Avoiding stairs wherever I can, not walking too far, resting when the pain gets bad – but Dr Novak's advice is to do a little movement every day, rather than let myself atrophy while I wait for the op. I'll recover more quickly if I'm stronger, he says.'

'Makes sense,' said Amy. 'Just promise me you won't overdo it.'

Grace nodded curtly. 'Now. Shall we have some breakfast? Crumpets and marmalade?'

This was a far cry from Amy's usual, rather purgatorial breakfast of black coffee and a chalky-tasting protein shake, typically quaffed on the Tube. It sounded wonderful.

'Are you sure you're all right making it?' Amy said, wincing. Grace rolled her eyes good-naturedly, but her frustration was clear.

'I know I'm not a hundred per cent at the moment, but I think I can manage opening a Warburton's packet and operating the toaster,' she said. 'If you want to make yourself useful, make another cup of tea – I always need two to get going in the mornings.'

Amy did as she was told.

Within ten minutes they were seated opposite one another sipping from steaming mugs of Yorkshire Gold and munching on perfectly crisp, buttery crumpets covered in the zestiest, zingiest marmalade Amy had ever tasted.

Seeing her blissed-out face, Grace said: 'Home-made with love by Barb's army of WI bakers. Tasty, isn't it?'

'*Insanely* good,' Amy concurred. She picked up a last shred of orange jelly from her plate with her fingertip and popped it into her mouth, relishing its tartness as it dissolved on her tongue.

MyFitnessPal would no doubt inform her later that this had not been a balanced or healthy breakfast. However, as her warming, scrappy old sloth rested on her satisfied stomach, Amy realised that – without question – it was the most nourishing meal she'd had in a very long time.

As she began to read through the massive dump of correspondence Carolyn had sent her since last week, Amy's pleasantly full tummy turned bilious. With every email and attachment she opened, it became increasingly clear that, while technically a step up, her new job was one that she'd never actually have applied for.

Carolyn had used the word 'commercial' to describe her latest venture, which seemed accurate enough. It was now obvious, however, that she'd omitted two others which were crucial to her vision for the imprint: 'women's' and 'fiction'.

Initially at least, it would specialise in the sort of novels Amy had deliberately eschewed her whole life: romances and sagas that promised laughter, tears and textbook happy endings. The role, in essence, was her worst work nightmare.

Amy suspected Carolyn had some inkling of this, but had chosen to ignore it – instead seizing the opportunity to get an editor she trusted on board with her pet project. For a moment, Amy felt annoyed that her boss had effectively used the Ground Zero of her personal life to sidestep the inconvenience and expense of recruiting an external candidate for the role. Then she remembered that, if not for Carolyn, she'd still be persona non grata in an office effectively run by her ex-boyfriend.

Beggars couldn't be choosers, Amy supposed. Besides, it was flattering that Carolyn felt she was the right person to get the thing up and running – even if Amy herself wasn't so sure. And what had Carolyn called this promotion in their meeting? *An opportunity for growth*. Amy told herself to focus on that, rather than her instinctive, nauseated reaction to stories full of silliness, sobbing and sexual euphemisms.

Among Carolyn's many messages was one with the subject line: 'Promoting our new imprint: IMPORTANT!' It had been red-flagged, too, and Amy opened it without further ado, keen to understand what could possibly justify shouty capitals *and* priority status.

Amy –
    We need to organise an event to mark the launch of the new imprint – celebrate the genre, etc.

PR budget tight – thus organisation likely to sit with you.

Suggest that you scout nearby locations that might work and ask for pitches/prices for hosting something of this nature. Also please consider catering, guest list, potential speakers for a panel, sponsorship, entertainment, & so forth.

Will leave with you.

All best,

C

Well, this was just perfect. Amy had never planned a major social event in her life – she'd not so much as organised a birthday party for a boyfriend, let alone a bash that was intended to impress industry bigwigs and attract the interest of up-and-coming writers.

And how was she supposed to pull a panel of expert, insightful speakers together when she knew next to nothing about the kind of fiction she was suddenly supposed to specialise in? Carolyn's emails were characteristically terse, but this was bordering on useless. Just finding out who was worth asking would involve a hell of a lot of work – and that was before Amy began trying to sweet-talk anyone into giving up their time.

Then there was getting to grips with who should be on the guest list, as well as the 'catering' and 'entertainment' Carolyn had mentioned – both of which, it seemed safe to assume, would have to be provided on a shoestring budget or via 'sponsorship'.

Finally, there was the small matter of the imprint this event was designed to publicise not actually *existing* yet – having no authors, no brand and no name . . . None of which it would acquire if Amy spent all her time addressing invitations and haggling over the price of hors d'oeuvres.

She took a deep breath and then let all the air back out of her lungs, trying to expel her stress along with it. Then, knowing resistance was futile, Amy resigned herself to spending some time googling for inspiration this afternoon. At least that way she'd have a few thoughts to share with Carolyn at their meeting next Monday.

Further down in Amy's inbox was another red-flagged missive, simply titled 'PHILIPPA FOTHERINGHAM'. She opened it with trepidation, and a grim certainty that her day was about to get even worse.

Amy –

Philippa Fotheringham is an old contact of mine – massive seller in the market I want you to target. Also coming out of contract with her publisher later this year.

Bringing her in is **top priority** for our new H-K imprint.

Inroads made with her agent – she is expecting a call from you this week.

All best,

C

PS: PF is based in Midlands – useful.

Amy groaned. Since Carolyn's message made no mention of who Philippa's current publisher or agent were, Amy would need to dig for the information without ruffling any feathers or raising suspicion. Carolyn was expecting that she'd do her best to poach Philippa for their new imprint once contact had been established – but rather unhelpfully she'd provided no context that would help Amy understand why Philippa might want to jump ship, or what could tempt her to sell her next book to someone she had no prior relationship with.

As for 'PF is based in Midlands'... Would it have killed Carolyn to indicate a city? A county, even? Philippa might live anywhere from Hereford (which was practically *Wales*), to Derbyshire. Knowing where this writer spent most of her time would certainly help when it came to wooing her – not to mention organising their first meeting.

Amy checked her watch; it was only 10.38 a.m., but she could already feel a heady mix of hormones, outrage and exhaustion sloshing around in her bloodstream. Sighing, she stood up and strode across the kitchen to reboil the kettle and hunt down a snack.

As her workday drew to a close, Amy faced a truth almost as unpalatable as some of the other truths she'd confronted today. It appeared that in the process of getting to grips with her new position as reluctant romance editor slash event planner, she'd drained her gran's fridge of milk, massively depleted her teabag supply and eaten an entire packet of Jaffa Cakes – all of which she should replace, ideally before Grace returned from her afternoon WI meeting.

Bertie – quite possibly the neediest dog in the world – had barely left her side all afternoon, snuggling and snoring in his basket at her feet, or even whining to jump up on her lap for short periods. Now, as Amy began to search for her handbag and keys, he padded after her, his soulful little face full of concern at the prospect of abandonment.

'Sorry, Bertie,' Amy told him, 'you're going to have to cope with no attention for half an hour or so. I need to pop to the shop.'

As she said it, her mouth went dry. But she was going to have to go there sometime, and it might as well be now.

As Amy crossed the bridge into Old Rowton and made her way towards the high street, her heart kicked up a gear. Trying to get a handle on its fluttering, she reasoned that she should have expected this: while Hari had never been particularly attached to his parents' shop, it was a place with associations Amy couldn't ignore – and it was a long time since she'd been there.

As she stepped across the threshold of R. J. Chauhan's Mini Mart, though, she was surprised by the sudden presence of a golf ball-sized lump in her throat. It refused to be swallowed away and her eyes resisted all inducements not to start weeping.

Remember him as he was, Amy told herself firmly as she swept away tears. *Focus on how lucky you were to find each other when you needed one another most.*

Scenes in which she and Hari starred flashed before her eyes like old home video footage. She and Hari, young and impetuous despite their bereavements, popping into the shop to buy snacks after they got off the bus back from college. Hari trying to cadge extra pocket money so they could escape the village for the night in the year before he'd passed his driving test.

On several occasions, Amy recalled with a smile, she and Hari had actually hidden at the sound of his mother's high heels clicking on the strip of tiled floor that separated the back office from the shop. She was a kind but imposing woman: the sort who'd always insist they mustn't spend their afternoons unproductively, then manhandle them in the direction of her dining table and hover until every scrap of homework was complete. Amy pictured herself and Hari stifling giggles as they crouched behind a stack of Kellogg's cornflake boxes.

God, she'd loved him. And she missed him – especially now. Especially here.

'Are you all right there?'

The voice asking the question was unfamiliar but friendly – bright enough to cut through Amy's fog of fond memories. She looked up, only to feel as though she were seeing a ghost. She was staring into eyes that were so like Hari's, the woman who owned them could have been his twin.

Amy had no idea what to say, but after a few beats of silence she managed to mumble: 'Jaffa Cakes. I need Jaffa Cakes. Where are you keeping the Jaffa Cakes nowadays?'

Shit. She sounded like some sort of chocolate orange addict, jonesing for her next fix.

A bemused line appeared between the woman's dark, perfectly arched eyebrows. She was taller than Amy by several inches and had long, lustrous hair casually swept up in a high, unruly bun. Around it, she'd tied a shocking-pink silk scarf.

'Biscuits and stuff are here,' the woman said, smiling and pointing. 'Let me show you.'

Once the woman had retreated, Amy grabbed the Jaffa Cakes, two cartons of semi-skimmed milk, a bunch of bananas and a box of Gran's preferred teabags.

When she went to the counter to pay, the woman had a slight smile on her lips and interest written plainly in her richly lashed eyes. She scanned the barcode on the first carton of milk, then said, 'You're Grace Perry's granddaughter, right?'

'Yeah. I'm Amy.'

The woman grinned.

'I'm Nisha,' she said. 'Nisha Chauhan. This is my aunt and uncle's shop. Hari was my cousin.'

Amy smiled weakly and sniffed. She swiped at her eyelashes, which were suddenly glistening again.

'I'm sorry,' Nisha said, sounding troubled. 'I didn't mean to upset you. Auntie Binita says you two were very close.'

'We were,' Amy said. 'And you haven't upset me, honestly . . . It's actually nice to hear his name mentioned – it's been a while. I've been living in London for years, though I'll be back here for a few months, now.'

'Really?' Nisha said, placing Amy's milk into a flimsy-looking plastic bag, then adding the rest of her groceries on top. 'Well, if you're looking for local friends while you're back, look no further! Meg and I will *totally* adopt you. And you absolutely have to join our book group. You work in publishing, don't you? You'd be perfect! And it'd be so nice to have someone else there below the age of seventy, ha ha!'

Wow, Amy thought. The village grapevine was clearly as healthy as ever. Back in London the people who'd lived in the flat downstairs from hers barely knew her name, let alone what she did for a living.

Also, Nisha had mentioned Meg. Could she really mean Meg Ainsworth? Surely not, Amy thought – by rights, Sam's sister should have a starring role on *Made in Chelsea* or be in the process of launching her own fashion and accessories line. Amy remembered Meg as willowy, glossy and beautiful: a classic, pretty posh girl.

Before Amy could formulate any sort of response to her promised 'adoption' by Nisha, or her urging to join the local book club, Nisha was tearing a scrap of paper from the till roll and insisting Amy write her mobile number on it.

'Brilliant!' she trilled, briefly reminding Amy of a brightly coloured songbird. 'Book group meets every month, usually at the pub – I'll text you the details of the next one. And maybe let's go for a coffee or brunch or something? It would be *so* nice to get to know you.'

'Okay,' Amy said, feeling more than a little in awe of Nisha's warm openness and strength of personality.

'I'll set something up,' Nisha said, smiling. 'Oh! And it's five eighty-five for your shopping, please.'

'Great, thanks,' Amy said, tapping her card on the reader.

'No problem . . . Oh! Hi!' Nisha's voice rose at the same time as her hand, which she was waving in the direction of the shop doorway.

Amy twisted around so she could see who Nisha was shouting to and immediately wished she hadn't. She also wished that she'd paid for her stuff and exited the building five minutes ago.

Sam Ainsworth was striding towards them, the last light of a changeable spring day blinking though the shop's large front windows to illuminate the gold in his hair and the glow of his skin. He cut an irritatingly radiant yet solid figure – like an angel thrown out of heaven for poor conduct, forced to take on corporeal form. *Urgh.*

'You two must be old friends!' Nisha cried gleefully, as though she were doing them a tremendous favour by reminding them they knew one another.

'Something like that,' Sam said, smiling. He slid his eyes from Nisha to Amy, who resisted the desire to stick her tongue out at him and settled for scowling instead.

Sam had come to a stop in front of the wine shelves. He was wearing rich-blue jeans and a grey marl T-shirt with a plaid shirt thrown on top, and had slightly battered-looking Nikes on his feet. If she hadn't known him, Amy might have assumed he was a normal sort of guy.

However, she did and he wasn't, so she said: 'What's the occasion? Hot date with a debutante? Surely there's something in your wine cellar that would do?'

She had no idea why she felt the need to reopen hostilities after all these years; it was like a reflex. An immune response. A defence mechanism.

'The only things in my cellar right now are spiders,' Sam told her, immediately rising to the challenge and seeming to relish it. 'And while it's *charming* that you're taking such an interest in my love life, this is for my sister. She's cooking me dinner tonight.'

'Trust me, I have zero interest in *any* aspect of your life,' Amy said.

'Obviously,' he nodded sarcastically. 'That's why you're stood here sniping at me when you could be halfway home by now.' He gestured at her shopping in its branded bag: goods for which she had clearly already paid.

'Oh, I'm sorry, *Your Lordship*,' Amy griped at him, a pink flush starting to bloom on her face because, in all fairness, he had a point. She willed it away. 'Should I have vacated the premises the moment you arrived?' she asked. 'Left the area so you could wander the aisles unperturbed, like a royal?'

'Heaven forbid! If you had, I'd have missed out on this scintillating conversation.'

Sam sounded cool but his eyes were bright with mischief – lit with the familiar nervous energy they'd often exhibited during his spiky exchanges with Amy at sixth form. He was clutching two bottles of wine, one in each hand.

'Er . . . ?' came Nisha's voice, shaky and uncertain. 'If that's for Meg, Sam, I can tell you she'll prefer the one on the right. The New Zealand Pinot Noir.'

'Thanks, Nish,' Sam said, his shoulders relaxing a little as he refocused on the task at hand. He put the bottle he didn't need back where it had come from, then made his way past Amy to the counter. This was the closest he'd been to her since the long-ago night when they'd kissed. She willed herself not to react in any way whatsoever.

'So,' Nisha said into the uncomfortable silence, which was punctuated only by the brief slap of Sam's debit card on the machine. 'Seems you two *aren't* old friends after all. My bad.' She made a comedy wince face, and Amy laughed.

'We're mortal enemies,' she explained.

'More like frenemies,' Sam countered. 'There were definitely *some* moments where we got on.'

'None that I can recall,' Amy said, entirely dishonestly.

'We must remember things differently then,' Sam said, and there was an edge to his voice – a pointedness that sounded dangerously close to flirtatious.

'I'd better get back,' said Amy, suddenly feeling like her skin was too tight. 'It was great to meet you, Nisha.'

'You too, Amy!' Nisha gushed. 'I'll text you. We'll do something soon, yeah?'

'Sure,' Amy nodded, smiling. It was a long time since anyone had so innocently invited her to be their friend.

'I'm off too,' Sam said. 'See you later, Nish.'

He and Amy both moved towards the shop's exit, shoulders and shopping bags colliding awkwardly as they tried to move down the same narrow gap between shelves.

Briefly, they were so close that Amy caught the scent of him: clean, but somehow deep and woodsy, too. It was like cedar and citrus fruit cut with herbs.

Amy felt heat rush up her neck again, and this time it flooded her cheeks before she could calm herself. She wanted the shop floor to rise up and consume her – *anything* to prevent Sam from noticing that a second's proximity to him had left her so flustered. Ever the well-bred gentleman, he merely gestured for her to go in front of him, then held the shop door open so she could leave first.

Back on the high street, he looked down at her – probably a whole foot down, since she was in flats. Determined not to appear cowed, she lifted her still-pink face to look right back at him.

'It was . . . nice to see you, Amy,' Sam said, sounding gentler and less testy than before. He raised a hand in farewell and turned to walk away.

Amy stood still for a few seconds, breathing hard and trying to regain her composure. For the briefest, most infinitesimally small moment, she found herself wondering if he'd meant it.

Chapter 9

Over the following fortnight, Barbara made good on her threat to claim Amy's help with several upcoming events. In between establishing contact with agents, reading the manuscripts they submitted and trying to source potential sponsors for the launch event that would celebrate her as yet unnamed imprint, Amy was corralled into taking part in a Sunday-afternoon litter pick *and* giving up the following Saturday morning to man a stall at the village bake sale.

The very idea of a highly organised, people-powered clean-up event was bizarre to Amy, who'd lived for so long in a busy city that she'd become inured to a constant low level of outdoor mess. The notion that streets, hedgerows and watersides could be pristine and rubbish-free almost didn't compute – and she was similarly confused by her neighbours' willingness to clear up other people's trash. It seemed Rowton's engaged, enthusiastic villagers were a breed apart from the tunnel-visioned Londoners who thought nothing of discarding a half-read *Evening Standard*, McDonald's wrapper or takeaway coffee cup on the steps down to Baker Street Tube.

While Amy wasn't what Barbara would have called a 'litter critter' herself, neither was she particularly keen on collecting the mangy detritus of other people's day-to-day lives. And yet, the previous weekend she had wandered around the village armed with a black sack and a metal grabber, plus instructions to focus her efforts on a specific stretch of the grassy banks either side of the stream.

Grace, who wasn't fit to collect litter herself, helped to co-ordinate other people's efforts from the sidelines, ensuring that tea and coffee were available for volunteers and supplying replacement rubbish bags as and when they were needed. Barbara, of course, was commander-in-chief of the army of villagers who'd turned up to help – and to Amy's eyes, it *was* an army: somewhere between twenty and thirty people of all ages, none of whom were afraid to get their hands dirty in pursuit of keeping Rowton tidy. Several individuals, Barbara's long-suffering husband Dave among them, were even sporting waders – presumably so they could walk into the stream and pluck errant crisp packets, Coke cans and fish and chip papers from the water should this prove necessary.

Sam Ainsworth had appeared shortly after Amy's arrival, not bothering to hide his amusement at the sight of her in a pair of borrowed, bright purple wellies with turquoise polka dots all over them. Not only were they the least stylish things she'd ever had on her feet, they were also a good two sizes too large – and she rapidly discovered it was pretty difficult to maintain an air of elegant disdain in footwear fit for a circus clown.

'You look as though you're in costume,' Sam had said, his face lit up by a wry grin. 'About to act in a play about the sort of person who helps out at community events.'

Eyeing his mud-spattered Hunters and lightly weathered Barbour jacket, Amy had seethed, 'What are you even *doing* here, picking up after the commoners? Isn't there a hunt that you could join? A gentlemen's club you should be propping up the bar in?' She'd stopped short of folding her arms and scowling like a stroppy teenager, but reigning in the gesture had been a Herculean effort.

'You're the newbie here, Amy, not me,' Sam said, supremely self-assured and unbothered by her sarcasm. 'I've attended almost every litter pick Barbara has organised in the past five years. And let me tell you, just in case you're in any doubt: that is *a lot* of litter picks.'

Amy resisted the urge to laugh at this, first because he

was infuriating, and secondly because she felt stung by this evidence of his genuine involvement in village life. She still hadn't forgiven herself for allowing video calls to take the place of actual visits to her grandmother for months on end, or Grace's subsequent reluctance to tell the truth about her hip. Sam's clear confidence that he belonged here also needled an old, long-dormant feeling of not fitting in – the sense of being different that had made running off to London appealing, but which was really borne out of being the awkward, introverted new kid with an absent mum and a dying father.

'Whatever,' had been Amy's rather weak retort, after which Sam had slunk away to join his sister – as well as a young girl of around seven, who Amy assumed must be an extended family member. She was blonde and sweet-looking, sporting a mischievous grin that Amy couldn't help warming to.

Meg was tall and slender, just as Amy remembered, with hair a few shades lighter than Sam's: it was long, poker straight and a strawberry blonde colour, its paleness shot through with natural streaks of copper here and there. Where his skin was beige in tone, hers was peachy – the sort of complexion that seemed designed to blush prettily at compliments. She had hazel eyes – a different tone to Sam's, but the same shape, with the same 'don't need mascara, unlike you mere mortals' lashes. Like her brother, Meg had enviable bone structure and full, pink lips. In short, she still looked every inch as though she were destined for a terribly tasteful, terribly expensive society wedding – yet she, too, was wearing wellies and a somewhat scrappy jacket, and had a bin bag in her long-fingered hand.

Meg had nodded at Amy and thrown her a smile when their eyes met. Why were she and Sam *here*, Amy couldn't help wondering as she returned her smile, rather than living in smart London apartments or lofts in New York? From what she could remember, their parents were hardly the sort that grown-up children would rush to spend time with.

Cool, distant, snobbish and old-fashioned, Roger and Pamela Ainsworth were generally unpopular in Rowton – particularly Roger, the current Viscount. Perhaps this held the key to Sam and Meg's regular appearances at events like this, Amy thought. Maybe, in exchange for whatever obscene sum of money each of them was advanced to live on every year, they were required to do a little fence-mending with the villagers – obtain some positive PR for the family so its senior members could carry on in the same, blasé manner they always had.

Once Barbara's volunteers had all received their instructions and the litter pick began, Amy had filled her refuse sack with rubbish as cheerfully as possible – though she was followed for much of the morning by Simon, the village postman. He was a history buff with no off-switch: a man whose enthusiasm for discussing World War Two, the development of Britain's canal network or the downfall of Napoleon knew no bounds, and whose ability to talk at length to a disengaged listener was legendary. As Amy discovered during the course of the morning, he also seemed to have appointed himself Rowton's most eligible bachelor.

When she returned her grabber to Barbara, glassy-eyed and exhausted by Simon's pontificating – not to mention his awkward attempts at flirtation – she'd caught Sam looking at her. Smirking, he'd flicked his eyes towards her companion and chuckled as he dropped two bags of rubbish into the back of Dave's truck, which would shortly be headed to the tip. Somewhere beneath the drone of the postman's lecture on the Battle of Stalingrad, Amy had heard the angry rush of blood beating against her eardrums.

She hadn't seen Sam since, but she'd continued nursing her annoyance anyway. No doubt he'd turn up at the bake sale this morning to continue his 'I'm just a regular guy' routine, Amy thought, as she hefted a folding trestle table into position and swathed it in one of the brightly coloured gingham cloths Barbara had provided.

The table was one of eight, now arranged in lines on either side of Old Rowton high street. The cobbles beneath them made for a lack of stability that necessitated much padding of the haphazard gaps between the ground and the ends of their flimsy metal legs.

In spite of her grandmother's encouragement, Amy hadn't bothered trying to make anything for the event. 'It would be daylight robbery to make anyone pay for anything *I* cook,' she had insisted, 'even in the name of a good cause.'

Grace, on the other hand, had managed to produce two batches of oat and raisin cookies, a gigantic tray of white chocolate blondies and a Victoria sponge – aided and abetted by Amy, who was chiefly responsible for several periods of intense whisking, bending to put in and remove things from the oven and three huge piles of washing-up.

Amy set out her wares on several of her grandmother's oldest china serving plates – pretty but worn platters that she'd deliberately mismatched for a worn-in, vintage look. She arranged some soft pink peonies in old glassware, too – beautiful blooms cut just this morning from a massive plant in Grace's back garden. Amy placed them alongside the baked goods as a final finishing touch, then stood back to admire her stall.

In a departure from her usual 'cocktail parties and avocado toast' content, she even snapped a picture and uploaded it to Instagram with the caption: *Saturday fun where I come from.* Before posting, and even though she knew it was mawkish, she added a heart emoji – as if to confirm to anyone who might come across the image that her pleasure in dressing the table was sincere. Somewhat to Amy's own surprise, it had been.

A moment later, she felt a presence behind her and immediately knew that the shadow falling across hers belonged to Sam.

'All your own work?' he asked.

Amy snorted and turned to face him. 'Only the styling. I've never made a cake or a biscuit in my life.'

Sam was standing next to Meg. The little girl from the litter pick was with them again, dressed in dungaree shorts and a rainbow-striped T-shirt. There were large square plasters on both her knees, and they'd become slightly grubby at the edges – as if to indicate that no amount of cuts or scrapes could stop her from pursuing her next adventure. The sight made Amy smile and catch her eye.

The girl smiled back brightly, and Amy noticed she had dimples in exactly the same position as Sam's. She *must* be related to the Ainsworths, somehow . . . Then it hit Amy that she was being incredibly, *unforgivably* stupid.

Could it be that this girl was Sam's child? She looked more than enough like him for that to be a very real possibility. What's more, the presence of a daughter would certainly explain why he wasn't tearing up the streets of Chelsea every night or playing the venture capital game in Silicon Valley. But if he was a father, who was the little girl's mother? And was he married? Divorced? Still romantically involved with whoever he'd cared for enough to procreate with?

The questions buzzed around in Amy's brain. She felt a throb of some awful feeling that seemed part anger, part agony as she turned her gaze on Sam, searching for clues that he might have what Hugh would call a 'significant other'. She cringed inwardly at the clumsiness of the phrase, as well as her interest in the private life of a man she didn't even *like*. There was no ring on Sam's left hand.

He was holding a stack of three cake boxes – the professional-looking kind with shallow trays and tall, clear plastic lids you could see through. He caught Amy's eyes as they lingered on his grip on the top box, which contained twenty-four home-made Viennese whirls.

'Before you say anything, Amy, no Rowton Hall staff were involved in the production of these tasty treats. It's all our own work. Mostly Meg's.'

'I— Er. I didn't imply otherwise,' Amy stuttered, grateful

for this opportunity to pass off her gawking as standard-issue snark.

'I could hear you thinking it.'

'Rubbish.'

In truth, she had been halfway to forming some witty quip that would have suggested a professional hand in their efforts – at the very least in the biscuit piping, which appeared flawless. However, she thought it best to maintain a wounded silence now.

Meg took the little girl by the hand and they hurried over, taking the cake boxes with them. Barbara was waving at them to set up on a vacant table, on the opposite side of the street a few metres away. 'Good luck with the sale,' Sam said as he made to go after his sister.

'Luck?' Amy asked, wrinkling her nose. 'It's selling goodies for the WI, not climbing Everest.'

'Has nobody mentioned there's a competitive element to all this?' Sam asked, his eyes all innocence but a wicked smile threatening to take over his face from the bottom up.

'Since when?' Amy huffed.

'Since always.'

'Gran and Barbara didn't say anything.'

'They probably forgot. It's one of those things everyone here just knows: whoever raises the most from their bake sale stall wins dinner for two at the Oak – donated by Jed, of course, rather than paid for out of the day's profits.'

Amy emitted a noise that was supposed to be dismissive, but instead made her sound as though she was experiencing breathing difficulties. 'I can live without a free dinner,' she said, rolling her eyes at him. 'And surely *Your Lordship* has the usual five-course meal awaiting him this evening. Why would you need pub grub?'

'I think we both know that *needing* the dinner's not the point,' Sam said confidentially. 'It's the winning that counts. Or at least, it always used to be.' He grinned meaningfully, showing off his mouthful of annoyingly straight white teeth, and Amy fought the urge to punch him.

Back at college, she'd made beating him in exams and routine tests her focus in English lessons – an obsession she hadn't bothered to keep secret. Even though they were consistently on course to achieve the same overall grade, she'd wanted to know that Sam's twelve years of expensive private education hadn't made him better than her at reading books or writing essays. She had also wanted *him* to know that.

'I am an adult now, Sam,' she said, desperate to sound dignified but unable to stop glowering at him. 'Unlike *some* people, it seems.'

'So I see,' Sam laughed, and strolled off after Meg towards their cake stall.

Amy did brisk business when the bake sale got under way – and in spite of her insistence that she didn't care about winning a free pub meal, she gloried in the speed at which her stash of white chocolate blondies sold out.

She also saw with satisfaction that Sam and Meg's Viennese whirls were going, but not yet gone. Was it so wrong that she wanted to beat him? Probably. But there was no point denying the impulse.

Grace appeared about an hour into the event, on the arm of a familiar figure. The sight of them together made Amy start and double-take, but there was no mistaking it: her grandmother was strolling slowly up the high street with Mr Bradley, Amy and Sam's old English teacher and – in their final year of sixth form – the college principal. He was greyer and leaner than she remembered, but still wearing his old uniform of slacks, brogues, a button-down and a smart jacket.

What. The. Hell?

'Amy!' Mr Bradley exclaimed when they reached her stall. 'It's a delight to see you. Grace tells me you're doing wonderfully well for yourself in the world of publishing.'

He always spoke like this, she recalled: he was formal

and scrupulously polite, with an old-fashioned cadence that made him sound like someone in a period drama.

Amy cleared her throat, not sure how to respond. She felt wrong-footed by his physical closeness to Gran, as well as a little like she was seventeen again. She half expected him to launch into a lecture on Chaucer's *Canterbury Tales*, or the importance of irony in *Nineteen Eighty-Four*. It was bizarre, seeing him out of context – like encountering a llama in a library.

'Er,' she began, 'yes. I work for Howard-Knight. I'm setting up a new imprint here in the Midlands, so I'll be back in Rowton for a little while.'

'And Nisha tells me you're to join our book group,' he said. 'What a merry party we shall be.'

'Yes,' Amy said. 'I'm looking forward to it. Can I get you anything while you're here? Gran – anything for you? I'm afraid your blondies are all gone, but I still have cookies and Victoria sponge.'

'Oh, I'm all right, thanks, love,' Grace said. 'Don't like to get high on my own supply.'

Amy boggled at her, then made a mental note to ask Gran what she and Barbara had been watching on Netflix lately. *The Wire*? *Breaking Bad*, perhaps?

'I think I spy coffee and walnut cake over there on the Ainsworths' stall,' Mr Bradley told Amy apologetically. 'I'm afraid it's my absolute favourite.'

Amy grimaced. She loved coffee, but putting it in cake was just *wrong*. It was typical that Sam would produce such an abomination.

'You're sure you wouldn't prefer a piece of Victoria sponge? Gran *did* make it, after all . . .'

'Well,' Mr Bradley said, the tops of his ears turning slightly pink as he glanced down at Grace, wearing an expression that Amy could only describe as adoring. 'Perhaps one of each, then.'

Amy boxed up Mr Bradley's cake and strained her eyes

to see past the crowd at Sam's table. She felt restless and antsy – alive with the need to win, in a way she hadn't been for a long while.

The next hour or so was a blur of greeting and serving people until the bake sale wound towards an unofficial end. Most stallholders had sold almost everything they'd brought with them, and foot traffic had seriously decreased as lunchtime approached. Nisha had only a small box of her delicious-looking home-made samosas left, while Barbara's remaining rocky road easily fitted into an old biscuit tin. Amy saw that her stall, and Sam's, were the most depleted. He'd sold everything apart from a chunk of his vile coffee cake, while she had only a handful of cookies left over.

People began counting up their earnings, and Barbara made her way up and down the high street, bagging up coins by type and taking note of how much each volunteer's offerings had raised.

'Well, my goodness,' she announced after she'd visited every stall. 'This has never happened before, but we have a *tie* on our hands, ladies and gentlemen!'

Amy couldn't help an eye-roll at this. Barbara sounded like a Channel Five game show host.

'Amy, on behalf of our dear friend Grace, and Sam, with the lovely Megan and Pearl helping him, have raised identical sums for us this year!'

So, Sam's maybe-daughter was called Pearl. A very pretty name, Amy had to concede, that wasn't self-consciously upper class. At the same time, she felt herself groan. Tying with Sam in a competition was almost worse than losing to him, though she didn't know why.

A ripple of applause sounded among the stallholders and the few in-the-know villagers who'd hung around to hear Barbara's verdict.

'Of course,' Barbara went on, 'this does present us with a challenge. We only have one free dinner to give away.'

'Amy should have it,' Sam said loudly, nodding in her

direction. She heard several appreciative coos at this, which dialled her irritation right up to eleven.

Why did he *always* have to play the part of Mr Nice Guy when in truth he was anything but? She felt suddenly furious. This was a person who'd barely even looked at her, let alone supported her, when their mutual friend had died – even after they'd shared *that* kiss.

'No, no,' Amy said. 'You should have it. I didn't even bake what I sold today. I just put things in boxes and counted out change.'

'But you still gave up your time,' Sam said reasonably. 'And you might enjoy a visit to the Oak. As you've probably noticed, it's had a bit of a facelift. The new menu is great.'

'But I didn't win it fair and square,' Amy argued, her voice brittle and petulant. Thank God Meg and little Pearl – whose behaviour at this moment was decidedly more mature than Amy's – were already sloping off in the direction of the pub.

'*Fine*,' Sam said, striding towards her stall with purpose. 'I'll buy one of your biscuits and then you will have won.'

'They're no longer for sale,' Amy said churlishly.

Sam was standing opposite her now, on the other side of the trestle table – its red-and-white checked cloth covered in chocolate smears and cookie crumbs.

'Have you gone mad?' he said quietly. 'Just give me a bloody biscuit and let's stop this. People are looking.'

'Only because you decided to play Prince Charming,' Amy hissed at him, irrationally angry. 'I mean it, I am *not* selling you a cookie.'

'Amy,' Sam sighed, picking up the pink Tupperware container she'd put the last few biscuits in, 'I was genuinely trying to be nice when I said you could have the dinner.'

'Bullshit,' Amy said. 'You just love that everyone around here *thinks* you're nice. This was a chance to look magnanimous – to be the lord whose largesse knows no bounds. To show off in front of—'

She almost said 'your daughter', but stopped herself. It

would have been cheap to bring a child into this stupid squabble – and it would have made Amy look as if she'd been snooping, trying to find out about his life. *That* wouldn't do at all.

As she tried to master herself, Amy thought she saw something like hurt shadow Sam's sunlit features. Next time she let herself glance at him, though, he just looked pissed off.

'*Amy*. I can't help the family I was born into, but you know as well as I do that I try my best not to let it define me,' he said in a low, heated tone that made her skin prickle. 'Generally my philosophy is that what other people think of me is none of my business – but you seem determined to *make* it my business. To prove publicly how much you dislike me, even though we've not seen one another in more than ten years.'

'I—' Amy started, but the words died in her throat. His righteous anger, plus the presence of a child he might well have fathered, combined to make her question how complete a picture she had of adult Sam, despite her instinct that he'd barely changed since their teenage years.

For a moment, they simply stared at one another. Thankfully, most of their fellow villagers – including Nisha, Grace and Ken – were making their way back towards the bridge or meandering in the direction of the Oak. Amy guessed that, from a distance, it must look as though she and Sam were having a cosy tête-à-tête rather than furiously bickering in hushed tones.

'Now,' Sam said, 'I'm going to take a biscuit and leave you a two-pound coin in exchange, and then you can get your pub voucher from Barb and we can both go home.'

'*No*,' Amy said, insistent for no reason she could clearly define. 'Give – me – that – box.'

She lunged for it, pulling it back towards her across the table. Sam instinctively drew it in the opposite direction and Amy yanked at it again. They were suddenly engaged in a Tupperware tug of war, which Amy knew on some fundamental (yet conveniently ignorable) level was utterly insane.

'You're being ridiculous,' Sam seethed.

She was, and she knew it.

'No, *you* are,' Amy retorted. 'This is . . . bullying. This is *theft*!'

'For the love of God,' Sam sighed, his fingertips still firmly stuck to the plastic. 'It's not theft if I want to pay you for the bloody thing!'

'Your money's no good here,' Amy announced tartly. 'No doubt *that's* a phrase you've never heard before.'

'Honestly, you'd be surprised,' Sam said darkly. He leaned forward a little and tried to extract the cookie box from Amy's grip, pulling it down and towards himself just as she heaved it in the opposite direction.

What happened next was like something from a comedy sketch show. Sam lost his footing on the uneven cobbles beneath his feet, accidentally throwing his weight too far across the already wobbly table – and as Amy pulled the container away from him, he came with it.

At the same time, Amy lost her grip on the Tupperware and fell forward, towards Sam, as it flew out of her hands. Their combined weight collapsed the trestle table, folding it in on itself so that for a few seconds they were sandwiched together, pressed up against one another until the hinge snapped and its two halves flopped to the ground. It was long enough for Amy to get a faceful of the skin between his shoulder and his jaw – and to notice he smelled the same as he had that day in the shop: warm and deep, but fresh as well.

They landed in a heap of soon-to-be bruised limbs, covered in crumbs from the gingham tablecloth, which was now lying beneath them like a picnic blanket.

'*Shit*,' Sam said. 'Amy, are you okay? I am so, so sorry.'

'I think I'm all right,' she said as she scrambled to free herself from the wreckage. Sam was already on his feet, and when he offered her a hand up she wasn't too proud to accept it.

His expression was pained. Mortified, even. His obviously sincere regret bothered Amy, so she said, 'It was my fault, too.'

'Oh it was *definitely* your fault, too,' he replied. He dropped her hand, then. 'I'm still sorry, though. I should have known better than to argue with you . . . We never were any good at just letting things go. I hope you're not hurt?'

'I'm fine,' she assured him, brushing biscuit fragments off her T-shirt.

'Well, I'm glad you two are all right,' someone boomed, 'but that's more than can be said for my blasted table! What on earth got into you? It was like watching a pair of hungry kids fighting over the last chip.'

'Sorry, Barbara,' Amy and Sam both mumbled, shamefaced. For a second their eyes met and it felt like that time she'd caught them and Hari, aged sixteen, with a six-pack of cider cans. All three of them had begged forgiveness and pleaded with Barbara not to rat them out to their parents or guardians. To their knowledge, after confiscating the booze and severely reprimanding them, she never had.

'I'll pay for the damage,' Sam said.

'You will *both* pay for the damage,' Barbara informed him. 'No more heroics – doesn't look like Amy is a fan of chivalry. You can split the cost of a new table between you, and in the meantime, you can clear up what's left of this one.'

After Barbara had stalked off, Amy and Sam gathered the splintered remains of the table they'd smashed and packed it into the vast industrial waste bin at the back of the pub.

'Jed won't mind,' Sam assured her. 'He'll probably find the whole thing hilarious when I explain. Listen . . . I really am sorry about what happened. Can I buy you a drink, perhaps – by way of apology?'

Amy wavered. Some impetuous, impulsive part of her wanted to say yes. But what happened then? If they bought drinks and sat down together as though they were friends, what could she safely say to him that wasn't snide or sarcastic or bitter? And what could he have to say that she'd want to hear?

Did she *really* want to know whether the cute kid in the dungarees was his? For some reason, she knew she didn't – at least not right now. If Pearl *was* Sam's daughter, Amy would have to process this information properly and it would inevitably adjust her view of him. She felt a strong desire to avoid doing *that* for as long as possible.

'I should probably go and shower the cake crumbs out of my hair,' she said. 'Thanks, though.'

'Right,' Sam said. 'Of course. If it's okay with you, by the way, I'll suggest to Barbara that she gives Grace the free dinner. I have no idea why I didn't think of it before. I'm sure she and Ken would love that, and she did bake the best stuff today.'

'*Ken?*' Amy demanded, one eyebrow raised. 'You mean Mr Bradley?'

'He's Ken to me nowadays,' Sam told her sheepishly, as if he'd been caught sucking up to a teacher outside the staffroom.

Amy nodded. 'Good idea,' she said. 'I should have thought of that, too.'

'Okay. Well. See you, then,' Sam said. He turned and walked towards the front door of the pub without looking back. After a few moments Amy shook herself, then began strolling in the opposite direction – wondering why on earth she'd waited to see if he might.

Chapter 10

The following Wednesday morning, Amy was enjoying a fresh cup of coffee and a peanut butter bagel.

Well, she was *trying* to enjoy the bagel; Bertie was sitting at her feet whining every time she took a bite, his big brown eyes so mournful she could hardly stand to look at him.

'Bertie,' she said, '*do one*. You've had your breakfast.'

'Peanut butter's his favourite,' Grace said, looking up from her latest Agatha Christie. She'd read each and every one of them, she'd explained to Amy – but some of them so long ago that she had no hope of remembering whodunnit, which meant she could enjoy them afresh.

Disappointed that his whimpering was having no effect, Bertie stepped up his campaign for a bite of Amy's bagel by barking at her.

'You're ruining my breakfast,' she told him, 'and on this, the first morning of our new Nespresso era.'

After too many miserable mornings spent trying to satisfy herself with Gran's instant, Amy had cracked and bought a proper coffee maker for the kitchen. It made a change from throwing every spare penny at new accessories, she supposed – she'd certainly get more use out of it than she would the latest Mulberry.

'This little sausage must be the greediest dog in the country,' she said to Grace. 'He's driving me mad.'

'He is who he is,' Grace said, shrugging. 'You can't train the personality out of a dog, any more than you can a person. He has many qualities besides gluttony to recommend him, don't you, Bertie?'

The dog pointedly ignored her, his attention totally focused on the plate in front of her granddaughter.

Just as Amy decided to relent and allow Bertie to lick the leftover crumbs from it, the doorbell rang. The little dog shot off towards the front of the cottage, barking at the top of his lungs and with his tail swinging from side to side at speed.

'For goodness' sake,' Amy moaned, racing after him. When she got to the end of the hallway, she picked him up and tucked him under one arm so she could get to the door and open it.

Simon stood on the other side in his postie's uniform, a clutch of letters in his hand and a fancy-looking parcel at his feet.

'Morning, Amy!' he cried. 'And how are you today, Bertie?' He reached across the threshold to scratch beneath the dog's chin. Bertie promptly licked his hand, presumably to check for possible food remnants.

Grace, having made her way slowly down the cottage's small corridor, took Bertie from Amy so she could pick up the parcel and examine it. It was addressed to her. She put it down inside, then took the letters and sorted through which of them were hers, placing them on top of the smooth black box.

'Looks interesting,' Simon said, nodding towards it. 'Swanky, too. Gift from a secret admirer? Should I be jealous?'

Grace had warned Amy after the litter pick that listening too politely to one of the postman's history lectures would give him the wrong idea, and it seemed she had been right. The note of disappointment in his voice would have made Amy feel sorry for him if his general air hadn't been so entitled – and if his question about her post weren't so blatantly nosy.

'I seriously doubt it,' Amy snorted. That said, she couldn't think of many people she knew who'd send her something this posh-looking for no clear reason . . . In fact, this sleek package reeked of vintage Hugh.

Amy felt a creeping, scratchy sort of dread crawling up

her spine. She hadn't heard from him in almost a month, and quite frankly she preferred things that way. If this *was* a gift from Hugh, what would it mean?

'Ach,' Simon said, throwing Amy what he seemed sure was a winning smile. 'Girl like you? You must have people queuing up for dates.'

Grace scrunched up her nose in disapproval. '*Girl?* Good heavens, Simon, she's thirty-one years old!'

At this, Simon's face turned roughly the same shade as a plum tomato.

'I'll take the term as a compliment,' Amy told him, not wanting to encourage any kind of crush but unable to bear the sight of him wilting beneath Gran's withering frown. 'It's a while since I've been ID'd buying wine in Tesco.'

He smiled at her bashfully, and the look on his face made it plain that he was searching for something else to say. *Not today, Satan,* Amy thought.

'Well, nice to see you, Simon,' she said briskly. 'I need to get a shift on and start work.' In truth, she also felt a compelling need to find out what was in her parcel.

'Oh, bye, then . . . bye . . .' the postman mumbled, retreating reluctantly, as if he didn't have a sack full of other items to deliver.

'Nicely done,' Grace said after Amy had shut the door behind him. 'Being able to extricate yourself from a conversation with that man is a skill it usually takes newcomers years to develop. You've gone native in a matter of weeks.'

Amy felt a little glow of pride, then glanced down at her parcel. The box was made of thick, matt black cardboard and the large cream label bearing her name and address was handwritten in a sweeping, elegant script. When she opened it there was another box inside, protected by puffy wads of pale tissue paper. It was made of the same dark, high-quality card as the outer parcel – but this time topped with a proper lid and tied with rose-pink grosgrain ribbon rather than neatly taped shut.

Even the air that had been trapped inside this package reeked of luxury and expense: it smelled floral but powdery as it wafted up at Amy, reminding her a little of Chanel No 5. With real trepidation, she pulled at the ends of the ribbon, then eased the lid off the inner box to reveal what was in it.

Hmmm. This was . . . unexpected. Beneath delicate layers of fragrant, gossamer-light tissue was an array of costly items that – presumably – had been put together by Epitome London, the 'lifestyle concierge service' whose logo was embossed on the inside of the box's lid. What in the name of God was a lifestyle concierge service, Amy wondered. And why would anyone need one?

As she looked at the items more closely, any doubt as to whether Hugh had sent them completely dissolved. She felt a strange, sinking feeling – a weird mix of annoyance, alarm and temptation.

Every item in this package was the sort of expensive, high-end indulgence she struggled to afford but felt inexorably drawn to. These were the kind of items that had seen Amy run up a credit card balance that occasionally kept her awake at night – but which Hugh could lavish on her with barely a moment's consideration.

There was a huge, highly scented candle from a high-end French perfumer in a fragrance so delicate and beautiful it made her sigh. There was also a bottle of bath oil to match it: a chunky little cut-glass vial with a cork and crystal stopper. It had probably cost more than most people in Rowton spent on the weekly shop, which – at the same time as thrilling her – made Amy feel slightly sick.

On one side of the package was a bottle of her favourite, very expensive red wine and a massive slab of her preferred dark chocolate – the artisan, 'bean to bar' sort that didn't come cheap but promised subtleties of flavour that, at least to some degree, justified its wince-worthy price tag. The scent of it, seeping from beneath layers of gold foil and thick paper wrapping, was mouth-watering. Amy buried the confectionery beneath a handful of scented tissue paper before the desire to tear it open and devour it became irresistible.

Finally, snuggled in a black cardboard frame at the bottom of the box was a selection of carefully curated skincare products. They bore the label of a famous Harley Street clinic: one that Amy had frequently told herself she couldn't possibly afford to set foot in, even with plastic in her pocket. As she read the labels on the elegant boxes that contained cleanser, moisturiser, serum, eye balm and high-factor SPF, she actually *whimpered*.

This was her dream routine, there was no use denying it – and it had clearly been designed by someone who'd seen photographs of her face, presumably provided by Hugh. Again, she fought an urge to prise open the expensive boxes, withdraw the glass bottles she knew they housed and discover the scents and textures of the potions within. Instead, she placed each one back into its perfect recess so they stared up at her enticingly, imploring her to give in to their promise of a preternaturally perfect complexion.

But Amy knew that wouldn't be *all* she was giving in to if she chose to throw caution aside and slather her face in 'silk and honey quenching cream'. She was aware this gift was her own, personal kryptonite – and that Hugh knew it, too.

It seemed beyond doubt that inspiring conflict in her – playing up to her weakness for fancy stuff – had been his intention. Somewhat shamefully, she had realised since their break-up that this was a key part of his modus operandi: by showering her with the 'finer things' he knew she craved, he gradually, insidiously indebted her. And for six months, she had let him.

How many times had she gone along with what he wanted because she felt, on some ill-defined level, that she *owed* him? It had taken the shock of the proffered engagement ring to jolt her into standing her ground and saying no. Now, it appeared, Hugh thought he could revert to their old pattern from a distance, despite having ruthlessly edited Amy out of his life mere weeks ago for failing to fall in with his plans.

Looking wistfully at the box in front of her, so alien in Grace's hallway and yet so appealing, she had to hand it to him: after a month of silence, this was a strong move. Tucked into a pocket on the side of the box she spotted a small sealed envelope, again dressed with the Epitome London logo. Amy's stomach griped as she reached for it, her bagel threatening an untimely return. She knew she had to read it, but she *really* didn't want to.

> *Amy,*
>
> *Please consider this a peace offering – and a token of how sorry I am that you felt the need to leave the London office as a result of my behaviour. As you know, I was devastated by our parting, and that hurt manifested in ways I now regret. I hope these little gifts will brighten life in the sticks for you while you're away. I also hope that your absence won't be prolonged. I miss you.*
>
> *With humble apologies, and in anticipation of future friendship,*
> *HH x*

Oh. Dear. God. There was a lot to unpack, here.

First – although probably not foremost – Amy bristled at 'life in the sticks'. Admittedly, this was a phrase she'd previously used herself when she described where she'd lived before heading to London . . . But for Hugh to talk as if she'd moved to some culturally barren backwater was different. It was patronising. She felt suddenly protective of Rowton, its unassuming prettiness and its quirky, good-hearted residents, in a way she wouldn't have imagined possible just a few short weeks ago.

'Good heavens,' Grace said from over Amy's shoulder. 'He spins a good line. Nice present, too.'

'*Gran*,' Amy said, shaking her head at the invasion of privacy. Grace was right, though: Hugh's message read like something from a previous century.

There was something self-consciously Mr Darcy-ish about penning a *mea culpa* like this, which would have been all very well if the apology had felt sincere. However, there was nothing in this note that acknowledged the truth of how badly Hugh had reacted to a mess that was largely of his own making. Amy hadn't *asked* to be proposed to, let alone a thousand feet up in the air. As for her 'feeling the need to leave' London . . . The implication was that it might all have been an overreaction on Amy's part: an unnecessary step, rather than a move directly inspired by his very heavy hint that if there was no chance of a reconciliation between them, she should consider her position professionally. At best, he was being disingenuous – and at worst this was a blatant attempt at gaslighting.

Then there was that final line about her absence, and his hope that it wouldn't be for long. *Seriously*? He'd insisted she leave his flat inside hours of their break-up, then reduced her to a quivering wreck within five minutes of bumping into her at work. After making it clear that he couldn't stand the sight of her, did he really think a posh candle and some snazzy moisturiser would convince her they could comfortably coexist again? It made Amy queasy to think he believed she could be so easily – if expensively – bought. She might have been persuadable once, but she didn't want to be that person anymore.

She snapped several photos of the package and card, then opened WhatsApp and typed a message to Kit. She needed to sense-check her reaction to this with someone who'd give her a no holds barred opinion, and Kit could always be relied upon for those, provided you could raise him.

Amy: Just received this from Hugh. WTAF? 🦨

Two blue ticks. Thank God.

Kit: OMFG 😶

Kit is typing . . .

Several minutes later, Amy concluded that Kit clearly wasn't typing. Or if he was, it was taking far too long.

Amy: Well??? What does this mean? What do I DO?

Kit: Sorry, back now – was just messaging Julius 😍

Amy: 🙄 Not a question for now, but who TF is Julius?

Kit: A very smart, somewhat nerdy sex god who is thus far annoyingly resistant to my charms 😔
Am trying to wear him down with words, since – unbelievably – my hot bod alone doesn't have him convinced 😱

Amy groaned and instructed herself to dig deep for some patience.

Kit: Okay, so re: what this means . . .
Tbh I am shocked but not surprised by this development.
Hugh thought by chucking you out of his swish flat and making you question your job security, you'd realise how shit life was without him in your corner.
Being so harsh and acting so fast was a power play – his Blitzkrieg, you might say.
You disappearing altogether was NOT in his plan.
Basically, you've flummoxed him by fucking off.

Amy frowned at her phone as she read Kit's words, all of which clanged with the ring of truth.

Amy: What are you saying? That he didn't intend for me to take him seriously when he suggested we shouldn't work together?

Kit: Hmmm. I think he wanted you to take it seriously enough that you were scared, the massive bastard.

HOWEVER, he didn't think you'd have such an easy out. He didn't expect you to up and disappear to a different part of the country by the time the week was done.

My spies (aka Jo on reception) tell me there was quite the row between him and Carolyn on the Monday when you weren't at your desk. First he'd heard of it all apparently.

Amy: God. I feel bad if it's caused an issue between them. That's awful.

Btw, I take issue with the phrase 'easy out', given I'm stuck editing romance novels, bleurrrgh 🤮

Kit: I'm pretty confident Carolyn can take care of herself. And at least you still HAVE a job.

Back to the point: H took his scare tactics too far. A month in, he's realised you're not coming back with your tail between your legs because life outside London is too awful to bear. So he's changed tack – decided to remind you of the luxe life you could be leading with him down in the Big Smoke. You get the carrot now, not the stick.

She surveyed the contents of her gift box again and sighed. It was some carrot.

Alone after Grace's departure for a catch-up with Barbara, Amy spent the morning looking through a stack of manuscripts she'd been sent by the various literary agents who were aware of Carolyn's plans for the new imprint. Despite her avowed aversion to romantic fiction, a few of them seemed promising – the prose sharp and the plotting unexpectedly twisty.

All the while, Hugh's gift stared at her from the corner of the room. Not sure what else to do, she'd stashed it there first thing and resolved to deal with it later – though she wasn't at all sure what she'd really meant by that.

Amy had been uncomfortable about this stuff being lavished on her before she'd sought Kit's view on the matter, but now she felt worse – and her disquiet was growing. Keeping the present felt like tacit acceptance of Hugh's machinations; maybe it even signalled that she would ultimately be taken in by them. That idea made her chest tighten with indignation and stiffened her resolve.

Without thinking too hard about what she was doing, Amy got to her feet and crossed the kitchen to open what Gran called her 'useful junk' drawer. She fished around inside it in search of an envelope and something she could write on, eventually finding a box of note cards adorned with cutesy drawings of sausage dogs. They weren't exactly her style, and nor would the image of a doe-eyed miniature dachshund with a ball in its mouth do much to convey the seriousness with which she hoped her words would be taken . . . But sod it. This would have to do.

She grabbed a pen from the drawer, too, then leaned on the kitchen worktop and began to write.

Hugh,

It was very kind of you to send me some things to enjoy while I'm away from London, and I appreciate the thought. However, I'm sure you understand why I can't accept them.

Now that you and I are no longer in a relationship, I think it's important for us to try and rebuild a professional rapport – and that means keeping things as businesslike as possible. This is such an elaborate gift that I feel like it muddies the waters a little.

I hope you're well, and that everyone else at HQ

is, too. Perhaps I'll see you if I'm ever in London for meetings.
  All the best, and thank you again for the gesture.
  Amy

There. That was polite but firm, and she'd explained herself as well as she could. She sealed the card inside its envelope and placed it inside the gift box. With what she considered impressive resolve, she then plonked the present back into its original packaging, covered the address label with a giant orange Post-it note and redirected the whole thing to Hugh's flat.

Before she could change her mind, Amy pulled on her trainers and jacket and picked up her handbag to head straight to the village post office. There was no time like the present for getting rid of *this* present. Bertie whined as she made for the door and Amy felt her heart squeeze. She really was weakening when it came to this mutt.

'*Fine*,' she sighed theatrically, snatching his lead from its hook and fastening him into his harness. 'You can come along for the walk.' Bertie wagged his tail and pressed his cool, wet little nose to hers as she clipped the lead into place. She couldn't help smiling and kissing the top of his head.

Just over half an hour later, the deed was done. Amy had messaged Kit an image of the parcel while in the post office queue. She'd captioned it with a string of woebegone, sobbing emojis and the words: *Tell me I'm doing the right thing before I rip this box open, run back to Gran's and commence an evening of Self Care for Millionaires.*

She'd held her nerve and paid for return postage on the box despite his lack of reply, but as she and Bertie rounded the corner onto Grace's street, she felt her phone buzz.

Kit: WHOA. You sent it back? That's bold – fair play. Wonder what his next move will be . . . 🫣 😬

113

This was a question Amy hadn't considered.

Before she could contemplate whether returning Hugh's gift might have been stupid – whether, in fact, simply *ignoring* it would have been a better way to handle his attempt to reach out to her – she stopped in her tracks.

The unmistakable sound of a lawnmower was drifting over the back garden fence. Surely Gran wasn't out there, pushing it? Had she come back from Barbara's and started mowing before Amy could prevent her?

Slightly panicked, Amy opened the front door of the cottage and strode through to the kitchen, then dropped her phone in shock as she looked through the window.

Sam Ainsworth – *Sam bloody Ainsworth* – was slowly and methodically directing Gran's ancient orange Flymo around the little rectangle of grass beyond the patio. He was wearing sun-bleached, dusty jeans, a thin, ancient-looking T-shirt that clung to his torso and a pair of gardening gloves. The name 'Oliver Mellors' flashed through Amy's mind like a firework, lighting it up before crackling away to nothing.

Stupid, she chided herself. *He's the snooty lord of the manor, not Lady Chatterley's hot gardener.* Yet here he was, gardening. Looking hot. This last fact was one Amy decided to ignore in favour of wondering what the hell he was playing at.

She shook herself and bent down to pick up her phone from the floor. As she straightened again, new pieces of the 'Gran's cottage looks perfect' puzzle fell into place. What was it Barbara had said? *Grace is well-loved in this village. Dave and I aren't the only ones pitching in.*

As a person who enjoyed a nice bouquet but could barely keep cacti alive, Amy hadn't given much thought to who might be tending Gran's garden while she was less mobile than usual. Now it seemed clear that Sam was the person responsible for keeping the grass neat and Grace's prized plants in bloom. She tried to unpick his motivation for this apparently selfless support and rapidly discovered she couldn't make sense of it. Showing up at litter picks and bake sales was an easy way to virtue-signal an interest in village life, but this was something else – something Amy couldn't explain away, and which made her feel irritated. Prickly with discomfort.

Should she knock on the window and acknowledge him? Offer him a cup of tea? What was the etiquette for finding the local landowner, who was also your sworn nemesis, doing chores in your grandmother's back garden?

Before she could formulate any kind of game plan, Sam looked up and caught her staring. He turned the mower off, ran a hand through his rather unkempt golden hair and nodded awkwardly in Amy's direction. He thrust his hands into his pockets and took a breath deep enough that she could see the air go in and out of him, swelling and then loosening his chest, from several metres away. Then he came towards the back door, seeming to have settled an argument with himself.

Amy unlocked and opened the door and Bertie scampered out to greet Sam, who immediately laughed and leaned down to pat him.

'Hi,' he said, when he was upright again. He was flushed, though it wasn't particularly warm outside – and this, coupled with his ruffled hair and scruffy clothing, unsettled her. He looked too normal. Too earthy. Too . . . *real*.

'Hi,' Amy said back, becoming aware a moment too late that she was gawking at him.

The stripes of colour lighting up Sam's cheekbones brightened. With a jolt, Amy realised he was embarrassed.

'I . . . I'm sorry to intrude like this,' he said, sounding sincere. 'I did knock, and when no one answered I thought now would be a good time to see to the lawn. I try to pop by when I won't disturb Grace. Or you, now. I have a key to the side gate and one for the shed.'

Amy nodded.

'Can I get you anything? Tea? Water?'

'No, thanks,' Sam said with an anaemic smile. 'I'm almost done. Don't trouble yourself – I'll lock everything up and let myself out once I'm finished.'

'OK,' Amy told him. 'If you're sure.'

'I am,' he confirmed.

Amy coaxed Bertie back into the house with the promise of a dog treat, then closed the door behind them. She sat at the kitchen table, deliberately placing her back to the windows so she wouldn't be tempted to look out. She also turned up the volume on Spotify's latest 'Made For You' playlist in a bid to prevent herself from listening for the slam of the shed door, or the scrape of a key in a lock.

She'd set herself the task of finding out everything she could about Philippa Fotheringham in advance of their meeting this Friday, and before long she'd fallen down an online wormhole into what felt like an alternate universe: a place with its own celebrities, superfans and even its own lexicon. Apparently, 'HEA' stood for 'happy ever after', while 'HFN' meant the protagonist of a novel obtained 'happiness for now' by its final page. Amy also discovered that a 'cinnamon roll' was not merely a tasty baked treat, but a well-known term for a romantic hero who was 'super sweet'. Her mind boggled.

Meanwhile, every blog and book review she read further strengthened Amy's confidence that Philippa could be relied upon to produce what her audience called 'autobuys' – books they would always purchase because they had total trust in her to satisfy them. From a professional standpoint, this was exciting – a far cry from her usual experiences with authors who might be critically acclaimed, but struggled to entertain readers en masse.

Only when Gran came home and put the kettle on did Amy return to the here and now. 'Ah! Sam's been, then. Did you see him?' Grace asked, glancing through the window at the freshly trimmed grass.

'Briefly,' Amy confirmed, feigning nonchalance.

'He's a good lad,' Grace said, mostly to herself. 'Nothing

like his father, thank heavens. Insisted on helping me out with the pruning and such when he heard about my accident – said he remembered from years back how precious I am about the garden.'

Amy merely hummed in acknowledgement of this, not trusting herself to ask questions or pass comment.

It was much later that she realised an obvious query – and one she could easily have needled Sam with – had completely passed her by. The whole business with Hugh and his parcel of posh gifts had clearly knocked her off her game.

Any other time she'd have demanded to know why Sam was mowing the lawn himself – making a show of performing manual labour when surely the estate had someone on the payroll he could have sent instead. Today she'd simply ogled him, then offered him a cuppa.

Chapter 11

Amy's first impression of *And So We Meet Again* – Philippa Fotheringham's latest five-star-rated novel – was not good. Its cover showed a bosomy woman staring up into the smouldering eyes of a tall, dark man with a jawline so sharp it could be used to chop logs.

She needed to read the book before meeting the woman herself tomorrow lunchtime, and she'd been putting off the task all week – but with just over twenty-four hours until their appointment, Amy had run out of excuses.

She supposed the book's appeal must be the strong sense of inevitability that hung over the characters from the opening pages, rather than any doubt as to whether Voluptuous Vamp would eventually enjoy a tryst with Chiselled Chin Man. From the looks on the faces of its cover stars, it seemed pretty clear what was going to happen when the people in this story 'met again'.

Yet several hours after first picking up her Kindle, Amy was still engrossed in the tale of Lady Sarah Bamford and handsome but wholly unsuitable Thomas Montgomery, her recently deceased father's estate manager. Bertie, curled up next to Amy on the sofa, grumbled in his sleep as she reached for a biscuit from the tin on the side table.

I have dreamt of Thomas Montgomery often since leaving my family's estate for my husband's, Amy read, her eyes skipping across her e-reader's screen at speed. *In sleep and awake I have pictured his face: dark eyes, plush lips and that angular jaw I so often wanted to press my lips to. I've imagined his broad shoulders, thought of his clever and capable hands. I've recalled the contained strength of his body, revealed fleetingly in brief movements: the mounting of a horse; the lifting of a heavy trunk; the push to open a stiff, unyielding door. And now he is with me, and we are alone at last . . .*

'EARTH TO AMY?' Grace boomed, at a volume loud enough to finally reach her. 'I've asked you three times now if you'd like a cup of tea.'

'Oh,' Amy murmured, 'sorry. Yes, please.'

'What are you reading?' Grace asked, cocking an eyebrow. 'You've been buried in it all morning. It must be good.'

'Er—' Amy stuttered. 'Well. It's research.'

Then she decided to be honest. 'Actually, it *is* pretty good. It's the latest from an author called Philippa Fotheringham – I'm meeting with her tomorrow.'

Amy could tell her cheeks were flaming. She felt an odd sort of shame at having been caught enjoying this book – partly because she'd spent years railing against romance in all its guises, but also because she'd previously considered herself far too smart to be sucked in by a story whose ending she could predict from page one. As it turned out, matters weren't quite so simple.

'Ah,' Grace said. 'I've read a few of hers. Entertaining, well-written romps with just enough racy bits, I find.'

Amy felt her eyes grow wide. She was no prude, but she had zero desire to begin a discussion on fictional sex with her seventy-four-year-old grandmother. Slightly at a loss for words, she nodded and said, 'That seems a fair assessment.'

Grinning at Amy's embarrassment, Grace rolled her eyes and left the room.

In fairness, it probably shouldn't have surprised Amy that Gran had read some of Philippa's books. This week's research had already proved beyond doubt that she was wildly popular, and that signing her would be very much the coup Carolyn had claimed it would be. Via self-publishing and then through book deals with several small houses, Philippa had sold more than a million copies of her works.

These comprised around twenty full-length novels as well as several short stories and compilations, all of which were available digitally, with some in paperback.

Meanwhile, @Philippa_Writes had in excess of 20,000 Twitter followers, over 17,000 Facebook fans and a not too shabby Instagram following of 4,759. These were the kind of numbers anyone on Amy's old literary list might only ever have dreamt of. There was no question that Philippa Fotheringham had a loyal and expanding army of readers, even if – perhaps to her discredit as a publishing professional – Amy had never heard of her until recently.

From the author blogs and photos published on PhilippaFotheringham.com, Amy had gleaned that the woman herself was both self-assured and formidable – an impression that tallied with the scant information Carolyn had shared, and which Amy felt was well worth having before they got together in person. Philippa beamed warmly at website visitors from a professional-looking portrait, but her posture was ramrod straight and there was a keen intelligence in her eyes that reminded Amy of her boss. She might not dress as sharply as Carolyn – there was a lot of lilac and more than one waterfall cardigan in Philippa's wardrobe, based on the evidence Amy had seen so far – but it seemed likely that whatever relationship existed between the two women was built on a foundation of shared intelligence and business acumen.

When Grace returned to the sitting room with just one mug of Yorkshire Gold, Amy frowned. She took the proffered tea and placed it on a coaster just next to her, then asked, 'Are you not having one?'

'No,' Grace replied. 'I'm off out for coffee at the garden centre with a friend.'

'A *friend*?' Amy said, frowning again and noticing her grandmother's fresh lipstick. 'Does this friend have a history of handing out detentions for late coursework? Is it someone who's permanently dressed like a well-to-do TV historian and – inexplicably, in my view – actually *likes* coffee cake?'

Now it was Grace's turn to blush. '*Yes*, if you must know.'

At that moment, the doorbell rang. Amy leapt up to answer it and found Mr Bradley on the other side, looking as neat and dignified as ever in a pressed shirt, jacket, tie and matching pocket square. Amy felt a sudden swell of warmth for him even though he was ridiculously dressed up for a stroll around displays of shrubs and bedding plants. He'd made a special effort to look nice for Grace, which signalled sincere affection for her.

'Come on in, Mr Bradley,' Amy said.

'Oh dear, please call me Ken,' he said, smiling.

'*Ken*. Sorry.'

'Don't bother, Ken!' Gran called from further inside. 'I'm ready – on my way to you now.'

The moment she stepped across the threshold of the cottage to greet him, he gently kissed her cheek and arranged himself so she could take his arm. Although they were only walking as far as his car, Amy's heart gave another little squeeze at her former teacher's reflexive consideration for Grace. Everything about his conduct was old-fashioned and fussy, and it should have made Amy roll her eyes – but it didn't.

Something inside her suddenly twinged with fresh consciousness of how *in*considerate Hugh had sometimes been. She cringed at her own stupidity: why hadn't she seen it at the time? He'd lavished attention on her, taken her to nice restaurants and spent inordinate amounts of money on holidays – but everything had been on his terms, and she'd been too dazzled to notice until he confronted her with an engagement ring.

She sighed and flopped back onto the sofa, reaching for her tea mug with one hand and her Kindle with the other. She might as well finish Philippa Fotheringham's book now she'd started it – and it *was* work, after all.

The following afternoon, seated on the train to Birmingham, Amy tried not to think about how badly she needed her lunch with Philippa to go well. It was rare for Amy to woo an author with such a strong history of successful publishing, and despite all the reading and research she'd done over the past few weeks she still felt like a traveller in a foreign land. Romantic fiction, it turned out, wasn't all the same: it was a rich and complex field in which you could become expert, and Amy was barely proficient. What's more, the stakes were high today: Carolyn wanted Amy to bring Philippa in for H-K and would *not* be impressed if she messed this up.

Determined to present what felt like inexperience as the 'fresh pair of eyes' Philippa Fotheringham's work could benefit from, Amy had booked a table at a classy-looking place with a Michelin star and a tasting menu that sounded both appealing and unfussy. She'd got the sense from Philippa's agent that she wouldn't take kindly to fish-flavoured foams, desserts dressed up as breakfasts or main courses served in smoke-filled silver domes. Within moments of arriving at the restaurant, Amy felt an intense rush of relief that she'd followed this instinct.

Philippa was already waiting for her, resplendent in a salmon-pink silk shirt. Its deep V-neck showed off Philippa's high shelf of a bosom, which Amy couldn't help thinking would not have been out of place in one of her Regency bodice-rippers. She had a mane of thick, glossy, professionally blow-dried hair that Amy could tell was expensively highlighted. Strands of white and silver mingled with cool blonde streaks, which enhanced rather than covered up Philippa's greys. She was a very attractive woman in a take-no-prisoners sort of way: the curvy, pastel-shaded, ultra-feminine antithesis of Carolyn in looks, yet possessed of a very similar vibe.

'Amy!' Philippa boomed, in a gloriously broad Birmingham accent. 'It's lovely to meet you. This place is all right, isn't it?' Like the voices of all proper Brummies, Philippa's had a melodic, sing-song quality. Almost every word was pronounced as though it had somehow acquired extra vowels.

'I'm glad you like it,' Amy said, smiling. 'The menu looks great.'

'It does. None of the nonsense with liquid nitrogen that you often find in such establishments. I mean, what's that all about? I went somewhere last year where they were dishing out freeze-dried popcorn for pudding and calling it art. Honest to God, I'd rather have had a Mr Whippy with a flake.'

Amy laughed. 'I think we're safe here. And if you'd prefer a 99 for afters, just let me know – I'm pretty sure I saw an ice cream van on the way from the station. I'll even shell out for strawberry sauce.'

'Now you're talking my language, bab.'

Bab. *Wow*. Amy couldn't remember the last time she'd been called that – her grandad had been the family's Digbeth native and he'd been dead for twenty-five years.

Amy and Philippa agreed to share a bottle of rosé and some fizzy water, settling into a comfortable conversation as they waited for the first of their seven mini dishes to appear.

Having finished *And So We Meet Again* last night, Amy had already started another of Philippa's books – a contemporary romcom this time, *Katie McGough Starts Over* – and she was able to share her genuine enthusiasm for these novels, as well as chat with the author in depth about plotting, settings and characters.

As she tapped her Kindle screen yesterday evening to award Lady Sarah and Thomas's tale a five-star rating, Amy had reconciled herself to her affection for Philippa's novels on the basis that, if you were so minded, you could enjoy a J. R. R. Tolkien book without actually *believing* in hobbits. Surely, she reasoned, the same could be said of true love.

'So, tell me about you,' Philippa said, during a lull between their menu's savoury and sweet courses. 'Carolyn's sung your praises – probably louder than I've ever heard her crow. But she says you normally work on literary fiction.'

'That's right,' Amy said. 'This role is a bit of a departure for me, but it came along at an opportune time and I'm confident I have something unique to bring to it. I was very happy to be considered.'

'Sounds like there's a story there, chick,' Philippa winked.

Amy grimaced, forgetting to keep her poker face in place.

'It was something to do with a man, I assume. You needed to make a sharp exit?' Philippa pressed on, her green, almost feline eyes narrowed inquisitively.

'Something like that,' Amy said, not too keen on elaborating. 'It was rather awkward and Carolyn was excellent about it.'

Desperate to avoid any mention of the Hugh disaster, Amy proceeded to explain – without blowing her own trumpet *too* loudly – the work she'd done with a range of impressive authors Philippa had heard of. She confessed she was new to commercial fiction, but stressed her experience with positioning books so as to make their publication compelling news events that the media might pick up.

'She knows a bright spark when she sees one, does Carolyn. Always did,' Philippa smiled. 'I hear she's left organising some big launch event for the imprint in your capable hands.'

Amy stifled a moan at this. She had a few potential sponsors, and speakers, but still no venue – and she and Carolyn had a catch-up call scheduled for next Thursday, during which her boss would surely demand a progress report.

'Thank you, that's kind of you to say,' Amy said to Philippa, trying to shrug off the dread that descended on her each time she thought about the party she was supposed to be hosting. 'I'm intrigued, though . . . How is it that you and Carolyn know one another?'

'*Oh*,' Philippa laughed, 'has she not told you? Bless her, she's probably trying to spare my blushes.'

'No . . . ?' Amy said, sensing she might soon regret having asked this question.

'We have an ex-husband in common,' Philippa said mildly. Amy almost choked on a mouthful of sparkling Acqua Panna.

'I married her first husband after she split up with him. It was a *slightly* messy business, but not too acrimonious – Carolyn had met someone else anyway when I took up with Harry. Our paths crossed a few times afterwards because we moved in similar circles . . . We were both young and working in PR in London back then. Once I got to know her, it wasn't too long before I realised I liked Carolyn more than the bloke I'd married, ha ha!'

Amy could feel that her eyes had grown cartoonishly round, but she said nothing and nodded sagely – as if what Philippa was describing was a perfectly standard situation.

'He and I were divorced within the year,' Philippa went on. She said 'year' to rhyme with 'her'.

'When I told Carolyn I'd left him, she said she wasn't surprised. She said, "Philippa – he thought he was getting a sweet young Stepford wife with you because he didn't reckon on the brains beneath the blonde hair, boobs and Brummie accent." She was absolutely right. *Anyway*, we've been good friends ever since. She's been on at me for a few years to come on board at H-K – ever since my books really started selling. I told her she had to find me the right editor first.'

Amy gulped now, fully realising the pressure Carolyn had put her under.

'Don't look so worried, bab,' Philippa said as two portions of strawberry mousse with freshly made shortbread appeared on the table. 'I think you and I are going to get on famously. Anything you don't know about romance, I can teach you . . . Though for what it's worth, I can spot a tender heart at fifty paces – and you, my dear, are the proud owner of one.'

Amy shook her head as they tucked into their tiny ramekins.

'Honestly,' she said, 'it would be a thrill to work with you if you do choose to sign with us – but in my personal life, I'm . . .' She thought back to what Kit had said in his kitchen on the afternoon of what she privately called The Balloon Disaster. 'Well. I'm known as a bit of an ice queen.'

'Nonsense,' Philippa said with authority. 'You just haven't found the right man to thaw you out.'

Philippa winked at her again, and Amy's inability to find an appropriate response was conveniently covered by the arrival of a waitress bearing a silver tray with coffee, petits fours and the lunch bill, which she discreetly handed to Amy.

'Trust me,' Philippa said, smiling confidently as she took a cocoa-dusted truffle from the plate before them. 'The ending to your love story's nowhere near written yet.'

Chapter 12

On Sunday morning Amy made her way to the village cafe for brunch with Nisha. She felt weirdly jumpy – a little as though she were going on a first date and wanted to make a good impression.

She needn't have worried. Nisha sauntered in a moment after Amy had arrived, waving as she approached the table. She was wearing a wide, sincere smile, bright pink lipstick and a rainbow cardigan so twee it made Amy's teeth hurt. This woman was so unabashedly *herself* that it was almost intimidating – or it would have been if she weren't so sunny and unassuming.

'Ohmygod, I'm *so* glad we're finally doing this!' Nisha said, pulling up a chair at their tiny table for two. 'I've been mega excited about it.' Her enthusiasm was infectious, and Amy found herself saying, 'Me too,' as she cast her eyes around the wood-panelled, pale blue-painted room, then over the double-sided menu.

This place was nice, she realised, as her attention was caught by the gigantic, vintage-looking coffee machine behind the polished wood counter. The intoxicating smell wafting from it took her back to the day she'd returned to Rowton with Kit in tow. How had it taken her this long to come in here?

The cafe was nothing like the old greasy spoon it had been thirteen years ago, and all the food on offer sounded mouth-watering. Her stomach rumbled in eager anticipation.

Amy was aware she'd taken on a little extra padding during the past few weeks; her skinny jeans were noticeably tighter around the waist. However, when she reread the words 'crispy Belgian waffle with maple syrup and berry compote', she couldn't bring herself to ignore them. The way to stave off a wardrobe crisis, she reasoned, was more exercise. Back in London she'd gone to the gym a few times a week, and while she couldn't honestly say she missed its testosterone-tense atmosphere or eau de sweat aroma, she should probably try and replace it with something over and above walking Bertie. As dogs went, he wasn't the most energetic – and his four-inch-long legs weren't really cut out for long-distance rambles.

Now that real pasta, proper butter and home-made cakes had returned to her life, Amy found she was loath to give them up again in favour of protein shakes and cauliflower pizza bases. Indeed, she hoped never again to experience the travesty that was 'courgetti bolognese'. If regular runs meant she could gleefully add an extra sprinkle of Parmesan to her dinner without needing to replace all her trousers, she would do it – and gladly.

'I'm having the waffles,' she said decisively. 'What are you going to go for?'

'Bacon bap,' Nisha said, 'with lashings of ketchup.'

'And to drink?'

'Hmmm, a caramel latte with whipped cream and sprinkles, I think,' Nisha said.

For a second, Amy wondered how this would mix with freshly fried streaks of salty meat. She rapidly decided not to think about it.

'Right,' she said, 'I'll go and order. My shout, since you were kind enough to invite me out.'

'Awww, thanks!' Nisha smiled. 'But only if the next one's on me.'

When Amy returned to the table, Nisha wasted no time in asking what, if almost anyone else had posed them, might have been considered an unrelenting barrage of questions. Her first priority was determining whether it was true that Amy and Sam had argued over a Tupperware box and destroyed one of Barbara's trestle tables at the WI's most recent bake sale. Dimly, Amy wondered how Nisha had even heard about the incident. Then she reminded herself that little escaped the notice of Rowton's most engaged residents. How *hideously* embarrassing; this surely meant that Gran had heard about the episode, too, although she hadn't mentioned it.

'Sadly, that is true,' Amy told Nisha, cringing. 'Not my finest moment – or Sam's. However, *he* has form: he can usually be relied upon to cause arguments, in my experience.'

'Weird,' Nisha said, wrinkling her nose and eyeing Amy with an expression that sat somewhere between puzzled and suspicious. 'You're literally the only person I know who doesn't *love* him.'

Amy rolled her eyes. ''Twas ever thus,' she said. 'Sam was always Mr Popular, but we didn't get on in sixth form either – even though both of us were close to Hari. *He* spent a fair bit of time telling the two of us to shut up and stop bickering.' She smiled fondly at the memory of her old friend, then thanked God, the universe or whatever benign force might be out there that a waitress had just appeared with their drinks.

Amy didn't want to get drawn into a discussion of her history with Sam, or the reasons for her hostility to him. She sensed that Nisha, with her happy disposition and apparent propensity for seeing the best in everyone, would struggle to understand Amy's unique yet powerful antipathy towards him. She certainly wouldn't accept it without a full and complete disclosure of what had passed between Amy and Sam immediately before and after Hari's death – and Amy had no intention of sharing *that* story.

'Meg reckons the three of you had kind of a *Dawson's Creek*-type vibe,' Nisha mused, taking a sip of her coffee – which looked more like an ice cream sundae than a beverage befitting a fully grown adult. 'Y'know, pretty girl, torn between two handsome boys – the best friend and the one she loves to hate.'

Amy swallowed a mouthful of flat white too fast, then coughed as it burned its way down her oesophagus. 'Nope,' she said bracingly. 'Not at *all*.'

This statement was at least fifty per cent true, and therefore landed with sufficient weight that Nisha nodded, seeming to believe her. Amy felt her confidence return.

'It sounds like Meg watched too much TV back in the day,' she joked.

'Oh, and now,' Nisha agreed, laughing. 'We both do. We're obsessed: just coming to the end of yet another rewatch of *Gilmore Girls*.'

'The two of you are close, then?' Amy asked as two plates of delicious-looking food arrived.

'Yeah,' Nisha confirmed as she peeled back the top layer of her sandwich to ensure it was sufficiently sauced. Evidently, it was. She replaced the bread and took a bite, chewing contemplatively. As Amy dug into her waffle, Nisha explained: 'Meg and I are besties. I moved to Rowton about six years ago and we've been friends ever since.'

'And what brought you here?' Amy said. She might as well ask her fair share of searching questions, she thought; it seemed unlikely that Nisha would mind.

'Well, Auntie Binita left the shop just under a year after Hari died,' she explained. 'But a few years after that the manager she'd put in place wanted to retire. It looked as if she might need to let the business go, but I volunteered to take it over so it could stay in the family.'

'How is Mrs Chauhan?' Amy asked. She never had got into the habit of calling her by her first name.

'She's okay. She moved to Nottingham,' Nisha said. 'My parents, brother and sister are all there, as well as my nan on my mum's side. Dad and Uncle Rav were brothers, and Auntie B always got on well with Mum.'

'Got you,' Amy said, nodding, feeling glad that Hari's mother was among people who knew and loved her. She'd lost so much here, and the village must have been steeped in memories of her husband and son; it was no wonder she'd wanted to get out of Rowton for good. Amy could empathise, although she was softening towards the place – even more so as she ate her breakfast.

'The move got me out of a tight spot, to be honest,' Nisha went on, catching a glob of ketchup with the tip of her purple-polished index finger before it could land on her cardie. 'My nan was all for getting me married off, and I really wasn't up for it.'

'No?'

'No. It was all, "Premal is a doctor and from a very good family", and I was like, I want to *fall in love* – not audition fifteen suitors and then pick the one with the most solid pension plan. Luckily my parents were cool with me escaping.'

Amy laughed.

'Are you with anyone, Amy? Did you leave your heart behind in London?'

Nisha's interest was so genuine that Amy wavered – her stock response that she simply didn't go in for soppy stuff withering before she could force it out of her mouth.

Instead, she said: 'Er. Well. I *was* with someone, but I definitely didn't leave my heart with him. We split up just before I moved back. In fact, it's *why* I moved back.'

'Eek,' Nisha murmured. 'Sounds dramatic.'

'D'you know what, it really was,' Amy said, lifting a last, syrup-coated square of waffle to her lips. 'Would you believe, he asked me to marry him after only six months, with absolutely no warning? In a hot-air balloon . . . even though I'm terrified of heights.'

'No way,' Nisha said, wide-eyed. 'I mean, it's *sort of* romantic, I guess . . . But, like, nobody wants to be proposed to while they're shitting themselves that they might plummet to the ground and die.'

'Quite,' Amy agreed, surprised to find herself laughing.

She had no idea why she was telling Nisha all this, except

that it felt as though she were expelling some toxic substance her muscles had been clinging onto. Nisha's company, it turned out, was the conversational equivalent of a sauna.

'We were very compatible on paper,' Amy continued. 'Similar careers, similar interests, similar life goals . . . People said we made sense together. But—'

'No SDS,' Nisha finished for her. 'Absolutely classic.'

'No . . . what? What's SDS? It sounds like a chronic disease.'

'Far from it,' Nisha said, her fuchsia lips widening in a knowing smile.

How was that lipstick even still *on*, Amy wondered, resolving to ask for details later.

'SDS,' said Nisha grandly, 'stands for *Stomach Drop Sensation*. It's the magic. You know, the warm glow you get deep down in your gut that means someone's just *right* for you. It comes from your heart and your body and your brain all at the same time. It's awesome and scary, like a force of nature – like magnetism or gravity, or something.'

Amy tipped her head to one side, trying hard to appear amused rather than discomfited. 'Is this a term you've coined yourself, or does everyone else already know about it? Am I the only one who didn't get the memo?'

'Anyone who'd *need* a memo about SDS must have a serious lack of it in their life,' Nisha said, shaking her head in disapproval. 'Are you telling me that you've never, even for a moment, felt it? Not even a semi-stomach drop? Or a stomach *dip?*'

She looked shocked and . . . *Yes,* Amy decided, saddened. A little like Kit had when Amy denied ever having had a kiss that could be described as a 'knee-trembler'.

'Er. I . . . Maybe a tiny stomach dip?' Amy conceded, not sure why she was admitting to this. 'A fraction of one? I don't know . . . It was a very, *very* long time ago.'

'It counts,' Nisha said triumphantly. 'You wouldn't remember it otherwise.' Amy signalled to their waitress and ordered another round of coffees, mainly so she wouldn't have to agree.

'It's a long time since I felt the SDS,' Nisha sighed as their empty plates were cleared. 'Rowton's lovely, but it has a serious dearth of eligible hotties.'

Amy nodded, worried that if she passed comment on any of the local men she'd give the impression she might be interested in dating one of them.

'I mean, there's Sam, of course,' Nisha went on. 'Ridiculously good-looking and newly available. But definitely not my type.'

'Right,' Amy said, her tone determinedly disinterested – despite the curiosity suddenly fizzing in her stomach. *Newly available*?

'Yeah,' said Nisha, scraping chocolate-dusted whipped cream off the top of her drink with a teaspoon. 'He's too clean-cut for me. Too neat. Too nice. I like my men a bit scuzzy – there's less pressure. Alex from the pub, for instance – I'd *definitely* go out with him if I could catch him between girlfriends.'

Amy pictured the auburn-haired, thick-armed deputy manager of the Oak: a man with arty tattoos, a deep rumble of a laugh and a ready, toothy grin. She could easily picture him on Nisha's rainbow-clad arm, she decided.

Then, foolishly, she asked a question she'd already swallowed once. 'You think Sam is *nice*?' Her voice sounded scathing. Her tone dripped with incredulity.

'Like I said earlier, everyone does,' said Nisha, shooting her another questioning glance. 'According to Meg, Tilly *finished* with him for being too nice – too much like a mate. One day there were rumours of a wedding, then the next she was just gone. Poof!'

Amy felt her stomach do a backward roll. Why had she eaten such a huge, sugary breakfast?

As for the idea of Sam getting married ... That was weird. Somehow not believable. Surely he was too deeply annoying, too faux normal and authentically argumentative for anyone to want to knit themselves to him for eternity.

'Who's Tilly?' Amy asked, cursing herself for not reining in her nosiness.

'Tilly Wexmore-Yates,' said Nisha impressively.

'Seriously?' demanded Amy, her mouth falling open.

Tilly Wexmore-Yates was on TV – not in anything Amy usually watched, but she was nonetheless someone most people had heard of. A popular presenter and 'roving reporter' figure on both the BBC and commercial channels, she was known for fronting programmes about consumer issues at home and abroad.

Tilly had the sort of long, pale blonde mermaid waves that less trichologically blessed women pined for. She was tall and slim, but with curves in what a tabloid newspaper might have called 'all the right places'. Her huge blue eyes were set in a sweet, princess-y face. Like Sam, she came from money – but even though Tilly's accent was plummier than his or Meg's, Amy suspected the Wexmore-Yateses were what the old Viscount might call 'new money'.

'*Seriously*,' Nisha said. 'I've no idea what happened between them, obviously, but I hear the older Ainsworths were disappointed. Supposedly they were very keen on having her for a daughter-in-law.'

'Oh,' Amy murmured hollowly. Then, realising this was the ideal chance to dig for further information, she said: 'What about the younger members of the family?'

She hated herself a little for this, yet itched for Nisha to answer the question that lay beneath the one she'd actually asked.

'Pearl? I don't think she was too bothered.'

'Right,' Amy said, frustrated.

'I mean, what seven-year-old tomboy wants to share their favourite person in the world with someone as girly and glamorous as Tilly Wexmore-Yates?' Nisha said, side-eyeing Amy as she spoke. 'And Uncle Sam is *definitely* her favourite, much to Meg's disgust.'

'Always the way,' Amy said, shamelessly generalising to cover what felt oddly like relief. 'Typical, isn't it?'

'Uh-huh,' Nisha nodded, glancing at Amy again, her eyes alight with interest. 'Though to be fair, he does an awful lot with her – he has since she was a baby. Despite being such a very dislikeable person.'

ABORT, *ABORT*! yelled a voice in Amy's head. She needed to move them off this topic before she showed any further sign of being too invested in it – even though her brain was buzzing with more questions. Meg was Pearl's mother? If so, who and where was her dad? And she must have had her young . . . At nineteen or twenty, Amy calculated. She could only imagine how badly *that* had gone down with the Viscount – especially as there was no sign Meg had ever been married.

'Oh! Before I forget,' Amy said, as if what she was about to say next was so urgent it warranted a complete change of subject, 'you need to tell me when the next book group meeting is – and what I need to read.'

In truth she wasn't mad keen on joining, but mentioning it seemed prudent at this juncture.

'Yes!' Nisha cried. 'I'm so glad you brought that up, I've been meaning to tell you. It's on Wednesday and the book is *And So We Meet Again* by—'

'Philippa Fotheringham,' Amy said. 'How uncanny. I've just read it.'

'Ohmygod, it's *amazing*, isn't it? I flippin' LOVE Philippa. I'm her biggest fan. Like, biggest *ever*.'

'Oh, really? Ha! If you can believe it, I went for lunch with her on Friday – it was a work thing.'

'SHUT. UP.'

Nisha's mouth had dropped open, her bright pink lips a pretty neon 'o'.

'Yes,' Amy said, laughing. 'The publishing house I work for . . . Well. It's totally hush-hush at this stage, but we're trying to get her to sign with us.'

'Ohmygod,' Nisha repeated with quiet reverence, 'you actually met her? What was she like?'

She was flapping her hands, fanning herself as if to try and stem her excess of excitement.

'She was kind of badass, to be honest,' Amy said. 'I liked her a lot. I hope I'll get to work with her.' All of this was true, which – given her position on the idea of courting Philippa a few weeks ago – represented quite the turnaround.

'*Good*,' Nisha said emphatically. 'That's such a relief. It's awful when you meet someone who's had dealings with one of your heroes and it turns out they're an absolute plonker in real life.'

'Where am I going for the book club meeting?' Amy asked.

'Oh, sorry! I forgot that bit. The pub,' Nisha said.

'Perfect.'

'Come at half past seven. We usually get bar snacks as well as drinks, so maybe don't have dinner first,' Nisha went on.

Amy nodded her assent and slurped the last of her second coffee.

Nisha did the same, then checked her watch – a lilac and white plastic Casio with a digital display. It was the kind of thing you'd buy for a pre-teen, but on her it looked funky. Altogether, Amy thought, Nisha had the kind of style you couldn't acquire by dint of reading the right magazines or having an unlimited budget to spend at Net-a-Porter.com. It was clear she wore what made her happy, rather than what others considered fashionable or appropriate. In combination, Nisha's rainbow garments formed a look that was cooler than the sum of its parts. They gave her a signature aesthetic that was much more interesting than anything Amy had seen on Instagram lately.

Maybe she needed to readjust her own mindset, now that she was living back in a place where what you said and did seemed to matter more than what you wore . . . Where she was under less pressure to appear sleek or sport the latest must-have accessories than she was to show up at Barbara's next litter pick. It would certainly render the prospect of opening her monthly credit card statement less scary.

'I should probably get back,' Nisha said, 'do an hour or two in the shop before it closes. I've left Part-Time James in charge this morning, so God knows what state the place will be in by now.'

Amy understood from previous conversations that 'Part-Time James', as Nisha called him, was a pleasant young man and a good worker so long as there was someone telling him exactly what to do. What he lacked in initiative his placid nature made up for, but it wasn't advisable to leave him alone for long periods.

The two women hugged and said goodbye outside the cafe, Amy venturing back towards the bridge and Nisha heading in the opposite direction.

As she wandered through the village and down past the clock tower, Amy could feel the swell of the coming summer in everything around her: there were roses in bud, a gentle warmth in the air and the smell of freshly cut lawns on the breeze.

Her mind flickered to Sam: Gran's volunteer gardener and apparently the world's coolest uncle. She had a strange sense of being on the other side of something important – as if she were seeing it distorted through stained glass or reflected, weird and misshapen, in a fairground mirror.

Either Amy was right about Sam, or other people were. Surely the coexistence of both versions of this man was impossible – would cause the kind of space–time paradox that made the universe unstable.

Ordinarily, Amy wasn't arrogant enough to assume she had better intel than literally everyone else within a five-mile radius. However, on Sam Ainsworth she had the inside track – *she* had information that others didn't.

She knew that he'd kissed her into a state of blissful, terrified vulnerability, then shrunk away as if she were diseased: that he'd opened her like a book he'd spent years wanting to read, then closed her with a *snap* just as she felt ready to share her story. She knew that he said things, made you believe he meant them and then didn't follow through.

After Nisha's philosophising, Amy was also grimly aware that the only 'stomach drop sensation' she'd ever experienced was with Sam – and that her feelings about that were too complex to unravel right now, or possibly ever.

Finally, and most importantly, she knew what nobody else in the world knew: that she'd eyeballed her mobile phone for days, *weeks*, endlessly refreshing her emails and jumping out of her skin every time there'd been a knock at the door after Hari died. And Sam had never once shown up for her.

He was the first and last boy she'd ever waited for, ever sobbed into her pillow over – and she had never forgiven him for it.

Chapter 13

When Amy arrived back at the cottage, she knew immediately that something was wrong.

Barbara was sitting at the kitchen table next to Gran, who was clutching her friend's hand tightly, as if to steady her. Grace's eyes were shiny with tears that occasionally slipped down her cheeks, but Amy could see anger in them as well as acute distress.

Barbara was weeping too, and it was a pitiful sight: like seeing the decrepit man behind the curtain after believing for decades in the Wizard of Oz. Her proud features were pinched with anguish, and her shoulders – which Amy had always thought of as broad enough to carry any burden and strong enough to resist whatever weight might be dropped on them – were slumped. She looked heartbroken. Hopeless.

Mr Bradley was there, too, standing awkwardly in the corner by the kettle, poised to make tea though it was clear that a round of brandies might have been more welcome. Dave, Barbara's husband, sat on the other side of the table. Bertie was curled in a ball on his lap, and Dave was stroking the dog's floppy little ears ceaselessly, apparently in a daze. His face was pale and he wore a vacant, helpless expression. If Amy didn't know better, she might have been prevailed upon to believe he'd seen a ghost.

'What . . . what's happened?' Amy said. 'Is everything . . . ?'

She let her voice trail off before she finished her question. What was the point? It was abundantly clear that everything was *not* OK.

Had someone died, or received a terrifying diagnosis? Amy didn't think so. Trouble like that wouldn't account for the fury she could see Grace struggling to contain.

Barbara shook her head and took a deep, shuddering breath. 'Don't worry, Amy – it's nothing affecting your gran. It's . . . it's us. We're going to have to leave our house.'

'What?' Amy asked, genuinely not understanding. This didn't make any sense – the words seemed to have been divorced from their usual meanings. She and Dave had lived in their house for more than thirty years, as far as Amy knew. What on earth could she mean, they'd have to move now, at their time of life?

It wasn't lost on Amy that Barbara's first instinct upon seeing her concern was to reassure her that Grace was all right. Barbara might be gruff, but she was *good*. She was kind, always able to bestow compassion on those who needed it without making a song and dance of offering support. When Amy's dad had died, Barbara had popped in and out of the cottage almost daily, sometimes with a ready-to-reheat home-made dinner, and other times with a pint of milk she'd miraculously sensed they needed. She'd even stop by with library books for Grace, or music magazines she thought Amy might enjoy.

Barbara had been there for Grace in the most mundane, unshowy ways – the ways that only people who loved you like family, cared for you in their blood and bones, could be. Now *she* was distraught, clinging onto Grace as though a five-foot septuagenarian in need of a hip replacement was the anchor who'd keep her attached to the life she and Dave had built together.

'I had a visit from young Sam Ainsworth earlier,' Barbara said, her voice flat, weak and scratchy, as if sobbing had strained her vocal cords. 'It seems his father – the Viscount – is selling off a parcel of property in Rowton for the sake of cash flow. *Liquidating some assets*, I believe is what it's called. Our house is among the places to be sold. So's the pub.'

Amy gripped the edge of the table with her fingertips and crashed into a vacant chair.

'Sam came to your house to tell you you're being *evicted*?' Amy said hotly. 'How *could* he?!'

'It isn't Sam who's doing this,' Barbara continued, reaching for Amy's hand and patting it. Amy burned with outrage at this intervention on Sam's behalf – this willingness to defend, to *excuse* the person who'd delivered such a devastating blow to a woman who couldn't have deserved it less.

'He thought . . .' Barbara began, then stifled a sob. She took another gulp of air, exhaled slowly and tried again. 'He thought it would be better coming from him than some faceless minion on the phone – or, God forbid, by letter. We've first refusal on buying the place, he said, and he wanted to tell us as soon as possible so we could try and get something organised. But there's no way we'll get a mortgage at our age – neither of us is even working anymore.'

Amy became aware that she'd taken Barbara's hand and was now holding it gently between her own. 'What about savings?' she asked.

'We've enough to keep ourselves, but nowhere near what we'd need to buy the cottage outright,' Dave put in miserably. He shook his head, as if in disbelief, and it struck Amy that his state of shock was a result not only of the Ainsworths' decision to sell their home, but also of Barbara's despairing reaction to it. How many years had it been since they'd met a challenge she couldn't overcome or encountered a problem she didn't feel equal to fixing? Amy was willing to bet it had been decades.

'And . . . and there's no way to persuade the Ainsworths out of this?' she asked, though she already knew that getting Sam's father to change his mind about anything was nigh on impossible. Roger Ainsworth's reputation for being cantankerous, selfish and implacable went back further than Amy could remember, and she didn't imagine his heart was likely to begin bleeding for others at this late stage in his career.

'No,' Barbara said, 'ours is one of the last few cottages

in Old Rowton that the estate still owns – and they're the most valuable and easiest to sell. This is about offloading stuff that'll bring in the most cash.'

Amy made a face and snorted angrily. 'You'd think the lord and lady of the manor were on the poverty line, not living in a stately home and swanning around in Chanel. Don't the Ainsworths own half the village? *Surely* there must be other property they can sell? You know, places that people who've reliably paid their rent for half their lives aren't living in.'

She was breathing hard and felt hot all over. Rage was building in her like a wave that threatened to engulf every other feeling. It made her feel sick to think that Sam could have any part in this – nauseous and sad and disappointed, but also *vindicated*. And he *was* involved in what was happening to Barb and Dave, for all Barbara's insistence that it wasn't his fault. He would be the ultimate beneficiary of his father's cut-throat decision-making: the one who inherited his family's massive fortune.

'I think you'd be amazed if you knew what Roger Ainsworth has already done for the sake of keeping himself afloat,' Grace said, her own face like thunder. 'There's a fair few places in new hands since you were here last, Amy. This isn't the first time he's sold off land or buildings, reportedly to pay some bill or other on the big house.'

Amy exhaled loudly, but expelling her breath from her lungs was a poor vent for her fury. 'So let me get this straight: ordinary people like Barbara and Dave lose their homes – and Jed might lose the pub – so Roger and Princess Pamela can keep living in *Downton fucking Abbey*?'

'Amy!' Grace yelped. '*Language!* Think of Ken.'

Amy glanced sheepishly at her former teacher, whose strong aversion to swearing was all too familiar from her college days. He waved a hand at her in understanding that, if any occasion called for the F-word, this was probably it.

'That's about the size of it,' Dave confirmed. 'We've got to be out within six months.'

'I can't believe they can do this,' Amy said, her voice thick with tears.

'They can, and they are,' Barbara sighed, 'even though we were assured *long* before we retired that the house was ours until we kicked the bucket. I've met with Roger several times over the years, and I made sure to double-check the situation when I got my pension lump sum. With that as a deposit we could have bought somewhere smaller, on the other side of the water, maybe . . . We could have got a mortgage, then, while Dave was still working. We *should* have.'

Amy winced at Barbara's tone, heavy with disappointment in her own judgement – judgement that, in all fairness, had probably never failed her until now. Thanks to Gran, she was also aware that most of Barb's pension payout had been spent on helping their son, Mark, pay for university and get onto the housing ladder. It was beyond unfair that such generosity should come back to disadvantage her like this, to make her vulnerable at this point in her life.

Seeming to recover a little of her usual stoicism, Barbara said: 'Still. Six months is much more notice than most landlords would have given us. I'll start looking around tomorrow to see if there's anywhere local we might be able to afford – though I don't rate our chances.'

'I'll help in any way I can,' Amy said.

'Thank you, love,' said Barbara, nodding. 'Sam's said the same. He has a few contacts that might be useful – other landowners that might have places coming up for rent.'

Amy folded her arms and scowled. She bit down on her lip in order to keep from launching into a tirade about this being the absolute *least* Sam could do; ranting wouldn't help anyone, and it would only upset Barb more.

'That's good,' said Grace. 'I'm sure he'll do whatever he can for you.'

'Oh God, not you as well,' Amy burst out, her temper finally fraying. 'Am I the only one here who's joined the dots between Barb and Dave losing their house and Sam inheriting millions of pounds? He's the good cop to his father's bad cop, but they're on the same side! Sam *profits* from this in the end! He isn't the good guy here – he's just really great at handling his own PR. He'll have everyone eating out of his hand by the time he's the Viscount, which will no doubt facilitate some nefarious agenda he's yet to reveal.'

'I must confess, Amy, I think that's a rather cynical point of view,' Mr Bradley said softly. 'I know you and Sam never saw eye to eye, but it seems to me he's doing his best to be helpful in a very difficult set of circumstances.'

'You're all mad,' Amy said. 'I can't believe any of you are standing up for him.'

'*Amy*,' Grace said, severely enough that her granddaughter felt chastened. 'Nobody's standing up for him. He hasn't *done* anything. This is an awful situation, but it isn't his doing. It's Roger at the helm, just like it's always been. I'm well aware there's long been some issue between the two of you, but you might want to consider that we know him better than you do these days. This is the most time you've spent in the village since you were eighteen, after all.'

Amy looked at the kitchen floor, not wanting to meet Grace's eyes. She sighed and scrubbed a hand over her forehead, wishing already that she hadn't made such a show of herself.

'It means the world that you're in our corner, Amy,' Barbara said, 'but Grace is right. Sam isn't the enemy here, so I don't want you wading in and having another ruck with him on our behalf. It wouldn't make any difference anyway.'

Amy nodded and swallowed hard, trying to tamp down her exasperation.

'On the subject of *rucks*,' said Grace, 'I heard about your little disagreement after the bake sale – not at all becoming of two adults over thirty, if you ask me.'

Amy winced, wishing powerfully that Gran hadn't brought this up.

'I know you have your own reasons for disliking Sam,'

Grace went on, eyeing Amy in a way that made her wonder if her gran had X-ray vision, 'but they have nothing whatsoever to do with this. Promise me you're not going to try taking him to task or screeching him into submission. I believe him when he says he's already doing everything he can.'

'Fine,' Amy said tonelessly, struggling not to launch into a rage-fuelled explanation of how she knew first-hand that what Sam *said* didn't always have much bearing on what he *did*. 'I promise.'

Mr Bradley cleared his throat. 'How about that tea then?'

'Forget it, Ken,' Grace told him, sounding suddenly exhausted. She got up from the table to grope in the old dark-wood drinks cabinet in the corner. 'I don't know about everyone else, but I could certainly do with something stronger.'

'Right,' Ken said, opening a cupboard and pulling out a series of short cut-glass tumblers.

'Make ours doubles,' Barbara said, tipping her head towards her husband.

'Mine too, please,' Amy said, nodding in sympathy – though she already knew that no amount of strong booze, even at this tender hour of the day, would wash away the bitter, fiery taste of her own anger.

Chapter 14

By the following Wednesday afternoon, Amy thought she'd done a fairly good job of simmering down. Work had been a welcome distraction from thoughts of Barbara's devastation and Sam's involvement in it, and it was easy to sink into her emails, submissions pile and to-do list now that she felt like she was making progress with them.

She'd already signed several authors for Howard-Knight's new imprint, and found herself genuinely excited about publishing their stories; while all were about love in one form or another, they were far from a homogenous mass. Some were gritty, some were sad and others were funny, while several tackled issues such as racism, poverty and homophobia. In addition, the writers she'd be working with were ethnically, culturally and socially diverse – far more so than was usual for H-K.

Carolyn was thrilled with how things were shaping up, and to her own surprise Amy felt proud of what she'd accomplished. Between them, they'd decided to name the new imprint 'Torch' – in honour of the many flaming emotions the characters in its stories would feel, but also in celebration of its mission: to publish smart, modern, illuminating women's fiction.

According to Kit, Carolyn had made a point of shouting about Amy's successes so far at H-K's latest company meeting, much to the annoyance of Hugh. 'Caro is singing your praises,' Kit had live-texted her. 'Hugh looks bloody LIVID – like someone just keyed his car.'

Amy had also managed to obtain several important sponsors for Torch's launch event: a local up-and-coming gin distillery that would donate cocktails, a catering firm prepared to provide a luxury dessert cart, and a tea company that had offered hundreds of flavoured infusions for free, provided their name was on the recyclable cups it was served in.

In addition, all the new authors Amy had signed were happy to attend the party and take part in a group Q&A, and Amy was hopeful that if she could get a contract in place, Philippa Fotheringham would be willing to come on board too. There was plenty more still to organise, but it was a decent start.

Amy's main, niggling worry was where on earth they'd hold the event – she'd had little interest from the hotels and conference centres she'd contacted, probably on account of her shoestring budget. She was going to have to raise it with Carolyn on their catch-up call tomorrow, and was already bracing herself for a dismissive 'just get it sorted' reaction to any plea for assistance.

As she checked her emails one last time and closed her laptop – logging off at 5.30 on the dot for a change – her phone pinged with a notification. She'd been added to a WhatsApp group: Rowton Readers. This was good timing – Amy was heading to her first book club meeting tonight, so if she needed to bring anything other than herself and a willingness to chat about *And So We Meet Again*, now was the time to find out what.

Nisha: Everyone, can we please welcome PUBLISHING PROFESSIONAL Amy to the group! She'll be joining us tonight for the first time and I for one am EXCITED 😄 ✨

Bless Nisha, she was lovely. But also, cringe.

There followed a flurry of messages from numbers Amy didn't recognise, but which came from WhatsApp profiles that thankfully had names attached.

Megan A: Welcome Amy! x

Kenneth Bradley: Welcome Amy.

Si Smith: Really looking forward to seeing you Amy! Xx

Eek. The postman's enthusiasm for her company made Amy nervous, but before she could dwell on it another new message arrived.

Sam: Hi.

What fresh hell was this? Sam was in the book club?

Amy racked her brain, trying to remember whether anyone had mentioned it before.

She drew a blank, then instantly began berating herself for not having asked – for not having thought of this on her own. *Of course* Sam would be in any local group that was dedicated to reading. Not only was he apparently on a mission to seem as involved as possible in every community initiative Rowton's residents could think up – he was also, or at least *had* been, a true lover of stories.

Despite being a 'publishing professional', Amy had met few people in her life who seemed to adore novels, plays and poetry in the same way she did. Grudgingly, she admitted to herself that Sam was one of them.

Before she could start feeling warm or sentimental about his love of literature, however, she reminded herself how irritating she'd found watching him tote *The Ragged Trousered Philanthropists* around college. She'd accused him of vapid preening on the fourth or fifth day he brought it in, only for him to launch into a well-informed sermon on why George Orwell had been right about its status as a classic.

This had annoyed her all the more, and the conversation had descended into trivial sniping until Hari broke it up by threatening to withdraw lift privileges. He'd passed his driving test by this time and had begun taking the three of them – the only Rowton residents who attended – to sixth form every day. The thought of having to catch the bus to Stratford-upon-Avon at the crack of dawn each morning was enough to silence both Amy and Sam. As she recalled, this wasn't the last time Hari had held the prospect of a return to public transport over them in order to break up an argument.

Gah.

Could she get out of tonight somehow? Perhaps she could fabricate a work-related excuse . . . But Nisha would be beyond disappointed if Amy didn't turn up. She'd gone out of her way to befriend Amy, and her febrile adoration of Philippa Fotheringham – as well as Amy's personal knowledge of the author – meant this was a meeting she'd been looking forward to all week.

Amy gritted her teeth and tapped out a message.

Amy: Hi all, thanks again for inviting me! Looking forward to it x

Nisha: ☺ Just a reminder, too – we're not at the pub tonight

Oh . . . ?

Nisha is typing . . .

Nisha: There's a large private party in & the bar is closed – so Sam has v. kindly offered to host us at Rowton Hall. Ideal setting for discussion of Lady Sarah and Thomas, right?! 🔥

Shit.

Just when Amy had written the evening off as likely to be unpleasant, Nisha had to go and prove her wrong. It was going to be excruciating.

Amy had sat in the grounds of Rowton Hall many times, typically without permission. However, she'd never set foot in the house itself – and unlike most people around here, she'd never had any desire to.

It was a huge, imposing structure made of sand-coloured stone, symmetrical and elegant in the way of most Regency mansions. Its array of vast sash windows glittered in the late-evening sunlight as she approached, each one as tall and wide as a standard doorway would be in a normal home. Two neoclassical columns stood on either side of the property's entrance, and a further four decorated its frontage, holding up a large triangular frame that featured the Waverley coat of arms.

It was beautiful, but Amy reminded herself that she'd long ago resolved not to be impressed by it. A vague feeling of intimidation, however, was harder to banish. The sheer scale of the place made her feel even smaller than usual, and – although it was odious – the sense that someone like her didn't belong in a place like this hung on her like the smell of old cigarette smoke.

When Amy got nearer, she saw that Sam was standing in the doorway ready to greet people and direct them inside. It took an effort to keep her feet moving in his direction when everything in her was vying to turn back, go home and bury her head in *Unforgettable You*, another Philippa Fotheringham book. The more of them she read, Amy had told herself, the better: a strong knowledge of the author's back catalogue could only help with getting her to sign a deal.

As she drew closer to Sam, Amy thought she detected a stiffening in his shoulders – but it vanished before she could be sure, any tension she might have imagined replaced by his usual easy grace. He was wearing jeans and a pale blue cotton shirt – slightly oversized, with the sleeves pushed up. He looked precisely as you'd expect an off-duty aristo to look: confident and polished in an understated sort of way. His hair was slightly too long, and tousled in a manner that implied he – or someone else – had spent the afternoon clawing at it.

'Amy,' he said when she was finally standing in front of him.

'The very same,' she said drily.

They remained still for a few awkward seconds, looking at one another as though fearful that a wrong move might prematurely inflame hostilities.

'Am I allowed in?' Amy asked, raising an eyebrow.

'Of course,' Sam replied, briefly shaking his head and then stepping aside. 'Apologies. Long day. I think that's everyone now you're here, so I'll show you to the drawing room.'

The drawing room. Good lord. Imagine having so much living space in your home that you had to give all the rooms with sofas and armchairs different names. Parlour. Sitting room. Morning room. Smoking room. Amy was certain Rowton Hall had them all.

Sam led her into an entrance hall that could only be described as . . . Well. *Stunning.* It was wide and high-ceilinged, and the floor was tiled black and white with alternating slabs of what Amy thought must be marble, arranged in a simple pattern that highlighted their smooth gleam. The walls were of the same bare stone as the building itself, but decorated with gilt lamps and priceless artwork in heavy, ornate frames.

Amy's eyes were drawn inexorably inwards, towards a broad staircase that led up to a round arch. Through this she could see a chandelier, a bust set atop a red marble plinth and the outline of yet more stairs. There was a landing that jutted from the upper floor into the hallway, delicately suspended above it. The mezzanine was edged with wrought-metal railings painted old gold, their rich colour illuminated by the light spilling in through the massive windows that sat behind it. When Amy looked up at the ceiling – every inch of which was decorated with a mural featuring creamy-skinned Adonises and ample-bosomed women – her breath caught in her throat. *Damn it.* She hated that she was wowed by this.

She swallowed, forcing herself to remember that the extravagance of these surroundings was apparently maintained by periodically turfing villagers out of homes they'd rented for decades, or selling out business premises from beneath hard-working people like Jed.

Since that afternoon in Gran's kitchen, she'd discovered the extent of Roger Ainsworth's 'asset liquidation' and the depth of Rowton residents' antipathy to him. Determined that the Hall would never end up in the hands of the National Trust, he'd spent years impoverishing the wider estate in favour of investing in the house – so much so that he'd been dubbed 'the Vampire Viscount' by one local blogger. Furthermore, Roger was insistent that Rowton Hall must remain a private home – never open to the public and not available to commoners for functions such as conferences or weddings, which might have brought in vital income. This position seemed to sum up his selfishness and snobbery, and made it all the more remarkable that people were willing to give Sam – and apparently his sister – the benefit of the doubt.

Amy and Sam made their way up the stairs and along a corridor in silence, their feet barely making a sound on the thick oriental runner beneath them. Sam led her through a pair of dark-wood double doors into the drawing room – another impressive space with rich decoration and lavish furnishings, though not particularly tasteful in Amy's opinion. This part of the house was doubtless among those the senior Ainsworths had renovated to their own liking.

The walls were adorned with paper in a bold carmine shade, its metallic fleur-de-lis pattern glinting in the sun that came through the sashes. Heavy swags of burgundy velvet framed the windows, and the huge but rather uncomfortable-looking sofas were covered in the same fabric. Elsewhere, the mahogany wood and oxblood leather of the remaining furniture combined with the room's general *redness* to make Amy feel almost oppressed. Once the doors closed, she could almost believe she'd been swallowed – gobbled down into the greedy belly of some hostile beast.

'Amy!' Nisha cried, the second she walked into the room. She patted the space next to her on a two-seater Chesterfield and Amy duly sat down, her stomach squirming like a bag of angry snakes. She shucked off her denim jacket and put her tote bag between her feet.

'Have you met everyone before, or should we do introductions?' Nisha asked.

'I think I know everyone already,' Amy replied, looking around the room. Mr Bradley was here, perched in a high-backed armchair, though Gran had declined to come along this evening in favour of relaxing with Bertie, Miss Marple and a new box of After Eights. Simon was sitting next to Barbara and Dave on one of the velvet couches; Dave looked very much as though he'd been dragged here against his will. In another chair – the oldest, squishiest-looking one in the room – sat Meg. She smiled at Amy tentatively, but with sincere warmth.

'What can I get you to drink, Amy? Wine? Beer? G&T?' Sam asked.

What – you mean you don't have a tray of champagne cocktails available for guests upon arrival? The jibe was on the tip of Amy's tongue, but she determinedly bit it back. She had enough decorum to understand that picking a fight with Sam in his own house wouldn't be a good look – and while the very sight of him made her itch with annoyance, it seemed clear she was the only one with a problem. Even Barb and Dave were here and sipping politely from pint glasses, despite the nightmare situation Sam's father had put them in. This, as well as Sam's willingness to open up the house to visitors, confirmed it for Amy: Roger and Pamela must be away, somewhere far enough afield that there was no chance they'd appear to interrupt the evening's event.

'Glass of red, please,' Amy said. 'I'm not fussy – whatever you have open.'

Sam nodded wordlessly and a few moments later passed her a large glass of what she decided was Pinot Noir. It was delicious: smooth, light and an almost translucent dark cherry colour.

'Now we're all assembled,' Mr Bradley said, 'I'm going

to ask Nisha to kick us off tonight by explaining why she nominated this novel for everyone to read. Nisha?'

Nisha grinned girlishly, took a swig of rosé wine from her glass and said: 'Well. Philippa is my *fave-of-all-time* author, as some of you know. I love romances, and I loved this story – I think it's maybe her best yet.'

'I see,' Mr Bradley nodded. 'So in large part, this was about bringing a book you found particularly entertaining to the group – allowing us the privilege of sharing in one of your passions.'

Amy smiled to herself and reasoned that she should probably take notes as Mr Bradley pressed Nisha for why she felt it was Philippa's best work. Ever the kindly teacher, he was the perfect unofficial chairperson for tonight's meeting – and probably every other, she suspected.

'So how did everyone else feel about the novel?' Mr Bradley went on, and one by one the book club's members shared their thoughts.

Dave struggled to articulate his view, so Barbara explained on his behalf that he'd chiefly enjoyed the sex scenes. Simon said he'd found the book's exploration of social class interesting, while Meg lamented the fact that Lady Sarah's life choices had been so circumscribed by her gender. Mr Bradley himself said he'd found the story affecting, and its style unusually poetic. In particular, he praised the dramatic scene where Lady Sarah's family seat burns down in the manner of Jane Eyre's Thornfield Hall.

'Now, Amy,' he said, turning to her. 'I understand you have a personal – possibly even professional – connection to this author. So we must all assure you that whatever passes between us in the sacred confines of book club will stay confidential.' He smiled, pleased with his own little joke.

Amy blanched as she felt all eyes turn to her. Sam's seemed to be staring hardest, full of interest and wry amusement.

'That's right,' Amy said, trying to keep her tone measured and neutral. 'I recently met up with Philippa for work, although I can't tell you any more about that at the moment. As for the book . . . I've never been into love stories, so even picking this up was a slightly odd experience for me. Out of character. I did enjoy it, though – more than I expected to.'

She couldn't help noticing that Sam's eyes were still on her. His lips had curled into a pert smile, just a smidge away from smug.

'That's interesting, Amy,' Mr Bradley said, and she turned her attention back to him. 'Is it fair to surmise that, since you moved back to Rowton, you've begun working on a type of fiction you're less familiar with?'

'Definitely,' Amy said. 'This genre is a new challenge for me.'

Her former teacher nodded, in a 'we'll come back to that later' sort of way. He turned to Sam and asked, 'What thoughts on the book were uppermost in your mind?'

'I inhaled it,' Sam said. 'Read it in a day.' Then, seemingly unable to resist, he added: 'Unlike some, though, I wasn't surprised by that. I hadn't assumed it would be bad simply because it's popular.'

'A striking point, which I think we should explore further.' Mr Bradley nodded, seeming to have missed altogether that Sam's comment was a pointed dig at Amy. 'Why is it that so many people assume entertaining novels have less value than more – quote unquote – *serious* books? We might wish to remember that in his day, Charles Dickens wrote the latest must-reads – yet now his stories are considered part of the literary canon and are studied in schools.'

'It's rooted in a kind of snobbery, I suppose,' Sam said, looking directly at Amy in a way that made her toes curl and her blood boil. 'A form of prejudice.'

Other people were nodding. 'Give me a romance or a thriller any day of the week,' Barbara said. 'I can't be doing with these books where there's no punctuation and it's all one long chapter. I like nice, clear breaks in a story so I can peg the washing out, go for a walk or make a cuppa without losing the plot.'

'Personally,' Sam said, unable to stop himself grinning as he goaded her, 'I think it's a little *pretentious* to assume that a story can't have depth or emotional resonance simply because it satisfies its readers, or leans into tropes they find entertaining.'

Amy could feel her pulse rate rising by degrees. He'd suggested – and in front of a room full of people – that she was pretentious. Was he kidding? He lived in a *literal mansion*. And the more she looked at it, the more certain she was that the wallpaper in here contained flecks of real gold leaf.

'I'd even argue,' Sam continued, impervious to the glare Amy had now fixed on him, 'that someone like Philippa Fotheringham has a more difficult task crafting a book than some of the literary wunderkinds who turn out stream-of-consciousness screeds with no clear structure, characterisation or themes.'

'Now who's being judgemental?' Amy demanded, unable to contain herself. 'I've worked with some amazing literary authors whose books mean an awful lot to people.'

'I don't doubt it,' Sam said, shrugging. 'But I'd be willing to bet you'd never say one of *their* books confounded your expectations simply by being readable.' He smiled at her.

'I never said anything about feeling *confounded*,' Amy cried, her voice edging dangerously close to shrill. She asked herself if she really was prepared to be lectured by a man who was a key beneficiary of the awful situation Barbara and Dave were in, only to find the woman herself staring daggers in Amy's direction. The subliminal message delivered was: *don't you dare bring it up, young lady – it isn't your place.*

'I thought you implied that you began this book with some trepidation, only to discover – to your shock – that it wasn't total rubbish,' Sam said into the momentary silence.

'I did not!' Amy cried, then took a deep breath to help calm her rising temper. 'I merely intimated that love stories aren't usually to my taste.'

'That's because you still consider yourself too cool and clever for them,' said Sam, sounding utterly sure he had her number. His voice was tinged with something like disappointment – as though he'd been hoping she might have got past her teenage narrow-mindedness.

The thing was, he *didn't* have her number. Even if a part of Amy had traditionally sneered at romance novels because she thought them basic, her lifelong aversion to this stuff had far deeper roots than intellectual vanity.

There was danger in absorbing, in *believing* the message that love could conquer all – that everyone had a soulmate, that your happiness could depend completely on being adored by an 'other half'. Being a romantic had hampered rather than enhanced her father's happiness; he'd never married, never even had a serious partner after Lily left him. And then he'd died young. His life hadn't been miserable, but it had frequently been painful and, in some ways, lonely.

'No, it's because—' Amy began, not at all sure where the sentence she'd started would lead her. Before she could worry about whether these stinging memories of her dad's heartache were written all over her face, she was interrupted by Mr Bradley, who loudly cleared his throat as if to remind both her and Sam that there were other people in the room.

Everyone seemed to be swivelling boggle eyes from her to Sam and then back again, like they were spectators at a tennis match. Amy sagged in her seat, heavy with embarrassment.

'And *that*, ladies and gentlemen,' Mr Bradley said, 'is merely a taste of what I had to deal with for the full academic year I spent teaching these two. Never before or since have I met two students who so wildly disagreed over *everything*. Really, it's no wonder at all that I went for promotion. Being principal of the entire college was, quite frankly, less stressful than getting them through their second year of A levels would have been.'

There was a ripple of grateful laughter from around the circle – a palpable sense of relief that this witty intervention had defused a potentially explosive row. If anyone in the group suspected there was more to Amy and Sam's clash than a desire for robust academic debate, they were British enough to pretend otherwise.

Within a few moments, genial conversation about the novel had resumed. Amy half-heartedly participated in discussion of Lady Sarah's heroic character arc, the role of privilege in the story and its surprisingly dark, unflinching portrayal of poverty in Georgian England.

She remained tight-lipped during scrutiny of the central relationship between Sarah and Thomas, and determinedly resisted catching Sam's eye when the chat moved on to key romantic moments. During a long back-and-forth on the fiery sexual tension that drove the two apparently mismatched protagonists towards their happy ever after, Amy stared at the floor.

'Well, thanks to all of you for an evening of scintillating conversation,' Mr Bradley said, casting his eyes around the room as the rest of the book club finished their drinks and the meeting wound down. 'Do we have any nominations for our next read, before we all head home?'

'How about something a little darker, in the interests of balance?' Sam asked. 'There's a thriller that came out a couple of weeks ago, *The Loner Next Door* by Alex Swift. I've heard good things.'

Amy glanced at him. He could have used this as another opportunity to needle her, but he hadn't. She wondered why.

There were no objections to Sam's idea, so members of the group began saying their goodbyes and departing.

'Is it okay for me to use the loo before I head home?' Amy asked, not quite knowing or caring whether she was addressing Sam or Meg with this question. In truth she could probably have coped without going to the loo, but Simon was watching her, gimlet-eyed, and she knew he'd insist on giving her a lift home if she didn't scramble out of his way fast enough.

'Of course,' Sam said. 'Head through the door over there

and then up the corridor. Bathroom's the fourth door on your left.'

'Thanks.'

Amy left the room through a different exit to the rest of the group, heading in the opposite direction to the entrance hall. As soon as she was alone, she let go of a deep breath that she hadn't even realised she was holding.

She made her way up a dimly lit corridor that seemed to go on for miles. It had doors to left and right, then a pair of double doors set into the far wall at its end. This place was dizzying – like something out of *Alice in Wonderland*, Amy thought. How many years must it have taken infant Sam and Meg to learn their way around it?

Suddenly aware she'd lost track of how many doors she'd gone past, Amy stopped. *Shit*. From here, it wasn't even possible to work out which one she'd originally come out of. She'd have to take a punt – try the next door on the left and, if that was wrong, the two on either side of it.

She felt uneasy as her hand closed around the heavy brass handle – almost as if she were snooping, though that wasn't her intention. Wandering around Sam's family home without a guide felt a little like spying on him.

As she pushed into the room Amy realised within seconds that she was in the wrong place. This wasn't a bathroom, it was a . . . What *was* it? Nothing in here made any sense. Furniture, much of which was dusty and damaged, was piled haphazardly into a corner. The carpet was grey with grime and the cream wallpaper – some Victorian-style pattern with bluebells – was peeling.

There was a greenish-black stain spreading outwards from one corner of the ceiling, and a musty smell of damp that Amy assumed must be emanating from it. On a table beneath the cobwebbed sash window sat boxes of ancient-looking taxidermy: everything from birds to butterflies, suspended in time for study or sport but long since abandoned.

Heart beating fast, Amy backed out into the corridor again

and closed the door gently behind her. She tried the next door along and immediately understood that she'd made the wrong decision. This was another forsaken, mildewed space, stuffed to the gills with random objects that clearly hadn't been touched in decades: books, mirrors, candlesticks, a shotgun ... Even a children's doll's house complete with miniature beds, wardrobes and chairs. There was something almost spooky about a toy that looked as though it had been left mid-game, then never played with again. It made Amy think of Miss Havisham's stopped clocks and rotting wedding breakfast.

Horror-struck, Amy rushed back out into the corridor. She felt almost sick with shock. How many of Rowton Hall's rooms were like this? The contrast between them and the spectacular entrance hall wasn't so much a gulf as a yawning chasm. Their crumbling condition certainly threw Roger Ainsworth's approach to estate management into sharp relief – though if large sections of Rowton Hall were in this sort of state, the place was surely a money pit with little hope of restoration, no matter how much land and property he sold off.

The door she'd just crashed back through swung flush into its frame, closing with a soft click that made her shiver. From this side of it, you'd never guess at the mess within. There was something tragic, as well as sinister, about this secret side to the house: a sense of beauty going to waste, of history being allowed to moulder and decay. While Amy didn't believe for a minute that anyone needed to *live* in a building like this, letting something so elegant and lovely fall apart for the sake of not sharing it seemed utterly shameful.

Trying to steady her breath, Amy resolved to turn around and try one of the doors further back towards the room where they'd held book club – though even locating that would be a challenge now she was so disorientated.

'Amy ... ?'

Sam was behind her, his voice low and cautious.

'Sam! Oh my God, I wasn't poking around, I swear to you – I—'

'You got lost. It happens,' he said flatly. 'No doubt you've seen some of the less salubrious corners of the Hall, now: the grand inheritance you're always so fond of reminding me I'll come into one day.'

Amy had no idea what to say to this, so she simply nodded. How could she have known there was so much wrong with this place? She had nothing to feel bad about, she told herself: even if Rowton Hall *was* a white elephant, Sam's family was still ridiculously wealthy by any normal standard.

'Yes is the answer to your question, by the way,' Sam said as he walked with her down the corridor, then pointed at the bathroom door she'd failed to find by herself.

'I . . . I didn't ask a question,' she pointed out.

'I could feel you thinking it,' Sam sighed. '*Is much of the house in that sort of mess?* Yes. I come from a long line of spenders and hoarders. They'd buy things, collect things, then never throw them away. Over several generations, whole wings of this place have been shut up and forgotten about simply because the prospect of clearing them is prohibitive – too expensive and time-consuming.'

'Oh,' was all Amy managed to say.

'I'll go back to the drawing room,' Sam said. 'Fourth door on your right when you come out. Meet me there and I'll see you out.'

If Amy had been feeling snippy, she might have asked whether he wanted to escort her off the premises to prevent any further espionage. Instead, she just said, 'Fine.'

She went from the bathroom back to the drawing room with no detours, either deliberate or accidental. Sam was waiting for her, alone; Simon had obviously given up on hanging back, if he'd ever considered it. Amy breathed a sigh of relief.

Sam walked her back to the grand entrance hall, the quiet between them stretching like a rubber band that threatened to snap.

'Amy,' Sam said as she turned to say goodbye. 'I'm sorry

about earlier. I went too far – let it get personal when we were talking about the book. It isn't for me to draw conclusions about why you do or don't like certain things. Though I *am* baffled as to why you of all people have ended up editing romance novels.' He risked a small smile, here – a slight quirk of the lips that nevertheless reached his dark eyes.

'It's OK,' Amy told him. She figured she should let him off after invading his family's privacy. 'As for the work thing . . . It's a long story. It wasn't my choice. And you weren't *completely* wrong, I have been pleasantly surprised by some of the manuscripts I've been sent.'

'Maybe you'll tell me about it sometime,' Sam said, though Amy couldn't think when. It wasn't like they were friends; they weren't going to meet up, split a pizza and bond over their work woes.

'Do you . . . *Argh*,' Sam started. 'Don't take this the wrong way, please – I don't want to sound like a patronising twat—'

Amy look at him blankly.

'Do you want me to walk with you?' he asked. 'It's dark out there, and—'

Only a proper arsehole would knowingly let you go alone.

Eighteen-year-old Sam's voice came back to her, as clearly as if it were speaking to her now.

'*No,*' Amy cut in, sounding sharper than she'd intended. 'I mean . . . No. Thank you. I'm a grown woman. I'll be fine.'

'Really, I'd feel far happier if you let me come along – or drive you, even.'

I'll follow you at a respectful distance if I have to, but I'd really rather not stalk you back to your gran's.

'I'd prefer to go alone,' Amy insisted. 'I'll be perfectly safe – home within a quarter of an hour, cup of tea in hand.'

'Well then,' Sam murmured, dejected but too wary to push her. 'Goodnight, I suppose.'

'Goodnight.'

On the way back to Gran's, Amy reflected that it was probably less than ideal to be walking through the village by herself at this time of night. But the prospect of Sam seeing her back to the cottage set off some peculiar combination of fireworks and alarm bells inside her. She knew the simple act of strolling across the bridge with him might open a Pandora's box of memories. Excitement. Nisha's dreaded stomach drop sensation. And then, inevitably, abandonment. Hurt.

Once home, Amy got into her pyjamas, double-cleansed her face and applied a soothing night serum. As she examined her reflection in the bathroom mirror, she wondered – not for the first or last time – whether she'd done the right thing by sending back Hugh's gift. Perhaps those Harley Street potions might have helped with the fine lines around her eyes, which looked deeper all the time despite how little she'd laughed recently.

She climbed the stairs to her bedroom and picked up her phone so she could set her alarm. There was a WhatsApp message waiting for her.

Sam: Did you get home okay? Please let me know.

It seemed childish not to reply.

Amy: Yep – safe and sound.

Sam: Great. Goodnight x

An electronic kiss? God. There was a time when she'd have dined out on that for weeks, clung to it like a talisman. Now, given that she so frequently felt she might genuinely hate Sam, it just confused her.

Goodnight, she wrote in reply, sinking back onto her bed and sighing in irritation. And then, unable to prevent herself:

Amy: x

Chapter 15

Amy awoke sweaty and unsettled, having dreamt she was lost in a haunted house that looked a lot like the forgotten corners of Rowton Hall. In it, she'd sprinted from room to room, growing ever more distressed as she searched for someone who may or may not have been Sam.

Bleurrrgh. She shoved the already dimming memory of the dream aside, then sat up in bed to sip from the glass of water on her bedside table. She felt anxious in an ill-defined sort of way – maybe a result of weekday wine drinking, she told herself, which she didn't do very often. Amy threw back her covers and eased herself out of bed. She hoped a hot shower would sort her out – she needed to get up and steel herself for this morning's call with Carolyn.

She was going to have to admit there was still no venue for this ill-considered party her boss wanted to throw, *and* try and prevent Carolyn from railroading her into saying she'd plough on with the search for a location alone. If this event was going to happen before the summer was out, they were rapidly running out of time to get it organised – and a little help from Carolyn, whose force of personality varied only between 'irresistible' and 'hurricane strength', would be worth weeks of dedicated effort from lesser mortals.

An hour later Amy was washed, dressed, lightly made-up and waiting for Carolyn to dial in to their Zoom. As she sipped her coffee, trying to decide how to broach the subject of needing more support with the launch event for Torch, she decided to send Kit a Slack message.

> Amy: Have you seen Carolyn today? I need her to help me with something . . . What sort of mood is she in? *Prays*

He replied within seconds.

> Kit: Unclear. I've just seen her arguing with Hugh through his office window but that's standard – they're basically in a blood feud at this point. Working here's like being in the mafia now, just with books. Everyone's been sucked into a family, his or hers.

Before she could reply to him Amy's computer pinged, notifying her that Carolyn had joined the meeting.

'Yes, yes, *fine*. But I'm afraid I have to go,' Carolyn said, presumably to whoever she was speaking to on her mobile. 'We'll catch up later. I'm on another call now. Ciao.' She put her phone on her desk, then looked into her webcam.

'Amy!' she said, wriggling her shoulders slightly as though to try and shake off the irritation her previous conversation had inspired. 'So. Tell me how things are going.'

It was always this way with Carolyn: no 'how are you' preamble, no questions about her day so far or chit-chat about her personal life. Amy proceeded to provide a rundown of everything she'd achieved since their last meeting, relieved that it gave a good account of how hard she was working.

Having deliberately left any mention of the party until last, Amy finally took a breath and said, 'Now, on the subject of the launch event – I'd be really grateful if we could discuss a couple of things—'

'I'm going to stop you there, Amy,' Carolyn said, holding up a hand. 'I've been meaning to grab you for a chat about this since last week.'

Oh, shit. Was Carolyn already aware somehow of how much more was still to be done? Amy wondered if she should brace herself for a bollocking. Then a wild hope seized her. What if Carolyn could see how much Amy already had on her plate, and had decided not to bother with an event that, quite simply, was going to be an absolute ball-ache to arrange? Amy's heart swelled at the prospect of a reprieve.

'Torch needs to make a real splash when it launches – garner the sort of publicity that it, and your hard work building it, really deserves,' Carolyn ploughed on. 'We need to think big, then think *bigger*.'

Just like that, Amy's optimism shrivelled like a punctured party balloon. As she arranged her face into an impassive rictus grin, she asked herself what she could possibly have done to deserve this. Far from reducing the stress that the public launch of Torch was causing her, it was evident Carolyn's intervention was about to make matters worse.

'I had a lovely dinner with Philippa shortly after you and she met,' Carolyn continued. 'She was thoroughly impressed with you, but just as importantly *very* interested in the idea of a book event that focuses on romance. It fired us up – made me think we could possibly do more than just crow about ourselves. If we widen the focus, we could really make our mark within the genre – establish Torch as a brand that's blazing the trail for popular, unapologetic fiction that's funny, sexy, historical, topical and satisfying.'

'Right,' Amy said, nodding blankly. 'So what does this . . . mean, exactly? In practical terms.'

Carolyn frowned briefly, frustrated that Amy hadn't yet caught on.

'The original launch event idea is toast,' Carolyn said brusquely. 'Forgotten. Finito. Instead, we're looking at a festival. Imagine it, Amy: an outdoor extravaganza during the August Bank Holiday weekend. Authors, publishers and readers all coming together to proclaim their *love* of love stories.'

Amy's mouth had gone dry. She gulped from her mug of now lukewarm coffee, asking herself if it were possible that Carolyn had taken some mood-altering drug before work this morning.

'I . . . I wasn't aware you were such a fan of the genre,' Amy said weakly.

'Oh lord, Amy, I love a bodice-ripper as much as the next person – but this is *business*,' Carolyn said, rolling her eyes. 'This is a commercial opportunity: a chance for us to own this growing trend – this idea of romance reading as almost rebellious. We want to nourish the developing notion that picking up a romance novel can be a *feminist act*, a reclaiming of joy.'

'I see . . .' Amy said for the sake of buying time, well aware that she needed to come up with a response that at least *implied* she understood what the hell Carolyn was talking about. 'It's . . . I suppose it's like Charles Dickens, isn't it?'

'What is?' Carolyn asked, her eyebrows knitting.

'Well. In his day, his books were . . .' Oh *God*, what had Mr Bradley called them? 'Must-reads! But now we have GCSE classes reading *Great Expectations*. Just because fiction is popular, that doesn't mean it's unworthy.'

'Quite,' Carolyn said, looking suddenly impressed. 'So, we're moving from a launch party to a much broader event, of which our imprint will be the host and *at* which we'll make a fuss about how groundbreaking we are. I'm thinking themed food and drink. I'm thinking press coverage and social media hashtags. I'm thinking merchandise! The sky's the limit.'

Amy felt almost faint with dread. When she told Carolyn they had nowhere to hold this 'festival', she was surely going to be sacked. But there was no sense in putting off the inevitable . . .

'It sounds amazing,' Amy said, not entirely dishonestly. 'But in terms of the venue, we need to—'

'Oh, yes! I'm afraid that whatever you've already lined up may prove unsuitable now we've reconsidered the scope of the event. I'm assuming there'll be no budget implications if we cancel, since you haven't expensed anything yet?'

Amy considered giving Carolyn both-barrels honesty and admitting that, actually, she hadn't had anywhere sorted in any case. She discarded the idea immediately, simply agreeing that it wouldn't be a problem to 'move' the event to another location.

'Marvellous, because I have the perfect place lined up,' Carolyn said. 'I think you're going to be as excited as I am when we discuss it properly – but I have to jump on another call in a moment. Are you okay to join a RomFest kick-off meeting this afternoon? Say 3 p.m.? The MD of the venue will join, too – he's already agreed that if I push the button on this he'll support you with organisation. I think that would be helpful, now that the scale of this thing has spiralled somewhat.'

RomFest? Dear God.

Amy instructed herself not to turn her nose up at Carolyn's chosen terminology and instead focus on the fact that – against all odds – the universe seemed to have thrown her a bone here.

'Yes, I'm free then,' Amy said. 'Just send me the meeting details.'

'Marvellous,' Carolyn said. 'And Amy – good work so far on this. Torch is shaping up in precisely the way I'd hoped it would. I know heading up this project was rather a forced decision on your part – and that it probably wasn't your dream to take on the launch of a romance imprint – but my faith in you clearly wasn't misplaced.'

'Thanks,' Amy said, practically breathless with shock. This was the most effusive praise Carolyn had ever given her, and they'd worked together for the best part of a decade.

'Until three, then,' Carolyn said, her ringing mobile already in her hand. 'Hello, Penelope. Yes, I got your email. And no, I do *not* understand—'

Amy shuddered and pressed the 'X' in the corner of her screen. She felt immensely grateful for her own good luck, as well as decidedly sorry for Penny in Accounts.

* * *

At around ten to three, Amy flipped the kettle on to make a cuppa and clicked into the RomFest email Carolyn had sent her a couple of hours ago. It contained a Zoom link but not much else, and it was addressed to both Amy and 'MD@RHE.co.uk'. What the heck was RHE when it was at home? Royal Horticultural something? She supposed she'd find out shortly.

Cup of tea in hand, she settled down at the kitchen table with Bertie jumping around her feet in the hope she might have brought biscuits, too.

'Sorry, pal,' Amy told him affectionately. 'Gran and Ken ate the last of the garibaldis this morning.' The two of them had gone to an art class this afternoon – a regular fixture on what Amy had begun to realise was a rather packed social calendar. Grace – despite having to be careful not to overdo it – had a busier and more varied life than her granddaughter, not to mention a functional relationship with someone who seemed to adore her. Not that Amy herself was bothered about finding a new boyfriend; based on this morning's conversation with Carolyn, it was clear she'd have more than her fill of sappy nonsense between now and September.

Amy was first to dial in to the meeting, so she left the Zoom window open and clicked away to answer an email from an agent she'd just started working with, then check the latest news on the *Guardian* website. This she did while absent-mindedly singing along to Sam Fender on Spotify.

Her computer chimed and a voice said: '*Very* melodic. Glad to see you're still into angsty rock about class struggle – it would have crushed my whole belief system if I'd caught you listening to Steps.'

What the fu—

Amy told Alexa to stop playing, then scrambled to find the Zoom window – now buried beneath about seven others. Even before it surfaced, she knew what it would show.

The grim meaning of the letters 'RHE' was suddenly made

manifest. At the very least she could take a good guess at it, based on the fact that Sam Ainsworth's face was grinning at her from her laptop screen. Rowton Hall Estates? Rowton Hall Enterprises? It didn't matter. The salient point was that Carolyn seemed, inadvertently, to be in the process of destroying her life.

Ignoring his jibe about her musical taste, Amy said: 'I'd ask what on earth you're doing in this meeting, but *how* you've ended up in it seems a better question. I thought your family didn't do "venue for hire" stuff. My understanding was that the very idea was beneath you.'

'It certainly isn't beneath *me*,' Sam said. 'Hence my attendance this afternoon.'

Amy scowled at him. 'That doesn't answer the question.'

'Carolyn – your boss, I believe – is acquainted with my mother from years back,' Sam explained.

That figured, Amy thought. Posh people didn't seem to follow the 'six degrees of separation' rule, whereby everyone in the world was connected via a chain of so many acquaintances. It was more like a rule of two or three degrees, the whole thing concentrated by having been to the 'right' schools, debutante parties and polo matches.

'Somehow,' Sam went on, 'with a little help from me, she managed to convince Pam, and then my father, that an outdoor event like this would be highly profitable and not too disruptive.' That also figured. Carolyn was doggedly determined when she wanted something, but also excellent at making whoever she was working on believe her plans were all their own bright idea. 'I said that as MD of the estate, I'd do all the necessary work to make it happen. As you can probably imagine, the prospect of a healthy return for *no* investment of his own time or effort was too tempting for Roger to resist.'

Amy couldn't help noticing that Sam referred to his parents by their first names. It felt almost derisive – like he disapproved of them. That said, she always called her own mother Lily; Mum felt like a title you had to earn, and

Lily – though Amy rarely felt resentment towards her – had never put the necessary work in.

'You didn't think that working with me on this might be . . . Well. Hideous?' Amy asked. 'You didn't think that perhaps you should *not* involve yourself in my professional life, given how much we dislike each other? At the very least you could have given me some warning. I was at your bloody house last night!'

Sam frown-smiled at her indulgently, as though she were being very silly. It made her want to punch him in the face, or – failing that – angrily slam down the lid of her laptop. She sighed, knowing she couldn't do either.

'I didn't know you were involved until late this morning,' Sam said. 'Carolyn called me to confirm everything – after she'd spoken to you, I believe. Something about checking there'd be no budget problems caused by moving the event. Only at that point did she tell me this festival would be a celebration of all things love-related. And up until then, she'd never mentioned your name. You might also recall that you only revealed last night that you were working on this kind of fiction, which came as quite the surprise.

'Also, for the record: I don't dislike you. I never have.'

He said this softly. Sincerely. The words seemed to whack Amy in the solar plexus, so she resolved to ignore them.

'We can't even get through an encounter at the village shop without arguing,' Amy pointed out. 'Mr Bradley had to intervene last night in order to prevent bloodshed in a discussion about a *book*. How can you possibly think we can work together on something as ambitious as this?'

Sam shrugged. 'Because we have no choice. Contracts are already signed. Rowton Hall is hosting RomFest, and you and I are in charge of it. I'm sure we'll manage.'

Ping.

Carolyn had joined the meeting.

'Ah,' she said. 'You two are getting acquainted. Excellent. I've no doubt you'll end up fast friends, if you aren't already.'

Amy choked slightly at this, then coughed to cover her incredulous reaction.

'We actually went to sixth form college together,' Sam said, seemingly amused by Amy's discomposure.

'Oh, splendid!' Carolyn cried. 'I did wonder whether your paths had crossed . . . Don't you think Rowton Hall is a wonderful choice of venue, Amy? When I realised it was so local to you *and* the inspiration for one of the country's favourite Regency romances, I had to make sure we got it. We'll be using the beautiful gardens and woodland, with the house as the ultimate picturesque backdrop.'

'It's . . . brilliant. Yes. Amazing,' Amy said, trying and failing to sound enthusiastic.

Carolyn tipped her head to one side, perturbed. 'I know we've shifted the goalposts somewhat today, and doubtless this is a lot to take in,' she said. 'Which is why I'd like you to have this Friday off.'

'What?' Amy asked, forgetting to be polite. Carolyn didn't do days off – she'd been known to send work emails on Christmas Day, and rarely understood other people's quite normal need for downtime.

'Well, not *off*,' Carolyn continued, and Amy fought not to roll her eyes. *Here comes something else I won't like.* 'I want you to make your way to a scary story festival that's happening up north – see how it all works and get some inspiration.'

'I suppose that makes sense,' Amy conceded, nodding her head. 'Looking at how another genre comes to life at an event would probably be helpful for me, having never done anything like this before.'

'Indeed,' Carolyn said, smiling with satisfaction. 'The event is in Robin Hood's Bay, near Whitby – presumably because of the Dracula connection – so not *too* difficult for you to get to. I'd suggest the pair of you drive up on Friday, so you're there for when it kicks off the following morning. I've already taken the liberty of organising tickets and accommodation.'

Hang the hell on.

The pair of them?

Amy felt her face growing red as she fumbled for an excuse not to do this, having said mere moments ago that the trip was a good idea.

She could not – absolutely could *not* – spend a night away with Sam. She groped around in her brain for a reason she could offer up that wasn't juvenile, unprofessional or faintly ridiculous, and came up with nothing.

She became aware that her mouth was hanging open when Sam said, 'That sounds great, Carolyn. I've no doubt the experience will be very illuminating.' His tone was serious and sensible, but there was laughter in his eyes.

Fantastic. Now Amy would be written off as unreasonable – lacking in commitment to her new job – if she tried to backtrack. Would it have killed him to say, Sorry Carolyn, I can't rearrange my weekend at such short notice? Unlike Amy, Sam didn't work for H-K; he could have politely declined the offer with very little loss of face. And anyway, hadn't he said contracts were already signed? Carolyn was locked into hiring Rowton Hall's grounds even if Sam point-blank refused to set foot in Robin Hood's Bay in the rudest manner imaginable.

'That's settled, then,' Carolyn said. 'I'll leave you two to talk among yourselves about arrangements. And perhaps we can schedule another call for Monday, so you can report back on what you've seen. I daresay you won't be dialling in separately in future, either, what with your being in the same village, ha ha!'

Fuck. Another bombshell. Somehow, they just kept coming.

'Now,' Carolyn motored on, 'let's do a quick brainstorm – note down every idea we've had so far with regard to this event, as well as any challenges we can see on the horizon. We'll see where we're at with a little analysis today, then regroup to discuss how your reconnaissance might help us make the right decisions.'

Amy stifled a groan, strategically bending to retrieve a notebook from the other side of her laptop screen in order to hide the queasy expression she knew was on her face.

Carolyn *really* didn't want a full rundown of the concerns Amy had about planning RomFest right now. But if she'd been honest enough to offer one, Amy knew 'spending time with Sam Ainsworth' would have been right at the top of the list.

Shortly after she logged off from work for the night, Amy's mobile began to ring. She hoped it was Kit, so she could rant to him about the utterly ludicrous day she'd had – but when she picked it up from the table, she saw Lily's name lighting up the screen.

Hmmm. Conversations with her mother were rarely helpful and often infuriating, even when Lily had the best of intentions. But it was weeks since Amy had spoken to her, and what if something important had happened? What if something was wrong? Gingerly, Amy tapped the 'answer' icon and put the phone to her ear.

'Hello?'

'Darling!' Lily gushed, her formerly British accent now a weird, semi-Californian twang. 'I'm so glad you picked up.'

'Of course,' Amy said, wondering already if answering this call had been a mistake. Lily sounded perfectly relaxed, which implied there was no crisis. 'What time is it there?' Amy asked, trying to sound upbeat.

'Just coming up to ten in the morning,' Lily said. 'Sky's blue. It's gonna be a beautiful day. But I need to talk to you – I'm a little worried.'

Great. Just what Amy needed: something else to be concerned about.

'Okay . . .' she said cautiously. 'What's wrong?'

'I've just pulled a three-card spread for you,' said Lily.

Amy closed her eyes and pinched the bridge of her nose. *This* was what her mother was calling about from the other side of the Atlantic? A trio of tarot cards?

'And?' Amy asked, willing herself not to be too obviously exasperated.

'All major arcana cards. Very unusual. Significant.'

As far as Amy was concerned, what Lily was describing had no significance whatsoever. She knew from previous conversations with her mother that a three-card spread supposedly offered insight into someone's past, present and future – though Amy privately considered this an absolute load of hogwash.

She pressed her lips together, determined not to say as much out loud.

'Your first card was the wheel of fortune. Reversed,' Lily said gravely. 'Have you had some bad luck lately? Have you been forced to make some change you weren't very happy about?'

Amy sighed. This was deeply annoying. When she admitted to Lily that she'd split up with Hugh, changed jobs and temporarily moved back to Rowton, her mother would be more convinced than ever that the cards spoke true.

'Kind of,' Amy told her, grudgingly. 'I don't want to get into it now, and I promise you I am *fine* – but I'm back at Gran's for a while. I got a promotion at work and it required me to be outside London. Also, Hugh asked me to marry him and I said no, so we broke up. I realised I just couldn't do it, and he . . . Well. He wasn't pleased.'

'Ah,' Lily said sagely. 'That explains a lot. Your present card – the second one I pulled – is the tower. I found that a little alarming. But now I think it's connected to all the change you're experiencing. You have to let the chaos and revelation you're going through lead you into a new phase of your life. Embrace the transformation.'

Amy huffed out a weary breath. Short of quitting her job, she had very little choice but to 'embrace' everything that had been thrown at her lately. 'Mmm-hmmm,' she murmured, humming her agreement with Lily so as not to invite further questions about the state her life was in.

'And then the future card – well. I'm less concerned about this one, though it does indicate a big shift for you,' Lily continued. 'The moon, reversed, suggests you need to start paying attention to your dreams – to all the subconscious messages the universe may be trying to deliver to you. You must listen to what your innermost voice is telling you, confront how you really *feel*.'

Right now, Amy's innermost voice was telling her to end this conversation as quickly as possible – so she was pretty sure her mother wouldn't want her to pay attention to it at this precise moment.

'Right,' Amy said. 'I see.'

'Do you?' Lily said, sounding sad and sympathetic. 'I know you're sceptical, Amaryllis, but I do think this spread offers a very strong picture of where you're at in your journey. I think you'd find the cards very instructive if you'd open your mind.'

Urgh. Almost no one had the audacity to call her Amaryllis – at least not to her face.

'If you know I'm *sceptical*, why do you insist on doing readings for me?' Amy demanded. 'I mean, how accurate is it anyway, from thousands of miles away? And shouldn't you *ask* someone before you start consulting the universe about their fate? Surely there's some rule against tarot-ing without consent?'

'You're my daughter!' Lily cried. 'My intentions are pure – I'm very confident the universe is clear on that. Of course I'm going to check in on you from time to time. There are only good vibes flowing from me to you, you know?'

Only good *vibes* is about right, Amy thought. She couldn't remember the last time her happy hippy of a mother had helped her in any practical way.

'So tell me about your new job,' Lily said.

Amy offered an edited version of how she'd come into her new role and what it involved.

'I'm no longer surprised by your cards,' her mother

commented. 'You say you're working with the heir to the Hall on this festival project?'

'I'm afraid so,' Amy confirmed.

'Oh? I seem to remember you were quite fond of him as a teenager.'

Amy flinched. 'You're thinking of Hari.'

'No,' Lily insisted. 'I'm not. I may be an . . . *effervescent* sort of person, but I'm not an idiot. And I care for you. As if I'd forget that your best friend died in a car wreck.'

'I hate to break it to you, Lily, but your memory is definitely faulty if you think Sam Ainsworth and I were friends.'

'I never said you were *friends*. I said you were fond of him. And I do wish you'd call me Mom.'

'Just like I wish you'd call me *Amy*.'

'I remember your letters from your sixth form years,' Lily went on, ignoring her. 'Always full of complaints about how crazy he made you. You did your best to hide it, but of course I could always tell you had a colossal crush on him.'

'What, because you have *the sight*?' Amy asked, sarcasm finally bursting through her determined politeness. There really was only so long she could feign understanding of Lily's bizarre melting pot of beliefs, or maintain patience with her pontificating.

'No, because I'm *your mother*,' Lily said.

'Well, it's nonsense anyway,' said Amy, though her voice lacked conviction even to her own ears.

'Just take care,' Lily told her. 'Remember the moon: that card means now is not the time to bury your feelings or push aside inconvenient emotions.'

'I don't *have* any inconvenient emotions!' Amy cried. 'Apart from exhaustion, or annoyance perhaps – I'd already done a full day of work by the time you called me up to start divining my future. I should go. I need to make a start on dinner – Gran'll be home soon.'

'Sure,' Lily said. 'Give my love to Grace. And darling – one last thing.'

'Yeah?'

'I'll send you a moonstone. They're full of feminine power and excellent during times of change.'

'Right. Thanks.'

'Trust me, I think you're going to need it. *Remember the moon.*'

Amy shook her head at her iPhone. The moment she put it down, what she would need was a very large G&T.

'Bye, Lily. Speak to you again soon – preferably about something other than the portents of my doom.'

'You're not doomed – you're just evolving!' Lily said. 'Or at least the universe *wants* you to be. Love you, kiddo. Take care.'

'Love you too,' Amy said. And despite their unconventional dynamic, she meant it.

Chapter 16

Carolyn's claim that Robin Hood's Bay 'wouldn't be difficult to get to' from Rowton was thoroughly debunked on Friday afternoon.

In Carolyn's head, it seemed, everything north of the Watford Gap blended into an amorphous mass of 'not London', where nothing was far away from anything else. In practice, the journey from South Warwickshire to the North Yorkshire coast took almost five hours – made longer by heavy traffic and a series of delays on the M1.

Amy had insisted on driving. There was no way she wanted to be dependent on Sam for transportation, in the way she'd always been when she and Hugh went anywhere by car. Even though it was years since London-dwelling Amy had undertaken a trip of this length, she'd got herself insured on Grace's pale blue, rarely used, twelve-year-old Nissan Micra and informed Sam via text that she'd be making her own way up north.

Somewhat logically, but much to her annoyance, he'd immediately asked if he could travel with her. Amy had hoped that the prospect of being driven by a woman would feel somehow emasculating – an idea that, along with jibes about the relative skills of male and female drivers, had sometimes surfaced during discussion among Hugh's car fanatic friends. Sam had no such scruples; in fact, he was profuse in his thanks when Amy reluctantly agreed that it would be cheaper, and more environmentally friendly, for them to travel together.

The prospect of having to make conversation with Sam all the way to their destination was unthinkable, so Amy had put together a lengthy playlist of music from their youth in the hope of limiting their interactions to only basic, necessary exchanges. Perhaps a little foolishly, Amy hadn't considered the sort of atmosphere that several hours of songs from their teenage years might produce inside the Nissan as it trundled along. She was by no means a sentimental person, but nevertheless felt swept away by a tide of nostalgia as tracks by Editors, Arcade Fire and Bat For Lashes blasted from the tinny-sounding stereo. The sense of wistfulness for something lost – as opposed to just some*one* – was palpable; it was a weird, shared pining for the people Amy and Sam used to be, as well as the friend who was no longer there with them. Neither of them acknowledged it.

When Bat For Lashes' cover of Springsteen's 'I'm On Fire' began seeping from the speakers, Amy's resolve not to react finally crumbled. She couldn't handle those lyrics in that small a space – not with him next to her. She pressed a button on the car's stereo and allowed a Radio Four current affairs show to cut through the tension between them.

As they pulled up to their B&B at just after eight o'clock, Amy sighed with relief. The guest house was a tall, thin, three-storey building within sight of the sea, whitewashed with black-painted window frames. Next door to a pub, it perched at the top of a steep, winding lane that led down to the beach. The sky was still pale blue despite the hour, and the air drifting in through Amy's open window smelled salty and clean.

They parked at the rear of the B&B on a tiny scrap of concrete that claimed it was a car park, yet contained only three small spaces – two of which were taken. Amy thanked her lucky stars that Grace's car was little; squeezing in here might otherwise have proved impossible.

'You okay?' Sam asked her.

'Yeah. Just glad to finally be here.'

'No doubt,' Sam said. 'Thanks for driving. And for the tunes – I'll have to follow you on Spotify.'

'Ha. You'd probably hate most of my playlists, to be honest. I refer you to your earlier comment on my love of angry songs about the decimation of the working class.'

'I only said you enjoyed that stuff – not that I *didn't* enjoy it,' Sam pointed out.

Amy shook her head at him and opened the driver's side door. 'I can't deal with you being pedantic right now. Mainly because I've been desperate for the loo since we went past York.'

Sam laughed. 'You head in, I'll bring the bags,' he said. 'Leave me the car key so I can lock up.' He smiled broadly, showing the dimples that Amy could almost forget he had until they appeared, to dazzling effect. She rolled her eyes, refusing to be moved.

Unable to ignore the urge to pee any longer, she did as he'd suggested and went inside. The young lad on reception – probably nineteen or twenty, but somehow made to look younger by his uniform of smart trousers, shirt, waistcoat and tie – pointed Amy in the direction of the nearest bathroom. After using the toilet, she splashed cool water on the back of her neck. Grace's old Micra wasn't blessed with air conditioning, and the car had become uncomfortably warm and sticky in the late-May sunshine.

When she rounded the corner back into the B&B's entrance hall, Sam was remonstrating with the boy behind the main desk, speaking in hushed tones that Amy could tell did not bode well for their stay.

She moved to stand beside him. 'What's up?'

Sam looked at her with a pained expression.

'It can't be that bad,' Amy said bracingly. Then she felt her own face fall. 'Oh God. Is there some problem with our rooms? Do we even *have* rooms? Have they doubled-booked on us?'

'Er. Sort of. In a manner of speaking,' Sam said.

'What does *that* mean?' Amy snapped. 'Will you just tell me what's going on, please?'

The boy behind the reception desk flinched, apparently having realised that dealing with Sam was infinitely preferable to explaining the situation to Amy.

'They have double-booked us – but in the sense that they've booked *both* of us into one room,' Sam told her, speaking so quietly that she initially thought she'd misheard him.

'WHAT?' she cried, as the words Sam had spoken tessellated into understanding. 'How? *Why*, for pity's sake?'

'It seems Carolyn wasn't one hundred per cent clear when she organised this that we weren't . . .' He halted, reddening slightly, then made himself continue: 'She wasn't clear with the person on the phone that we weren't a couple.'

To Sam's credit, he sounded less than thrilled at this turn of events, though Amy had no idea why he looked so flustered. It wasn't *his* fault it had happened.

'According to Matthew, here' – Sam gestured at the now terrified-looking receptionist – 'Carolyn said *two guests* and gave our names, never thinking to explain we needed separate rooms.'

'That's about t' size of it, yeah,' Matthew put in, rubbing the back of his neck uncomfortably, his warm Yorkshire burr doing nothing to soften the blow of the frankly terrible news he'd just delivered.

'This is not happening,' Amy said firmly. 'It's like something out of a made-for-TV movie. It's Hallmark Channel stuff. I refuse to accept it. I simply will *not*.'

Sam side-eyed her. 'You watch the Hallmark Channel?'

'No, I bloody well don't!' Amy hissed through gritted teeth. 'But I know it *exists*. And I'm serious: I will not partake in this . . . this . . . *bullshit*.'

Sam was smirking – almost grinning – at her now.

'I see nothing funny about any of this,' Amy fumed, feeling seriously tempted to kick him in the shins. 'We need to find somewhere else to stay.'

'Oh, you'll not find anywhere in the village tonight wi' rooms,' Matthew said blithely, backing even further away from the reception desk when he saw the look on Amy's face. 'What I mean is, this scary story thing's got the whole place booked up. All day there's been folk arriving dressed up like vampires and ghosts and the like. The Vic – the pub next door, I mean – their rooms are full. I reckon it'll be t' same story all over.'

Amy sighed. 'So what do you recommend, bearing in mind it's taken us five hours to get here?'

To her horror, she realised she was perilously close to tears. Exhaustion had combined with a feeling of utter helplessness to create the sort of angry frustration that usually found its release through her eyeballs.

'Amy, it's OK,' Sam said, gently resting a hand on her shoulder. 'I'll . . . I'll sleep on the floor, or something. We're just going to have to muddle through. It's only one night.'

Amy shook him off, overwrought. Being stuck in the car with him had been bad enough; the prospect of trying to sleep in the same room as him was horrendous. Being anywhere near Sam, she'd begun to understand, muddied what ordinarily felt clear: that she did not, and never could, like him. Somehow in his presence she seemed to forget this.

She was minded to call Carolyn right now and shout the odds, demand an apology for this epic, embarrassing screw-up – but she knew there was no point. Carolyn and melodrama were like oil and water: they simply didn't mix. However justified Amy's ranting might be, it would glance off her boss's Teflon-tough carapace without leaving the slightest mark.

'I can set you up wi' a camp bed,' Matthew said warily. 'I know it's not ideal, but it's probably t' best we can do. You take your key and I'll follow you up, if that's all right.'

'That would be great, thank you,' Sam said.

Taking this as permission to escape, Matthew handed Sam a long, old-fashioned silver key with a label stating 'Room Three' attached to it, then shuffled off up the corridor. Sam shouldered both his bag and Amy's, then moved in the direction of the spiral staircase Matthew had bobbed his head at before disappearing.

Amy's shoulders sagged. 'This is a disaster,' she moaned.

But for lack of any other option, she followed Sam up to the first floor and into their room.

It was one of those spaces with too much furniture, too much wall art and a profusion of scatter cushions that – if Amy were being uncharitable – she'd have said gave the room the air of a padded cell. Everything was cream, beige or rose pink.

It was pleasant enough: clean, fresh-smelling and neat. However, when her eyes drifted to the bed, she emitted a yelp of horror. A smattering of deep red flower petals had been arranged in a gigantic heart on top of the soft velvet bedspread, and there were chocolates on both the pillows.

'Don't. Say. A *word*,' Amy hissed as she began sweeping the petals into a tiny wastepaper basket she'd pulled from the corner. Wisely, he didn't – but she could *feel* him laughing.

This whole situation was catastrophic; the room's self-consciously romantic vibe the worst imaginable backdrop for a night spent in forced proximity to someone from whom Amy was determined to keep a safe distance.

Aside from anything else, Gran and Barbara had extracted more promises of silence from her before she'd left Rowton this afternoon – and it was respect for them that had so far convinced her not to take Sam to task. Barbara insisted he was doing his best to help, and had muttered some explanation of how Sam was supporting Jed with a plan to try and keep the pub. Privately, Amy was of the view that 'regularly propping up the bar' probably didn't amount to much practical assistance aside from boosting its profits – but she kept this to herself.

At that moment, a rap on the door signalled Matthew had arrived with the promised camp bed. He shouldered the thing into the room with some effort. It looked ancient, rickety and positively unsafe – but by the time it had been dressed with sheets, pillows and a duvet, it at least resembled a bed. It was squeezed alongside the small double that sat in the centre of the room, in the only area with enough available floor to accommodate it. The set-up was hardly going to make for a clear demarcation between one bed and the other, but it seemed that, short of reconfiguring the whole place, there was nothing to be done.

With an air that suggested he'd discharged his duty, Matthew asked if that was all for now. When Sam confirmed he could be on his way, the boy smiled the beatific smile of one who had just been granted salvation and no longer had reason to fear the eternal fires of hell.

'I'll sleep on that,' Amy said after he'd left, gesturing at the camp bed and then asking herself why she was being so noble. By rights, she should have looked forward to the spectacle of Sam's six-foot-something frame hunched on top of a structure that was much too short for his legs and very possibly wouldn't take his weight.

'You absolutely won't,' Sam told her. 'I couldn't let you.'

'Let me?' Amy demanded, both eyebrows up in defiance. 'Aside from you very much *not* being in charge here, there's the small matter of me being quite a lot smaller than you. That bed is clearly designed for a child – not an actual adult man.'

'An actual adult man,' Sam said, smiling. 'I think that's probably the politest way you've ever described me. I seem to recall being referred to as "that upper-class arsehole" for at least six months at one point – and that was only when you *weren't* pissed off with me.'

'Where was the lie?' Amy asked, shrugging her shoulders.

'I like to think I'm not an arsehole, if I'm honest,' he said, sincerely enough that she squirmed slightly. 'As to the other thing . . . I'm not going to argue that I didn't grow up obscenely fortunate – at least in some ways.'

Amy bit her lip to save launching into a 'poor little rich boy' tirade. While her foray into Rowton Hall's dusty, dilapidated corners – and Sam's brusque, uncomfortable references to his parents – implied the Ainsworths might not be the happiest of families, this hardly compared to the heartbreak Barbara, Dave and Jed were facing.

In the end, all she said was, 'Good of you to admit it.'

Sam looked at the ceiling and sighed. 'I've never denied it. But like I said to you during our argument at the bake sale, I don't want to be defined by it. Privileged isn't *all* I am. Though I suspect thinking of me in those terms always made things easier for you.'

'What's that supposed to mean?' Amy asked, frowning.

'Nothing,' Sam said briskly, shaking his head. 'It meant nothing. Forget I said it. I don't know about you, but I could do with a drink. Shall we try the pub next door?'

'I . . . Er . . . Oh, *fine*,' said Amy, finally losing the will to protest at this reminder that there was chilled white wine just a short walk away.

'After you,' Sam said, holding the door open for her to walk through.

Amy mock-simpered at him as she passed, still wondering what he'd meant – and feeling somehow, very annoyingly, as though he'd won this particular argument.

Chapter 17

By the time she'd made her way through a large glass of Sauvignon Blanc, and Sam had sunk a cold beer, Amy had arrived at the troubling conclusion that she was enjoying herself.

Having shelved thoughts of Barb, Dave and Jed in favour of sharing her views on the latest must-see TV, several (non-romantic) books she and Sam had both read and the transformation of the village cafe from greasy spoon to stylish brunch spot, she'd managed to relax. In fact, despite the stressful drive, the double-booking disaster and the presence of someone she'd long considered her nemesis, she felt more serene than she had in weeks.

Perhaps it was the wine – a full bottle of which had recently appeared on their table after Sam's trip to the bathroom. More likely, it was the fact that she'd drunk it on a pretty empty stomach; the bar snacks still being served by the time they got there were tasty, but nowhere near as substantial as Amy would have liked.

It would also have been dishonest of her not to admit that Sam was good company, so long as she could put aside all her very valid reasons for feeling hostile towards him. It was a long while since she'd been forced to confront several inconvenient facts: first, that he was clever and funny, and able to talk about pretty much anything. He'd argue his point if he felt strongly about an issue, but – unlike most of the men Amy had spent time with in her London life – didn't feel the need to pretend expertise where he had none.

Secondly, Sam was an attentive listener. Amy was used to dealing with people – particularly the men in her professional environment – who seemed not to pay attention to anything she said. By contrast, Sam asked pertinent questions and actually listened to her responses. He seemed genuinely interested in the vagaries of the publishing industry, as well as her vivid report of meeting Philippa Fotheringham.

Thirdly, he still had that face, those eyes, that *mouth*. Those uncompromisingly square shoulders. Regarding him over the top of her wine glass, Amy noted a sharpening of the features that, in youth, had lent Sam an air of wholesome, boy band loveliness. During the years when she hadn't seen him, they'd become more characterful versions of themselves. They came together to form a whole that was greater than the sum of its parts: the sort of beauty you could paint or photograph, but never properly render in only two dimensions. Up close and in person, it was compelling.

Foolishly, and in no small part thanks to the alcohol she'd consumed, Amy decided to test her feelings – tread on the thin ice that separated her common sense here and now from the deep-water memory of her teenage crush on him. What would it be like to kiss him again, she wondered, allowing her eyes to linger on his full lips for a moment? Her heart thumped, and the sudden sense that her stomach was dissolving confirmed what she already knew: it would be electric. Alchemical. It would change her state, transform her from one thing into another – morph her into some soft-centred, boneless person she barely recognised. The idea should have horrified her, but it didn't quite manage to. Instead, she shivered in nervous fascination.

'Amy . . . ?' Sam said. 'Are you still with me?'

'Sorry. What?'

'You were miles away,' he said, brow furrowed in concern. 'Are you tired? D'you want to head back and go to bed?'

At the word *bed*, Amy jumped and stifled a hysterical laugh.

'Sorry, I'm fine,' she insisted. 'What were you saying?'

'I was just saying that my niece is apparently obsessed

with you. According to Meg, she thinks you look like Snow White but – and I quote – you're "way too cool to hang around waiting for a handsome prince to kiss you". I told Meg to let her know she has your number.'

Amy laughed. 'That's terrifying. Summed up by a seven-year-old. And I've only met her a couple of times!'

'She's a smart cookie,' Sam said fondly. Amy's heart clenched involuntarily at the sight of his proud smile.

'You two are close?' Amy asked, though she already knew the answer.

'Very,' Sam said. 'I adore her.'

Amy nodded. Despite having met up with Nisha and Meg several times lately – and having crossed paths with Pearl during coffee dates or Prosecco-fuelled film nights – she was none the wiser about the little girl's parentage. She didn't like to ask, but it was clear that – whatever the reason for Pearl's father's absence – Sam had stepped in as a male role model for her.

'I don't suppose you know the whole "Meg and Pearl" story, do you?' said Sam. 'You're too polite to pry, and Meg struggles to talk about it.'

'Oh – no. I haven't asked her anything,' Amy confirmed, pleased that he'd read her correctly. She wasn't uninterested in other people's lives, but having grown up without her mother – and then during her father's illness – she'd been the object of more impertinent questions than she could ever have hoped to count. This was one of the reasons she'd found city anonymity so appealing. It wasn't in her to mete out the same treatment to others who might have experienced trauma; in general, she reasoned that people would tell her as much as they were comfortable with in their own time.

As if to prove the point, Sam said: 'Meg got pregnant with her at nineteen – she was living at home but up and down from London a lot at that stage. Partying too hard, in with the wrong crowd, generally just sad and lost . . . All the posh girl clichés.' He flashed her a knowing look.

Amy grimaced – out of sadness for a lonely-sounding Meg, rather than judgement of her behaviour. She hoped Sam could tell the difference.

'When she told her wanker of a boyfriend she was expecting,' Sam went on, 'he made it very clear he wanted nothing to do with the situation. He's barely ever seen Pearl, which suits us just fine: last I heard he was coked up to the eyeballs and running some members-only nightclub in Ibiza.'

'Wow.'

'Yeah. At the time, I was living in New York. I went over there for a few years after graduating, did a few different jobs in advertising and tried to work out what to do with myself. I'd decided I was going to study for an MBA and was all set to head back to London – I knew she wasn't doing well, that I'd left her too long . . . Then I got this desperate call from her and realised I had to get back to Rowton immediately.'

'I don't quite understand,' Amy said, treading as carefully as she could – fearing she might step on a conversational landmine at any second. 'Where were your parents at this point?'

Sam took a sip of wine, then set down his glass and looked at her levelly. 'Pressuring her to have an abortion she definitely didn't want.'

Ah. *Boom.*

Amy blanched and closed her eyes. 'Because they thought she was too young?'

Sam laughed bitterly. 'God, no – because they were worried about the scandal it might cause. They'd wanted her married off by twenty-one to a duke, or the scion of some multibillion-pound business – not that they were fussy about *which* business. A baby born "out of wedlock", as they put it, was not part of their plan for keeping up appearances.'

'That's awful. *Beyond* awful. I'm so sorry she went through that,' Amy said. She meant it, too: the thought of terrified, teenage Meg being browbeaten by her pompous, puffed-up father made Amy feel sick.

'Yeah, so am I,' Sam murmured. 'Once I got back from

the States, I stood between her and Roger – made it clear I wasn't going to allow my sister to be manipulated or forced into anything she didn't want. He's never quite forgotten that I defied him. Of course, irony of ironies, the second Pearl was born, all bonny, blonde and blue-eyed, everyone fell in love with her. Then Meg became this amazing, wonderful mother and her so-called sins were forgiven.'

'So you came off worst, in the end?' Amy breathed, still trying to take all this in.

'Oh, I don't know,' said Sam. 'I did my fair share of night feeds and nappy changes, but I'm not the one who's ultimately responsible for keeping another human being alive. And I got my MBA done – at Birmingham, in the end. As far as my relationship with my father's concerned, standing up for Meg was just the final nail in the coffin. We've been at loggerheads for years, pretty much since I started making a nuisance of myself at boarding school.'

He smiled mischievously, offsetting the wistfulness that had crept into his voice.

'How old were you then?' Amy asked, arching an eyebrow. She filed away the idea of Sam making up bottles of formula and wrestling nappies onto a newborn for consideration later.

'Oh, God . . . Eight, maybe?'

She laughed. 'In that case, it really is no wonder you ended up at a state sixth form college for A levels . . . I'm amazed it took that long for the nation's independent establishments to blacklist you.'

'I wasn't ever actually *blacklisted*,' Sam said, finishing the last of his Sauvignon. 'I did bounce around a bit, though. Several schools strongly "suggested" to Roger and Pam that I might be a better fit elsewhere.'

Amy laughed again, in spite of herself. 'I can't approve, you know – *my* high school was in special measures. We had to share textbooks in every lesson – one between two if we were lucky, because there were never enough to go around. People got kicked out for carrying knives or doing drug deals in the corridors. It was chaos.'

'I won't pretend that sticking two fingers up at private schooling doesn't make me sound like an absolute tosser,' Sam conceded. 'But these places – the ones I was sent to, anyway . . . they're stifling. Designed to squash the life out of you. I'll never be sorry I got out.' He shuddered, then – visibly affected by whatever grim memory had surfaced. Amy just nodded – willing, for once, to accept that his experience might have been more complicated than she'd thought.

'We should go,' Sam said. 'Early start, and all that.'

'I'm going to feel rotten after all this wine,' Amy groaned. 'And no doubt I'll look like something near dead.'

'It's a horror book festival,' Sam pointed out. 'You'll fit right in.'

Without thinking, Amy threw him a sarcastic grit-grin and then whacked him on the arm. Neither of them said anything else as they gathered their things and made their way to the door.

Back at the B&B, the atmosphere shifted. The camaraderie that had been fuelled by ambient pub noise and crisp, ice-cold alcohol felt suddenly fragile and nebulous. They were awkward with one another again – embarrassed to be stuck in the same too-small space.

'You use the bathroom first,' Amy said. 'I have a complicated skincare regime – you won't want to wait around for me to finish it.' Sam nodded, then headed into what was essentially a jumped-up shower cubicle and shut the door behind him.

He was back within a few minutes, his hair slightly damp and wearing plaid pyjama pants and a soft grey T-shirt. Amy couldn't look at him. There was something obscene about seeing him in his nightwear, even though it revealed no more than ordinary clothes and was entirely family-friendly.

She grabbed her washbag and the navy satin pyjama shorts set she'd brought to sleep in, wishing powerfully that she'd opted for some sort of unsightly, unsexy head-to-toe coverall instead. The last thing she wanted was for Sam to think she was in any way attempting to *attract* him – but it was either the vaguely flirty PJs or knickers and a vest top, which on balance seemed significantly worse.

She needn't have worried. By the time she'd double-cleansed, brushed her teeth and then applied eye balm, night serum and an intensive moisturising cream, Sam had fallen asleep. He was bunched up on the camp bed and breathing heavily.

Refusing to let herself focus on his slightly parted lips, the dark fan of his eyelashes on his cheeks or the slow rise and fall of his chest under the covers, she manoeuvred her way around him and clicked off the light.

When Amy awoke at 6.57 to sunlight streaming through the B&B's thin curtains, she blearily picked up her phone to discover a selection of WhatsApp messages from Kit – several of which had been sent just a couple of hours ago.

At 2.34am:

Ames, the hot nerdy sex god is at Queer Karaoke!!!
Can't sing, sadly – every note is flatter than a witch's tit.
But he's SO BEAUTIFUL.

At 4.46am:

OMG I think I'm in love 🤍
Finally snogged him.
Julius = best kisser EVER. But refuses to bone until we've been on a proper date 😩

At 4.52am:

Almost forgot to ask!!!
Did you resist a ransacking from the heir to the estate?
🍆 🌙 💦

Full disclosure, I'd definitely have thrown him one despite his apparently evil tendencies.

Amy sighed and put the phone back down in favour of assessing the extent of her hangover. Pleasingly, she didn't feel too bad.

Like an idiot, she'd confided to Kit yesterday evening that she and Sam had a) been sent on a joint research mission by Carolyn, and b) thanks to her casual ineptitude were stuck sharing a room. When he'd responded, she'd felt briefly convinced she could hear him laughing all the way from London.

Right now, Amy could hear the shower running in the bathroom and prayed that Sam had had the foresight to take his clothes in there with him. Seeing him in a towel would be mortifying. Worse than mortifying, if she was truthful with herself.

In fact, the mere *sound* of the water was provocative. She forbade her mind to wander for fear it would conjure images of damp, golden skin, rippling back muscles, soap-soused shoulders . . . At that moment, her stomach seemed to fall out of her body and down through the thick, patterned bedroom carpet. She put her hands over her ears and shut her eyes. No, no, *no*. This couldn't happen.

For a mad moment, she considered texting Nisha for her official definition of 'stomach drop sensation'. It would have been pointless, of course; inevitably, the response would have been something along the lines of 'Ahhh, you just know it when you feel it!'

So, Sam was hot. He was attractive. This news was hardly revelatory – she could handle it. And it didn't mean she had to amend her views on what they were to each other, which was *nothing*.

In fact, Amy reasoned, she should probably have expected that at some point she'd feel physically drawn to him again. There was precedent. She was a grown woman, she had *needs* . . . Though she had to admit it was a very long time since they'd felt quite so urgent.

She picked up her iPhone again and sent a message to Kit, as if to ward off her own lustful thoughts.

> Amy: Obviously there has been ZERO ransacking. First, we have to work together thanks to Carolyn. Also, I DON'T LIKE HIM.

To Amy's amazement, Kit's reply was almost immediate. She surmised that he hadn't been to bed yet and would probably crash at some point within the next half hour.

> Kit: Just like you couldn't even remember his name? Lololol

Amy stuck her tongue out at the phone screen, then buried her face in her pillow.

To Amy's intense relief, Sam emerged from the bathroom fully clothed. She sent up a silent prayer of thanks to whichever force was on her side this morning.

Unfailingly polite as always, Sam offered to walk up the high street and fetch them both coffees so she could shower and get ready in private. More than half an hour later, just as she was putting the finishing touches to her makeup, he returned with a double-shot cappuccino – her morning favourite.

After a hearty breakfast, she and Sam made their way to the festival HQ. They discovered the event was spread across several locations in the Robin Hood's Bay area, all of which were within easy walking distance of one another. Having been provided with maps and wristbands that guaranteed their entry to various 'scary stations', they set off for a talk entitled: 'The Undying Appeal of the Bloodsucker'.

In support of Matthew's claim that the whole village was full of festivalgoers, almost everyone Amy and Sam saw was in full costume or sporting an item of clothing that declared their allegiance to a specific author or story. She lost count of the amount of *Child of the Night*, *Doctor of Doom* and *Valley of Shadows* T-shirts she saw; there was even a drinks cart selling cocktails that looked horribly like cups of real blood.

She and Sam snapped photos of every quirky stall, souvenir and festival feature they saw, noting that the event's presence on social media was key to its success. Not only had Instagram and TikTok done a lot of heavy lifting when it came to promoting the festival; excerpts from the day's headline sessions were being streamed live and there were competitions running that rewarded engagement with particular hashtags.

After a scary story-themed lunch in a local restaurant – a seafood pasta dish masquerading as some kind of entrails stew, which Sam thought was hilarious and Amy felt was in very poor taste – they meandered through celebrations of sci-fi horror, psychological terror, slasher fiction and post-apocalyptic novels.

Amy marvelled at the scale of it all. Hundreds – probably thousands – of readers were united in their enthusiasm for books that would rob most people of the ability to sleep for a week. Several well-known authors were here: writers whose names she recognised and whose work she knew, despite not having any professional or personal interest in the horror genre.

'What do you make of it all then?' Sam asked her as they grabbed plastic cups of 'Psycho Chef's Sour Citrus Punch' – otherwise known as fresh lemonade – on their way back to the B&B's car park.

'I think . . .' Amy began, making a face as she took a sip of her strongly acidic drink, 'that we have a *lot* of work to do if we're going to pull off anything as successful as this. But I also think a romance festival could be even bigger and better.'

'Agreed,' Sam said, sucking lemonade through his straw and immediately breaking into agonised coughs. 'Bloody hell, that stuff's undrinkable.'

Amy laughed. 'I actually quite like it. Once you get past the initial eye-popping sensation, it's very refreshing. Trust you to want something sweet and sugary.'

'Nah,' Sam said playfully. 'Yet more evidence that you've got me all wrong, Ms Perry. Why would I want cloying and syrupy when I could have spiky and bitter? In food and drink, as in life, I've always had a fondness for the astringent.'

'Yeah, right,' Amy said, refusing to consider this comment's possible subtext. 'I'll remind you of that next time I see you spooning three sugars into your tea – which I *did* notice at breakfast, by the way.'

'Touché,' Sam grinned, clambering into the passenger seat of Grace's Nissan and buckling his seat belt.

On the way home, Amy took care to keep the conversation impersonal, encouraging Sam to fill half a notebook with thoughts and ideas they could share with Carolyn on Monday.

After dropping him back at Rowton Hall, she went home to the cottage and readied herself for bed, trying to keep her brain from buzzing – instructing it to stop raking relentlessly over little things he'd said, the shape his lips made when they were wrapped around a wine glass, or how weirdly intimate it had felt to shower in a room that smelled like him.

Her phone buzzed and she snatched it up eagerly, expecting some kind of 'goodnight, thanks again for driving' text from Sam. Instead, it was Kit:

So. Just got up. Am now wondering . . . Precisely how intense is your crush on the sexy Viscount-to-be after a full 24 hours in his company? Honest answers only, on a scale of 1–10

Amy groaned and put her head in her hands, wishing for approximately the millionth time that he didn't know her so well.

Amy: 11.
I hate myself right now.

Chapter 18

On Monday morning, Amy made her way over to Rowton Hall so she and Sam could dial in to Carolyn's RomFest meeting together. Resistance to pairing up in this way was futile, Amy knew; it would lead to awkward questions about their ability to work together, and while those concerns were probably completely valid, she didn't need the hassle of dealing with them.

Over coffees made by Sam and a box of croissants Amy had picked up from the village bakery on her way over, they organised the notes they'd made while up north and came up with a selection of clear proposals for Carolyn to sign off.

'If I didn't know better, I'd say you were almost excited about this,' Sam remarked as he tore a pain au chocolat in half.

'I'm excited about the PR potential,' Amy parried. 'I think we've got some great ideas here.'

One of these was to celebrate the variety of forms romance novels could take, in the same way as the scary story festival had highlighted the genres within the genre. RomFest could offer content on everything from romcoms and tales of Regency rakes to tragic contemporary tear-jerkers. They'd also decided to lean into honouring beloved romance tropes: Amy had come up with the idea of pitting them against one another and encouraging attendees to choose between 'teams'. Hashtags would be used to discuss the various merits of 'fake dates' versus 'soulmates', and 'enemies to lovers' stories on social media. As she explained this to him, Sam had scribbled on a scrap of paper, then turned it around to show a drawing of a T-shirt with 'Team #EnemiesToLovers' emblazoned on the chest. Amy had beamed at him. Carolyn was going to love it.

They'd also discussed ideas for themed food and drink: hot and spicy burritos in a nod to some of the steamier fiction on offer, and – Amy's personal favourite – the Ice Queen cocktail: a freezing cold rum concoction topped with warm coconut cream, designed to melt its way down through the drink. She'd seen something like it in the mirrored Mayfair bar Kit had taken her to for her birthday: a night out that, now she looked back on it, felt as though it had taken place several years ago rather than just a couple of months back.

Amy was grateful that she and Sam had so many work-related things to talk about; while they were discussing the RomFest budget and what insurance policies they'd need, she couldn't drift into dangerous daydreams.

As they sat next to one another waiting for Carolyn to log in to their meeting, Amy stiffened her spine and tried to create enough distance between herself and Sam that their arms, legs and hands wouldn't accidentally collide. His closeness was unsettling. He smelled like coffee, chocolate and that cedar and grapefruit scent he always wore. Depressingly, even the slightest hint of it now agitated her.

Suddenly, Carolyn appeared on Amy's laptop screen – but she had her back to the camera. She was talking to someone, though he or she was obscured by Carolyn's shock of silver hair. Whoever it was, Amy didn't envy them.

'. . . do *not* see why you need to be involved,' Carolyn was saying. 'Really, given the circumstances and your previous, very vocal objections to this project, it seems entirely inappropriate for you to plug in at this stage. I've already made my feelings on the subject known to your uncle, and—'

At the word 'uncle', Amy felt her mouth compress into a thin, horrified line and the acid in her stomach begin to burn.

Sam cleared his throat. 'Carolyn?' he said politely. 'Sorry. I just wanted you to be aware that Amy and I were already dialled in.'

'Ah. Yes. Hello, there,' she said, turning to face them. She was completely unabashed; far from embarrassed at being caught mid-rant, Amy could tell she was absolutely livid at the subject of her rant. If looks could kill, Hugh – now visible to Carolyn's left – would have been reduced to a pile of smouldering ash by the fireballs shooting from her eyes. Amy rather wished he had been.

'As you can see,' Carolyn said waspishly, 'Mr Howard here is keen to join us today and understand our plans for Torch, and the RomFest event that will launch it.'

'I see,' Sam said. 'Hi there, it's good to meet you.'

Amy merely nodded, not trusting herself to speak. This was her punishment for sending back Hugh's gift to her, she realised. *This* was the 'next move' Kit had said Hugh would make.

'Actually,' Hugh said, his voice a lazy drawl that, infuriatingly, implied he had more important places to be, 'you and I have met before.'

'Oh?' Sam looked nonplussed.

'At Queen Mary's College, Winchester,' Hugh said. 'You, ah, *left* after the fifth form.'

Oh my God, Amy thought. Hugh was *smirking* – as if he thought reminding Sam of being encouraged to leave boarding school would wrong-foot or humiliate him. She looked sideways at Sam, and when their eyes met, his were full of mirth. He grinned, all white teeth, dimples and devilish indifference. Amy fought the urge to laugh, as well as a flutter of attraction.

'Oh, yes!' Sam said, 'I'm sorry, I remember now. And you're right: my head of house and I had some irreconcilable differences that peaked during GCSE year – I'd say my departure came as something of a relief to the old man.'

Amy stifled another giggle. Hugh's eyes narrowed.

'I hear the two of you went on some sort of *research trip* this past weekend,' he said.

'That's right,' Sam confirmed, glancing at Amy as if to

ask whether there was a reason for Hugh's hostile attitude, and in puzzlement at her uncharacteristic silence.

Understanding landed on Amy like a bucketful of ice-cold water. Somehow, Hugh had got wind of Sam's involvement in the RomFest event – and it was clear he didn't like the idea of Amy working so closely with another man. Really, it was almost laughable: Amy herself wasn't thrilled about being thrown together with Sam Ainsworth, but Hugh's dislike of the idea was almost enough to convince her of its merits.

'Why don't you take me through the fruits of your labours?' Carolyn said. 'Fill me in on what you discovered and how we can learn from it.'

Between them, and somewhat to Amy's surprise, Sam and Amy effortlessly outlined their experiences in Robin Hood's Bay, followed by their skeleton plan for RomFest. They embroidered this with ideas for the creative touches that would help to bring it alive – and as Amy had predicted, Carolyn practically squealed at Sam's T-shirt suggestion.

'This all sounds very expensive,' Hugh said, sounding so snide that Amy almost felt embarrassed for him. 'As finance director, I'm really not sure I can sign off on the kind of budget you'll need for so much frou-frou and froth. Where's the ROI?'

'You won't need to,' Sam said smoothly. 'Most of the cost is being met by Rowton Hall Estates, as per my earlier discussions with Carolyn. We'll take on the majority of the risk, on the basis that we'll profit from RomFest. H-K will get its costs back, plus a little more – but the primary benefit for Torch will be exposure, in line with your goal.'

At this, Hugh looked positively murderous. Carolyn's face was lit up by the sort of grin Amy imagined she usually wore at the funerals or prison sentencings of her very worst enemies.

'I did attempt to explain all this before our call today, Hugh,' Carolyn said. 'I think this leaves very little to chat through, so let's regroup in a week or so and see where we are. Excellent work, Amy – and you, Samuel. I'm impressed you've come together so quickly as a team.'

This comment, Amy thought, was almost certainly for Hugh's benefit: deliberately needling, designed to hit him where it hurt – and to show him that she fully understood why he'd chosen to turn up this morning.

'Thank you, Carolyn,' Sam said. 'I rather wish we had a recording of you saying that, though – our old A level English teacher, who refereed *many* an argument about our set texts, would never have believed it of us. Can you imagine, Amy?'

Hugh's usually pale complexion had turned puce. His light blue eyes were bulging. Evidently, he'd had no idea there was any kind of prior relationship between Amy and Sam – and the revelation was not welcome.

As Amy shook her head, she felt an odd blend of horror and hysteria rising inside her. On the one hand, this was all very amusing. On the other, it was *she* who'd have to deal with the fallout of Hugh's inevitable meltdown – and she was suddenly sure that, whatever form it might take, a meltdown was definitely coming.

'What,' Sam said as Amy clicked her laptop's trackpad to exit their meeting, 'was *that* all about?'

Amy stared out of the window, pretending her attention had been caught by a blue tit perched on a nearby shrub. For a host of reasons she chose not to untangle, she really didn't want to explain to Sam that Hugh was her ex-boyfriend. Nor did she want to admit that she'd refused a proposal of marriage from him; that she wasn't *only* back in Rowton for the sake of spending time with Grace or that, in fact, her whole 'romance book editor slash living with Gran again' situation had arisen because she'd chosen to flee from a man she was suddenly mortified she'd ever dated in the first place.

Without actively deciding to lie, she allowed a series of half-truths out of her mouth. Hugh was well known at H-K for picking up and putting down pet projects at a moment's notice; he took a keen interest in any changes of direction for the firm, since he expected to become CEO one day; there was no love lost between him and Carolyn, and Amy had recently heard from Kit that their difficult professional relationship was rockier than ever just lately.

This seemed to satisfy Sam's curiosity, and Amy hoped that her relief at his acceptance of the story wasn't visible on her face.

'Well, my money would be on Carolyn in any confrontation between them,' Sam said, laughing. 'She'd wipe the floor with him. He'd be reduced to a husk, which would please several of my old school friends, actually . . . When I first implied I remembered Hugh, I was fudging – but now I recall he was a pretty objectionable character.'

Amy shifted uncomfortably in her seat. 'Oh. Really?'

'Yes,' Sam nodded. 'Nothing physical, not that sort of a bully – but very single-minded, always willing to use his money and position to his advantage. And very much the sort who'd kick a nervous, homesick first-year when they were already down for the sake of impressing his friends.'

'Urgh. That's horrible,' Amy said, feeling slightly sick. She didn't doubt anything Sam had just said. In fact, she admitted to herself, schoolboy Hugh sounded a lot like H-K Hugh, if rather less subtle in his pursuit of popularity.

'Well, hopefully he won't bother coming along to any more meetings,' said Sam. 'Now he knows he hasn't got to stump up the cash for amusingly named cocktails, hashtag T-shirts, Portaloos or public liability insurance, he'll no doubt lose interest in RomFest. He certainly doesn't strike me as the romantic type – more one of those sociopaths you meet in slasher fiction about bitter, jilted boyfriends.'

At this, Amy felt like her stomach was suddenly on a spin cycle.

'Fingers crossed you're right,' she said, swallowing hard, 'and that's the last we'll see of him.'

But even as she uttered the words, she knew she didn't believe them for a moment.

* * *

In the fortnight that followed, Amy and Sam got together a couple of times a week to work on RomFest. She grew almost resigned to the physical side effects of this contact with him: the thumping of her heart, the prickling of her skin and the racing of her thoughts in delicious but dangerous directions she definitely hadn't authorised.

The rest of the time, Amy was focused on her day job: editing manuscripts, meeting with agents and authors, liaising with cover designers, copy editors and audiobook producers, and helping to firm up marketing plans for Torch's first releases.

When she wasn't working, she spent time with Grace – provided she could catch her in between dates with Mr Bradley, whose refrain of 'call me Ken!' still hadn't had the desired effect on Amy. She also continued bonding with Nisha and Meg over brunches, evenings in and even a shopping day in Birmingham – during which they met up with Carla, an old university friend Amy hadn't seen in years.

It was novel for her to have female friends after a lifetime of being more comfortable with boys or men – a pattern that had started in part because, as a small child, she'd spent the majority of her time with her father.

As a little girl she'd felt more comfortable with the male of the species, while the workings of fellow females – not to mention their elaborate games and social hierarchies – seemed scary and mysterious. Nevertheless, Nisha and Meg had begun to fill the Kit-shaped hole in Amy's day-to-day life, and she genuinely enjoyed spending time with them – even though they'd ribbed her relentlessly about her 'night away' with Sam.

While on the surface the three of them had little in common, Amy had discovered that their differences didn't run as deep as the qualities that drew them together. Nisha's rainbow-hued outfits and sweet hopefulness were undercut by a sharp mind and a surprisingly pragmatic view of the world. Meanwhile, Meg's gentle calm belied the steely core that had seen her resist intense pressure from her overbearing parents, then ignore years of idle gossip about her status as a single mother. She was now a successful painter who exhibited regularly in small galleries throughout the country, and also ran free art classes for young people at local schools and colleges.

It turned out Pearl was a student at the village state primary – a source of endless fascination to Meg's old school and university friends, many of whom already had their toddlers' names down for Eton, Harrow or Cheltenham Ladies' College. Amy couldn't help being impressed by Meg's determination to do things her own way – not because she felt it was any kind of sacrifice to eschew private schooling, but because she could admit that the decision had been difficult for Meg. She'd faced a barrage of criticism from Roger, Pamela and other extended family members, as well as the worry that Pearl might be treated differently from the other children – or even bullied by them – because of who her grandfather was. As it turned out, she was happy as a clam in Butterfly Class: thriving academically and popular with a mob of local friends who adored her.

If it occurred to Amy that she was able to disregard Meg's birthright to privilege while holding her brother to a completely different standard, she didn't dwell on it. The fact was, she needed as many reasons as she could find to ensure Sam stayed in very specific mental boxes: 'work colleague', 'posh person I don't particularly like' and 'eventual inheritor of estate kept solvent via villagers' misery' were chief among them.

As the two of them spent afternoons discussing festival plans and dividing up tasks based on which suited who best, it became clear that Carolyn's assessment had been right: they made a good team. Even worse, certain parts of Amy – both bodily and spiritually – now seemed to have regressed, inconveniently reincarnated as their former teenage selves. Despite regular admonishments from her brain, these found Sam so physically bewitching that she occasionally struggled to breathe.

If being near him was problematic, being away from him was almost as bad. She thought about him more frequently than could possibly be justified, and his image floated into her brain at the most unsuitable, potentially embarrassing moments. During a discussion with Philippa Fotheringham – who'd now signed on as a Torch author, to Carolyn's delight – Amy accidentally transposed the name Sam for Thomas. This confusion of a fictional romantic hero with their handsome, very real and now mutual acquaintance prompted a peal of jubilant laugher from Philippa. 'Don't worry, your secret's safe with me, bab,' she'd said with a wink. 'Though I'm not sure how much of a *secret* it is, really . . . I don't think even I could write the kind of sexual tension that's permanently sizzling between the two of you.'

For the sake of quelling her crush, Amy regularly refused Sam's invitations of a drink after work, always insisting that she needed to get back to Grace, cook a meal or attend some other work-related engagement. Being in any kind of social setting with him seemed risky. It would muddy what ought to remain clear waters, particularly if there was alcohol involved.

Amy could no longer deny to herself that she was attracted to Sam, but remained convinced she still didn't *like* him. They were work colleagues who got on surprisingly well, but they weren't – and had never been – *friends*. These were the mantras she repeated daily, and which she'd resolved to chant until such time as RomFest was over and done with . . . Or until she miraculously stopped wanting to inhale lungfuls of his cologne every time he walked past her.

It was a relief that June's book club meet-up was cancelled. Amy wasn't sure how she'd have coped with sitting opposite Sam in a pub, debating the merits and flaws of *The Loner*

Next Door in some wine-fuelled variation of their sixth form altercations. The argument they'd had last month had been bad enough, and that was before she'd been forced to spend time with him – or started fantasising about how his golden hair might feel if she were to run her fingers through it.

However, Amy's satisfaction was short-lived when it became clear that the decision to postpone discussion of Alex Swift's latest thriller was so that a group 'field trip' could take place instead. According to Nisha, the book club went to the Royal Shakespeare Theatre in neighbouring Stratford-upon-Avon to watch a play a few times a year – and as a relative newbie, Amy was very much expected to join them.

As it turned out, though, tickets for the chosen play – selected by Mr Bradley and as usual a surprise to the rest of the attendees – were unavailable for another couple of weeks. This granted Amy a fortnight's reprieve from sitting in close proximity to Sam in a dimly lit room, as well as the opportunity to think up an excuse for not attending. For this, she was profoundly grateful.

On the afternoon of 20 June, Amy arrived at Rowton Hall with a sick feeling in her stomach. This was the last place she wanted to be today – and Sam was the last person she wanted to be anywhere near, despite her burgeoning obsession with his lips. She'd accepted his request to meet a few days ago without looking properly at her calendar – and annoyingly, what they needed to talk about couldn't be put off until tomorrow.

As she skirted the wooded area she'd always loved so much and made her way up the drive past green, carefully manicured grass and a glut of blooming rose bushes, she wished she hadn't come. She could have said she was ill; in truth, she *felt* ill. This was the first time she'd ever been in Rowton on the anniversary of Hari's accident – the first time she'd ever been among other people who'd remember it or want to mark it in some way.

It wasn't that Amy ever forgot it herself, or wanted to; it was more that the grief she still felt at losing him had form here, in a way it never had in London. It was a conspicuous, weighty absence: a dark, glaring void that followed her around to all the places where she imagined Hari should be. It was a black hole that, today, pursued her relentlessly, threatening to suck her in.

It had started this morning when Nisha – with the very best of intentions – had sent Amy a message to say she was thinking about her on what she knew would be a tough day for them both. This simple, thoughtful act of kindness had seen Amy dissolve into a tearful mess over breakfast, and Grace demand to know why her granddaughter was weeping into her Weetabix.

Hari had been more than a friend to Amy – more than someone to hang out with after college or talk to endlessly about favourite bands. Having lost his own father at around the same time John Perry died, Hari had been Amy's partner in navigating grief; a comrade in the same desolate, interminable trenches – someone who truly understood. His death had inspired mourning all of its own, but it had also sharpened the pain of her dad being gone. Suddenly, there was no one in Amy's life who knew what it was like to occasionally wake up in the morning, smell fresh coffee from downstairs and think he might be sitting at the kitchen table, reading the paper and preparing to berate her for sleeping in so late.

Somehow, her sadness over Hari always stirred Amy's deep reserves of heartbreak for her father. As she stood on the threshold of the Hall and rang the doorbell, she brushed away tears and cursed herself for putting on mascara that morning.

Sam greeted her with his usual warmth, offered her a cup of tea and gestured for her to make herself comfortable at the large old table they often sat at during RomFest meetings. She'd seen recognition in his eyes when she first walked into the room, despite his attempt to make sure things felt normal: he knew that she was sad, and he understood why.

This clear comprehension of her feelings didn't comfort Amy. In fact, it made her powerfully, irrationally angry. If he understood what Hari had meant to her, why had he stayed away immediately after his death? Why had she been left with no one to cry with, reminisce with, be fucking *livid* at the universe with? Throwing her an empathetic glance now was the textbook definition of too little, too late. To her surprise, and feeling stung, she found herself wishing *if only it wasn't*.

During their conversation, which took in final decisions on catering and confirmation of the day's line-up of guest speakers, Amy was reticent and occasionally combative. Ordinarily scrappy and opinionated, she crossed the line into belligerent and sullen – but in a feat of forbearance that was enough to make Amy wonder whether he'd had a personality transplant, Sam didn't rise to her criticisms or sarcasm.

His calm resignation to her bleak mood did nothing to allay it. If anything, it darkened it further. When they'd finally come up with a physical layout and timeline for RomFest – the meeting's main objective, and the blueprint that would allow on-the-ground preparations for the event to begin – Amy closed her notebook, shut the lid of her laptop and swept them, along with her collection of coloured fine-liners, into her tote bag.

'Amy . . .' Sam said, his voice low and urgent but gentle. 'Stay. Have a drink with me.'

Amy bit her lip and shook her head, but it wasn't a gesture that meant 'no'. It was more a plea for him not to say anything further, a signal that she didn't want to hear anything that might start her crying.

Seeming to understand this, Sam crossed the room – a modest home office space with Ikea furniture, a microwave and a kettle – and pulled an already open bottle of Pinot

Grigio from the fridge beneath the countertop. He looked at her to check her reaction, lifting the bottle aloft by way of enquiry. When she didn't speak, he opened a cupboard, took out two glasses and poured large measures of the wine into each.

He set one down on the table next to her, then drew up the nearest chair and turned it so he was facing her. They were so close their knees were almost touching. The gap between them was like a synapse: a space across which electrical impulses flowed, invisibly but irresistibly.

'It's always a shit day,' said Sam heavily. 'Never not awful. My guess is it's hitting harder for you than usual, being here?'

Amy sighed and nodded, her eyes filling up despite all admonishments. She took a gulp of wine as tears began to course down her cheeks.

Sam sipped from his own glass. 'I still miss him, too. He was the best of us.'

Amy nodded again and sniffed, then berated herself as the knowledge that she was not a pretty crier made its way to the forefront of her mind. As if she should *care* whether Sam might think she looked awful while she desperately tried not to sob.

'I should have been a better friend to him,' Sam stated. Amy lifted her head, her eyes connecting with his. She couldn't understand the regret that was written in them; to her knowledge, he and Hari had been thick as thieves right up to the end. In the fictional movie of their lives, Hari had always been the quietly handsome, clever best mate to Sam's flashier, more confident main character, but Hari preferred it that way. He'd never felt overshadowed or unseen – at least, not in a way he didn't want.

Was Sam worried he'd somehow eclipsed Hari, to his detriment? Amy was confident that wasn't the case, and for a split second contemplated offering Sam that reassurance. Then she remembered how little comfort he had offered her in the aftermath of the accident, and her anger at him flared again.

In a few massive mouthfuls she saw off what was left of her wine, feeling it go to her head almost immediately.

'I should go,' she said, her voice scratchy and tight. She stood up too fast but righted herself before she could stumble. She snatched up her bag and jacket and made for the door.

'Amy, wait—' Sam was right behind her. She didn't just hear his words, she *felt* them, warm on the back of her neck. His hands settled lightly on her shoulders, turning her around to face him.

She didn't want to look at him. She was too furious, too mixed up, too weak-kneed. Just as she resolved to shake him off and run for it, she felt his fingertips on her face. He lifted it gently, tilting her jaw. His dark eyes locked with hers, large, bright blue and glassy with tears, then scanned her features, seeming to take in every freckle, quirk and flaw.

Was he going to kiss her?

She was suddenly, acutely aware that she would definitely *let* him kiss her. In truth, she felt seized by a powerful desire to stand on her tiptoes, press herself against him and *make* him kiss her.

Then his thumbs were brushing at the damp tear tracks beneath her eyes. She leaned into the touch, feeling all the tenderness of it, desperately wanting to lose herself in it. They were both breathing hard.

As if it were too much effort to hold himself upright any longer, Sam let his shoulders loosen and lowered his face towards Amy's.

She felt a rush of wanting him so strong that it drowned out every other feeling. Her lips parted in anticipation, in readiness to ignore all reason and follow this elementary, instinctive desire for him wherever it might lead.

She rose up on her toes to meet him, then felt frustration twist in her chest as he simply allowed his forehead to settle against hers. Her gaze lingered on his perfect, ridiculous, infuriating mouth. The air between them tasted sharp and clean, the cool crispness of wine undercut by something sweeter. *Him*.

Sam sighed, and it was a rough, almost broken sound that made Amy's skin tingle.

He swiped again at her wet cheeks. Weirdly, she was still weeping.

'Don't cry, Amy,' Sam murmured, the soft movement of his lips disturbing the air between their mouths. 'I can't stand to see you cry.'

It was the wrong thing to say.

With a jolt that was almost physically painful, she remembered the burning humiliation – and then the sheer misery – of waiting for him to reach out to her after Hari's death. Too right, he couldn't stand to see her cry.

She recalled how stupid and worthless she'd felt at the realisation that his interest in her had been so shallow and short-lived; that it probably always would have been, with or without Hari's accident. She remembered how furious she'd been with herself for briefly believing someone like Sam – a storybook-style hero, the handsome prince from a fairy tale – could really fall for a short, stroppy, bookish girl with a breeze-block-sized chip on her shoulder.

As she twisted away from him, his eyes widened in surprise. He stepped back, embarrassed, then stepped forward again, awkward and indecisive.

'Amy, I—'

'No,' she said, shakily. '*No*. It's too late to try and be there for me now. I need to leave.'

In fact, her whole body hummed with the need to stay.

Forcibly, she recalled the devastated look on Barbara's face on the day she'd discovered her home was to be sold. She considered Jed: landlord at the Old Oak for as long as Amy had been alive, now facing eviction so Sam's parents could keep living in their dilapidated relic of a house. And for all Barbara's protestations, as far as Amy could tell Sam had done nothing about any of it.

'This,' Amy muttered grimly, gesturing at the space between them, 'can't happen.'

'Amy,' Sam said, 'please can we talk, there are things I want to—'

'No,' she insisted. She held both hands up to him in a 'don't shoot' gesture. 'All we ever need to talk about is this festival. Getting it set up and then over with. That's it.'

He frowned at her, but for what felt like the thousandth time today chose not to argue. 'If that's what you want.'

Amy nodded curtly. She wanted so many things in this moment, most of which made no sense whatsoever. But *this* was what had to be done – it was a reassertion of the smart, self-preserving practicality she'd spent a lifetime cultivating. It was a return to normality, to an existence where avid teenage crushes lived in their proper place: the past.

'It is,' she said, backing further away from him towards the door.

Sam scrubbed his hands over his face, like he was trying to wake himself from an especially disorientating dream. When he looked at her, his eyes were harder than she'd seen them in weeks: shuttered, as though she was no longer permitted access to whatever truths they might reveal.

'Whatever you say,' he said bitterly.

Amy couldn't decide whether he sounded dismissive, angry or hurt – but as she made her way back through Rowton Hall's winding corridors and out through its magnificent entrance, she told herself it didn't matter anyway.

Chapter 19

As June became July, Rowton-in-Arden was bathed in the sort of summer sunshine that felt like a fresh gift every morning. Villagers tended their blooming gardens as if they were longed-for children, petrified at the prospect of a hosepipe ban. The grassy banks either side of the stream yellowed and wilted. Every evening's air was barbecue-scented, and the Old Oak did a roaring trade, its beer garden constantly full of locals and visitors enjoying chilled drinks in the hot sun.

The glorious weather provided a stark contrast to Amy's mood, which remained dark – her equilibrium still upset after her confusing near kiss with Sam. Determined to reassert their professional boundaries, she went out of her way to avoid being alone with him, but – in typically aggravating fashion – he plagued her thoughts whenever she lowered her guard.

She even had several dreams not unlike the one she'd experienced on the night after the Rowton Hall book club meeting – though these new versions of the narrative all concluded with Sam, hungry-eyed and intense, happening upon her in some deserted, long-forgotten corner of the manor. Such fevered imaginings always saw her startle awake, sweaty, disorientated and filled with longing.

Terrified that he might somehow intuit his sleep-thief status from simply looking at her, Amy took to conducting as much of their business as possible via email or online meetings. On several occasions she deliberately scheduled face-to-face appointments in Birmingham, Leicester or Nottingham on the same days she was due to catch up with Sam, meaning that their conversations had to take place virtually.

On one day, to her private chagrin, she even fabricated such an engagement for the sake of steering clear of him. After long hours spent cafe-working in Leamington Spa, she dialled in to a meeting with him and claimed she'd been rushed off her feet with agent and author meet-ups since 10 a.m. The barista who'd served her several coffees, a mozzarella melt and innumerable glasses of water had raised his eyebrows at this, but wisely said nothing.

In addition, it had become clear that Hugh had no intention of stepping back from RomFest or the launch of Torch – even though it was perfectly obvious his input was neither needed nor welcome. Sam seemed to find this both baffling and amusing, remaining polite in the face of his posturing and, occasionally, the sort of outright rudeness that Amy thought thoroughly deserved one of Sam's trademark witty takedowns – or failing that, a punch in the face. Her concerns about Hugh's ongoing presence in Torch meetings, her email inbox and her life in general simmered on a low light. She knew that, at some point, she was going to have to deal with him – but it made little sense to bring their inevitable confrontation forward.

As well as staying on top of work – which now included the editing of Philippa Fotheringham's next title, *Love to Hate You* – Amy had her grandmother's upcoming operation to think about. Grace had been called for surgery in just over a week's time, and the cottage needed to be made ready for her recovery period. Amy cleaned the house from top to bottom, ensured their supply of books, magazines and box sets was in order, and organised everything so that Grace would have no need to trek up and down her perilous stairs, aside from to get up in the mornings and head to bed each night. She also tidied the bathroom and kitchen, streamlining the contents of drawers and cupboards so that, once she was back on her feet, Grace would be able to do basic things for herself quickly and efficiently. Amy knew her gran would want to maintain as much independence as possible while her hip healed, and was determined to do everything she could to enable that.

Any alarm she felt about Grace going under the knife was

squashed – at least outwardly – by the mask of unrelenting positivity she maintained during every discussion about her grandmother's hip replacement. The notion that something might go wrong, and the reality that general anaesthetics always come with risks, were permitted no part in conversations and granted zero purchase on Amy's thoughts – as though refusing to acknowledge her deepest fears would shrink and ultimately nullify them.

Given the volume of things on her mind, it perhaps wasn't surprising that Amy forgot all about the book club's planned trip to the theatre. It was only when Nisha messaged the group about who was willing to drive that Amy remembered it was that evening – and therefore a little late for her to start scrabbling for a reason not to go.

As it turned out, she was one of the few book club members with access to a car; bowing out wasn't an option unless she was prepared to prevent others from enjoying the performance or consign them to spending huge sums on cab fares. Reluctantly, she agreed to meet Barbara, Dave and Simon on the corner at 6.15 in Grace's faithful Nissan Micra, ready for their journey into town.

Since he had business in Old Rowton in the afternoon and they'd both be on that side of the bridge, Mr Bradley had volunteered to drive Nisha and Meg. Grace, meanwhile, couldn't face the prospect of being confined to an uncomfortable seat for several hours, and had opted to stay at home with Bertie. With Philippa's approval, Amy had given Grace access to a proof copy of *Love to Hate You*, which she was already nose-deep in by the time Amy finished work. She barely noticed when Amy kissed her cheek, ruffled Bertie's floppy ears and said goodbye to them both.

Amy had deliberately avoided asking Nisha or Meg whether Sam would be joining them – though it seemed reasonable to assume he wouldn't, given there was no mention of his travelling with them. He didn't respond to any of the messages that flew around in the Rowton Readers WhatsApp group, and when Amy – to her shame – checked whether or not he'd read them, she discovered he was offline.

The relief Amy felt at concluding he wouldn't be coming was only intensified when Mr Bradley revealed the play he'd got tickets for was *Much Ado About Nothing* – the Shakespeare she and Sam had studied for A level, then bantered about on the night they'd ended up kissing. Her sense of having escaped an awful fate was undercut with something else, though – her certainty that the night wouldn't be as much fun without him there. It was infuriating.

Since her return to Rowton, Amy reluctantly admitted to herself, Sam had begun to loom just as large for her as he had in their teenage years. She fought the pull of him now in the same way she'd railed against it then – but the world burst into full, blazing colour when he was around and then faded back to monochrome when he wasn't. In London, she'd been content to live in many and varied shades of grey. From here, that existence increasingly looked flat, dull and incomplete.

Around thirty minutes after they'd first set off – and having banned Simon from speaking so she could concentrate on a parallel parking manoeuvre – Amy pulled the Micra into a small space on a side street around the corner from the theatre. They'd agreed to meet the others outside the main entrance, so had only a short walk to find them. Within seconds of exiting the car, Dave blithely asked, 'What's this play all about then? Normally I look them up on Wikipedia but I didn't get around to it today.'

Before Amy could give him the brief rundown he was after, Simon began a detailed lecture on Shakespeare's comedies and the place of *Much Ado* within the wider canon of his works. Amy saw Dave's eyes take on the sort of vacant glaze she remembered some of her less engaged classmates sported during Mr Bradley's lessons.

When Simon started espousing the virtues of 'the so-called problem plays', she felt compelled to intervene on Dave's behalf. His expression had slackened, and he had the look of someone who'd just received terrible news from a doctor rather than a 'quick summary' of the events in *Measure for Measure*.

By now, the group had reached the steps that led up to the main entrance to the imposing but elegant theatre building. As Simon droned on behind her, Amy spotted Nisha, Meg and Mr Bradley waiting for them a short distance away. Knowing he'd probably listen to her, but cringing at her awareness of the fact, she turned to suggest to Simon that now might be a good time to pause the conversation, head inside and grab a pre-show drink. Before she could say anything, however, she stopped short. A metre or two back, among the crowd of people making their way towards the theatre's large double doors, was Sam.

At his side was a slender woman with long, pale blonde hair. Amy guessed she was the best part of a foot taller than her, and she had on a pair of expensive-looking gladiator sandals whose ties wrapped up and around her golden, tanned shins. On Amy, the straps would likely have come up as far as her knees, and against her pale skin they'd have made her calves look like raw poultry, trussed and ready for roasting.

The woman wore next to no makeup – just a slash of bright, perfectly applied poppy-red lipstick. Amy didn't need anyone to tell her that the woman next to Sam was Tilly Wexmore-Yates – his supposedly *ex*-girlfriend and the woman his parents had wanted him to marry. A little like Sam himself, she was somehow more beautiful in real life than in pictures or on TV. Amy spotted several passers-by staring at Tilly, then whispering to one another excitedly – presumably confirming that she really *was* that woman they'd seen on *The One Show* last week.

Amy felt suddenly relieved that she'd made time to change before coming out this evening. Despite her determination to stay away from Sam, she'd recently found herself making an extra effort with her appearance on the off-chance she might bump into him – a habit she hadn't allowed herself to interrogate. Tonight she was sporting dark denim skinnies, a soft, egg yolk-yellow silk shirt and a blue beaded necklace that matched her eyes. Her hair was loose, falling in gentle waves that almost touched her shoulders. It was a little longer and decidedly less sleek than it had been when she'd first come back to Rowton – partly because she hadn't bothered to find a local hairdresser, but also because she'd discovered she rather liked what Kit had always called 'its natural movement'.

In need of comfort – and for the sake of not appearing interested in Sam and Tilly – she pulled her phone out of her bag to text Kit, rapidly realising she had nothing to say. She certainly didn't want to tell him she was standing outside the theatre with a well-known TV personality – he'd only get excited, which was precisely the sort of reaction she didn't need as she tried to ignore Tilly's elegant radiance.

What were she and Sam *doing* here, Amy wondered. Were they on a date? Perhaps they were back together. Maybe they'd never properly split up, which threw his recent tear-drying and face-caressing behaviour into pretty sharp relief. Amy forced these thoughts away in an effort that felt like dry-swallowing a massive, awkwardly shaped pill.

Whatever might be going on between Sam and Tilly, it didn't matter. Amy didn't care. It was none of her business.

A little too late, Amy realised she was staring. She coloured and looked away, only to hear Meg cry, 'Sam! There you are!'

Oh, *hell*. Did this mean he and Tilly were joining them?

Amy stared at the pavement, willing her face to cool down and her heart rate to slow.

By the time she looked up again, Sam and Tilly had closed the gap between themselves and the rest of the book club, while Nisha, Meg and Mr Bradley had moved down the steps to greet the newcomers. All together, a rather mismatched group of nine was now gathered at the side of the theatre's huge, wide-open doors.

Sam stepped forward, his hand at Tilly's back, clearly intending to introduce her. Amy felt a hot, angry sensation in her chest, as though her heart had been friction-burned.

'Evening, gang,' Sam said, smiling. 'I hope it's okay with you all if Tilly joins us for a drink before the play starts. She and I have had some business together today, and she wanted to say hi.'

He nodded towards Meg here, signalling the warm friendship between his sister and his . . . well. *Whatever* Tilly was. Amy couldn't be entirely sure what Sam meant by their having 'business together', but by now she'd read enough romance novels to recognise a euphemism when she heard one.

'Of course!' and 'Absolutely!' came chorusing from all directions. Tilly was clearly popular with those who'd already made her acquaintance, and an object of fascination among those who hadn't. Amy bit back a groan, though she felt intense relief that Tilly wouldn't be with them all night.

'Amy?' Sam said. She forced herself to look up at him, painting a smile on her face that she hoped wouldn't look as insincere as it felt. *He* looked almost nervous. Guilty, maybe, or as though he might feel sorry for her.

There was no way Amy could let Sam labour under the misapprehension that seeing him and Tilly together bothered her in any way. She refused to give him the satisfaction of believing it made her uncomfortable or – heaven forbid – jealous.

'Of course! Sorry! I was a thousand miles away,' she said, shaking out her hair and standing up straighter. 'Such a mad day at work.' Then she turned to Tilly and said, 'I'm Amy. Great to meet you.' The smile she flashed in Tilly's direction was so wide and sweet it could single-handedly have won the Oscar for Best Supporting Actress.

'Likewise,' Tilly said, smiling back with the quiet, innate confidence of a naturally gorgeous person. A person who Amy felt sure would *never* get lost inside her boyfriend's stately mansion, or have a physical fight with him over Tupperware, and almost certainly hadn't spent her formative years being referred to as 'spooky doll girl'.

* * *

Forty minutes later, the Rowton Readers were settled in their seats and awaiting the start of the show.

In yet another sign that some divine force had set its will against her, Amy was sat next to Sam; not merely in the same room as him, which she'd imagined would be bad enough – but in the immediately adjacent square foot of space.

The air between them felt like it was full of static – as if a single word or the briefest physical contact might cause an electric shock. Amy felt wretched and furious, for reasons she chose not to unravel.

Among her many complaints was the effect his fragrance had on her. Really, did he have to smell so bloody *wonderful* all the time? Also, she considered it a personal affront that his stupid *face* – which she hadn't seen up close in weeks – was glowing. A light sprinkling of freckles had appeared across his nose since the last time they'd met, and his eyes seemed to have darkened in contrast with his hair, which suddenly boasted sandy, sun-brightened streaks.

Amy stared resolutely at the programme she'd bought on the way in, pretending to read the director's explanation of her vision for this 'fresh, modern and feminist' rendition of a four-hundred-year-old play. The words wobbled in front of Amy's eyes as phrases like 'repressed emotions', 'eavesdropping' and 'deception of the self' failed to hit their intellectual mark.

Instead of focusing on what was in front of her, she struggled to subdue a rising tide of memories: visions of herself and Sam being instructed by Mr Bradley to read the roles of Beatrice and Benedick during Year Twelve English lessons. 'One might as well make the most of your natural tendency to spar,' he'd said.

BENEDICK: *It is certain I am loved of all ladies, only you excepted.*
BEATRICE: *I had rather hear my dog bark at a*

*crow than a man swear he loves me . . . You always
end with a jade's trick: I know you of old.*

How would she bear this? There couldn't be a more awkward
play for the two of them to sit through together. Amy twisted
her hands in her lap, then fidgeted in her chair.

Sam nudged her with his elbow. Reluctantly, she looked up.

'Are you okay?' he whispered, his thick, honey-coloured
eyebrows drawn together.

'*Fine,*' she whispered back, in a tone that strongly suggested
she might be plotting his imminent murder.

'I don't understand what's going on here,' he said, his voice
low and deliberately even. He was trying to sound calm but
not quite succeeding. 'Have I done something?'

Amy scowled at him as the answer to his question took
shape in her mind: *You turned up here tonight with a woman
you're almost certainly shagging – and for no sane reason I
can fathom, it's made me want to ugly-cry.*

Instead of saying this out loud, she hissed: 'I don't know,
have you?'

Sam rolled his eyes and Amy sensed the right side of this
argument sliding away from her at speed.

'If there's a reason why you've been avoiding me,' Sam
told her, 'I wish you'd just say.'

'I am *not* "avoiding you",' Amy said derisively, performing
an inverted commas gesture with her index fingers. 'I've been
busy. Setting up a new book imprint single-handed is quite
a lot of work, believe it or not.'

'Is this the part where you imply I have no idea what
having a real job feels like because I'm the son of a lord?'
Sam asked, his voice hot and indignant. Goosebumps broke
out on Amy's forearms, exposed in her thin shirt.

'You're being ridiculous,' Amy muttered, feeling almost
intoxicated by the slip in his composure. 'I haven't said
anything of the sort.'

'You didn't *need* to, Amy. You're obviously pissed off

with me about something, it's written all over your face. And typically, the thing you find it easiest to punish me for is being "posh" – whether or not that has anything to do with the actual problem. So go on, let me have it: shouldn't I be in the royal box, or at a fox hunt, or stoning some peasants to death, et cetera, et cetera? Or – and *here's* a novel idea! – you could just *be honest with me*. Tell me what's on your mind, or *ask* me the question you want answered. I'd never lie to you.'

Amy stared at him in surprise, feeling like he might as well have punched her in the stomach. Fruitlessly, she scrabbled for something to say back. Every caustic retort she came up with fell short, and as the spotlights lit up the first actors who walked on stage, her mouth was still hanging open.

Throughout the first half of the play, Amy's shock was replaced by a fizzing, smouldering anger. There were several moments when she seriously considered whether she had the physical strength to strangle Sam but, to her dismay, these thoughts quickly degenerated into wondering what the stubble on his throat would feel like under her palms . . . Whether he'd protest if she cupped his jaw with her hands, then covered his glowering lips with hers.

The moment the interval began, Sam was up and out of his seat. He was at the end of the aisle, and thus able to make a sharp exit without clambering over anyone – a smooth, wordless departure he completed within seconds. Amy swallowed a sudden swell of disappointment.

'Blimey, someone needed the loo sharpish,' Simon said loudly from a few seats away. Dave – seated on Amy's other side – shuffled and snorted. He'd been half asleep since the second his backside hit the red velvet-covered cushion of his chair over an hour ago, and if he'd overheard any of her earlier exchange with Sam, he already seemed to have forgotten it.

'Is your young man getting you a drink, or shall I?' Dave asked Amy, as though it were common knowledge that the two of them were – as he would no doubt have put it – 'courting'.

'Er . . . I shouldn't think so. He has absolutely no reason

to be buying me a drink,' Amy said, bewildered. After seeing how enraged she was at news of their home's forced sale, how could Dave possibly think there was anything going on between her and the Viscount's heir? It was baffling.

'Wine, then?' Dave asked, evidently feeling no need to explain himself, or ask any questions that might help him improve his understanding of the nature of Amy and Sam's fraught relationship.

'Better not,' Amy told him, despite an overpowering urge to down a G&T. 'I'm the designated driver, after all. A lime and soda would be great, though, thanks.'

Dave and Barbara went in search of the bar, as did Meg and Nisha. Seconds later, Mr Bradley excused himself to go to the gents. To Amy's dismay, Simon took this opportunity to slide across the vacant seats between them and temporarily occupy Dave's.

The last thing Amy needed right now was a one-sided conversation with someone who paused for breath so rarely it was a wonder he wasn't oxygen-deficient. Alas, the moment Simon was settled he began explaining the reasons why *Much Ado About Nothing* was, 'in many respects, the original romcom'.

Amy resisted the urge to point out that she'd previously studied this play, had a first-class degree in English Literature *and* worked in publishing – latterly specialising in the very genre he was so avidly telling her about. She was abundantly grateful when the rest of their cohort – still minus Sam – reappeared, and even more so when Dave insisted he had no intention of playing 'musical bloody chairs' with the postman and wanted his original seat back.

As the lights dimmed and the audience readied themselves for the second half of the play, Amy felt a sick sort of dread settle in her stomach. Had Sam actually *left*? Had their argument bothered him so much he'd felt the need to publicly abandon the evening? In theory, the possibility should have made her feel like she'd won something: the upper hand, their latest argument, the most recent round in their lifelong war of wills. Instead, it left her cold and confused – and with a gnawing, sharp-edged sensation that, somehow, she'd lost.

Her panic rose as spotlights once again illuminated the stage – the actors playing the night watch tramping out and immediately prompting laughter. Amy tore her gaze from the empty seat beside her to watch, then felt someone sink into the chair to her right.

She didn't need to look over to know it was Sam – just like she didn't need to glance up to know that the sky was blue, or stare at the stars to be sure they were there. Relief flooded her, closely followed by alarm. Her reactions to him were too intense, too erratic, and she knew it. Her feelings were horribly confused, totally inconsistent and all incompatible with one another. Everything was becoming ungovernable: senseless and resistant to reason. It absolutely terrified her.

He nudged her in the same way he had earlier, catching her eye and looking at her gently through the darkness.

'Truce?' he whispered, dipping his head towards hers. His breath warmed her ear as she nodded, a little too eagerly.

'In that case . . . here,' he said, pressing something shockingly cold into her hand. She gasped involuntarily and heard him smother a laugh, then looked down to examine whatever freezing thing he'd given her.

She swiped frost from the side of a small cardboard tub to discover the words 'Ginger Spice Gelato' written there. He'd bought her ice cream.

'Peace offering,' he said quietly.

'Thanks,' she said, and swallowed hard.

'I hope it's okay,' he murmured, slightly embarrassed. 'I debated all the options and then took a punt.'

'It's fine,' Amy whispered softly, peeling back the lid so she could start surreptitiously eating and taking great care not to let him see her smiling face.

It was perfect – her favourite flavour. And she was almost sure he knew it.

Chapter 20

In the week after the Rowton Readers' theatre trip, Amy saw more of Sam than she had in the previous three or four weeks. On an almost daily basis, her head now did battle with her body – her brain attempting to exert control over her unruly physical reactions to his presence.

'Stomach drop sensation' seemed a poor moniker for what she experienced every time he leaned to read something over her shoulder. When the heat from his body warmed her skin, his arms bracketed hers or their fingers accidentally brushed over her laptop's trackpad, Amy felt like life snapped into high definition – as if all other sensations were pale, feeble excuses for feelings.

To make matters worse, her mind continued to turn traitor at every opportunity. Left unchecked, it would set her adrift on a sea of daydreams that involved the sort of clinches she'd never previously imagined enjoying in the workplace – not even when she worked with Hugh, her actual boyfriend.

Stubbornly, Amy told herself that stress must be behind her inability to keep her lustful yearning under proper control. With RomFest now less than two months away, the pressure to make it a success was intensifying.

Tickets went on sale this coming Friday, and Amy knew that the more they sold, the easier it would be to get more authors, journalists and 'bookfluencers' to help promote it or come along on the day. By dint of supporting the festival, these big names could help to establish Torch as the new place to be for proud writers and readers of an often-derided genre – a genre Amy had come to enjoy, but perhaps more importantly respect over the past few months.

When a broadsheet columnist she spoke to about a possible feature asked her whether the world really *needed* more books about women falling in love, Amy's earnest defence of her authors' work had surprised even her. It did, she'd said, because people's lives were made brighter by entertaining stories that – at their best – were inclusive, insightful and emotionally resonant. Amy had also pointed out that there was something worrying – and perhaps rather revealing – about the ease with which books about unhappy, abused or even murdered women were accepted as 'serious', while stories about them having fun, strong friendships and satisfying sex were deemed vapid or unrealistic. She'd scored Torch and RomFest a two-page spread in a popular Sunday supplement, titled: 'Shining A Light On Love: why it's time to take romance seriously'. Carolyn had been so thrilled with the piece that she'd actually phoned Amy to congratulate her on the morning it came out. This, Amy knew, was an unheard-of level of appreciation from her usually tight-lipped boss; the professional equivalent of hell freezing over.

During their next online catch-up, Hugh – prompted by Carolyn – had offered Amy a grudging, lukewarm 'well done'. After he and Carolyn had left the call, Sam openly and scathingly wondered what his problem was. 'It's like he'd prefer for the whole enterprise to fail,' he'd said. 'Which makes me wonder whether he understands what the job of finance director actually entails. Or maybe it's that he *assumed* it would go badly, which doesn't speak too highly of his judgement. No one sensible would ever bet against you.' At this, Amy had demurred and turned pink, then quickly changed the subject.

It had been decided that *Love to Hate You*, Philippa Fotheringham's new book, would be the first Torch title to publish, not least because it could be made ready to hit e-readers only a few days after RomFest. Exclusive merchandise specific to the novel – including 'chilled-out night in' bundles containing chocolates, cotton pyjamas and a special, RomFest-only edition of the e-book – would be available at the event. Even better, the author herself would be there in person to talk about her work.

Amy's busy schedule was put on pause when the day of Grace's hip replacement operation arrived. She had booked the day off, as well as a few days post-op to ensure she could devote her full attention to her grandmother. On the morning of Grace's surgery, Amy and Mr Bradley both went to the hospital with her and waited until she was taken down to theatre.

In recent weeks, it had become clear to Amy that her ex-English teacher and college principal was beyond besotted with her gran – that his 'courting' of her was truly in earnest. Amy had frequently found herself holed up in her bedroom or hanging out at Nisha or Meg's in order to avoid feeling like the third wheel while Grace and Mr Bradley watched documentaries or old episodes of cosy-crime dramas. Meanwhile, dinner times either involved all three of them, or consisted of a solitary ready meal for one because Grace and her beau were out and Amy was alone.

Now, Mr Bradley looked ashen. The moment Grace was out of earshot, he clutched Amy's hand and sighed: a heavy exhalation that morphed into something scarily like a sob.

'Oh Amy, my dear, I'm sorry,' he said as he straightened up, dabbing at his eyes with a proper pocket handkerchief. Dimly, Amy wondered where on earth you could even buy such things nowadays. She decided this wasn't the time to ask.

'Don't apologise,' Amy said, patting his hand awkwardly as he loosed his grip on her. 'I understand. I'm worried, too. I won't be able to rest until she's come round and the doctors tell us the surgery went well. Probably not until I've got her home, tucked up on the sofa with Bertie and a Miss Marple.'

'She's a wonderful woman,' Ken said, his voice wobbly and waterlogged. 'I hope you know how highly I think of her. How much I value and enjoy the time we spend together. How grateful I am to have found someone to . . . to *love* again. At my time of life.'

Love? Amy was not prepared for this.

'It's going to be all right,' she said firmly, gently placing her hands on his shoulders and looking him square in his kind, smile-lined eyes. '*She's* going to be all right.'

In truth, Amy was feigning a level of calm confidence she didn't truly feel – but it rather seemed as though one of them needed to keep it together.

'I can't bear to think of losing her,' Mr Bradley said shakily. 'After my wife died, I never thought I'd find another partner – let alone one I could adore so completely.'

This was all deeply embarrassing – but beneath the mortification that came with hearing a man she *still* couldn't call by his first name profess undying devotion to her grandmother, Amy felt something else. She was moved. Tears had sprung to her eyes and, although she felt worried for Grace, they weren't born of anxiety or fear for her gran.

'My dad,' Amy said quietly, 'always said he could never love anyone again after my mother left us. Losing her crushed him for good.'

'I know it did,' Mr Bradley said, nodding and seeming to pull himself together somewhat. 'It was a shame for him – he was a good man. Falling in love is a game of chance, to some degree: one never knows when or where the feeling might appear. But being willing to play it is key, and that's difficult after heartbreak.'

'You think he could have, then? Fallen in love again, I mean? You think it was . . . a choice not to?'

'Oh, that's not for me to say,' said Mr Bradley, clearly concerned he'd upset her. 'I meant no offence.'

'No, I know you didn't,' Amy reassured him. 'I'm just interested in your perspective. You and Gran have both overcome bereavements – moved on in a way he never did, even though he was so much younger.'

'Indeed. I suppose that when I refer to a game of chance, I do mean one has *some* choice: it's a question of either keeping your cards close to your chest, or deciding to show them, come what may.'

Amy nodded. 'So you're saying that whether you can fall in love depends on how risk-averse you are?'

'Essentially, yes. Though as I said, it might also be a question of readiness to play.'

'You've lost me, Mr Bradley.'

'Call me Ken, my dear, I beg of you. I think we're a little way past formalities after this morning.'

'Sorry,' Amy said, wincing. '*Ken*. Maybe it's the extended poker metaphor, but I don't understand. I suppose I always thought my dad staked his heart on my mother and then lost it forever. Are you saying he folded too soon?'

'I wouldn't presume to judge. But perhaps he decided to be a spectator for a while, rather than a participant in the game. That may have been a conscious decision – one that arguably made sense while you were young and he was your sole carer.'

Somehow, despite her anxieties about Grace's operation, RomFest, Hugh's mind games and her increasingly intense, Sam Ainsworth-focused fantasy life, Amy registered the significance of this. Perhaps she'd misunderstood things – believed her father too broken to find love again, when in fact he'd merely been putting it off until she didn't need him so much. How was he to know that, by the time she was thirteen, he'd have terminal cancer – that he'd miss his chance to try again?

'Well, this has all been quite illuminating, though I'm suddenly aware I have no idea how to play *any* card games,' Amy said, smiling.

'In my experience, when you find the right partner, you tend to figure out the rules as you go,' Ken said, a slight but perceptible gleam in his kind eyes. He beamed knowingly at her when she didn't respond.

Feeling a change of subject might be prudent, Amy said: 'Why don't I fetch us some coffees, then head back to the cottage and take His Majesty for a walk?'

'So long as you're sure,' Ken said, tentative. 'What if she wakes up while you're away?'

'I think,' Amy said, peeling herself up off the uncomfortable plastic chair she was stuck to, 'that based on everything you've said this morning, you're the first person she's going to want to see.'

As the words left her lips, she finally understood that Grace's initial reluctance to tell Amy about her accident wasn't only down to the distance that had grown up between them, or Grace's fear that she'd pull her granddaughter away from her busy London life if she frightened her.

It was also because, with Ken to support and care for her, Grace didn't really *need* Amy – at least, not as much as Amy had thought. The realisation stung, more keenly than she'd ever have expected it to.

As Amy pulled up to the kerb outside the cottage in Grace's car, she heard her phone chime from deep inside her handbag.

Kit: How's your gran? Did the op go OK? Please let me know when you can. Love you x

Amy felt a rush of affection for him. Plenty of people assumed that Kit was as trivial and self-obsessed as he sometimes pretended to be – but that couldn't be less true. He was thoughtful, honest and loyal. As best friends went, he was a worthy successor to Hari. She smiled as she wondered how well they might have got on, then typed her reply.

Amy: There was a slight delay getting her down to theatre so she's still in. I've popped back home to take Bertie out. Ken's there in case she wakes up.

Kit: Ken? As in your old teacher?

Amy: I know right?
However, it seems they're, like . . . in love??? 🙁

Kit: Yes!
WRINKLY ROMANCE!!!
Totally here for it.
Text me later?

Amy: Promise x

It came as no surprise to her that Kit was fully on board with the idea of Grace having a boyfriend. Since meeting his latest squeeze at Queer Karaoke some weeks ago – the slender, shy, bespectacled economist he'd been lusting after for months – he'd been the most infatuated and soppy that Amy had ever known him.

She climbed out of the car, locked it and made her way to the front door of the cottage, which was practically buried beneath a burst of blowsy peach roses. It was another blisteringly hot day, but the air was thick – heady and syrupy, suggestive of imminent rain.

Once inside, she fastened Bertie into his harness and lead, then closed the door on the house and strode in the direction of the bridge. Without consciously deciding to, she wandered across it, then up Old Rowton high street.

No fewer than five separate people stopped her to say hello as they passed her on the pavement, and all of them asked after Grace. Living here wasn't necessarily *better* than being in London, Amy thought – but it wasn't worse, either. Idly, she wondered where she'd be this time next year – though Ken's recent revelations seemed to confirm that her cohabitation with Grace would come to a natural end once her grandmother was back on her feet.

Amy had reached the edge of the village, right up to the boundary of the Rowton Hall grounds. The estate's little wood beckoned, shaded and cool. Bertie pulled on the lead, straining to head in the direction he was most used to. For some reason, Amy was reluctant to head in there today. She felt fragile and edgy, but the sweat gathering at the small of her back and speckling her temples won out – being out of the hot sun for a while would be blissful.

She let the little dog direct her, but before they were fully through the gate that led into the copse, Amy jumped at the sudden sound of a car engine. A glossy, deep blue BMW with the top lowered was making its way down the main drive, away from the mansion and onto the road Amy and Bertie had just crossed. At the wheel was Tilly, smiling and sun-kissed. The sight of her here, halfway through the day and sporting a casual, strappy sundress, removed all doubt from Amy's mind: she and Sam must have patched up whatever had previously gone wrong between them. They were seeing one another again.

When Tilly spotted Amy, she grinned and waved. 'Hey! CUTE dog!' she cried as the car glided by. 'See you soon!'

See you soon?

Urgh. Amy didn't *want* to 'see her soon'. Or ever again, in fact.

This was irrational and completely unfair, given Tilly seemed perfectly lovely and had done nothing to deserve Amy's dislike. Bertie was whining, desperate to escape the glare of the sun and scamper around in the sheltered undergrowth of the wood. She stomped after him, cursing herself. Cursing *Sam*. This bitter, uncomfortable feeling was his fault, she was certain – though if she'd been asked, A level English-style, to find evidence for this opinion, she knew she'd have struggled to locate any.

Beneath the canopy of trees, the muggy air was only marginally less oppressive than it had been on the high street. Amy let Bertie's lead out to its full length, allowing him to explore a little. She decided they'd do one short circuit in here and then she'd head back to the hospital. With any luck, Grace might even be awake by the time she got there. Her phone was in her pocket, the ringer turned up high so she could be reached the moment her gran came out of surgery.

When Amy and Bertie got to the far side of the wood where the trees thinned, she heard voices. One of them was Sam's. She edged closer to the low murmur of conversation, peering between gnarled old trunks and trying – for no reason she could think of – not to be seen.

'As I've been arguing from the very beginning,' Sam was saying, '*this* is what's going to secure our family's place at the Hall, now and in years to come: events on our terms, but which bring in significant profits.'

He was talking about RomFest, Amy had no doubt. But she was shocked at the phrase 'secure our family's place at the Hall'. Sam sounded exactly like his father: committed to staying in their crumbling stately pile at any cost.

'We'll see,' his father drawled. So it *was* Roger he was talking to. 'I still think it's folly – a lot of fuss on our private land that will doubtless lead to damage. You've always been fatally naive – stupid and idealistic from as far back as I can remember.'

Stupid? Ouch. Amy felt an odd stab of something like protectiveness, then repressed it – but not before she could think that while Sam Ainsworth was many things, stupid wasn't one of them.

'We *will* see,' Sam told him, somehow keeping hold of his audibly frayed temper. 'You agreed to this on the basis that I might prove a case for commercial use of the grounds – so long as I did all the donkey work and dealt with the money. Current projections are promising. You may yet be able to instruct the renovators to deal with the mess in the old card room.'

What the *fuck?* The old *card room?!* In the context of people being forced out of their homes, the very idea of refurbishing a space whose original purpose was to host Regency-era games of whist was objectively disgusting. Suddenly, Amy felt sick.

'I rue the day I ever let you anywhere near the estate accounts,' Roger grumbled. 'It isn't often I question my own judgement, but appointing you to manage things was a colossal error.'

'An error you're stuck with,' Sam deadpanned, 'since no one else of sound mind would be willing to do the MD's job on the terms *I* do. And let me reassure you: I think it's clear to most people how rarely you wonder whether you might be in the wrong.'

'In my grandfather's day, an heir like you would have been disinherited,' Roger hissed.

'In your grandfather's day, an heir like me would have died at the Somme,' Sam said scathingly – and Amy could virtually hear the accompanying eye-roll. 'If you thought there'd be any advantage to disinheriting me, you'd have done it years ago,' Sam went on, blithe and calm. 'Whether you like it or not, preserving this place is part of my future – and I intend to ensure there's something *left* to preserve when the time comes. You can decry this event, and the strategy behind it, to your heart's content – but I assure you, I know what I'm doing. Unlike most of our ancestors, I wouldn't risk my own financial security on a self-indulgent whim.'

Bile burned the back of Amy's throat as her stomach turned over. She swallowed back vomit, rage, disappointment and . . . Shit. *Tears.*

In a flash, she realised that as her attraction to Sam had grown – as she had failed to check it, struggled to keep it in its box – she'd also begun hoping she could like him again.

She'd almost believed, and some part of her had *wanted* to believe, that his intentions were good. That his motives were as pure as the rest of Rowton's residents always claimed.

She'd been right, though; he wasn't on their side, any more than the wolf was on the side of the sheep. Sam cared about this house, his family's legacy and patching up the holes in their supposedly threadbare finances – not about the 'ordinary people' of the village, plenty of whom still depended on the estate for their homes and livelihoods. He also, apparently, cared about Tilly Wexmore-Yates.

She'd heard enough. Being careful not to step on anything that might snap or crack underfoot, she gently backed away from the trees she'd concealed herself in. Staring around her, she felt almost dazed – as though she'd stumbled out of a nightmare and back into reality again, only to discover the real world was just as horrible as her dream. Everything she looked at undulated before her eyes, waving and shimmering in soft focus. It was a few seconds before she realised the wood looked watery because she was crying.

She hated Sam for this – possibly more than ever. He'd *almost* had her – he'd so nearly convinced her that her judgement was off, with his ginger spiced ice cream and the revelations about his sister and niece. She'd been so close to trusting that there was more to him than she thought, that he'd changed . . .

Lightning suddenly flashed overhead, illuminating the dense canopy of leaves above her. Seconds later, thunder rumbled and she felt the first spots of rain hit the bare skin of her arms. *Great.*

It was only then that she realised Bertie had been awfully quiet the whole time she'd been spying on Sam and Roger. This was most out of character for a six-kilogram sausage dog who managed to sound like a pack of crazed Alsatians every time anyone rang the doorbell.

She looked down to discover she was still clutching the plastic handle of his lead with the long line attached and his harness dangling from its end.

The dog himself, however, was gone.

Chapter 21

Racked with panic, Amy stumbled back onto the wood's main path and shouted to her left, then her right. 'Bertie! BERTIE! Come back! *Please!*'

She was really crying now, harder than she had in years – as if the events of today had broken something inside her and the loss of yappy, scrappy Bertie had been the final straw. Tears were streaming down her face and her chest was heaving with deep, shaking breaths that kept turning into sobs.

Gran would never forgive her if she couldn't get Bertie back. *How* had he slipped his harness? She'd taken him for countless walks over the past few months, and nothing like this had ever happened.

What if he found his way onto the road and ran out in front of a car? He was the daftest, most coddled canine Amy had ever met. He had no road sense whatsoever and certainly no notion of his own mortality.

Then there was the storm. It had taken just seconds to set in and now thick sheets of rain were falling all around her. Thunder continued to crash at regular intervals and lightning frequently lit up the bruise-coloured sky. Bertie would be terrified. Soaking. Cowering somewhere, too afraid to emerge.

Amy herself was saturated, her T-shirt and skirt sopping wet and stuck to her skin. Her dark hair was plastered against her scalp and every inch of her was dripping and goose-bumped. As Rowton's month-long heatwave broke right over her head, the temperature of the air had plummeted. Shivering, she staggered in one direction and then another, calling, whistling and yelling. 'BERTIE! BERTIE! COME BACK! HERE, BOY!'

Exhausted and increasingly hopeless, Amy tripped on a tree root and crashed clumsily to the ground. When she clambered back up again her right knee was bleeding and her hands were grazed, both oozing red.

She hung her head, trying to tamp down her distress and think logically. She needed to get the dog back urgently, she had to keep looking for him – but at any moment Ken might call and tell her Grace had come out of theatre or woken up and asked for her. It surely wouldn't be long until she had to get back to the hospital – but how could she face her grandmother in this state? *God*. How could she ever face her again if she couldn't find Bertie, or if something awful had happened to him?

At the thought of his soft, wet nose never nudging hers again – the cold absence she'd feel beside her on the sofa if he wasn't snuggled up there, snoring, whenever Grace was out – Amy began sobbing harder. The silly little sausage had made her *love* him, and this was the result: this abject terror of losing him.

She tried to calm herself, but her heart felt like it was cracking – fracturing as she stood there weeping fat tears in the chilly rain. She cursed the violet clouds above her, overwhelmed with dread and frustration.

'Amy?! Amy! What the hell's going on? Are you hurt?' Sam was running towards her, having just emerged from a nearby thicket of trees. He was wearing running gear and, like her, he was drenched. His white T-shirt, now semi-transparent, was clinging to him and his hair was a mass of messy, rain-darkened waves.

'I'm *fine*,' Amy told him, her voice unsteady. She tried not to notice as he licked a raindrop off his bottom lip.

'You're *bleeding*,' Sam said flatly, 'and running around the wood, screaming.' He stepped towards her and she backed away a little.

'I'm looking for Bertie, okay?' she yelled at him, still sounding stricken. 'And I tripped. It's no big deal – just a few cuts and bruises.'

'Let me look,' he said. It wasn't a question. He came closer and as Amy tried to move beyond his reach, her back hit a tree trunk. She huffed out a breath, reluctantly settling against it as he took her left hand in his to examine it.

'We need to clean this up,' he said, 'and your other hand, *and* your knee. There's mud and grit in there, and you're freezing. Let's get you back to the house.'

'No,' Amy said, her tone suddenly clear and ice-cold. 'I'm not going anywhere with you.'

'What?' Sam demanded, annoyed. 'What have I done now? I thought we were OK again? Actually, fuck it. Whatever you're mad with me about, it doesn't *matter* right now. All that matters is getting you the help you need.'

'I don't need any help!' she spat back.

'Because you're clearly doing brilliantly,' he said sardonically. He folded his arms and stared at her, his gaze skipping over every feature of her face until it settled on her eyes. He sighed, all the fight seeming to drain from him. 'Please. Just . . . What can I do?'

'You can leave me alone,' she told him. 'Like I tried to tell you before, from now on we only talk about work – and only when we absolutely have to. The rest of the time I don't want to see you or hear from you. Ever. At all.'

Sam bent and put his head in his hands, then straightened up and shoved his sopping wet hair out of his despairing eyes.

'For God's sake, Amy, I can't keep up with your moods! One day you seem to hate me, then you . . . *don't*. And then we're back to this. I don't understand,' he groaned. 'I'm sorry I almost went too far that day we drank the wine – I know it made you uncomfortable. But I thought we were getting on, at least. Not hating every minute spent in one another's company.'

Amy said nothing, at a loss for an honest comeback that was sufficiently cutting. It was difficult to find one because in truth, she loved Sam's company. If she'd been able to forget who he was – who he'd been to her in the past – she might even have found herself capable of loving *him*.

This thought lanced through her like a knife. As he stood there, damp and dishevelled, beautiful and begging her to let him help in any way he could, she felt all the warmth of wanting him fight with the cold wash of rage that came with remembering the things she'd overheard.

'We will *never* get on,' Amy cried, steeling herself. 'Not after the things you said this afternoon. I heard you, ranting on about preserving the estate, the house, the fucking *card room* . . . You always said you hated all that stuff, poncing around college with your George Orwell novels and your weekly copy of the *Socialist Worker*. What was it all for? Shits and giggles? Was it all about winding up your dad?'

'So you're spying on me now?' he asked, his brown eyes narrowing.

'It was an accident,' Amy said, her chin jutting out like a petulant child's. 'But once I started listening, I had to be sure of what I was listening *to*.'

'And you're certain you've got it right, are you?' Sam countered, his voice low, almost dangerous. His face was so close to hers now that Amy could see each of the individual lashes framing his dark eyes. His pupils were blown wide and black in the gloom.

'You think,' he went on, 'that after eavesdropping for a few minutes, you have sufficient evidence to prove I'm the evil lord of the manor you've always *wanted* me to be? Was that snatch of conversation really conclusive enough for you to dismiss everything else I've ever said or done?'

Amy ignored this. 'What about Barb and Dave?' she cried, deciding to throw caution to the wind and hit him with something she felt certain would stick. 'What about Jed and the pub? Here you are, bragging to your father about how your grand plans for hiring out the grounds will turn fabulous profits – all while they're facing eviction in a couple of months' time. It makes me sick!'

Sam shut his eyes and dipped his head again, like it was weighted down by sheer misery. '*This* is what you think?' he said a moment later, through gritted teeth. He looked agonised. 'You think all this' – he gestured at the small space between them, presumably to indicate their joint work on RomFest – 'is me larking about trying to piss my father off and earn pocket money? Fucking *hell*, Amy.'

'Well, what am I supposed to think?' she shouted at him.

What am I supposed to *feel*, she asked herself. Because even now, as they stood yelling at one another in the rain, she could sense the snapping, crackling current of the attraction between them. Beneath the fresh, petrichor smell of the storm there was the citrus and cedar scent of his skin. In spite of everything, she wanted to lose herself in it.

'You've always thought about everything in the way that suits you best,' Sam said. 'Regardless of any and all evidence that might tell someone less bloody stubborn they were wrong.'

'Rubbish,' Amy said, scowling and shaking her head vigorously.

'What about Hari? You refused to look his feelings for you in the face because it wasn't convenient . . . And so did I, in the end.'

'You know *nothing* about Hari and me, or what we meant to each other,' Amy cried, 'and that absolute nonsense you've just spouted confirms it!'

'Some of us are capable of adding two and two, Amy,' Sam said. 'You seem determined to go through life believing they make five.'

'Well, we can't all be as clever as you, Your Lordship,' Amy snarled. 'We didn't all go to top boarding schools and have private tutors coming out of our arseholes.'

It was a low blow, and she regretted it instantly. The furious light faded from Sam's eyes and he stepped away from her suddenly, as if she'd slapped him.

'I understand,' he said quietly. '*You* don't, but it's

not for me to enlighten you. I'm not going to justify or explain myself, since you're determined to think so little of me. We'll do exactly as you wish: pretend we're merely colleagues with no prior connection, no . . . personal history.'

Amy's chest ached at the sight of him, dejected and hurt, unwilling to meet her gaze.

Before she could work out what to say next her mobile rang, its tinny trill cutting through the sound of the slowing rain. It was Ken.

'Hello?' Amy said breathlessly.

'Amy,' he said, 'she's out of surgery. Everything went as planned. She's still a little groggy, but ready to see you whenever you can get here.'

'Oh, thank God,' Amy sighed. 'Thank you. I'll be there as soon as I can.'

There was no point in relaying the Bertie disaster right now. If she was going to have to confess to losing him, far better to do it in person; it was the least Amy owed her grandmother after everything she'd done for her.

The storm seemed to be receding; the air felt almost steamy as the heavy rain gave way to a light, dwindling drizzle. Perhaps if she spent a few minutes looking for Bertie now before heading back to the car, he'd come out from wherever he was hiding.

She said goodbye to Ken and rang off, then looked up, feeling Sam's eyes on her. 'Gran's operation is done,' she said. 'Mr B says everything went fine.'

'I'm glad,' he said, sincerely, then looked away from her. 'That's very good news.'

'Sam—' Amy began, not really knowing where she was going with her sentence. At the same time, he blurted, 'At least let me help you look for Bertie—'

Then her phone rang again. She jumped in alarm. Had Grace taken a bad turn? When she pulled the handset out of her pocket, though, she saw it was Nisha calling. That was weird – she was very much a WhatsApp or text message sort of person.

'Nish,' Amy said, 'is everything OK?'

'I have Bertie here!' she cried. 'I saw him trotting down the high street in the rain, poor little love. I've got him in the back of the shop. He's wrapped up in a towel with a packet of ham slices, happy as Larry.'

'Of course he is,' Amy said, furious with him but intensely grateful for her good fortune, for the second time in as many minutes. 'He slipped his harness in the wood,' she explained. 'I'll be right there, just hang onto him.'

'Will do,' Nisha said cheerfully.

'You're amazing,' Amy said into the phone, 'a lifesaver. See you soon.'

'Bertie's OK as well?' Sam asked as Amy shoved her phone back into her bag.

'Yeah,' she said. 'At the shop. Gorging himself on Nisha's stock, no less.'

'Good. That's a relief, too.'

'Sam—' she tried again, but he held a hand up to stop her.

'I think you've probably said enough, Amy. Don't try to backpedal now, I'll know you don't mean it. Go and fetch Bertie, get those wounds cleaned up, and then go and see Grace. Please give her my love.'

Amy nodded, mute but tearful again at the sound of that word in his mouth. 'I will.'

'Thanks. I suppose I'll speak to you at some point on Monday, then. About *work*, of course.'

He turned and walked away, straightening his back and squaring his broad, sodden shoulders in the returning sunlight, now sliding serenely through fluffy white clouds. The gesture went straight to Amy's heart.

Chapter 22

As it turned out, Amy didn't speak to Sam on Monday. Or Tuesday, or Wednesday. In fact, it had now been more than a week since their row in the wood and she'd heard nothing from him.

Despite watching her phone and email inbox almost constantly, all she'd received were a few RomFest messages in CC – stuff he was copying her in on for the sake of completeness, and none of which addressed her directly.

She should feel happy about this. After all, he was doing precisely as she'd asked and restricting contact with her to what was professional and necessary. In reality, she felt edgy and bereft.

Grace, who was now home and recovering well from her hip replacement operation, had asked Amy repeatedly what was wrong. She was visibly glum, and knew her grandmother was worried, but what could she say? 'I've had a massive argument with someone I *always* argue with, so in theory I ought to be fine – but actually, I feel like I want to cry, sink my head into a vat of wine and eat all the chocolate I can lay my hands on. Not necessarily in that order.'

No. Any explanation of her mood that was even half true would only lead to more questions – none of which Amy was keen to answer. Instead of admitting to her confrontation with Sam, or to the fact that she missed speaking to him, she mumbled some vague nonsense about work stress and changed the subject each time Grace checked in on her. The routine was already wearing thin.

On Friday afternoon, Amy took the train into Birmingham for lunch with Philippa Fotheringham. In theory, their date was in celebration of the *Love to Hate You* manuscript being fully signed off and almost ready for readers to enjoy – but it was fair to say that Amy, despite the professional success this new novel represented for her, was not in a triumphant mood.

When she arrived at Russo's, the small but five star-reviewed restaurant they'd chosen for their meet-up, Amy saw that – like last time they'd got together for a meal – Philippa was already there. The woman was early for everything, which made perfect sense given all that Amy had learned about her since April. Like Carolyn, Philippa was the sort of person who wouldn't ever be caught on the back foot. Today, as always, her ultra-feminine exterior belied the ferocious businesswoman within. She was dressed in a frothy pink maxi dress that reminded Amy of the stuff other girls her age used to dress Barbie dolls in. Philippa's hair was freshly coloured and professionally styled – a voluminous, ashy blonde tumble of shiny waves that made Amy's inky, somewhat grown-out bob feel very drab by comparison.

'Bloody hell, bab,' Philippa said as Amy pulled up a chair and poured herself a cool glass of water. 'You look like you've lost a tenner and found a parking ticket. What's up?'

Amy was dismayed. She'd done her best to look cheerful even though she didn't feel it, donning a cherry-red, 1950s-style cotton dress with a sweetheart neckline plus matching wedge sandals. She ought to have known better, though; she'd come to understand that one of the reasons why Philippa wrote so well was her rare ability to read people, effortlessly and accurately. She understood what made others tick, which helped immensely when it came to crafting believable characters and the relationships between them – but God, was her talent inconvenient right now.

Amy sighed. 'I'm sorry, Philippa . . . Please don't be concerned that I'm in any way unhappy with *Love to Hate You*, or worried it won't be a massive success – because it certainly will be. I just have a few personal things on my

245

mind at the moment. But this lunch isn't about me, so let's not even go there – shall we order some fizz?'

'Oh, there's already some on the way,' Philippa said, grinning wickedly. Amy smiled and laughed for the first time since last week. At that moment, a smartly dressed waiter appeared with a bottle of Taittinger in an ice bucket, plus two cut-glass coupes.

When they'd both been poured a glass of champagne and enjoyed their first sips, Philippa said: 'I'm *very* much looking forward to your romance festival – are you and that strapping young lad all done now with the organisation?'

Amy took another gulp of her drink. 'Er – getting there, yes,' she said, trying to keep her face neutral.

'Honestly,' Philippa went on as she tore into a piece of the ciabatta the waiter had just delivered, then dunked it in olive oil and balsamic vinegar. 'He's a proper dish, isn't he? Looks like someone I'd make up for one of my historical romances.'

Amy could feel heat creeping up her spine and the sides of her neck. 'Er . . . sure. Yeah. I guess so.'

Philippa's carefully pencilled eyebrows shot up, though not very far. Amy detected very subtle Botox at work.

'*Ah*,' Philippa said, 'I see.'

'What do you see?' Amy asked, willing her face to assume innocence and not flush the same colour as her dress.

'I see we have one of my favourite romantic tropes coming to life in front of our very eyes,' Philippa said, her voice thick with glee. 'Correct me if I get any of this wrong, won't you – but as I understand it, you know this man from childhood, you didn't get on well as kids and there's been some disagreement since you've been back living in that lovely little village of yours.

'*Now*, however, you've been forced to work together on this project and you've discovered that despite all the bickering, you can't stop thinking about him. Don't deny it,' she said, flapping her diamond-encrusted hand dismissively.

'I saw the way you looked at one another during that meeting I was in a few weeks ago. And now here you are with a face like a wet weekend, just as the whole thing is coming to an end. This is classic enemies-to-lovers stuff – surely you've realised *that*, bearing in mind there'll be a whole area devoted to it come festival day? Aren't you printing T-shirts?'

Amy groaned out loud, and the waiter – who'd approached with the intention of asking if he could take their food order – turned on his heel in alarm. Philippa sloshed more champagne into Amy's glass.

'Oh dear,' Philippa said sympathetically. 'Is this news to you? The fact that you have feelings for him? Sorry to be the bearer.'

Amy sighed and sipped her drink again. The realisation that there was no point whatsoever in lying to Philippa felt oddly comforting. It would be good to finally unburden herself, and she reasoned she might as well volunteer the truth; Philippa would doubtless extract it from her anyway.

'It isn't news,' Amy said grimly. 'I think . . . I *know* I've always been attracted to him, at the same time as thinking he's too puffed up and privileged to be allowed. When we were teenagers, he was like this star: other people, girls especially, couldn't help themselves from orbiting around him. I hated that – I found it infuriating and shallow. I vowed I would never become part of his pathetic fan club.'

'Swooning over a good-looking, intelligent, well-mannered boy is pathetic?' Philippa asked, nonplussed. 'Sounds like rather a lot of fun, if you ask me.'

'To me, it *seemed* pathetic,' Amy explained. 'It seemed . . . weak. And then one night he kissed me. After which we barely ever spoke again until I moved back to Rowton.'

'I'm going to need more information about that kiss,' Philippa announced too loudly, her eyes round. She signalled to the hovering, increasingly anxious waiter that they still weren't ready to order.

'It was . . .' Amy groped for the right word. 'Special.'

Bollocks. Had she really said that out loud?

'*God* this is embarrassing,' Amy continued. 'But I'd never felt like that before. It was . . . huge. Emotion so big I couldn't contain it. My friend Nisha has this idea – this cringeworthy thing called the "stomach drop sensation". That night was the only time I'd ever had it until I came back here.'

Philippa nodded sagely, waiting for Amy to go on.

'Something horrendous happened a couple of days later, though. Our friend died in a car accident – my *best* friend. Sam wasn't there for me afterwards. It was like he forgot I even existed. I was so angry with him for that. So hurt.'

Perhaps her honesty was a direct consequence of so much fizz on an empty stomach, but this was the first time Amy had ever said these words out loud.

'I'm sorry about your friend,' Philippa said softly. 'But can I ask – did you reach out to *him* when all this happened? To Sam, I mean?'

'No,' Amy said, her eyes bright with tears she was trying to blink back. 'I didn't know how to. And I suppose I was waiting for him – waiting to see if he thought I was still worth bothering with when I was a grieving mess.'

'Hmmm,' Philippa said. 'I wonder how he felt during that time.'

'I don't think he felt anything. He was like a posh automaton from what I could see – totally emotionless. Stiff upper lip, and all that. And then he went off travelling, as his sort do when the real world's *too* real.'

Philippa frowned. 'Having met him, it seems pretty unlikely to me that he wouldn't feel *anything*. You were kids, weren't you? Eighteen or thereabouts? Based on experience with my two sons – both in their twenties now – I can tell you, lads that age aren't brilliant at showing their emotions, regardless of how rich they are.'

Amy made a face, unwilling to concede the point even though it was a reasonable one.

'Also,' Philippa said, 'and I hope you'll forgive me for this overstep, because when you work with me you have to get used to them – did you never think he might be waiting for *you* to reach out to *him?*'

At this, Amy shook her head. When she was in her teens, she hadn't considered herself the sort of girl boys mooned over or desperately hoped to hear from – especially not popular, wealthy, handsome boys like Sam. It had never occurred to her that she could possess that sort of power. But even as an adult, she realised, she'd been known to underestimate the feelings other people might develop for her. While Hugh's seemed mostly founded in his weird, possessive streak as opposed to genuine affection, she'd been totally blindsided by his decision to propose.

'Well. I'll leave that thought with you,' said Philippa. 'And I'll say one last thing before we put that waiter out of his misery and order some pasta. If I were writing this story, it would be nowhere near over yet.'

Amy smiled wistfully. 'Thanks for listening, Philippa – and I've no doubt if you were working on it, it would make an excellent novel. But it's real life, sadly, not a story with a happy ever after. No one's writing it.'

'That's where you're wrong,' Philippa said, patting Amy's hand and beckoning for the stressed-looking boy in the bow tie to come over to their table at last. 'Romances are powerful because – despite all crowing to the contrary – they draw on what's real. The novels matter to people because they recognise the feelings in them as true. And I would say this because I'm an author, but life is always a story. As for who's writing yours, I'd have thought that was pretty clear to such a clever young woman: *you* are.'

After a humongous dish of pasta arrabiata (only half of which she managed to force down) and a few bites of tiramisu, Amy's stomach was full enough that the Taittinger effect had worn off.

She'd managed to keep the rest of the conversation with

Philippa light and less personal, focusing on the marketing plans that had been drawn up so far for *Love to Hate You* – and which were set to kick off at RomFest. Between them, Amy, Carolyn and Philippa had ardent ambitions for this book. Their confidence that it would firmly establish Philippa as a household name was high, as was the hope that it would put Torch firmly on the map in the world of publishing.

As she sat on the train back to Stratford-upon-Avon, Amy tried to imagine how she'd feel in a month's time. *Love to Hate You* would be out there, hopefully topping book charts and bestseller lists everywhere. RomFest would be over and done with and – unless she performed a dramatic U-turn – she'd have no reason for any further contact with Sam.

They'd be reduced to casual, awkward acquaintances who saw one another only if they both turned up to book club meetings or happened to bump into one another in the village. She could see it now: the embarrassing, stilted 'how have you been?' chat that they'd struggle through if their paths accidentally crossed over the purchase of a pint of milk. Then the inevitable excitement would start, she supposed; increasingly frequent sightings of Tilly zooming in and out of Rowton Hall's grounds in her shiny blue car would give rise to rumours of a reunion, then a wedding . . . Amy's stomach lurched, drop-kicked by her own fevered imaginings.

Time and time again she'd replayed everything she and Sam had said to one another during their argument in the wood. But it was the ghosts of things *un*said that really plagued her.

I'm not going to justify or explain myself, since you're determined to think so little of me. What had he been too proud, angry or upset to tell her?

We'll do exactly as you wish: pretend we're merely colleagues. But what else *could* they be? What other options were there?

On some level, she knew this to be a wilfully stupid

question. The chemical fizz between them was sometimes so fierce she was amazed it wasn't visible to the naked eye. She didn't doubt he felt it too, though she had no idea what he thought it *meant*. In any case, in the context of his rekindled relationship with Tilly, it didn't speak highly of him that he'd referenced it at all – regardless of how obvious it was.

Amy's reverie was interrupted by a chiming from her handbag. When she extracted her phone, she saw that she'd received a text from Lily. She swiped and tapped to open it, only to discover an image of a tarot card captioned with three exclamation marks.

The card itself was a colourful image of a man in Renaissance-era clothing – blue stockings, a red shirt and some kind of long green waistcoat – seated on grass, with his back against a tree. Oddly, and somewhat annoyingly, it made her think of herself and the elm she used to lean against on her secret evenings spent in the wood at Rowton Hall. The man had three golden goblets at his feet. His arms were folded in a gesture of dismissal, disappointment or maybe even overwhelm. On the left of the image, what looked like a cloud was offering him a fourth goblet, but to no avail. A shining hand peeped out from the wisps of air depicted, clutching the cup by the stem and pushing it towards him – but the man seemed barely able to look at it.

Amy shook her head at the picture and sent a reply.

Amy: I don't know what this means . . .

Lily: It's the four of cups. What do you *think* it means? What vibe does it give you?

Rolling her eyes, Amy typed:

Well. I've just been out for lunch with one of my authors and arguably had more champagne than was sensible in the middle of the day. Maybe the dude in the picture has already had enough of whatever's in those cups – he definitely looks a bit pissed. So perhaps this card means 'don't be such a lush, Amy'. In which case, I take it all back: tarot IS real!

Lily: That's just the kind of response I'd expect from someone in the headspace to pull the four of cups. It's concerning.

Amy: But I DIDN'T pull the four of cups! Once again, YOU did it for me. Is there some tarot police force I can complain to about this? Some authority that can stop you doing readings for me against my will?

Lily: Of course not. And it's only bad form to read the odd card for you if my intentions aren't honourable. I've explained this plenty of times before.

Amy gritted her teeth, waiting for Lily to say more as the train sped away from the city and into sunlit, rolling countryside: wheat fields studded with vivid red poppies and vast expanses of dry grass dotted with cows.

After a few minutes, it became obvious that Amy was being punished for her sarcasm. She sighed and sent her mother another message.

Amy: OK, OK, I'll bite. Tell me: what does the four of cups mean? Am I really doomed this time?

Lily is typing . . .

Lily: It's a very significant card, Amy.

Sigh. Lily said that about literally every single card in the deck.

Lily: The four of cups generally speaks to our tendency as

humans not to see what's right in front of us. It demands a re-evaluation of your attitude and everything you think you understand. The hand coming through the clouds is the universe offering you a way forward – but it's on YOU to discover what that way forward is, then be brave enough to follow the path.

Amy: Right. So no pressure, then?

Lily: The cards are supposed to offer guidance, Amaryllis! I really think this one could help if you'd put your snark aside and do a little reflecting.

Right now, Amy wasn't in the mood for any more reflecting. In fact, some rapid deflecting was called for.

Amy: OK, I'll try. Thanks. For thinking and worrying about me, I mean – NOT for the unasked-for tarot reading x

Lily: You do that. You're welcome (for BOTH). And please know that if you ever need to talk about things or feelings that are troubling you . . . I know you have Grace – but I'd like the chance to try and listen. Love you x

Amy felt a rare swell of missing her mother then – of not having her quite close enough to lean on. For all her new age nonsense (as Amy saw it), Lily was determined, intelligent and strong: she and Amy were bonded by blood and shared these characteristics. In truth, their deepest natures weren't dissimilar – a fact that had been a source of fascination and occasional pain for Amy's father, who'd sometimes looked at her in wistful admiration and said, 'You're so like her, you know.'

She typed back:

Love you too. And thanks again x

She had no intention of calling Lily up for a heart-to-heart anytime soon, but she still appreciated the offer.

A few minutes before Amy's train was due into Stratford station, her phone began buzzing.

She'd turned the sound off so her fellow passengers wouldn't be notified every time her mother sent her a message – but even the *fzzz fzzz* of its silent ring was embarrassing, amplified by the movement of the handset across the metal tray-table Amy had pulled down to place her water bottle on.

Carolyn was ringing her. Briefly, Amy considered dropping the call.

Just lately, every time Carolyn appeared with no warning – even if only virtually – she was accompanied by bad news, or caused some minor catastrophe that Amy then had to contend with alone.

Amy still hadn't quite forgiven Carolyn for the debacle over the bedrooms in Robin Hood's Bay, not least because her boss – in a characteristic display of supreme indifference to the embarrassment she'd caused – had shrugged off her error with the vaguest of apologies.

Nevertheless, she *was* still her boss.

Reluctantly, Amy picked up the phone.

'Hello?'

'Amy!' Carolyn boomed, shouting over the sound of revving engines, car horns and the busy street she must be walking down. 'Glad I've caught you.'

Here we go, Amy thought. She tried to remember a time when the words 'glad I've caught you', spoken by *anyone*, hadn't preceded something awful that she didn't want to hear.

'Oh?' Amy said. 'Why's that?'

'There's been an exciting development on the RomFest front,' Carolyn announced.

Amy's heart sank. 'Really?' she asked, one hundred per

cent sure that whatever Carolyn's announcement was, it was far more likely to infuriate than excite her.

'Yes! The marketing team here has come up with a wonderful wheeze – since Philippa's book is another hot historical tale, they've suggested launching her talk with a dance!'

'Er. What?'

'A dance! There's apparently a local troupe who specialise in old-fashioned country dances – the sort that any Regency heroine would have known. They've agreed to come along and perform, and to teach the festivalgoers a few moves.'

'But we're holding the festival outside, not in a ballroom,' Amy argued.

'Oh, pish,' Carolyn said. 'What does that matter? We'll set up an outdoor dance floor with the Hall in the background. They're cheap, it will look fabulous and it's not as though we're pushed for space.'

Amy closed her eyes in despair, trying to process what Carolyn was saying. The last thing she and Sam needed at this late stage was *another* element of the festival to organise, insure and oversee.

'Here's the best part,' Carolyn went on. 'You and young Mr Ainsworth, as hosts of the festival, will lead the first dance. Isn't that the most wonderful idea?'

At this, Amy felt her soul leave her body. Her dead-from-horror spirit stared down at her corporeal form, laughing heartily at its latest misfortune.

At a loss for anything else to say, Amy asked: 'Whose idea was it?'

'Ophelia's – our new intern. Such a brilliant thought.'

Amy silently seethed at the oblivious, miles-away Ophelia.

'Amy? Are you there?' Carolyn yelled down the phone. Below her voice but above the general din of the city, Amy could hear a street vendor bellowing something about ice creams.

'I'm here,' Amy said heavily. 'Are you sure about this,

Carolyn? It seems a bit of a stretch at this stage – there'll be a lot to sort out if it's going to work. Not least the fact that I can't dance. *At all.* We might be advised to . . . reconsider?'

Please, for the love of God, reconsider.

'Nonsense,' Carolyn insisted. 'I've already spoken to Sam. He said the same as you – that he's a terrible dancer. But you'll have help! I've organised a private lesson for the two of you, and made it clear we need the steps you learn to be simple. He was quite game about the whole thing, such a dear. So buck up, Amy – you know how I feel about negativity.'

Utterly wretched, Amy leaned forward and rested her forehead against the back of the seat in front of her. *Of course* Sam had sold her down the river by being polite and obliging. *Obviously* it was going to be left to her – the person whose livelihood depended on Carolyn – to make a tremendous, possibly career-ending fuss if she didn't want to dance with him.

At the same time, Amy found herself wondering: how long could a country dance really last, anyway? She cast her mind back to the Jane Austen film adaptations she'd seen. The pivotal, intense scenes where hero and heroine came together at whatever ball they attended were usually no more than about three minutes long. Was avoiding three minutes of awkward swaying – or *whatever* they were going to have to do – worth pissing off the person who (metaphorically at least) signed her pay cheques?

Resisting the urge to bang her head against the nearest available hard surface, Amy concluded it wasn't.

'OK, Carolyn,' she sighed. 'If Sam says he'll do the dance, I will too.'

'Marvellous,' Carolyn said. 'Excellent. I'll be in touch next week about getting you prepared. You've no need to worry, I'm assured you'll be in excellent hands – and this is just the sort of creative, unique touch that will get RomFest, and Philippa's book, talked about in all the right places. Online and off.'

Grudgingly, Amy had to agree – but she was feeling far too cross to say so out loud.

'I'm just on the way back from a lovely lunch with Philippa, actually,' she said instead. 'Something tells me she's going to love this idea when we share it with her.'

'Indeed.' Amy could hear Carolyn beaming down the phone; little made her happier than browbeating someone reluctant into doing what she believed – usually correctly – *needed* to be done. 'Yikes! I must dash,' she said then, presumably having checked her watch. 'I have a meeting in a few minutes.'

'Of course,' Amy said. 'Have a good evening. I'll speak to you next week.'

'Lovely,' Carolyn said. 'Oh! And Amy – one last thing.'

'Yes?' Amy asked, sure for once that there was nothing further Carolyn could say or do to make her situation worse.

'I forgot to mention the costumes. Of course, if you're doing a Regency-style performance, you'll need to be dressed appropriately: empire-line gown, satin dancing slippers, probably some sort of headdress.'

At the word 'costume', Amy felt her breath catch in her throat. 'Empire-line gown' had her heart racing, and by the time Carolyn reached 'headdress', Amy genuinely wondered whether she was having a stroke.

For some reason, however, all that came out of her mouth was, 'Right. OK then . . . Bye.'

Chapter 23

'Okay, explain this to me again,' Nisha said to Amy as they sat in the beer garden at the Old Oak on Sunday afternoon. 'You've got to dress up like someone from the olden days and do a dance in public? With her brother?' She waved a hand to indicate Meg, who was sat next to her at the table with a pint of cider in her hand. For some reason, even after months of knowing her, it still surprised Amy that the daughter of a Viscount drank pints.

She took a sip of her own white wine spritzer and nodded. 'That's pretty much it, yeah,' she said, trying to sound as though the prospect were merely a minor inconvenience and not a thing she couldn't stop thinking about: the reason why the shadows beneath her eyes had deepened and her skin kept turning hot, then cool and clammy. 'Embarrassing, right?'

'It sounds wonderful to me,' Nisha said dreamily. Amy scowled.

'And think about it,' Nisha went on, her natural practicality surfacing in spite of her doe-eyed expression. 'It could be a lot worse – your co-host could be an ageing minger with bad breath, BO and nostril hair. At least you're getting to dance with someone hot. If it were me getting ready to be swept up in the arms of a handsome man dressed up like Mr Darcy, I think I'd be coming over all unnecessary.' She flapped her hands at her neck and laughed.

Meg made a face and mock-shuddered at the idea of anyone being in sexual thrall to Sam. Amy groaned in faux disapproval and willed herself not to turn pink – or indeed, 'come over all unnecessary', at least not where anyone she knew might witness it.

'Come on, Meg, I know you share genes with him but you can still *see*,' Nisha said, her eyes dancing with mischief. 'He's objectively gorgeous. It's no surprise to me that the equally beautiful Ms Wexmore-Yates is sniffing around him again.'

Misery churned in Amy's gut. She pulled her phone out of her bag and pretended to read a text message, resolutely refusing to look interested.

'I don't think it's like that,' Meg said, taking a sip of her drink. 'She's been up and down from London a couple of times lately, but they've mostly been wandering around the grounds at the house. Don't quote me on this, obviously, but it seems like it's all business between them nowadays. No idea what the visits are in aid of, though.'

'*Interesting*,' Nisha said, turning her gaze on Amy. 'What do you think?'

'About what?' Amy asked, play-acting indifference but sounding stiffer than she'd intended.

'Sam and Tilly,' said Nisha, exasperated. 'Keep up.'

Amy's stomach already felt like it was swimming with bile, but she figured that alcohol couldn't make matters any worse – and anyway, she needed some sort of fortification if Nisha was going to insist on talking about this. She chugged what was left of her spritzer.

'I think,' Amy said carefully, 'that it's none of my business.'

'Hear, hear,' Meg said. 'I didn't come out on a rare afternoon of freedom to discuss who my brother may or may not be boffing.' Pearl had gone out for the day with her school friend Max and his family to celebrate the boy's eighth birthday – and Meg clearly intended to make the most of this opportunity for rest and relaxation.

'Having said that,' Amy went on, as her brain asked her mouth what the hell it thought it was doing. It was moving without permission, forming words she hadn't planned to say. 'Tilly *is* his type. They look like they . . . fit. They make sense together.'

God, she sounded almost *mournful*, even to her own

ears – like she was confronting a painful truth she'd been avoiding. Which, to be fair, she kind of was.

'At a very superficial level, maybe,' Meg said, sipping at her cider. 'But I was never convinced they'd go the distance. They always looked more like friends to me than anything else – she never seemed to get under his skin. It was all very polite and *nice* between them, from where I was standing.'

At this, Amy felt the other woman's eyes sweep her face as though inspecting it for clues. She didn't raise her gaze to Meg's for fear of inviting questions – or, if Nisha had anything to do with it, an *interrogation* – that she had no idea how to handle. However, this moment seemed to confirm that Meg understood more about the messiness between Amy and Sam than Amy had given her credit for.

'I'm only saying this because I'm on my second pint,' Meg went on. 'He'd *kill* me for it – but I think he's holding out for a great, passionate love, like the ones in Philippa's books. Or those A level texts you used to argue with him about, Amy. I never saw the debates first-hand, but some evenings he'd arrive home and I'd almost be able to see the steam coming out of his ears. He's had the same look about him more than once in the past couple of months – notably after your throwdown at the bake sale.'

Amy cringed and made a 'please, let's not' face, but she couldn't help feeling that Meg was making a point.

'Has working with him made you like him any better, Amy?' Nisha asked innocently, scooping a handful of dry-roasted peanuts from the open packet between them. 'You *did* manage not to murder him when you went up north for that trip – which was pretty impressive given you got stuck in the same room.'

She'd raised a single, perfectly threaded eyebrow – as if she had Amy bang to rights. In a cop drama, this would have been the moment when Nisha – grey-faced and knackered after a long night of sticking it to the accused – triumphantly announced, 'See you in court, sweetheart.'

Amy steeled herself, then said, 'I feel exactly the same about him now as I did when we were kids. No offence, Meg.' This response had the advantage of being both ambiguous and entirely truthful.

Nisha frowned, then sighed dramatically and said, 'Such a shame. He'd make a lovely boyfriend. Part of me wishes I could bring myself to become obsessed with Sam instead of Alex . . . But the heart wants what the heart wants.'

Amy sagged with relief at the change of topic, while Meg shook her head fondly at her friend. 'I keep telling you: just *ask him out*. For all you know he might be obsessed with you, too. At the very least I'm confident he fancies you – he pops in and out of the shop more than anyone else I know. I've bumped into him in there at least three times this week and *every time* he's been buying a litre bottle of orange juice. Nobody needs that much OJ, unless they have some pathological fear of developing scurvy.'

Amy laughed heartily at this. Then she felt a presence behind her, someone standing in the way of the sunlight so its glare was no longer focused on the back of her neck. The respite was welcome, even though she knew instinctively whose shadow she was suddenly basking in.

'Hey, Sam!' Nisha cried. 'We were literally just talking about you.'

'Oh?'

Amy twisted her body on the bench she was sitting on, curling herself around so she could examine the expression on his face: a wry eyebrow raise, its confidence undermined by the wariness Amy could see in the set of his mouth and jaw.

She chose to focus on this, rather than on his legs – almost entirely exposed in football shorts. Dimly, she remembered that he played for some local amateur team. She knew what Kit would say if he were here: *He has the face and hair of a young Robert Redford and the thighs of Jack Grealish. If you had any sense, you'd climb him like a tree.*

Amy shook herself, then tried to refocus on the conversation that was happening around her.

'Yes!' Nisha was saying. 'Amy was just telling us about this *super*-romantic dance you'll be doing together at the festival.' She shot Amy a mischievous look.

'Er – that is *not* how I described it,' Amy cut in, mortified. Her face was burning.

'I meant to text and speak to you about that,' Sam said to Amy, his voice low and confidential.

'Before or after you agreed to it, which meant *I* had to agree to it?' she asked him, her tone bright but biting. 'This is the second time I've been bounced into something because your insistence on being Mr Affable has prevented you from saying no to things you *absolutely* should have said no to.'

'In my defence, Carolyn was very clever this time,' Sam said. 'When she described the idea, she made it sound – without explicitly saying so – as if you'd been party to the discussions that preceded it. It was only after I agreed to go along with it that she revealed she hadn't so much as spoken to you. I'm sorry, I feel terrible about it.'

To her immense annoyance, Amy believed him. He looked thoroughly abashed, and the conversational ambush he'd described was classic Carolyn. Amy shook her head, resigned and almost amused. 'The woman is a viper in a Max Mara trouser suit,' she said. 'I've worked with her for over eight years and she still manages to blindside me on a weekly basis.'

Sam smiled slightly at her surprisingly generous – if tacit – acceptance of his apology. 'At least it's only one dance,' he shrugged, still visibly embarrassed. 'Are you able to do the practice session next week? Thursday, I think it is.'

'Yeah, I'm in the village on Thursday.'

'Okay, then.'

'D'you want to sit down? Have a drink?' Meg asked her brother, her eyes sliding from him to Amy and then back again.

'No. Thanks. Better not,' he said tightly.

Amy felt a brief throb of dismay, then reminded herself how

insistent she'd been during their row in the wood that they would 'never get on'; that she wanted nothing whatsoever to do with him unless contact were work-related and completely unavoidable.

'You're sure?' Meg said. 'Not even a celebratory half?'

'No.' Sam shook his head. 'I'll leave you to it – I wouldn't want to interrupt your afternoon.'

As he walked away, Meg and Nisha stared after him, then looked towards Amy.

'OK, the sun's still out but it feels to me like the temperature in the immediate vicinity of this table just dropped about ten degrees,' Nisha said. 'What's happened? I know you two aren't the best of friends, but that was *chilly*.'

'We had a pretty major disagreement,' Amy mumbled.

'About what?' Nisha demanded.

'Work stuff.'

'Right,' Nisha said, rolling her eyes. 'The tension zipping back and forth through the air just then was *totally* about which stand should go where on festival day, or where to direct cars for overflow parking.'

Amy ignored this and turned her attention to Meg. 'I'm sorry, by the way. I know it must be weird for you that Sam and I are like this.'

Meg shrugged. 'Not so much weird as frustrating,' she said. ''Twas ever thus.'

There were layers of meaning here that Amy chose not to sift through. Then she remembered that Meg had said something about celebrating, when she'd urged Sam to join them. What was *that* all about?

Unable to prevent herself, she said: 'What did you mean earlier, by the way? When you mentioned a celebratory drink?'

'He's been working with Jed to build a business plan for the pub and find investors,' Meg explained, 'and they've finally done it. The deal's set to be signed and sealed tomorrow morning, so Jed will remain as landlord here. Nothing will have to change for him even though the estate will no longer own the place. It's a huge relief.'

Amy felt the cogs and wheels of her brain stutter and seize. This news was the equivalent of a stick through spokes.

'What . . . When?' she asked, feeling her eyes begin to bulge and her throat tighten up. '*How?*'

'You'd have to ask Sam,' Meg said. 'As I understand it, though, the plans have been in motion since the day Dad said he intended to sell.'

Amy swallowed hard and tried to work out how she felt.

She'd written off Sam's regular presence at the Oak as indicative of nothing more than a fondness for craft beer, despite friends' and neighbours' insistence that he was trying to help Jed. She'd been wrong – and worse, she'd thrown that wrongness at him in anger during their row in the wood.

Why the fuck hadn't he told her? Defended himself?

An irritating inner voice asked Amy why he should have had to. If he'd been so fundamentally mistaken in her, would she have felt it was her job to correct him? No. She'd have been offended. Disappointed. *Hurt.*

Amy shut her eyes and shook her head, like she was hoping the pieces of this kaleidoscope would arrange themselves differently if she gave them the chance. When she looked around her again, nothing had changed. She still felt awful – sad, stupid and to her horror, ashamed.

She needed to say something. The silence that had fallen demanded to be filled before it began sucking in speculation. Nisha was eyeing her suspiciously, clearly on the verge of saying something that would doubtless be unguarded and incisive.

'I need another drink,' Amy announced. She indicated Meg and Nisha's glasses. 'Same again? Final round, and some snacks to soak it up?'

Her friends indicated their approval and she dashed inside before anything further could be said.

Behind the bar, Jed was beaming, his round face lit with

pleasure and relief. 'Did you hear, Amy?' he asked as he pulled Meg's pint. 'It's all sorted with the pub sale. I'm investing, along with some partners – so there'll be no need for Wetherspoons to swoop in and screw the place up after all.'

'Meg's just told me,' Amy said. 'It's brilliant news.'

Jed loaded their drinks onto a tray, then added a bowl of chilli crackers, a packet of salt and vinegar crisps and a dish of salted cashews.

'It's a bloody feat, is what it is,' he said as Amy tapped her debit card on the reader he'd presented to her. 'Never thought we'd get it sorted. Sam's been a diamond. From glass collector to business adviser! He's a good man.'

Amy shoved her card back inside her purse, then shouldered her bag and picked up the tray with care.

'He is,' she said, feeling utterly joyless but almost sure she meant it.

Chapter 24

Amy made her way to Rowton Hall on Thursday morning with a bilious, jittery stomach. Since Sunday afternoon, she'd carried the weight of her own misjudgement like an albatross around her neck; her own words kept coming back to torment her, each time bringing on painful, full-body winces.

It wasn't lost on her that, having been wrong about Sam's involvement with Jed and the pub, she might also have made other mistaken assumptions. She'd thrown accusations around like confetti that afternoon they'd argued in the rain – but what had they really been based on?

Tell me what's on your mind, or ask *me the question you want answered,* he'd said to her that night at the theatre. *I'd never lie to you.* Back then, those words had felt like an empty challenge – hollow phrases designed to wrong-foot or manipulate her into revealing herself, overplaying her hand. Now she did Sam the courtesy of considering whether they might have been sincere.

Amy had no blueprint for apologising to him – mainly because she couldn't recall ever having done it before. In itself, this suddenly struck her as problematic. It seemed unlikely that every single disagreement they'd ever had had been entirely his fault, mostly because there'd been so many of them.

Today, she *was* going to say sorry. She needed to admit to him that she'd misconstrued things and now knew better. She wanted to try and make amends.

Within seconds of arriving at the Hall, though, any thought of approaching Sam for a calm, honest heart-to-heart went up in smoke. From a distance, she could see he was deep in conversation with another man at the entrance to the walled garden – someone tall, dark and well dressed . . . Someone who, as Amy approached, she noticed looked remarkably like Hugh.

God in heaven, it *was* Hugh. What the hell was he doing here?

The closer Amy got, the more certain she became that their discussion was heated – and that Hugh was becoming increasingly aggressive. Sam was leaning back slightly with his arms folded across his chest: a posture that spoke of deliberate control, of deciding against all provocation not to square up to a fight. Several times he raised a defensive palm as though to try and calm Hugh's ranting, but apparently to little effect.

When Amy reached them, Hugh was snarling. 'You always were a snake in the grass – totally untrustworthy – never on the right side . . . I remember you informing on Henry Atkinson, doing your best to make sure he was suspended after that incident with the first-year's textbooks . . .'

Sam looked like he was trying not to laugh, which seemed to infuriate Hugh all the more. 'In what universe is *that* relevant?' Sam said. 'I'd forgotten Henry Atkinson even existed until you just brought him up – but for the record, he fully deserved a suspension. Drowning some kid's books in the toilet just for the fun of it . . . He was a merciless bastard, which I assume is why you stayed close to him. What's he doing with himself these days? No, don't tell me – let me guess: he's in prison for some white-collar crime he claims is victimless.'

'I believe he's a trader in the City,' Hugh spat pompously.

'The perfect springboard from which to leap for that custodial sentence,' Sam said.

Before Hugh could hit back, Amy interrupted.

'Er . . . What's going on here?' she asked tremulously. Part of her was amused by their exchange of old school resentments, but another part felt deeply unsettled. Hugh had no reason to be at Rowton Hall, and no professional pretext she could think of for verbally abusing Sam. Amy was no egotist, but it would have been stupid not to consider that she might have some unwitting role in this altercation.

'I decided to stop by and make sure Ainsworth here was aware of some key facts,' Hugh said, his ice-blue eyes flinty and dangerous.

'About what? *Why?*' Amy asked.

'About you and me, Amy,' said Hugh, 'because from what I hear his attentions towards you have not been strictly professional these past few months. *Apparently* he's been carrying a torch for you since he was sixteen – a rumour I'd have found touching if it weren't so pathetic.'

Amy's blood ran cold, oxygen replaced with fury.

'How dare you?' she said, her voice steady but sharp. 'There *is* no you and me, Hugh – there hasn't been for months. Who I see, in whatever capacity, is absolutely none of your business.'

'So you admit you're sleeping with him then?' Hugh said, an almost maniacal triumph on his face. This unexpected crudeness took Amy's breath away. She stared at him, appalled and humiliated.

'Don't speak to her like that,' Sam said, his voice a low rumble that indicated his hold on his temper was slipping. 'It's completely uncalled for.'

'And you're her knight in shining armour, are you? Funny – she was always the independent woman with me. Apart from the fact that she let me pay for everything.' He shot Amy a leer that made her insides lurch.

Had he been drinking? She didn't think so. Perhaps this was just the natural end point – the most extreme manifestation she'd yet seen – of what Kit had called Hugh's 'possessive psycho streak'. Maybe it had always been in him to lose control like this, to become so entitled and erratic, once he felt like he was losing her. Why hadn't she listened when Kit had warned her Hugh might not be the benign actor she'd always believed?

At the same time, it was almost alarming that it had taken him until now to go full bonkers ex-boyfriend on her. How had her move to the other side of the country, plus her rejection of his 'I'm sorry' gift and subsequent refusal to engage with him, not convinced Hugh their relationship was over? Then the truth dawned on her and she felt like throwing something at him: he had only believed his chances with her were completely dashed when he imagined she was seeing someone else. *That* implied a change of ownership, a transfer of assets. Unlike her fundamental right to spend time with whomever she pleased, this was something he actually understood.

'This is outrageous, Hugh. You need to come with me. *Now*. I'm sorry, Sam, truly. I am *mortified*. As soon as we've said our goodbyes, I'll be back to start the training session as planned.'

'I can't let you disappear off with him—' Sam started to say. Amy exhaled loudly and felt surprised she hadn't breathed out a jet of flame.

'Neither of you is *letting* me do anything,' she said. 'I'm going to escort Hugh to his car on the basis that he'd rather that than I call the police, tell them about his threatening behaviour and ask them to move him on. Then he's going to drive away.'

'You wouldn't do it,' Hugh hissed, but she knew him well enough to see his confidence was shaky.

'Try me,' Amy said, staring up at him stonily.

After a moment's hesitation, Hugh sloped away from Sam and walked around Amy so that he was leading the way. With evident reluctance, he moved in the direction of the Hall's sweeping driveway. His silver Audi was there, polished to perfection and glinting in the sunshine.

When they reached the car, Amy folded her arms. She was going nowhere until he'd unlocked it, climbed inside and had disappeared entirely from view. She stared at him defiantly, daring him to change his mind about leaving.

Narrowing his eyes at her, he clicked a button on a high-tech key fob and the vehicle's wing mirrors swung out into position. 'This isn't over, you know,' he drawled. 'I'm not losing you to *him*, of all people. I don't care if he's been lusting after you since you were teenagers.'

'You. Are. Deluded,' Amy said. 'You and I are *over*, for good. Nothing you say or do is going to change that.'

'You'll be back in London before too long,' Hugh said, appearing not to have heard her. 'This little passion project of Carolyn's is going to bite the dust before the end of the year – the second my arse hits the CEO's chair. You're sensible, not some sentimental fool. When the opportunity arises to head up the lit fic division of H-K, you'll take it – and you'll leave lover boy back here without so much as a second glance. The ice queen I know and love will return.'

Amy felt sick. 'You don't love me, Hugh – you never did. And I'm not an ice queen, as it turns out. I just didn't love you, either.'

'What's that song?' Hugh said, mock-frowning, clearly enjoying her discomfort – believing he had her number. '"What's Love Got To Do With It"? It could have been written for us.'

'Goodbye, Hugh,' Amy said, slamming the driver's side door on him the moment he'd clambered inside. Unperturbed, he rolled the window down.

'And by the way,' she yelled, his smug confidence finally fraying her temper, 'you're completely wrong about our theme song. Have a dig for the right one on Spotify, it'll be the perfect listen on your drive back down south: "We Are Never Ever Getting Back Together".'

Propelled by rage and mortification, Amy made her way back to the walled garden. She had no idea what she was going to say to Sam when she reached him, but she felt an irrepressible sense of urgency.

It was embarrassing beyond endurance that Hugh had accosted him in his own home on her account. She could hardly bear to wonder what had been said before she arrived, though it was clear that – via some mysterious means – Hugh had got wind of the fact that she and Sam had once been more to one another than colleagues or argument-prone neighbours. Unable to fathom where he might be getting his information from, she tucked the question away for further investigation later.

Now, her priority was apologising to Sam. It struck her that the list of things she needed to say sorry for kept getting longer.

She ran through an aged red-brick archway and into a pretty, well-ordered space that consisted of a central lawn bordered by shrubs, rose bushes and multicoloured dahlias. It had been agreed that this was the ideal spot for learning and practising the dance she and Sam were to perform; there was plenty of open space, and they'd be shielded from prying eyes while they endeavoured to get the steps right. It would also facilitate a fairly realistic dry run for festival day, when they'd be dancing out of doors – probably in warm sunshine and with a hum of ambient, distracting noise floating through the air.

She scanned all four corners of the garden and felt her heart sink as she realised Sam had disappeared. Had he gone back to the house? Should she follow him? Maybe he'd decided to call Carolyn's bluff after all and tell her this was a mad idea – that he wouldn't partake in it.

Just as Amy had made up her mind to head back to the Hall and look for him, she heard footsteps crunching up the gravel path outside. Then Sam's voice: 'Thanks for agreeing to come along and help us today. I think I speak for my partner, as well as myself, when I say we're both a little nervous – neither of us has ever done anything like this before.'

His *partner*. She knew he hadn't meant it the way it

sounded, but the word still made her insides twinge. It seemed she was going to have to put her apology on hold for now; Sam – sounding as calm and courteous as ever – was clearly showing their dance instructor to the appointed spot for the day's lesson.

Sam started when he and the man he was with strolled into the garden to discover Amy already there. She felt flustered – almost like she'd been caught somewhere she shouldn't be. This was ironic, she realised, since she'd spent plenty of evenings on Rowton Hall land without permission in her youth, never once worrying that her presence might be illegitimate.

'Hi,' she said. 'I just came straight back here . . . I thought that made sense?'

'Of course,' Sam replied. His voice was taut and strained. She realised that, for the first time since their reacquaintance, he was properly angry with her – not just feigning outrage for the sake of their usual banter.

'Walter, this is Amy,' he said to the man on his right. 'My colleague and dance partner.'

'Delighted to meet you,' Walter said, bobbing at her politely and offering her his hand. His accent was Northern, but softly so; Amy imagined he might come from Derbyshire or thereabouts.

He was a solidly built man of late middle age with a thatch of thick, longish salt-and-pepper hair and a neatly trimmed beard. He wore round glasses and a pair of slim, smart trousers, topped with a shirt and waistcoat. The aesthetic struck Amy as an unusual combination of modern hipster and nineteenth-century dandy, but it suited him. She shook his hand and said, 'You, too.'

'Well,' Walter said thoughtfully, looking from Amy back to Sam. 'You're a bit of an odd couple, but I'm sure we'll soon have you in sync.'

Amy accidentally barked a laugh at this. An *odd couple?* It was almost like Walter knew them.

'Oh, I'm sorry,' he said, slightly pink. 'I meant nothing untoward by that – it was really a reference to your height difference. Ordinarily I'd try to partner a petite lady such as yourself with someone less tall and broad. But it's not a problem, as such.'

'Of course,' Amy said, 'please don't worry, I shouldn't have laughed. And what you're saying makes a lot of sense, I suppose – though I guess finding a suitable partner for someone as short as I am might be difficult at the best of times.'

'Not at all,' Walter said gallantly. 'I could happily partner you myself, if I weren't tasked with teaching you both.' This was probably true; he was maybe only about five feet seven or eight, so far closer in height to Amy than Sam at six feet and then some. Walter winked at her and she caught Sam rolling his eyes in frustration.

'Should we . . . make a start?' Amy suggested, tentative. It was abundantly clear to her that, having been the more relaxed of the two of them up to now, Sam was fervently wishing they didn't have to do this.

'Yes! Let's,' Walter said. 'I'll work with you two on your own for a while, and then the troupe will come and join us later so we can make sure you're clear on how a group of couples navigate their way around the floor during this dance.'

From the leather holdall in his hand, he pulled a Bluetooth speaker and a mobile phone. 'Amazing to think that we can do this without so much as a plug socket, nowadays,' he said brightly. 'Your Georgian counterparts would have required an ensemble of live musicians!'

Sam nodded, shifting from foot to foot uncomfortably. Walter didn't notice.

'Now,' he said, 'the first thing to tell you is that we're going to be learning a Regency waltz. Since the dance showcase is intended to help launch what I understand is a *very* romantic book, I've hit upon this as the appropriate routine. Waltzes were a new fashion from around the 1790s, but were considered controversial for a time; the waltz is a sensual dance that allowed couples to get physically close to one another and maintain eye contact in a way that many others didn't.'

Amy glanced at Sam again. His focus was fixed firmly on Walter, implying a determination not to meet her eyes. Unease pricked at her skin and she sensed Hugh's performance this morning had pushed them across some Rubicon, though she was yet to understand exactly what or how.

'The second thing for me to explain,' Walter went on, 'is that you'll be dancing to a slightly slowed-down version of a famous piece, "Michael Turner's Waltz" – often used in period films. Reducing the tempo a little will make the steps easier for you to stay on top of. The third and final point to make is that this dance is simple, repetitive and just two minutes long – nothing to be scared of. So! Shall we begin?'

Amy and Sam both nodded and shuffled onto the flat, freshly trimmed lawn. Walter circled them, pushing them into closer proximity and arranging their heads and hands just so. Amy's heart fluttered in her chest but Sam still refused to look at her.

An experienced teacher, Walter broke the dance routine into digestible chunks that the novices could learn, then thread together. There were sections where they were required to step away from one another and then come back again, and others where they had to raise their hands elegantly until their palms almost touched, only to withdraw them. It was an uncanny reflection of the way things had been between her and Sam since April, Amy thought; that constant push and pull of arguments and attraction.

It was odd and awkward, being so close to him – being expected to operate in such physical harmony with him – with an onlooker present. Amy was grateful that remembering what her hands and feet should be doing prevented her from losing herself in the moment – in the scent that rolled off

Sam's skin when he swayed with her, or the delicate pressure of his fingertips when they held onto hers.

The routine peaked with Amy and Sam's hands joined, their left arms forming an arc above their heads and their right arms wrapped around one another's waists. She gazed up at him, willing him to meet her eyes. She sensed a reluctance in him that had been entirely absent at any other time they'd been this near one another: a rigidity and restraint that spoke of extreme unease. It hurt to see how little pleasure he took in touching her.

Walter seemed oblivious to Sam's disquiet. 'I take it back,' he said after an hour or so of instructing them. 'You two are an excellent pairing – not a classic match, physically, but you have wonderful chemistry. You'll be a pleasure to watch on the day.'

Amy cringed.

'Let's break for some lunch, shall we? Then you can work with the group this afternoon,' Walter said.

'That sounds good,' Sam concurred. 'I've organised some food for you – it'll be up on the terrace. Please excuse me, though, I have a few things to attend to before we continue with the training.'

His stiff formality made Amy want to scream. She'd always railed against what she called his 'man of the people' routine, and had even claimed she'd prefer it if he simply embraced his natural difference from normal people and held himself apart. Now, she discovered, the punctiliousness she'd always assumed was his birthright looked wrong on him – like a bad haircut or an ill-fitting suit. She didn't like it. It felt like he was wearing a costume, and she longed for him to take it off again.

Over a variety of salads and sandwiches, Amy made polite chit-chat with Walter and silently fretted. Sam didn't reappear until the rest of the dance group had arrived, explaining that he'd eaten in his office while dealing with some work that couldn't wait. Amy wondered what had been so vital, then reminded herself that *she* was the one who'd insisted they shouldn't socialise in any way. If he had lied about being needed elsewhere, it was arguably in deference to her wishes.

The second half of the training session passed more easily for Amy than the first – mainly because she and Sam were no longer the only ones dancing. Other couples now whirled around them, and everyone periodically switched partners in a logical routine that wasn't complex but required concentration. At the end of the day, Walter announced that he was thrilled with their progress. 'Once everyone's in appropriate dress, it'll look even better,' he said, smiling at Amy's skinny jeans, striped vest top and flats. 'This is going to be a real moment on the day.'

That's one way of putting it, Amy said to herself.

She hung back as Walter and the dance troupe said goodbye to Sam and made their way back to the RomFest car park – already set up in a field on the far side of the Hall.

The moment they were alone, she said: 'Sam, I just want to say again how sorry I am about this morning. I can't even begin to imagine what possessed Hugh – what made him think he had any right to come up here and start mouthing off—'

Sam interrupted her. 'I think it's pretty clear what possessed him. You did,' he said bluntly.

'Sorry?'

'You didn't think the fact that you'd been in a serious relationship with him was worth mentioning to me at any point?' Sam asked. 'He's been a full-on twat in every RomFest meeting he's attended. He's gone out of his way to be difficult, especially with me – he's questioned decisions and insisted on bureaucratic bullshit at every opportunity, and it's all been about *you*.'

Amy didn't appreciate Sam's accusatory tone. Yes, she'd been economical with the truth – but she wasn't responsible for Hugh being an arsehole. 'I think it's been a little bit about him, too,' she said defensively.

Sam threw her a withering look. 'I'm not suggesting that you've been directing him from backstage – but I'd say the fact that you jilted him has rather a lot to do with him losing his shit.'

'*Jilted* him?' Amy cried, astonished. 'Is that what he told you?'

'Yes. He says you led him on, allowed him to shower you with affection and then refused to marry him after strongly implying that you'd welcome a proposal.'

'Oh my *God*,' Amy said, through gritted teeth. 'That is *not* what happened.'

'Perhaps not quite,' Sam said, 'but the break-up *is* the reason you're back here, isn't it? According to him, you did a moonlight flit after you refused his proposal. He says it was a power play designed to make him chase you – to make him beg to have you back on whatever terms you wanted.'

He grimaced, obviously disgusted at the idea, then went on before Amy could gather her wits to explain herself. 'The fact that you said nothing about ever having so much as dated him, *and* the fact that the role you accepted up here is hardly your dream job . . . Well. It all makes me wonder if he's right.'

Amy felt as if she was drowning. She was sinking under the weight of this absurd nonsense, yet was unable to shrug it off and come up for air because it sounded horribly plausible.

'He's a fantasist!' Amy yelled, almost desperately. 'I've done my best to completely ignore him since coming back to Rowton – I certainly didn't come here with any intention of provoking him to follow me. Trust me, that's the last thing I wanted. And honestly, I can't believe you'd give his version of events the time of day! You can't seriously think I'm the sort of person who'd behave like that?'

'It's shit, isn't it?' Sam said fiercely. 'Having someone think the worst of you when the evidence they have to go on is so flimsy – when their judgement's clearly impaired by their own preconceptions.'

His eyes had lost the guarded look they'd worn for most of the day. Their chocolate-coloured irises blazed with heat, and Amy quailed as he looked at her.

'Maybe you are *that sort of person*,' said Sam bitterly. 'Maybe you always were. Maybe this is the second time you've messed around with my feelings to achieve some end I never understood.'

'What?' Amy shouted, her fury swelling. 'Me, mess around with *your* feelings? That's . . .' She struggled, completely at a loss – unable to fully process the irony of this idea. 'That's *ridiculous*.'

'Is it? You've blown hot and cold with me constantly since coming home. One day everything's fine between us – we're practically kissing in my office – and then the next it's like you've remembered you're contractually obliged to hate me. I should have known better than to get swept up in all this again.'

He looked desolate – his shoulders slack and his head hanging low.

'All what?' Amy yelled, staring at him in disbelief.

'All *this!*' Sam bellowed, gesturing wildly at the two of them, then at the gap between their bodies. 'Please. *Don't* do me the discourtesy of pretending you don't know what I'm talking about.'

'I certainly don't know what you're referring to when you say I've messed around with your feelings deliberately, that I have *form* for it,' Amy said angrily. 'If I've struggled to understand a few things – to get some information straight over the past few months – then I'm sorry. But I've never, in my whole life, set out to toy with anyone's emotions on purpose.'

'What about Hari's?' Sam demanded.

'Oh my God,' Amy breathed, glancing up at the sky as if pleading for divine intervention. 'What the *fuck* has Hari got to do with anything? Why are you bringing him into this? It's painful and unnecessary.'

'I always wondered whether you kissed me that night for the sake of making him jealous,' Sam said simply. 'If your charming ex is to be believed, teenage me might have been on to something.'

Amy's voice died in her throat. She couldn't form words, let alone sentences.

'You didn't tell Hari about us,' Sam went on. 'You said you would but I know you didn't. Were you going to let him just see us together at Mike's party? Wind him up a bit so he'd finally tell you himself how he felt?'

He sighed, holding his head in his hands and clawing at his dark gold hair. 'I should have told him the truth. My best friend died not knowing I'd betrayed him by trying to steal the girl he was in love with. The girl that I was *also*, very inconveniently, in love with.'

Amy's eyes had grown so wide she worried they might fall out of her head. She was enraged, elated and completely confused.

'*You* kissed *me* that night,' she said after what felt like a lifetime of silence. 'Don't you think that pokes rather a large hole in this theory of me as some kind of arch manipulator?'

It was a good point, but it was incomplete – a half-truth. Even now she couldn't bring herself to be honest: to say that while he had initiated the kissing, she'd been desperate for him to do so.

'I know that,' Sam said wearily. 'But this is what you do, isn't it? Get so far beneath people's skin that they can't *not* kiss you. Or follow you halfway up the country.'

Fleetingly, Amy was reminded of what Meg had said the previous Sunday – her implication that Sam needed, *wanted* someone who was capable of moving him like this.

'And what about what you do? Or *don't* do?' she said. 'You dropped me like a stone after Hari died! It was like . . . like you couldn't be arsed with me when I was grieving. You only wanted sparky Amy, not sad Amy – or at the very least you wanted stiff upper-lipped Amy. I saw you actually *hide* from me once, you know – duck behind a wall so you wouldn't have to face me.'

She was shouting at him now, tearful and angry and out of control. 'Have you any idea how it felt? To have let myself get close to you that night – to have let myself open up – and then to be *ignored*? To be reduced, again, to being the geeky girl the village golden boy wasn't interested in . . . and to have lost my best – my *only* – friend too?'

'That's not how I remember things, Amy,' Sam put in. 'You were grief-stricken over Hari, and seeing the depth of your sorrow *broke* me. It proved beyond all doubt that he was the one you really wanted – just like everyone had always said. On top of that, I missed him myself *and* I'd betrayed him days before he died. I was eaten up with guilt. And never, not once, did you try to contact me. I'd put my cards on the table! I'd told you I had feelings for you. You said nothing. Even when Hari died, you said *nothing*.'

Amy felt like she'd been backed into a very tight corner – the same one Philippa had hinted might be worth exploring during their lunch date. Now she was there, though, she wanted out.

'What did you want me to say?!' she demanded, irate. 'That you were the centre of my universe? That I couldn't live without you? Did you need me to join your official fan club, like all the other girls in our year group, wear an "I Heart Sam" T-shirt under my clothes?'

None of what she'd said was remotely reasonable or anywhere close to fair, and Amy knew it. Baiting Sam like this, especially now, was beneath her. What he'd wanted was some basic assurance that she cared about him, and she hadn't been able to give it. She was struck by how stupid this was, given that she *had* cared about him. Given that she did.

Amy stepped towards him, not sure what she intended to do but knowing she had to come up with something.

'Don't, Amy,' Sam said, backing away. 'It's clear you think I'm some shallow, emotionless wanker who lives for adulation from anyone who'll offer it. I had hoped . . . I *had* hoped that over the past few months you'd come to realise I'm an actual person – not some privileged, shallow cipher with no feelings.'

Amy gaped at him, wishing she could rewind the conversation to the point where he said he'd been in love with her. It felt very far away now. Untouchable.

'Do you know what really kills me?' Sam said. 'It's that you've spent all the time we've known one another sniping at me for being rich – for being posh and not belonging in the real world. But who do you choose to live with, to almost *marry*? Some guy who, granted, doesn't have a title, but who I can assure you has a lot more cash in the bank than I do. A man with a family rather like mine, who even went to my school – and who, from what I can see, embodies the sort of snobbery, selfishness and superiority you always said you hated.'

All of this was factual. Incontrovertible. It was like a truth bomb had detonated, exploding every excuse she'd ever invented for disliking Sam – consuming the whole lot in a mushroom cloud, vaporising more than a decade's worth of pretence and obfuscations.

'You're a hypocrite, Amy,' Sam said, although he didn't need to. 'It wasn't my background you didn't like, it was just me. I finally understand that.'

She opened her mouth to protest, but once again words failed her.

'Once this infernal event is over with,' he murmured as he began to walk away, 'I promise you'll be rid of me for good.'

Chapter 25

Alone in the garden, Amy sank onto the lawn and put her head between her knees. Not sure whether she wanted to cry or scream, she found herself unable to do either. It was a while before she could think straight, or even move.

She'd spent years resenting Sam for ignoring her after Hari's accident – years nursing heartbreak at his supposed abandonment of her. She'd believed he lost interest in her the moment their stolen kisses and witty repartee seemed set to be replaced by weeping and chaste hand-holding at their mutual friend's funeral. She was stunned that, in fact, Sam had been tormented by his own grief, plus a sense of guilt that even now he had no idea was utterly misplaced.

At last she realised that he'd kept his distance from her not because he didn't care, but because he *did* – because it hurt him to see her in shreds over someone else. No doubt he'd thought trying to rekindle things with Amy would be a further insult to Hari's memory . . . Maybe he'd even felt trying to start something romantic with her while she was grief-stricken would amount to taking advantage.

Suddenly, she could see teenage Sam's motivations clearly – and not only did she understand them, she respected them. His diffidence had come from a good place: from wanting to honour a friendship he'd lost, and a determination to avoid muddying the waters for Amy, whose affections he was sure had all been for Hari.

That he'd been mistaken was as much her fault as his. Sam was right when he said he'd told her he had feelings for her but she hadn't said anything back. She'd been too afraid to verbalise the enormous, unruly emotions he provoked in her. She'd assumed that simply kissing him back would be enough.

Her perception of him as confident, privileged and popular had blinkered her to the reality that, in love, he could be just as vulnerable as anyone else. Worse than that, she'd used her inverted snobbery as cover for dismissing any notion that there might be more to him than met the eye. His background, which he hadn't chosen, had become Amy's pretext for convincing herself he was cold, selfish and shallow.

She lifted her head at the sound of a phone ringing. Hers. When she fished it out of her bag, she saw Kit was calling her.

'Hey,' she said thickly, 'what's up?'

She expected him to ask *her* what was up immediately, based solely on the weepiness he'd easily detect in her voice. But he didn't.

'I have news!' Kit gushed. 'BIG news!'

Amy tried to muster the enthusiasm that was clearly required for hearing it. 'Really? Come on then, spill.'

'Julius has asked me to move in with him – and I've said yes!'

'Wow,' Amy said, staggered. 'Like . . . wow. That's major. Are you sure you're ready?'

'I was born ready,' Kit said. 'He's the *one*, Amy – I've never felt like this about anyone before. I never believed I was capable! It's like he's rearranged me inside: feng shui'd my organs so that everything makes more sense. The connection we have, it's – it's like we were designed to fit together even though we're nothing alike. I'd trust him with my life. We want to take care of each other . . . and at the same time, I want to hump him every single chance I get.'

'But . . . it's quite early days for you, isn't it?' she asked gently. 'Aren't you a bit concerned you're rushing into this? I'm only asking because it feels risky to jump in with both feet after just a few months.'

'Oh, Amy, I might have known you'd be all sensible,' Kit said fondly. 'But please don't piss on my chips. I promise you, I've thought about this properly. Relationships always involve risk – you have to put yourself on the line to make them real. Julius put himself on the line by asking me to be with him and now it's my turn. It's what I want. When someone's right for you, you know it in your bones – and this is it for me, forever.'

Amy nodded, moved by his readiness to lay himself open for the person he loved.

'So you'll be moving to his place, then?' Amy asked. 'Whereabouts?' She assumed some leafy, affluent part of north London – probably not too far from where Kit lived now.

'Brighton!' Kit said. 'Can you *even?!*'

'BRIGHTON?' Amy near shouted. 'You're going to live in Brighton? You're leaving London?'

Her heart sank at the realisation that this meant she'd have no one in the city to go back to, should she decide to move again – unless she counted Hugh, which she very much did *not*.

'Yes,' said Kit, sounding vaguely annoyed. 'Julius works there, he owns a flat there and it's lovely! London's been pretty dull the past few months, to be honest, and I feel like I've done my time here. I can combine working remotely for H-K with coming into the office a few times a week – it's all squared away.'

'I thought you said Julius was an economist,' Amy said. 'Doesn't that mean he's based at some big, swanky bank in the City?'

'He *is* an economist,' Kit explained. 'But he's a professor at the university.'

'Right,' Amy said, realising she needed to sound much cheerier about all this if she wasn't going to upset him. 'A prof. Impressive. Well, I hope you'll be willing to welcome a regular house guest once you're settled in. I love the sea, but Rowton's about the most landlocked place in the whole country – slap bang in the middle.'

'Of course!' Kit said. 'I can't wait for you to come and see us, and meet Julius. You'll love him and he'll love you – of that I've no doubt.'

'Thanks,' she said. 'When's the big move happening?'

'Well, we've already started ferrying stuff down there. I'm expecting to be all moved in by RomFest – which I cannot wait for, by the way.'

'*Amazing*,' Amy said, glad she was managing to sound pleased for him. 'I'm really looking forward to seeing you, too.'

For a second, she considered telling Kit what had happened between her and Sam: all of it, the whole story, not just what had occurred in the previous few hours. It now struck her as significant that she'd been so determined not to before. In hiding how she'd once felt about Sam from her friend, she'd also been trying to hide it from herself.

However, she didn't – as Kit so delicately put it – want to piss on his chips. He was happy, in a celebratory mood, and she had no desire to bring him down.

'Listen, I've got to go,' Kit said. 'We're going to a roof terrace spot for dinner and I'm desperate for a shower . . . Is it hot up there, too? At least having a proper summer for once makes the Tube torture worth it.'

'Yeah, really warm,' Amy said. 'It's nice, though. Wait until you see the village in full bloom.'

'Oooh,' Kit said. 'Can't wait. I'll be in touch before but SEE YOU SOON! I'll be up the night before RomFest, but you know that already.'

'Great,' Amy said. 'And Kit? Just in case I forgot to say it before, I'm really happy for you. Really.'

'You did forget, but I know you are,' he said, and she could hear his grin all the way from the capital. 'Love you. Ciao for now!'

Chapter 26

'Amy, I know you're not crazy about doing this dance, but could you at least try to look a bit less miserable?' Nisha said on the morning of their planned trip to a period costume shop in Burton-on-Trent. 'I'm very excited about dressing you up in an early nineteenth-century gown and you're going to *ruin* it for me!'

Meg snorted from the back seat of Nisha's Ford Fiesta. 'I think what Nish *meant* to say there is are you okay, Amy. Because . . . well. Are you?'

'No,' Amy said baldly. She'd lost the will to pretend that she was fine; holding her feelings in tended to have what could only be described as mixed results, and it took effort to appear contented when she actually felt like crap. 'I'm about as not okay as I've ever been, actually.'

The combined effect of Kit's revelation and her showdown with Sam after their dance lesson had seen Amy sink into the bleakest mood she'd suffered since coming back to Rowton. She continually harked back to what Ken had said on that tearful morning in the hospital corridor: *falling in love is a game of chance, but being willing to play it is key.* Had Amy ever been willing?

Even at sixteen, when Sam Ainsworth had first appeared at college in a golden haze of charm and adulation, she'd shut down every inclination to desire him the way that others did. That blanket ban on feeling bewitched by him had lasted an impressive eighteen months in the face of daily temptation.

Later, every proper boyfriend she'd ever had had been carefully selected for their good looks, good conversation and good prospects – never because they did squiffy things to her stomach or made her blood feel like lava. She'd even chosen more casual partners forensically, picking people she knew she would never get emotionally attached to for brief flings that could be easily forgotten.

She'd been so closed off – so scared to make herself vulnerable – that when she and Sam crossed paths again, she'd embraced every reason she could come up with not to let herself feel the effect of being near him. She'd tried to ignore what he did to her, erecting as many walls as possible around her heart – no matter how flimsy the foundations they were built on.

'Are you worried about doing the big dance with Uncle Sam?' Pearl asked from next to Meg, bringing Amy back to the present. 'I'm sure he'll catch you if you fall over, he's quite strong.'

Pained, Amy closed her eyes and nodded. The seven-year-old hadn't meant this as a metaphor, but it had nevertheless sounded like a rather appealing one.

Today's road trip from Rowton to the costume emporium hadn't been Amy's idea – but the moment Nisha had heard there was a need for proper Regency attire, it was decided that its acquisition would become an event. Meg and Pearl were just as enthusiastic at the prospect of poring over reproduction fans, jewellery and dresses when Nisha had described the shop they were travelling to and showed them the website. After railroading Amy into a group afternoon out, during which she'd doubtless be prodded and pulled around like the 'spooky doll girl' she'd once been called, Nisha had offered to drive, and treat them all to pizza when they got home.

'Don't worry about everyone watching you,' Pearl went on sagely. 'You'll look lovely. Me and Uncle Sam think you're the prettiest person we know – he told me *he* thinks you look like Snow White, too.'

'Shhh,' Meg laughed, and poked her daughter. 'You mustn't go around telling other people's secrets, Pearl. If someone shares a confidence with you, you should keep it.'

In the rear-view mirror, Amy saw Pearl scrunch up her nose. 'Even if it's about someone *liking* someone else? That seems silly. Isn't it always good to hear someone likes you? Why not just tell the truth?'

'Out of the mouths of babes!' Meg said brightly, glancing at Amy and catching her eye.

'Indeed,' Amy said.

When did people grow out of Pearl's way of thinking, she wondered. In Amy's case, it was probably when she realised how much losing Lily had hurt her father. Somehow, in Amy's head, there'd been a conflating of John's occasional melancholy moments with his consumption of romances in all their forms. They'd become something frightening and destructive to Amy: misrepresentations that inspired you to want people and things you couldn't have in real life. That was the lesson Amy had learned, though she was sure now that her father hadn't meant for her to. And was it really one to live by?

After a ninety-minute journey they arrived outside Copthorne's: The Costumier, located on the old high street. It was set in a tall Georgian building – much like the ones in Rowton – made of red bricks that stretched three storeys high. The shopfront was painted a vibrant buttercup yellow, with the name of the store spelled out in gold and black letters above the door. Nisha clapped her hands. 'This looks like heaven!' she cried, pointing at the mannequins visible through the window. All were dressed in the sort of clothes Philippa Fotheringham was adept at depicting in her novels – usually right before she described their frenzied removal.

Inside, a woman who introduced herself as 'Mrs Thomasina Copthorne' greeted them. Dressed from head to toe in her own stock, she was stout, smiley and seemed entirely comfortable in her outlandish outfit: a shiny silk gown in deepest purple, bejewelled slippers and a feather headdress that added at least four inches to her already considerable height.

'Is it yourself, in need of a costume?' Thomasina asked, nodding her head towards Meg. 'When I spoke to whoever called me on the phone, I understood it was just one dress you were after, plus accessories.'

'That's right,' Meg said. 'But it was probably Nisha you spoke to, and it's Amy here who needs the outfit.' Meg gestured at her companions, then added: 'I believe my brother has been to see you, though. He's Amy's dance partner.'

'Pity,' Thomasina said, still focused on Meg. 'You have the right look for these Napoleonic-era gowns: peachy skin, ample bosom, graceful figure.' She turned to Amy. 'Your man's tall, isn't he? You're rather on the petite side, so it's an unconventional pairing . . . And we might find your dress options a little limited, too.'

Amy found herself liking Thomasina less by the second. 'Sorry to disappoint,' she said, as her heart hammered painfully at the costumier's reference to 'your man'.

'Nonsense,' crowed Thomasina, clapping her hands briskly. 'We'll find you something. It just might take a little longer.'

Amy stifled a groan as the woman looked her up and down, appraising her with the keen eye of the professional. She began pulling scraps of silk and linen from drawers – stockings and undergarments of types that Amy didn't recognise – then retreated upstairs to find some shorter-than-average gowns for her to try.

Just over a quarter of an hour later, Amy was transformed: Thomasina had coaxed her into a linen shift, around which she'd fastened traditional stays. Unlike her modern, wireless bras, the stays pushed Amy's modest breasts up and together in a manner that felt like it should be X-rated. Thomasina, however, was not interested in Amy's embarrassment, and proceeded to throw the first of several dresses over her head for inspection. With a gulp, Amy left the changing room to face her audience for the first time.

The stunned silence she met with convinced her that this gown was *not* today's winner. Made of shiny silk, it was as stiff as a board – the fabric so thick that Amy could barely move in it. Thomasina announced that it was a shade of period-appropriate 'old gold', but to Amy's eye the dress was simply orange: bright, eye-watering, borderline toxic *orange*.

'You look . . .' Meg began, evidently trying to find something positive to say. Next to her, Nisha stifled a giggle.

'I know!' Pearl cried. 'I know what that dress looks like – one of those sweets. You know, the ones Grandma and Grandpa have at Christmas time. The ones in the big purple tin.'

No longer in control of herself, Nisha guffawed and hid her face behind one of the scatter cushions that had been helpfully placed on the couch beneath them.

Meg bit her lip. 'I think you mean Quality Street,' she said in a strangled sort of voice, before snorting and allowing a fit of the giggles to overtake her.

'*Great*,' Amy said, placing her hands on her hips.

Nisha laughed harder. 'That's made it worse!' she shrieked. 'The sleeves look like the ends of the sweet wrapper! Oh God, Meg, which one is it that she looks like? It's doing my head in.'

Gasping for breath, Meg managed: 'I think it's the toffee penny.'

'Marvellous,' Amy hissed. 'I look like confectionery, and not even *good* confectionery. Everyone knows the only Quality Streets worth bothering with are the soft centres!'

Pearl had folded her arms, clearly disapproving of her mother and Nisha's behaviour.

To Amy's intense relief, Thomasina decided this was the moment to intervene. 'I think we should try another. Amy, let's go back into the dressing room.' Amy was only too glad to oblige.

The next gown was less ridiculous, but still not right.

'You look like a princess!' Pearl said when she saw her, while Nisha and Meg – fully recovered from their meltdown – ooohed and aaahed their approval.

'You don't look comfortable, though,' Meg said.

'I think it's too showy,' Amy agreed, gesturing at the chartreuse silk gown she had on. 'Too "look at me". This is an outdoor country dance, not a formal ballroom situation . . . And I don't want to stick out too much – especially as there's a real chance I'm going to put more than one foot wrong during the performance.'

Meg nodded. 'I think I agree. Too loud. Next one!'

'I wish we'd brought popcorn,' Nisha giggled.

The next dress was made of a creamy cotton muslin, spotted with pale pink flowers and trimmed with pink ribbon. 'It's beautiful,' Nisha said, 'but I think it's too pale. It doesn't do much for your complexion.'

'She's right,' Thomasina said, 'which means we should also discount these two here. Try the blue, and if that's no good I'll raid the children's section and see what we've got.'

The children's section? Every time Amy thought RomFest couldn't hammer her self-respect any harder, she discovered she was wrong.

She pulled the sky-blue gown over her head and prayed for it to a) fit, and b) not look terrible. It was made of a floaty georgette silk – a lighter-than-air sort of fabric that slipped easily through her fingers and seemed designed to make the wearer's movements look more graceful. The empire waist was dressed with a strip of simple cream lace, as were the edges of its short, slightly puffed sleeves. It had a low, square neckline that strongly hinted at a more impressive bosom than Amy had ever previously suspected she could boast – but the elegance of the dress undercut her fear of looking like one of the 'ladies of the night' from Philippa's books.

'Oh my *life*,' Nisha said when Amy emerged from the fitting room. She flapped her hands at her face. 'I think I'm going to cry!'

Amy reddened. 'Calm down, Nish, we're not choosing my wedding gown here.'

'Oh! I wish you were,' Pearl said dreamily. 'I think it

would make Uncle Sam very happy to marry you. And you look so beautiful.'

'You do look lovely,' Meg concurred, neatly ignoring this reference to her older brother so as not to prompt more gushing. 'That's the one, Amy. It makes your eyes bluer than I've ever seen them. It's stunning.'

A short while later, Amy had selected a pair of dancing shoes, a simple necklace of seed pearls and – at Nisha's insistence – a headdress. She'd point-blank refused anything involving feathers or flowers, opting instead for a band with cream ribbon that could be woven artfully through an updo.

'*I'll* do your hair on the day, Amy,' Nisha announced, evidently not prepared to trust Amy with such a vitally important task.

'Good,' Amy said. 'I'm useless at anything other than putting a wave in it with the GHDs.'

Thomasina rang up Amy's bill. 'I told you we'd sort you out,' she said smugly. 'You'll look wonderful. Send me some photos, would you?'

Grateful for her help, Amy promised she would – and that she'd make sure the shop was tagged in some social media posts.

The four of them arrived back in Rowton tired but a little giddy after their adventure. They headed to Meg's tiny two-up, two-down cottage and hunkered down in front of the TV with cold glasses of orange cordial. It was already past Pearl's usual dinner time, so Nisha ordered a pile of pizzas and sides from the Italian in the next village. Before long, they were tucking into huge slices of quattro formaggi, chunks of fried courgette and breaded mozzarella sticks with Pearl's latest Disney obsession, *Turning Red*, on the TV.

To Amy's amusement, Pearl fell asleep before the end of the movie – her head resting on Nisha, who had also drifted off.

'Bless her. It's been a busy day,' Meg cooed.

'It has. She's a lovely kid, Meg,' said Amy.

Meg laughed under her breath. 'I meant Nish.'

Amy stifled a hoot, realising this was the first time in days she'd felt so light.

'She's lovely, too,' Amy said, smiling. 'An absolute force, but lovely.'

'I hoped I'd get a chance to say this away from eager ears,' Meg said, suddenly conspiratorial, 'so I'll take this one. I'm sorry Pearl was so . . . indiscreet earlier. About Sam. I hope it didn't make you uncomfortable.'

'No more so than I was already,' Amy sighed.

Meg nodded. 'I gather there's been some argument. Worse than usual?' She arched an eyebrow, and Amy knew she was trying to add levity to a conversation that already felt fraught.

'There were some harsh words, some home truths . . .' Amy pressed her fingertips to her forehead and groaned. 'I think I've misunderstood a lot of things over the past few months – not to mention back when we were teenagers.'

'I always believed that something had happened between you that summer,' Meg said, in a way that made clear she wasn't digging for gossip. 'He never said anything, but it was obvious even though I was so much younger. He was devastated when Hari died, but losing you as well . . . His heart was broken, I think. My parents insisted he go travelling – pull himself together, get a fresh perspective . . . It was a disaster. He ended up in a Thai hospital with alcohol poisoning. He was seriously unwell.'

'Oh my God,' Amy breathed. Her heart contracted painfully at the thought of Sam so sick and so far from home. 'I had no idea.'

'Why would you?' Meg said kindly. 'I don't really know why I'm telling you all this, except it seems to me there's something between you even now. He's been different these past few months – more alive than I've seen him in a long while, as well as more prone to tearing his own hair out. And Pearl is *never* wrong, especially not when it comes to her Uncle Sam. If she thinks he's in love with you, there's a very decent chance it's true.'

'Oh, Meg,' Amy said, her chest suddenly heavy and her eyes prickling with tears. 'I've fucked up so badly. Made so many mistakes – assumed I knew all I needed to about what he was doing and why without ever just *asking* him. And I know what my problem is: if I'd asked questions, straight up, it would have seemed as if I cared about the answers. I've always been so terrified of letting that show.' Her voice cracked and she took a breath, then swallowed back a sob.

'Amy, I'm going to be honest here,' Meg said. 'I think that – for some of us at least – it *already* shows.'

'What's my tell?' Amy asked, grimacing, but appreciating Meg's attempt at humour.

'Well. For a start there was that tussle at the bake sale. Fisticuffs on Old Rowton high street over an oat and raisin cookie? After that, I think it was all of five minutes before someone first muttered "there's a thin line between love and hate". Much to Simon's dismay, naturally.'

'Oh,' Amy said, crestfallen. At that point, she hadn't even known *herself* how she felt.

'Can I ask you something?' she went on. 'I think I already know the answer, but I'd like to be sure. RomFest – Sam's involvement in it – it's personal, isn't it? It's his money he's investing, not the estate's.' Amy couldn't put her finger on precisely when she'd come to this realisation; it was as if it had always been there, sitting just beneath the surface of her consciousness, waiting for her to notice and raise it up.

Meg nodded her head, looking torn. Amy could tell she was breaking her word to Sam even by confirming what Amy had already figured out.

'And the plan is to put the profits back into the estate, right?' Amy continued. 'Even though that's not where the capital came from. It's to save the houses that were going to be sold. Prevent Barbara and Dave, and the other affected villagers, from having to move. Isn't it?'

'That's about right, yes,' Meg said reluctantly. 'Sam managed to convince my father to let him trial letting out the grounds at his own risk, on the basis that he'd stump up some cash for renovations if it worked. The money Sam's put into RomFest is his inheritance from our maternal grandparents. I spent my share on this cottage. The pub deal has helped with saving the houses, too – it means there's a bit more cash sloshing around for my parents, at least for now, and you know that's all they care about.'

Amy shook her head in disapproval she didn't bother trying to hide, then went on. 'And . . . when Sam talks about preserving the Hall – he doesn't mean that in the same way your parents do, does he?'

Again, Meg looked strained at having to confirm or deny Amy's speculations. 'No. It's a question of not letting the place fall apart, rather than having any desire to live in it. He and I obviously talk about it, and I know he'll involve me in any decision he makes even though he won't technically *have* to as sole heir . . . It may be that we can open up the house to tourists and keep a wing for the family; it may be that the whole thing goes into state ownership. But he doesn't want it to crumble away to nothing – neither of us does. It's a beautiful building. It shouldn't be rotting in private when it could be enjoyed by the public. But Amy,' Meg said seriously, 'you should talk to Sam about all this.'

'You're right,' Amy said. 'I do need to talk to him – about a lot of things, though I've no idea how or where to start. All this stuff, though. About the Hall, the estate, Barb and Dave's house . . . About whether Sam's intentions were good . . . I should have ignored my stupid, misguided assumptions and listened to what my gut – my *heart* – has been trying to tell me all along. I should never have needed to ask.'

Chapter 27

While there was no longer any question over Amy's feelings towards Sam – she had finally accepted she was full-on, crazy-obsessed, *epically* in love with him, and probably always had been – several other mysteries remained.

The first was why, if Sam had feelings for Amy, Tilly had been seen coming and going from the Hall so often lately. The idea that they'd simply been enjoying a casual fling for old times' sake made Amy feel sick, her jealousy so strong she worried it might corrode her stomach lining. It also tarnished Sam's halo somewhat, though Amy was loath to admit it.

The second mystery was how on earth Hugh had discovered Amy and Sam had previously been entangled. The list of likely informants wasn't long – in fact, the only person Amy could think of who had something resembling the full Sam and Amy story was Meg, and there was no way she'd shared it on the sly.

Thoughts of Hugh inevitably brought Amy back to the thorny issue of her ongoing employment at H-K. It was now clear to her that leaving London to set up a sub-office in a different part of the country hadn't put enough distance between the two of them – that in all likelihood, she was going to have to move on. The injustice of this stung her, and her gorge rose every time she imagined giving up the position she'd worked so hard for, because the alternative was never knowing what dick move Hugh might pull next. She couldn't trust him to let her go with grace, not because he particularly cared about her but because he resented her agency over her own life – her refusal to fall in with his plans. As Nisha might have said, the situation 'sucked hard' – but there was no point in complaining about how unfair it all was.

For what must have been the thousandth time, Amy cursed herself for getting involved with a man so strongly and inextricably connected to the firm that the end of their relationship could only ever mean her exiting it altogether. More than anything, she was gutted at the prospect of saying goodbye to Torch: an imprint she'd set up from nothing with a list of authors she'd hand-picked for their talent, tenacity and capacity to entertain. For all her initial reluctance to take on the project, she was proud of it and deeply reluctant to give it up – and the writers she'd forged relationships with.

Amy's most recent conversation with Carolyn had been uncomfortable: a one-to-one during which Amy described Hugh's demented performance at Rowton Hall and explained that, post-RomFest, she would have to begin searching for another job. Amy was open to roles in a variety of locations, and said she hoped Carolyn could see her reasons for needing to leave.

Carolyn, in typically clipped and unemotional style, had said, 'I understand. But I strongly suggest you do nothing further until you and I have spoken again on this subject – forces you're unaware of are in flux, and might well solve your problem. Under no circumstances will I accept your notice, and you must *not* try to hand your resignation to anyone else.' Amy had no idea what Carolyn was up to. Nor was she inclined to try and find out. However, she agreed not to contact any recruiters immediately – not least because with RomFest so close, she didn't have the time to deal with them.

On the night before the festival Kit arrived in Rowton, flush with the excitement of seeing Amy, his big move to Brighton and the prospect of meeting Philippa Fotheringham in real life. He'd come armed with two bottles of crémant, which Amy pointed out he'd mostly need to drink by himself. On a day when she'd be co-hosting and co-ordinating a major live event, not to mention dancing a waltz in public, the last thing she needed was a hangover.

After Kit had cooed over her costume and poured her the single glass of fizz she'd decided to allow herself, he said: 'Ames, what's going on? You look well, and you're saying all the stuff I'd expect you to the evening before such a big day, but you're not yourself. The lights are on but no one's home. Or maybe someone is, but they're screaming hysterically into a pillow.'

'Brace yourself,' Amy said, deciding not to sugar-coat anything she was about to say and feeling grateful she didn't need to. 'Since we last spoke properly, Hugh has revealed himself as a total psycho, Sam and I have fallen out in a way that I think might be irreparable *and* I've realised I am utterly and completely in love with him.'

'Okaaay,' Kit said, slurping from his flute. 'One thing at a time. Walk me through all this – tell me what's been happening and don't leave anything out.'

Amy did as she was told, her voice rising with rage as she ranted about Hugh's sudden appearance at Rowton Hall and then growing hoarse with tears as she described how comprehensively she'd convinced herself Sam was someone she couldn't even like, let alone love – only to discover she'd been catastrophically wrong.

'Oh God, Amy,' Kit said, draining his second glass of fizz. 'First, I cannot BELIEVE you never told me you'd copped off with him as a teenager. Major points deduction for withholding that information. Second, you weren't joking – it's a fine fucking mess you've got yourself into. I'm not so sure it's beyond fixing, though – not if you don't want it to be.'

'Really?' Amy asked. 'Because I honestly have no idea where to start.'

'Don't you?' Kit said, arching an eyebrow in disbelief and pouring the last of the first bottle of crémant into his glass.

Amy put her head in her hands, sighed and then straightened

up to look Kit in the eye. 'I need to tell him how I feel,' she admitted.

'And then some,' Kit said. 'Tell him, paint him a picture . . . Throw everything and the kitchen sink at it. Create an interpretive dance routine that leaves him in no doubt you're hot for his mind as well as his body.'

'There's already more than enough dancing in my immediate future,' Amy reminded him.

'Good point.'

'Also, he's refused to speak to me one-to-one since the row, even via email if he can help it. And he must have been avoiding me in the village – it's unusual for me not to run into him at the pub, the bakery or the shop,' Amy said glumly. 'It's been more than a week.'

'Well, he's not going to be able to avoid you tomorrow, is he?' Kit said. 'And what better place to make a confession of true love than a festival designed to celebrate it?'

'I have no map for any of this, Kit,' she told him. 'No frame of reference. No idea what I'm doing.'

'Nobody does when they fall in love, Amy. That's why it's called *falling*. You don't stroll cautiously into love via a predictable, tried-and-tested route. You don't get a pre-booked seat on the 9.40 from London Euston and then arrive in love fifty minutes later. It's supposed to be scary and exhilarating – like that moment where you reach the top of a roller coaster and know you're about to go whooshing down, screaming like a loon but loving every second of it.'

'I don't like heights,' Amy said. 'Remember?'

'Oh yeah,' Kit said, grit-grinning so sheepishly that even Amy laughed. 'The balloon. How could I forget?'

Amy woke up early without the need for her alarm. She scrabbled on her bedside table for her iPhone, read 05:28 on its home screen and sighed.

This was a stupid time to be up unnecessarily, but there

was no way she'd get back to sleep now; there was too much to do today, and too much at stake. Somehow or other, she needed to get Sam alone, apologise to him for everything and admit how she really felt. Alongside this last-ditch attempt to salvage things with him, she had authors' talks to oversee, social media channels to man and a Regency dance to perform.

The light streaming in through her bedroom window was pale and new, like the day was still being born. For some reason, this added to Amy's vague sense that something momentous was going to happen between now and when the sun set again. Such woo-woo imaginings were very unusual for Amy, and always made her think of her mother. She felt a sudden urge to speak to Lily, remembering what she'd said in one of her recent texts: that she'd like the chance to listen, should her daughter ever feel she needed someone to talk to. Amy did a quick calculation in her head and worked out that, in LA, it was around half past nine at night. Lily would probably pick up if she rang her.

Not pausing for long enough to talk herself out of it, Amy swiped and tapped her phone until it was calling out the long, drawling ringing sound signifying the distance this conversation would span.

'Hello?' Lily said, sounding alarmed. 'Amy? Is everything OK?'

Amy felt a pang of guilt. Her mother had assumed something must be wrong because she called her so rarely.

'Everything's fine, I'm safe and so's Gran,' Amy told her. 'I'm just up early. I felt like I wanted to speak to you.'

'Well, that's great,' Lily said. 'Big day ahead? It's the festival, isn't it?'

Amy was impressed that she'd remembered. She spent so much time talking about intangible, other-worldly things that it was always a shock when Lily revealed she had some idea of what was happening in the mortal realm.

'That's right,' Amy said. 'RomFest – complete with Q&As

and speeches from a variety of bestselling authors, stands that celebrate fans' favourite romance tropes, themed food and drink and even a Regency dance showcase.'

'It sounds wonderful,' Lily said. 'Your dad would be so proud of you. No doubt he'd have had a ball.'

'Maybe,' Amy said. 'I've been thinking a bit lately about how into romance he seemed, but how reluctant he was to try and find a new relationship after . . . Well. After you two broke up.'

She didn't want to say 'after you left us'. Far too loaded for any chat, pre-6 a.m., even if it was true.

'Oh?' Lily said. 'What's brought this on?'

'I guess I'm kind of . . . in a bit of a situation myself,' Amy admitted. 'Erm. I've discovered I have – have *always* had – feelings for someone I've hurt. And now I don't know if I can make it better or convince him that . . .' she swallowed. 'Convince him that I love him.'

'My, my,' Lily said. 'Can I assume we're talking about Samuel Ainsworth, the Viscount-to-be?'

'Yes,' Amy sighed. 'We are. Have you been gazing into your crystal ball again?'

'No,' Lily said, a wry smile in her voice. 'I just remember how you used to complain about him when you were at college – and how defensive you were about the idea of being friends with him when we spoke a few months ago. Also, he's *incredibly* handsome.'

'How have you divined that?' Amy asked, surprised.

Lily laughed. 'I googled him. Did some light Instagram stalking. Not everything I find out comes to me via the tarot deck, Amy. Though if you'll forgive me for saying I told you so, this morning's revelation *does* explain the four of cups. And the moon.'

It kind of did, but there was no way Amy was going to admit it.

'If you say so,' she grumbled. Then she steeled herself and said: 'I'm scared, Lily. What if I tell him how I feel and it doesn't change anything? What if he doesn't want me, after everything that's happened?'

Now she'd given voice to her fear, it took shape in her mind too. Amy imagined herself sliced open: raw, afraid and vulnerable but left to bleed out.

'You have to take the chance,' Lily said simply. 'Trust me when I say the *not* knowing will eat you up – to the point where you'll wish you'd just been honest, risked being rejected, faced the possibility that you might have to rebuild yourself afterwards.'

Amy was surprised by the soft, sad certainty in Lily's voice. Her tone was melancholic – like she spoke from personal experience.

'And you know this how?' Amy asked.

'Ask me some other time,' Lily said. 'Suffice to say that everything you've heard about me wanting to tread my own path, find myself, be free from responsibility . . . It's all true. But walking away from things – from *relationships* – that seemed too hard to handle has quite rightly had consequences for me. Doing the easier thing, the thing that feels like it's going to protect you . . . It isn't always easy, in the end.'

'Oh,' Amy breathed, thoroughly taken aback at what this implied.

'One thing I've learned,' Lily went on, 'is that when you love someone – in whatever capacity – you shouldn't hold back. You shouldn't play it safe, or try to hoard that love in case you lose it. Love doesn't work like other things – it's not mathematical. When you hoard it, it withers and dies. When you give it away, your hands are free to receive and you end up with more. It comes back to you in some form, bigger and stronger, even if it's from a source you don't expect.'

'That might be the wisest thing you've ever said to me,' she told her mother.

'And I say *a lot* of wise things,' Lily said, less serious now, 'whether or not you recognise them as such.'

Amy glanced at her clock. 'I should probably get going,' she said. 'But thank you, for your advice and for being so honest with me. It's helped. I'm glad I called.'

'Anytime, darling,' Lily said. 'Maybe come and see me for a holiday when you next get time off work. Or perhaps I could come and see you in the UK sometime.'

'Either, or both,' said Amy, 'I'd really like that. I love you.'

Chapter 28

Amy arrived at Rowton Hall just after seven o'clock, ready to help with whatever last-minute preparations were needed before the gates opened at nine. Amazingly, the event was a sell-out – and several magazines and newspapers had stated their intent to turn up, take photos and report on what one feature had already called 'the RomFest phenomenon'.

As Amy wandered around the stalls, stages and food and drink stations that had been set up over the previous week, she felt pride surge in her chest. She and Sam had done this: between them, they'd taken what had seemed a crazy idea and created something that promised to be great. As usual, Carolyn had been right. They made a great team.

He saw her coming and ducked into the house before she could reach him, clutching a clipboard as if to indicate there was something urgent he had to attend to. Dismayed, Amy got stuck in to helping one of the drinks vendors unpack stacks of recyclable cups, then with writing out the romance-themed cocktail menu in chalk paint on several large blackboards. As she artfully scribed the words 'Ice Queen: £6', she was confronted by how much had changed since she and Kit had drunk giant G&Ts in his kitchen after she'd refused Hugh's marriage proposal. He'd insisted then that there was a soft centre beneath the chilly persona she affected, and he'd been right.

She caught another glimpse of Sam as she surveyed the various stages that had been set up for authors' talks, then checked the T-shirt stalls to see if they needed any help. There was a variety of slogans on offer, all linked to stations around the festival that celebrated beloved romantic tropes: #historicalheroine, #forbiddenlove, #friendstolovers, #enemiestolovers and #soulmates. Again, he found an excuse to avoid her. It was miserable; every time he disappeared from view, determined not to be anywhere near her, felt like a punch in the stomach.

'This is fucking *crazy*,' Kit said when he arrived just after nine. His eyes swept up and down the fields to the rear of Rowton Hall, already alive with traders, volunteers, RomFest employees and the first guests. The car park was filling up, the distant windows of stationary vehicles glinting in the late-August sunshine. 'I'm amazed, Amy, and not because I didn't expect this to be great – but because even I hadn't imagined the size and scale of what you've achieved. Carolyn must be cock-a-hoop.'

'She seems pretty chuffed,' Amy said. 'She's coming later, so I hope she's as impressed in person as she's been from a distance.'

'Something tells me you have nothing to worry about,' Kit said, eyeing a nearby food stall that sold pancakes topped with edible prints of famous heroes' faces. 'As a young lad, I used to dream of smothering Mr Rochester in something edible,' he sighed immediately after buying one and squeezing a bottle of maple syrup over his plate. 'You, Amy Perry, have made a dream come true this morning.'

The day unfolded almost exactly as planned. By lunchtime, Rowton Hall's grounds were full of people in hashtag T-shirts, flower crowns (a last-minute innovation, and a popular one) and carrying 'RomFest'-stamped paper bags, presumably containing merchandise they'd bought. Food and drink vendors were doing a roaring trade, while the author talks and Q&As Amy had set up were going smoothly. People were smiling and laughing . . . There was joy in the air. Hope. A belief that love, whatever form it took and however it might end, was always worth celebrating. In spite of Sam's continued coldness, Amy felt elated.

As the afternoon wore on and Philippa's much-anticipated

talk drew nearer, Amy's nerves began to fray. She met Nisha at one of the large caterers' tents, where she'd kindly been allowed to store her costume for the dance showcase. As Nisha helped her into her stays and gown, then fiddled with her hair until it had been coaxed into an impressively authentic updo, Amy tried not to nibble on her nails or tap her feet.

'*There*,' Nisha said. 'You look perfect. Go get him.' Amy didn't bother to ask what she meant.

Walter had been given the job of compèring the dance showcase, and he made a great fuss of praising Sam and Amy's efforts before calling them to join him on the hardwood portable dance floor that had been laid especially for the event. Amy gulped and made her way towards him at the same time as Sam emerged from a crowd on the opposite side of the spectators' circle. It was all she could do not to gasp.

He should have looked ridiculous. He was dressed up like the lord of the manor she'd always sneered at him for being: leather boots, black breeches, a white shirt, plus a silk-fronted waistcoat and jacket with tails. The effect was magnificent. Heart-stopping.

When Amy got closer, she could see that the blue pattern on Sam's waistcoat almost exactly matched the shade of her dress. Had this been Thomasina's plan all along? If so, Amy couldn't help wondering why the hell she'd foisted the Quality Street monstrosity on her.

She smoothed down the soft fabric of her dress nervously and felt his eyes follow her hands, skimming over her body in precisely the way that the original designers of such gowns had intended. Silently, she thanked Thomasina for convincing her that the 'put them on display' stays were a must, if she was going to look authentically Regency.

This was the first time Sam had properly looked at Amy all day, and now it seemed he couldn't tear his gaze away. When his eyes met hers the familiar current of their mutual attraction sparked. Pure and perfect heat filled the space where witty barbs or complaints would normally be discharged to dampen it.

The small ensemble of musicians, positioned to the left of Philippa's little stage, struck up. The sweet, now familiar melody of the waltz sang through the air, and Sam took Amy's hand as they joined the rest of the dance troupe.

They didn't speak. As they began the dance, Amy found that anything more than remembering her steps would have been impossible. She slipped into a mesmerised, almost dreamlike state, only vaguely aware of Pearl standing at the edge of the dance floor, clapping and grinning.

Amy had been horrified at the thought of dancing in front of so many people, but now she was barely registering their presence. As the sound of string instruments soared, filling the warm summer air, she was utterly consumed by the magnetic ebb and flow of herself and Sam as they moved together.

She followed the steps Walter had taught them, briefly joining hands with other members of the dance troupe and circling them as she was supposed to. But she couldn't meet the eyes of the men who, momentarily, were her partners: her gaze was locked on Sam, just as his eyes were fixed on her.

As they returned to one another, Amy revelled in the familiar, almost gravitational pull of him – the fragrance she could detect rolling off his skin, the feel of his fingertips grasping hers and the firmness of his hold on her waist. As they stepped together, arms raised so that their hands were almost palm to palm, the intensity of Sam's stare was almost enough to ignite her. Their hands weren't supposed to touch, Walter had told them – but maintaining the prescribed few millimetres of distance was agony.

Each time the music drew them towards one another, their faces were so close that she could feel him breathing, taste his air – so near she could see the different shades of dark in his eyes.

When the music stopped, applause thundered around them. It was like a spell had broken. Amy placed her hand over

Sam's, which was still lingering at her hip – his arm wound around her so she was pressed close into his side. She wanted to stay there forever, to melt into him completely.

'Sam,' she said, 'I need to talk to you. *Please.*'

'I have to go,' he said, looking as dazed as she felt but twisting away from her.

On the far side of the floor was Tilly, stood among an array of cameras, clapping and cheering.

Chapter 29

Amy felt like the bottom had dropped out of her world. Everything was slipping away – sinking into an abyss – and she found she didn't care. She wanted to go with it.

She felt like howling. *Screaming.* But before her misery could find voice, she felt a smart tap on her shoulder. It was Carolyn.

'I never thought I'd see the day,' she said. 'Amy Perry in Regency costume, dancing for an audience.'

'Carolyn,' Amy said, recovering some composure, 'of course you were going to see the day. You literally *made* me do this.'

'That's a fair point,' Carolyn nodded. 'In any case, you were very good. *Both* of you were very good. You looked wonderful together.'

Amy flushed, then felt sick at the memory of Sam leaving her side for Tilly's.

'I'll find you once Philippa's talk is over,' Carolyn said, reclaiming her attention. 'I have an update on Torch and H-K that's pertinent to your decision about whether or not to stay on.'

Amy nodded. No doubt the 'Hugh is the new CEO' announcement was imminent. According to him – and out of sheer spite, rather than any sort of business sense – that spelled an end for the imprint this event had so successfully launched.

Up on stage, Amy introduced Philippa. Within seconds the author had her audience sitting in spellbound silence, lapping up insights into her writing process, hints about the content of her new novel and gossip about a possible TV adaptation of *And So We Meet Again*. Philippa was garrulous and down to earth – the perfect headline speaker on a day that celebrated reading for sheer pleasure.

She took questions, then sincerely thanked her army of fans for coming to see her. As they drifted off to make their final purchases from the few stalls that remained open, Philippa descended from the stage and Carolyn reappeared.

'Have we got some news for you, bab!' Philippa gushed.

Carolyn made an exasperated face. 'Let's find somewhere to sit down, shall we?'

She led them to one of the temporary picnic tables that had been set up for RomFest visitors to rest, eat and drink at, then said: 'Right. I won't beat about the bush.'

When do you ever? Amy thought.

'It's no secret that I don't see eye to eye with H-K's incoming CEO, and so I've parted ways with the firm.'

'You've resigned? Quit?'

'In a blaze of glory,' Carolyn smiled. 'And I'd like you to come with me, if you're keen.'

'Come . . . where?' Amy asked.

'Well, I should say with *us*,' Carolyn corrected herself. 'Philippa and I are setting up an independent house. We're both investing. Taking what began as Torch and expanding it.'

Amy was struggling to take this in.

'But how can you pick up the authors I've signed to H-K, take them with you and get away with it all?' she asked. 'Aren't there contracts in place? Doesn't H-K own all the manuscripts I bought? There must be legal issues that can't be got over without a fight . . . I mean, you're going to get the arses sued off you, surely?'

'Oh, I don't think so,' Philippa said with satisfaction.

'No,' Carolyn confirmed. 'Let's just say I've been at H-K plenty long enough to know where the bodies are buried – and believe me, there are a lot. The place is steeped in nepotism, which is deeply irritating but also leads to incompetent handling of appointments, financial and HR issues. Hugh's treatment of you these past few months has been *beyond* unprofessional – and that's just the tip of the iceberg.'

'God,' Amy said, gulping. 'We're not talking about abuse, or assaults or anything, are we?'

She thought better of Carolyn than to sit on something like this, but had to ask.

'Hmm,' Carolyn said thoughtfully. 'Not that I'm aware of. More about a culture of entitled idiocy. But let's face it, these things are on a spectrum – albeit at different ends.'

Amy nodded, recognising how right she was.

'In any case,' Carolyn went on, 'H-K doesn't want a commercial imprint like Torch as part of its stable – Hugh has made that quite clear. It's neater all round if they sign over the project to me, and if we all say farewell in a civilised fashion that doesn't involve spending lots of money on lawyers. We'll be a small start-up to begin with, and if you choose to be part of this new venture, very little will change for you compared with how you've been working since the spring.'

'And if I don't come with you?' Amy asked, though really the question was academic.

'Then it's back to the Howard-Knight offices for you, I should think,' Carolyn said. 'Hugh's announcing his new regime on Monday, I believe. Given the chance, my guess is he'll have you back at your old desk in a flash – or in the office next door to his if he can wangle it.'

Amy made a face and shuddered again.

'In that case, my choice is clear,' she said. 'Except . . . What are your plans, location wise?'

'I'd like to keep Torch based in this region,' Carolyn said. 'Philippa's here too, so it makes sense. Were you keen on heading back to London?'

'No, actually,' Amy said, realising this was true. 'Staying here or hereabouts sounds perfect.'

'Well then,' Carolyn announced, 'I'll have my lawyer draw up the necessary paperwork for your new role and send it to you ASAP. I suggest you submit your resignation directly to Julian, since I'm no longer in post. He should accept it without argument and will probably allow you to leave with immediate effect, so I can rehire you the following day. I've given him fair warning that if his nephew bothers you again there'll be severe consequences for both Hugh and the firm.' She grinned almost evilly at this. *To the victor the spoils,* Amy thought.

Smiling, she shook her head in disbelief. 'This is ... perfect. *Wonderful.* I'm ... overwhelmed. Thank you both so much.'

'*No* tears,' Carolyn said sharply, recognising the quiver in Amy's voice. She stood up, and Amy and Philippa mirrored the movement.

'Now. I think it's time for me to head off,' Carolyn said. 'I'll be in touch.'

Without further ado, she sloped off to the car park before she could be asked to pitch in with any of the RomFest jobs that staff and volunteers had now begun: litter picking, the reloading of unsold goods into vans and the deconstruction of a *lot* of flat-pack and foldable furniture.

'I'm off, too,' Philippa said, waving her preternaturally long nails in Amy's face. Amy reasoned they weren't well suited to manual labour.

'I'll speak to you next week,' Philippa went on. 'And by the way, bab – put that lovely man out of his misery. He's obviously mad about you. Write yourselves a happy ending, OK?'

'I'm afraid it might be too late for that, Philippa,' Amy said, determinedly holding back tears, even though Carolyn was no longer there to disapprove of them.

After changing out of her dance costume, Amy got stuck into packing pallets of unsold soft drinks into the back of a minivan. Generally, though, it seemed the vast majority of the day's food and drink had been bought by festivalgoers.

With a glow, she thought of what a good cause the RomFest profits would serve: keeping people like Barbara and Dave in the homes they loved. Her misjudgement of Sam had been sweeping, almost total, she realised again. His determination to make this event work, his insistence on obliging Carolyn and his tolerance of Hugh's rudeness had all been about achieving his desired outcome for others, not himself.

She felt someone standing behind her and breathed in a waft of fruity perfume. 'Amy? Can I have a quick word?' She turned to see Tilly smiling sweetly, apparently unaware that the mere sight of her made Amy feel as though her heart had been put through a shredder.

'What about?' Amy asked testily.

'I'd love it if you could sign this consent form for me,' Tilly said.

Amy felt like she must have blacked out – as if she'd missed a chunk of conversation that would have made the phrase 'consent form' comprehensible. What was Tilly on about?

'I don't understand,' Amy said eventually.

Tilly frowned and tipped her head prettily to one side. 'Did Sam not mention it to you?'

'Obviously not,' Amy retorted. This was torture. *Take him if you must,* Amy thought, *but spare me the bullshit.*

'Ugh, I did ask him to bring it up,' Tilly said. 'I need you to sign the form if we're going to include your dance in the documentary, and I really want to – it was just stunning!'

'Documentary . . . ?'

'*Yes,*' Tilly said. 'You know I do a bit of producing, as well as presenting? I've been working on a programme about the resurgence of romance: a celebration of the genre. I asked Sam if I could do some filming here today, and I've been up a couple of times already to interview him and get shots of the grounds and the festival prep. He was supposed to tell you all about it.'

She sounded annoyed.

Amy was baffled, but something that felt scarily like hope flickered to life in her chest. Meg had said she thought Sam and Tilly were all business . . . Had she been right?

'He didn't,' Amy said. 'But I'll sign the form. What channel is the documentary for?'

'BBC One!' Tilly grinned. 'And it should get mentions on *The One Show* and *Breakfast*, as well as a write-up on the website and presence on iPlayer. I'm *very* excited about it.'

Amy quickly took a wad of paperwork from Tilly, filling in all the fields she'd helpfully marked with crosses for participants' signatures.

'I already have forms from Sam and the rest of the dance troupe,' Tilly said as Amy scribbled away. 'I can't believe he never mentioned this . . . Still. I suppose you've had other things to talk about,' she smiled.

Amy shot her a look. 'Such as . . . ?'

'Old times! The future! He and I were *useless* as a couple but we were always good friends. He told me all about you one evening not too long ago. Said he'd been mad about you since you were children. Since he was *sixteen!*'

At the look on Amy's face, Tilly's confidence and enthusiasm waned. 'I thought you'd, ah, rekindled a lost love via working on this project . . . ?' she asked.

'It's not quite that simple,' Amy told her. But something about Tilly's rash, unthinking openness – and the phrase 'since he was sixteen' – struck Amy as significant. She thought back to her old theory on the interconnectedness of posh people: how the usual six degrees of separation shrank to three or even two, depending on how wealthy you were.

'Tilly,' she said, in a more polite tone than she'd managed up to now. 'Do you happen to know Hugh Howard?'

'Oh, yes!' Tilly said. 'Met him at a gathering a few weeks back in Mayfair. Charming chap. I couldn't believe he was involved in organising RomFest! I told him I'd been filming up here for a documentary I was working on, and the conversation came round to the festival. I couldn't help telling him how lovely I thought it was that an event designed to celebrate romantic fiction had brought two childhood sweethearts back together! Though Sam has refused to let me put *that* in the programme, the absolute shit.'

Amy sighed, half relieved, half exasperated. Tilly and Sam weren't sleeping together. It was Tilly who'd inadvertently told Hugh there was something going on between Sam and Amy. It all made sense, but – once again – not in the way she might have expected it to. The hope she could feel glimmering somewhere inside her ribcage burned brighter.

She signed a final form, then thrust the papers and pen back into Tilly's arms.

'Tilly, I'm really sorry, but I have to go.'

'Oh. Where?' Tilly asked, surprised by Amy's sudden urgency.

'There's something I have to do. Someone I have to see,' Amy said.

As she strode off, she pulled her phone out of her bag and messaged Kit:

At the top of the roller coaster. Going to go down screaming. Wish me luck x

Before she could stow it away again, his reply came through:

You don't need it. I love you. And FWIW: based on that dance, so does he x

Chapter 30

Amy had never told anyone she loved them before – not in the way she was planning to tell Sam.

She wasn't sure how she'd start: whether she should apologise for their last conversation before trying to explain herself fully, or just launch right in with three, unambiguous little words that left no room for misinterpretation.

Amy and Sam had never been very good at calm, sincere discussion . . . Maybe keeping it simple was the best way to go. But what if he still didn't want to talk to her? What if he refused to listen, no matter what she said?

Amy hurried around the festival site, in and out of tents and the remnants of merchandise stands. She even knocked on the doors of all the Portaloos.

She couldn't find him, but resolved to keep on looking.

An hour later, as the last trade vehicles made their way down the Hall driveway and back onto the road, Amy stopped for breath. Everyone had gone home.

Meg and Pearl had left hours ago. Ken and Grace had gone back to the cottage at around the same time, while Barbara, Dave, Simon, Nisha and Kit had announced their decision to head to the Oak after Philippa's talk. The place was totally deserted, and it finally dawned on Amy that Sam was gone, too. He'd sloped off without speaking to her – hadn't wanted to celebrate RomFest's success with her, even for a moment.

She picked up her things – her handbag, jacket and the garment bag with her costume in it – and decided it was time to admit defeat. Her chest felt like it was caving in, her heart collapsing into nothingness like a dying star.

It was getting on for eight o'clock but it was still very light, and the summer air was warm on her bare legs – clad in elegant, black linen shorts, worn with a broderie anglaise blouse made of cream cotton. She began walking but her feet refused to travel in the direction of the car park. Instead, she found herself moving towards the wood at the edge of the estate.

It was vaguely masochistic to go in there, she knew, but she couldn't help herself. This felt important. Necessary, for some reason. She sought out the exact tree she'd sat against all those years ago, then sank down in front of it, dumped her stuff on the ground and turned to lean her back against its thick, rough trunk. She sat there for who knew how long, only registering that she'd begun to cry when she tasted tears on her lips.

'Are you crying because you forgot to bring biscuits?' said a voice. *Sam's* voice. 'I was hoping for a Hobnob,' he muttered as he stepped closer.

Amy sniffed, not knowing whether to laugh or keep weeping. 'No such luck, I'm afraid. Though as I recall, that night it was ginger nuts.'

'I remember,' he said, dropping down next to her just as he'd done when they were teenagers. 'I remember everything.'

'*Sam*,' she said, burying her face in her hands, ashamed to even look at him. 'I don't know what to say. I had this idea that I'd find you and then, in the moment, I'd know how to tell you how sorry I am about EVERYTHING. But you'd disappeared, and I came here and somehow started crying and . . . *now* you turn up! Now, when I have a snotty nose and swollen eyes and mascara running down my face!'

'So . . . Do *I* have to say sorry? Are we arguing right now?'

'No!' Amy cried in alarm. 'I just – *argh*. I wanted to do this properly, like in a book or a film. And it isn't working.'

'So do it your way, whatever "it" is,' Sam said, daring to sound almost amused. He shifted slightly, and suddenly he was so close to her that their arms were touching. He felt warm. Solid. Safe.

'I've been an idiot,' Amy said, turning to face him. 'I've assumed things, got everything wrong and messed it all up. I picked and chose which facts I looked at and whose opinions I listened to based on what I *wanted* to conclude, which was that you were awful. And I *needed* you to be awful because . . .'

'Because . . . ?'

She sighed. 'I needed you to be awful so I wouldn't have to want you! Because it terrified me that you might not want me back . . . I'm not like you – I never was. I'm not confident or popular, or rich or cool. I might have made a career out of it, but I'm still the antisocial bookworm who hid out here to read when normal people our age went to parties.'

'Might I remind you that I liked that girl, Amy,' Sam said. 'Really. Like, a lot. I thought she was brilliant – the best person I'd ever met. I thought it was wonderful that she wasn't like me, or like anyone else, for that matter. I even liked how fucking *nuts* she drove me, arguing with me every day.'

'Why did you come here tonight?' Amy asked. 'And *don't* tell me it was so you could scav a biscuit.'

'I hoped you'd be here. I've been holed up with Roger going over the numbers . . . He's already got pound signs in his eyes after seeing how well we've done today, but I'm certain the houses that were at risk are safe. I understand from Meg that you . . . that you got a few things straight after our most recent argument. I saw Grace's car was still parked on the field, and here you are.'

'But you've been avoiding me all day,' Amy said. 'What's changed since you spoke to your sister?'

'I had to dance with you, didn't I? It was . . . unbearable,' he laughed.

'Oh, thanks a lot!'

By way of apology, he threaded his fingers through hers. Her insides illuminated at his touch, everything in her lighting up in a rush that left her breathless.

'What I mean,' Sam went on, 'is that it made me more desperate to kiss you than I've ever been in my whole life. Even more so than I was at eighteen. I couldn't ignore it, no matter how angry I was with you. And I realised something else, too. When Hugh accused you of messing around with me, you didn't correct him – you didn't tell him there was nothing between us. That made me . . . hopeful.'

Amy nodded. 'It was Tilly who let slip to Hugh that we were a thing,' she explained.

Sam puffed out his cheeks and shook his head. 'Of *course* it was. I was stupid for telling her anything. She caught me in a weak moment and the whole story came spilling out. There's a reason why she interviews people on TV, I suppose.'

'It doesn't matter,' Amy told him. 'I was just relieved to hear you weren't back together.'

'Me and Tilly?' Sam asked, incredulous. 'Rumours of our romance were greatly exaggerated last year, mainly by my mother. If you'd asked me whether I was seeing her, I'd have told you the truth.'

'I know you would,' Amy said, squeezing his hand. '*But*. In the spirit of being braver than I have historically managed, I'm going to tell *you* some things. First – and this isn't my story to share, but I think that at this point Hari would want me to – you don't need to feel guilty for what happened between you and me back then. Hari was working through some stuff of his own . . . Figuring things out. But I'm pretty sure he was coming to understand that he was gay.'

Sam's head snapped up, his eyes wide with shock. 'What? Why wouldn't he have told me that? He could have, of *course* he could have.'

'I know. And I think he probably knew that, too. But I suspect that, a little bit like me, he thought it might be easier to start afresh and explore other parts of his identity at uni. He'd already dealt with so much, losing his dad . . .'

Sam put his head in his hands, clawing at his hair as if that might help him process what Amy had just told him.

'I was so sure he was madly in love with you,' he said, shaking his head in disbelief.

'Nope,' Amy told him. 'We did love each other, but not in that way. Though I think it was helpful to him that people thought we were more than friends, and I generally didn't mind.'

Sam was shaking his head, looking shell-shocked.

'The other thing I want to say,' Amy went on, 'is that this – this *thing* we have, which as you're now aware terrifies me beyond belief . . . It's not just about bickering and kissing. I'm in love with you. Properly, completely and irrevocably. I've never loved anyone else, and I don't think I ever will. And I wanted you to know, even if you can't love me back after everything that's happened. Just because it's the truth.'

'I see,' Sam said, looking down. Frowning. 'That's . . . interesting.'

To Amy's astonishment, he began peeling his sweater up over his torso. Was he stripping off? Yes, she'd said she loved him – but she wasn't about to get jiggy with him in the wood.

He cast his navy cotton crew neck aside and pointed at his torso. He was wearing a RomFest T-shirt, but it wasn't the one she would have expected him to pick. It said: 'Team #Soulmates'. Underneath, he'd written their names in Sharpie, enclosing them inside a heart.

'Embarrassing, right?' he said, grinning. '*Terrible*. But that thing you said about wearing an "I Heart Sam" top under your clothes made me think of it. I need you to know that I have wanted you so much, for so long. I never stopped missing you, thinking about you or loving you. It's always been you, Amy.'

He pressed his lips to her cheek so gently that tears stung her eyes. He kissed her face again, and then again, inching his lips closer and closer to hers each time he moved.

She pushed her hands into his honey-coloured hair, feeling its smooth, cool softness against her skin. When their mouths met it was urgent, clumsy and warm. There was a hungry intensity between them – an impulsive connection that was passionate rather than polite. It was visceral, electrifying, earthy.

Being with Sam like this reminded Amy how alive she was. Every cell in her body fizzed with elation at his nearness; at the feel of his skin and the taste of his lips; at the scent of him, always the same – cedar and citrus, deep and fresh. Her heart felt like it might burst in her chest.

'So. Can I walk you home?' he asked, grinning. 'Kiss you some more outside the kitchen window?'

'I have Gran's car, remember?' she said, patting her pocket to jingle the keys.

'Ah,' Sam said, frowning.

'And anyway,' Amy told him, settling her head against his shoulder and breathing him in freely, fully, with no fear. 'I'm already home.'

Epilogue

'I can't believe you *knew*,' Amy said. 'Every time? Really?'

'Every. Single. Time. Your father was the same – blithely assuming he could climb in and out of windows without me ever noticing. The arrogance of youth.'

'Why didn't you ever stop me? Us?' Amy asked, aghast.

'It was something that you needed – you in particular, I think,' Grace said. 'And you were always a sensible girl. Usually back before dark, apart from on that one night Sam brought you home. The night we're talking about.'

'Ow!' Amy cried suddenly, feeling a hairpin scrape against her scalp. 'Nish, that *hurt*.'

'Sorry,' Nisha grimaced. 'Almost done.'

'We need to hurry this up,' Meg said, 'or we'll be late.'

As usual, she was ready before everyone else: beautiful and elegant in a simple dress made of fine, forest-green satin. It brought out the colour of her hazel eyes perfectly, and it was well chosen for an autumn wedding.

Outside the window, red and gold leaves were swirling in the mid-October breeze. The sky was clear: a pretty pale blue that promised not to rain on anyone's parade.

'*There*,' Nisha said with satisfaction. 'You look beautiful, Amy. And you look stunning, Grace.'

Nisha had piled Amy's hair – longer and wavier than she'd let it grow in years – into an updo not unlike the one she'd worn at RomFest. Grace, meanwhile, had too little hair for Nisha to interfere with – but she'd consented to having her makeup done and ended up looking like a movie star: all twinkling blue eyes, fire engine-red lips and luminous skin. She *did* look stunning.

'We'd better get going,' Meg said, looking at her watch again. 'The cars are outside. Pearl! Off the iPad now, please, it's time.'

The five of them made their way down Grace's impossibly narrow, impossibly steep staircase to find their special occasion shoes. It would have been borderline suicidal to put them on any sooner.

Meg, Nisha and Pearl got into their taxi and disappeared in the direction of the village church. It wasn't far – just the other side of the bridge – but too far to hobble to in heels.

As Grace and Amy climbed into their car and settled next to one another on the back seat, Amy picked up the thread of their earlier conversation. 'What on earth made you decide to tell me you'd sussed me out *today*, of all days?'

'I couldn't have you believing you'd got away with it forever,' Grace laughed. 'And I thought it was relevant, somehow.'

'As in . . . fate can bring people together in the most unexpected places?' Amy asked, nonplussed.

'*No*,' Grace said, rolling her eyes. 'As in, you have to show up if you want love. Put yourself out there. Be seen. You don't think Sam happened upon you in the wood by accident that evening, do you? Has it never occurred to you that he knew you liked that spot, had seen you there countless times before and took months to work up the courage to speak to you?'

It genuinely hadn't, even now. Amy felt her mouth fall open.

'And it wasn't an accident that you went back there on the night of the festival, either,' Grace went on. 'You were waiting for him, hoping he'd come so you could finally be honest with him. Amy, keep being honest. Keep showing up for one another, even when it feels scary or hard, and you'll never go far wrong.'

'That's good advice,' Amy said, sniffing. Knowing Grace was right.

'Now come on, no crying – you'll ruin that makeup Nisha's spent an hour putting on you. And we're almost there.'

The car pulled up outside the church and the driver helped them out – both women smoothing their dresses down gently, easing out the creases.

'Hey you,' said a voice in Amy's ear. 'You look wonderful.' Sam put his arms around her waist, and even through the deep red silk of her bridesmaid's dress she felt the warmth of his touch. He'd been waiting for her.

'Ken's a nervous wreck,' he whispered to Amy. 'The sooner you get in there, the better.'

To Grace, he said: 'You're the most beautiful bride I've ever seen. Well, so far.' He winked at Amy. 'I'll see you both inside.'

'Are you ready, Gran?' Amy asked.

'I am,' her grandmother said, standing proud in her simple, cream silk shift dress and jacket. 'Thank you, Amy, for giving me away.'

'It's my privilege,' Amy said, taking Grace's arm and readying herself to walk her up the aisle. Her grandmother was finally fully mobile again, able to move as freely as she ever had before her accident and operation.

Inside the church, friends and neighbours were gathered to celebrate. Kit and Julius – who'd rapidly earned his status as one of Amy's favourite people – had come up from Brighton. Even Bertie had been smuggled in and lay curled, quietly munching a bone, on Barbara's lap. If the vicar had noticed the presence of a black and tan miniature sausage dog among the congregation, he'd wisely chosen not to mention it.

As Grace and Ken said their wedding vows, Amy felt herself glowing with happiness – a joy that only intensified when she glanced behind her to see Sam watching her with pure adoration.

She smiled at him and knew she could make these same promises, offer this same commitment to him – knew that she wanted to.

And she suddenly knew too, that tonight – in a fit of uncharacteristic, crazily romantic hopefulness – she would ask him.

Acknowledgements

So, it turns out the 'difficult second novel' really is A Thing.

Writing a debut novel during a global pandemic was one thing; crafting a second while burnt out from the first, as well as continuing to navigate said global pandemic and all the stress associated with it, was quite another.

My first thank you goes to my husband, children, family and friends, without whom I simply couldn't have made it to the finish line. There were days when I cried, nights when I didn't sleep and finally, *finally*, mornings, afternoons and evenings during which the words flowed easily and abundantly. I was hugged, soothed, supported – and made lots of cups of tea – through all of them.

Self-belief is something I've always struggled with, so I'm fortunate that my stalwart agent, Kate Hordern, appears never to doubt me. Thank you, Kate, for your kindness and staunch optimism, and for refusing to allow my rampant perfectionism to eat me alive.

Jane Snelgrove, my editor at Embla, has kept faith with me throughout a tough year of writing. Thank you, Jane, for trusting me to deliver even during the dark days when it seemed that finishing Amy and Sam's story was too difficult a mountain to climb. We got there in the end, and I'm so proud of the book that – thanks to your expert guidance – did, in fact, find its happy ending.

More broadly, the whole Embla team are kick-ass wonder women. My thanks to everyone who has worked on Amy Perry; from the copy edit to the creation of the cover, collaborating with you all has been my absolute pleasure.

Finally, my most profound thanks to everyone who has picked up this book, in whatever form. Writing has been my only real ambition since I was a small child, and to know people out there in the real world are reading and sharing my stories is a dream come true. I don't take it for granted, and I appreciate every single reader.

This story originally came to me at a pretty bleak time – during a season of all our lives when many things seemed uncertain, and when none of us could be sure whether the world would ever be the same again. I don't think it's a coincidence that, in the end, it became a story that's largely about hopefulness – about seeing the best in each other instead of the worst. I hope it has brought you joy.

A Note from the Author

Rowton-in-Arden is a fictional south Warwickshire village, but plenty of places like it exist in the pretty part of the Midlands where I'm from. If you come for a potter round, you'll find Henley-in-Arden, Tanworth-in-Arden and probably several other Somethings-in-Arden – though none of them were the inspiration for Rowton, which is a shameless mishmash of several locations I've lived in and visited.

Laura Starkey

Laura was born in Warwickshire in 1982. She studied English & Related Literature at the University of York, then spent several years as a secondary school teacher before going on to work as a digital copywriter, editor and content designer. Despite her disbelief in real life 'meet cutes', Laura first encountered her husband on a Tube platform in London, in a plot twist worthy of any romcom (and she has read and watched a lot). She now lives in a small village in the West Midlands with her family, her book collection and a mini menagerie of pets. Laura is a graduate of the Faber Academy. Her first novel, *Rachel Ryan's Resolutions,* is also published by Embla.